SOMETHING
MORE
THAN LOVE

PATRICIA J. PARSONS

MOONLIGHT PRESS | TORONTO

For information or permissions:

Visit www.moonlightpresstoronto.com
Or email moonlightpressinfo@gmail.com

For Art who always encourages me to do the most outrageous things.

I was proud of the youths who opposed the war in
Vietnam because they were my babies."
~ Benjamin Spock
Times (London, May 1, 1988)

"To die is poignantly bitter, but the idea of having to
die without having lived is unbearable."
~ Eric Fromm

"Thank Heaven! the crisis—
The danger is past,
And the lingering illness
Is over at last—,
And the fever called "Living"
Is conquered at last."

~ Edgar Allan Poe, *For Annie*, st. 1

PART 1

"Deep in earth, my love is lying
And I must weep alone."

~ Edgar Allan Poe

ONE

THE UNIVERSITY OF VIRGINIA, EARLY SPRING, 1975

It was a frantic time for everyone. If I tarried a moment too long, I might end up in the war. It was now six years on since that fateful night in 1969 when, as a young undergrad, I sat in the television lounge in the student union building, beer in hand. It was November, and the news was full of the gruesome images of a war no one seemed to comprehend.

"Let us understand," Richard Nixon was saying into the camera. "North Vietnam cannot defeat or humiliate the United States. Only Americans can do that."

All around me, fellow students waved their plastic beer glasses at the screen, booing and hissing. For the first time since the war had begun, I became outraged. I was angry about the war, angry about what might happen to me – and for what? Mostly, I was angry at his arrogance. How dare he? And this, after all that America had suffered.

Thus, I cultivated a love for books and their natural abode – the academy – which would protect me in those terrible years. Had it not been for the war, I might have left the university after my first two beer-sodden years that were remarkable only for the number of fights into which I seemed to be able to embroil myself in residence. Indeed, I might have left to work in a hardware store, or sell encyclopedias, or even climb a mountain in Nepal. Such was the depth of my aimlessness. Only the bone-chilling fear of dying a grisly death on a foreign battlefield at a young age, fighting a war in which I did not believe, caused a miraculous turn-around in my scholastic career. Had I not had that epiphany that night while under the influence of alcohol, the Dean would probably have thrown me out anyway. But the years had drifted by in a haze of work and booze and one-night stands. Now, graduation loomed large, and the war dragged on.

My course was clear. More than a year before the completion of my dissertation, not knowing if I would ever, in fact, complete the requirements (which seemed a distinct possibility), I had begun to search for a position north of the 49th parallel. I would take refuge with our neighbours across the border in Canada, my excuse being that my penchant for English literature would be better served a step closer to its British origin, never mind that American literature was the point of my even being a doctoral candidate. Surely, Uncle Sam would see the light at some future date, and I would be able to return to my beloved hometown of Boston, Massachusetts.

I ignored virtually all possibilities of ferreting out a job teaching English literature to university freshmen in America.

I longed for a good appointment at the University of Toronto or, even better, McGill University, the famous English university in Montreal. I had a clearly romantic notion of introducing Francophone Canadians to the joys of American literature. I had even begun to read the *Montreal Gazette* whenever I was able and had developed a romanticized notion of living and teaching in what I perceived to be a totally foreign culture. I bought French-language tapes, then spent many a long, solitary evening in a vain attempt to make my Boston brawl sound like a *bona fide* Francophone accent. It was to no avail.

The offer finally arrived on a dull morning in March of 1975, when all was drawing to a head in Saigon, but uncertainty seemed to reign supreme. I had been glued to the television, as were many of my fellow graduate students, as our very futures hinged, at least to some extent, on what happened. At least I had been glued to the television when I was sober enough to comprehend what was happening. The public defence of my dissertation, *Scientific Cosmogony and the Myth of Immortality in the Works of Edgar Allan Poe*, had been an event of great importance to me. The fact that it had been excruciatingly nerve-wracking was the excuse I subsequently used for the inebriated state in which the letter found me. This state of intemperance was becoming quite familiar to me. I'd been wallowing in it since shortly after I was informed of my success by the terminally sour Dr. Archibald, Chairman of the English department, an individual who loathed the sight of me. I must admit the feeling was mutual.

When forced to confront me with the news, he looked as though he had a lemon stuck in his mouth. He was forced to inform me that I had, in fact, been successful in defending my work to the committee and assembled masses. I believe I expected him to say, "Congratulations, Dr. O'Hara." Instead, he simply said, "O'Hara, they've seen fit to pass you."

I shook the old man's hand and promptly went to the pub to get properly smashed.

From time to time during those three days, I came up for air and was reminded of some of the stark realities of my current situation. I knew that if the war didn't end soon, I would very likely receive my draft notice, whether I planned to head north or not. At least I'd be outside Uncle Sam's clutches if I headed to Canada. As things turned out, had the offer come even a month later, my career, and no doubt my life, would have taken a very different turn.

The letter was addressed to "Dr." Sean O'Hara. It was the first time I had been referred to this way since

3

my defence, and I was almost ashamed of how important it made me feel. It read:

"Dear Dr. O'Hara:
We are in receipt of your recent expression of interest in teaching at Dalhousie University. Your curriculum vitae is of interest to us, and we would welcome the opportunity to discuss your intentions of pursuing an academic career further. We will, however, need to interview you before the end of March. Please call the departmental secretary to set up the meetings, and we look forward to your arrival on campus.
Sincerely,
W. Tomlinson Ph.D., Professor & Chairman,
Department of English"

Dalhousie University? Had I written to them? Where in the world were they? Embarrassingly, I had to scramble around the library to find a map to determine the exact location of a city called "Halifax." It occurred to me that my fellow Americans and I were woefully unaware of much about our neighbours to the north. Perhaps that would change, at least for me.

Located on the extreme east coast of Canada, Halifax was actually closer to my current location than I had thought. And the end of March was only ten days away. With no other concrete offers forthcoming, I made the necessary arrangements and arrived in Halifax on the arranged date less than a week later.

As I drove into the city from the airport, I noted with some disappointment that the March weather seemed to be less than stellar. The roads glistened with wet snowflakes that seemed as large as cotton balls as they whipped onto the windscreen with the fury of an angry lover. The taxi driver said, "Always this way in March, eh," in answer to my inquiry about spring.

On the bright side, I discovered that Halifax is a quaint city with a character that almost defies

4

description. It boasted a waterfront in the process of restoration and a history that was probably more intriguing – or at the very least older – than that of most other Canadian cities. The university itself stretched some six or eight city blocks and turned out to be among the oldest universities in the country. It was founded as Dalhousie College in 1818, and my own proclivity for historical structures and documents drew me to the old stone administration building, which was like a compass pointing to True North.

The interview itself was unremarkable in every way, conducted by a panel of ageing academics clearly in need of some fresh blood, each trying to out-intellectualize the other. I could only imagine the *ennui* of the freshman students who were, no doubt, forced into lectures by these bored (and boring) men. I was informed that there were also women in the English department, but they were not in evidence in the selection committee. The whole experience resulted in a most pressing need to suppress a yawn.

After the interview with the department, I made my way to the Dean of Arts, whose opinion evidently carried quite a bit of weight in the selection process. He, too, was a white-haired academic, presiding over his domain much like a benevolent dictator. As his secretary appeared to be missing, I knocked on the imposing door between myself and the Dean.

"Enter," boomed the voice from within. I did as I was told and entered.

"Sit," he said as he gestured to a burgundy leather chair across the immense space of desk, and then we sat for what seemed like minutes but was rather seconds. He was a tall, balding man with severe features and a more severe tone of voice. He was quite the opposite of the rotund, pipe-smoking Dr. Tomlinson, the head of the English department.

"I'm Sean O'Hara," I offered when I finally found my voice. I couldn't determine why I suddenly felt so intimidated.

"Yes," he said, still staring at me. He held his hands as if in prayer.

His one-word sentences were beginning to make me feel even more uncomfortable, and I wished that I hadn't chosen to wear a tie. At that moment, it felt more like a noose that was tightening by the second.

"You look like him," he said enigmatically.

I hadn't the slightest notion of what he meant.

"Excuse me," then, as a bit of an afterthought, I added, "sir?"

"Poe."

I was still nonplussed.

"Edgar Poe. Are you wholly unaware of the fact that you bear a striking resemblance to the subject of your dissertation research?"

"Sorry, sir, I've never thought about it." Then, an amusing thought entered my skull, and I felt an overwhelming urge to share it. I did so. "Perhaps it's a bit like married couples. You know what they say – sir – the longer they're together, the more they begin to resemble one another." I snickered. He did not.

It was at that moment I looked up. I noticed a copy of a daguerreotype on the wall just behind his left shoulder. It was no more than four by six inches in size and framed in elaborate Victorian gilt. With the penetrating dark eyes, it was known to me in an instant. This very image had haunted me for hours at a time as I sat buried beneath the stacks of books about Poe, his life, his work. It was, of course, Edgar Allan Poe in about 1848, the year before his untimely death. With his high forehead, the deep bags under the eyes, and the full moustache, he probably did resemble me at that moment. I had even shaved off my long sideburns only the month before, thus adding even more to the resemblance.

"As you can see," he said, gesturing to the wall behind, "I, too, am an aficionado of Poe. His work has inspired many a sombre, aspiring writer, you know." He sighed deeply.

Another frustrated writer, I thought. I probably would have been, too, at the time, had I spent as much time on my writing as I ought to have.

The remainder of the conversation could hardly be termed an interview as such. We talked about Poe, my work, and the Dean's writing, which seemed to be in the mystery genre. In the end, it seemed clear to me that I would be offered a position, the thought of which was not altogether disagreeable.

The university was intimately small, and the city congenial. As a Bostonian, I was quite used to the North Atlantic's influence on the weather, notwithstanding the dismal March. And the Canadians I met were pleasant, if a bit diffident. Yes, I would not be unhappy with such a move. Thus, I became yet another displaced American.

TWO

HALIFAX, NOVA SCOTIA, FALL, 1975

Operation Frequent Wind was the code name for the largest helicopter evacuation in history. Saigon was emptied of American military and civilian personnel in an operation that also saw the evacuation of tens of thousands of Vietnamese. But not all. And we all watched those heartbreaking scenes of mothers trying frantically to thrust their children into the hands of the American soldiers on the helicopters hovering just feet above the roof of the American embassy. Even if they were left behind in a city overrun with Viet Cong, they desperately wanted a better life for their children. That is what happened two weeks after I confirmed that I would, indeed, accept the teaching position in Canada. It meant that I no longer had to fear the dreaded draft notice. As a scholar and a gentleman, however, I felt that I had to be as good as my word, and since no other university seemed to want me anyway, I packed all my worldly belongings in my ancient green VW Beetle and headed north along the I-95.

It was, as you may have figured out, 1975, and I was twenty-five years old. With the reckless confidence of youth and my new parchment proclaiming my Ph.D. in American literature in hand, I thought I knew everything. I would be the dashing young professor whom the coeds would discuss long into the night. They would live for my classes, and perhaps I would be caught in an affair or two. Relationships between professors and students were frowned upon even then, long before #MeToo. Still, it was not entirely out of the question, and there would undoubtedly be coeds who would be mesmerized by the young professor. Sadly, this scene, of course, was entirely a figment of my imagination and remained ever thus, fueled as it was at the time by youthful enthusiasm for learning, the crispness of the waning protest movements, and simple hormones.

The reality of the situation was of a virginal, figuratively speaking, young, not-so-dashing professor who realized that his career depended entirely on the approbation of his more senior colleagues, such as is the tenure system of our universities then and now. He knew that he would be studied and scrutinized in everything he did, from publishing his research to voicing opinions at faculty meetings. And, on top of everything, this young professor's deepest, most closely guarded secret was that he was horribly homesick here on this foreign campus.

I thought I knew everything, but I was yet to discover how little I really knew, a lesson that keeps returning to haunt my daily existence. I sometimes laugh aloud at myself when I think of the sweat and blood and tears I poured into the almost-never-ending research for my doctorate, analyzing and dissecting the work of a drunken, possibly drug-addicted genius in a misguided attempt to divine the wellspring of creativity. Ah, such are the pursuits of the young!

Seized by a romantic notion of the ocean and its inspiring qualities, I took a small house outside the city on the shores of St. Margaret's Bay. An inlet of the North Atlantic, the bay was beautiful, and the tiny house had an outstanding view of the water and the horizon beyond. I harboured a secret hope that St. Margaret, whoever she might have been, might still be haunting the shores and made a mental note to research the origin of the locale's name. Had practicality, however, played a larger role in my thinking than did romanticism, I might have reconsidered the wisdom of this choice. On more than one occasion, I thought that my old Beetle might not make the thirty-five-minute trip. I didn't cherish the thought of wintry mornings on that narrow, winding highway.

I had been in that first assistant professorship for only three months, a mere six weeks into the first semester, when I was summoned to Baltimore to make funeral arrangements for my grandmother, who had finally succumbed to her bad heart at seventy-five. My female ancestors had all lived to fairly old ages, while the males had been consumed at much earlier ages by their own passions for drink, smoke of various sorts, and work. This was my legacy.

As the only remaining male progeny in the family, either by birthright or marriage, it fell to me to arrange the funeral, escort my mother in her time of grief – although she and her mother had barely spoken in some years – and dispose of the matriarchal home that had been in the family since some indeterminate time in the 1800s. Although, to tell you the truth, I had never understood why Mama had never liked the house and why she didn't want it now. In fact, throughout most of my life, she had avoided it entirely, telling me on more than one occasion that she had been grateful in the extreme when my father had taken a job in Boston sometime during my infancy.

When I approached him about my need to absent myself from my academic duties for a week, the Dean was wholly unimpressed by my need to deal with a family tragedy so soon after the beginning of the semester, and he made his displeasure perfectly clear. I had quickly come to know that he had a well-deserved reputation for strictness and adherence to rules.

I can still see him standing above me, ramrod erect, hands behind his back, as I sat beneath his supercilious gaze.

"Dr. O'Hara," he said, emphasizing the "doctor" part, "Do you realize the seriousness of your

10

commitment to teaching these fledgling undergraduates? They will come to look to you for guidance and knowledge." He paced slowly back and forth behind his desk. "When you arrived on this campus, I was under the impression that you aspired to a serious career at the university. We cannot be letting one another down."

I agreed with him wholeheartedly and went anyway.

I had not been inside my grandmother's house in over five years. Mama may never have visited it when I was a child, but I had been packed off two or three times a year to spend some time with Grandmama. And now, here I was again, feeling as I had on so many occasions in my distant past. It was amazing to me how little it had changed. I imagined that it had changed rather little since it was built as well. As I stepped inside the front door, I was swept into the nineteenth century, a feeling that never ceased to wash over me when I crossed under the arch above the front door. My grandmother used to say that one of her ancestors had been responsible for the decor, which had been meticulously maintained over the decades.

The funeral itself was uneventful and not particularly mournful. After all, Grandmama Cecilia had lived a long life, and all her friends had left this world years before. It was a quiet affair. The priest droned on endlessly about life in the hereafter, a quaint concept that I could not quite grasp.

Later, we were faced with the disposition of Grandmama's worldly possessions. It posed little problem for us. My mother was at least helpful now that her own mother was dead and couldn't contradict her. Argument, it seemed to me, had been the cornerstone of their relationship. Mama seemed relieved that her mother would not be present for the reading of the will. Well, of course. She was, after all, dead.

We arrived at the offices of Grimshawe Bros. LLC on East Pratt Street in downtown Baltimore at five minutes to nine in the morning. Mama and I inserted ourselves into an elevator with the morning rush or, at the very least, the people who seemed to be late, judging from the buzzing about the time. Those were the days before everyone spent elevator rides with their eyes firmly trained on their smartphones. In this case, they had to balance coffee cups with iPods (remember those?) and briefcases while attempting to look at their watches tucked up under suit jacket sleeves. Men and women alike were attired in the uniform of the legal profession.

A navy-blue-suit-clad receptionist with a severe bun at the nape of her neck ushered us into the office of one Harold Grimshawe, the senior brother, or so it seemed, judging from the evident seniority of his apparent age. He looked absolutely ancient to me, just the sort of solicitor my grandmother would have trusted. As I looked around the office, it occurred to me that Grandmama must have chosen him not only because of his age but also because she probably felt right at home in his office. Clad all around in dark wood with brass accents, it looked for all the world like the den at the back of her old house.

"You must be Sean," Mr. Grimshawe said, raising himself with some apparent difficulty from the enormous leather chair behind his vast desk. He extended his hand, which I leaned across the expanse of desk to reach. He then looked at my mother, who was waiting patiently just behind me.

"Ah," he said, looking in her direction, "I finally meet Cecilia's daughter. Mrs. O'Hara, isn't it?" he said. "I have heard a lot about you."

"I'm sure you have," Mama said, taking one of the seats facing his desk.

I took the other while Mr. Grimshawe once again took his seat and began shuffling through a vast array of legal-looking papers. Had he lost her will?

After a bit more shuffling, he retrieved a folder from under several others. "So," he said, pushing his glasses farther up his nose, "we can begin."

"Sean, it has been my privilege to have been your mother's solicitor for five decades, and she was clear and explicit in her instructions about her will from the beginning." He pulled what looked like the actual will from the folder and continued without looking up.

"Cecelia, God rest her soul, came to see me about a new will immediately after her mother, Catherine, died. It has been updated several times since then, but there is one provision that has not changed from the very start."

He failed to mention exactly what that was, instead proceeding to read the will from the beginning.

Finally, he arrived at that point of the unchanging provision.

"Sean, I have no further information except this. Your grandmother wanted you to have a particular item."

As it turned out, that item was an old leather trunk that had been mouldering in a corner of the attic for many years. Even Mam knew nothing more. It was meant to be bequeathed to the first male offspring of this matriarchal line. I was the first and only male to spring from this line of ladies for an unknown period, and so it was now mine whether I wanted it or not.

Mama and I left the office wholly caught up in a conversation about what was next in terms of disposing of the house and its contents.

Over the next few days, I became so caught up in arranging for the auctioneer to dispose of everything else that Mama and I could not see our way clear to take home that I didn't notice my mother had taken it upon herself to ship the trunk home to Canada for me. When everything was finished in Baltimore, and I was readying myself for the long trip back to the university, I was grateful that I didn't have to deal with the dirty old trunk.

Curiosity had given me pause to consider the contents of the trunk several times during that busy week of the funeral. However, I had been otherwise occupied and hadn't pursued my interest.

Canada Customs, being what it was, then as now, the trunk was not available to me for pick-up for some two months after I had returned to Halifax. By that time, it was late in the semester, and I was too busy marking term papers from my freshmen students even to notice it. Considering the thickness of the mantle of dust that still covered it when it finally did arrive, it occurred to me that the customs officials hadn't even bothered to open it to check its contents. Busy as I was with those papers to mark and mandatory participation in other departmental activities, it had to harbour its mysteries for just a bit longer.

It was the night of the English department's Christmas party. It was an unusually mild December night, with a strong breeze whipping up leftover fallen leaves. More than once on the walk to the car after I left the festivities, I had the hallucinatory experience that the leaves were so many rats swirling about my feet in the darkness. I was momentarily overtaken by a feeling of panic. I was in no condition to drive and cannot now even remember anything of the drive home. Fortunately, we had received no snow yet that season, and the Royal Canadian Mounted Police, whose cars, not horses, patrolled the highways, seemed to have missed me.

I arrived home just after midnight, having imbibed more than my usual quota of holiday cheer, after which I must have stumbled my way down the old stone steps of the Faculty Club building. Unlike those party-goers who become more and more jolly as they sink into inebriation, I was given to despondency that was ever more pronounced during the Yuletide season. I only hoped that I had not said or done anything embarrassing since, even in my partially inebriated state (which I seemed to reach after considerably less alcohol than most other young men), I never lost sight of the fact that it would be a long road to tenure.

A leaden melancholy enveloped me as I trudged through the door of my silent little house. These feelings of gloom and loneliness were becoming my ever more constant companions, and I missed the cold crispness of the Christmases of my youth. Although my family Christmas memories were not entirely warm and jovial, resembling more a colloquium of learned colleagues than the quaint gathering of kinsfolk around the blazing hearth, I still saw the season in images conveyed by so many Yuletide cards. Oddly, I missed the familiar faces and the conversation. And over the years, my memories of family gatherings had warmed in my imagination as I embellished them with the longings of a thing neglected. The one singular, real memory of warmth was the remembrance of Grandmama Cecilia and her ancient old house in Baltimore, where I had been shipped off on Boxing Day after Christmas with my mother and father in Boston every year of my childhood.

Thus, I sat in my dark den, imbibing yet more of the holiday spirit, descending deeper and deeper into a haze of self-pity when a sudden sharp breeze through the open window blew the curtain back from where it kept out the night. I shivered slightly, thinking that I ought to close the window before the temperature dropped further. Then, I noticed a ray of pale gray light had fallen onto the dusty trunk and pushed deep into the corner of the room. The light gave it a momentary aura of unreality.

I placed my half-empty glass of some amber-coloured liquor on the edge of the heavy oak desk, which was my pride and joy, and then reached to turn on the small reading lamp. It lit just enough of the desktop to mark student papers or write in my journal while I was still enveloped in darkness. I arose from my leather chair rather shakily and was momentarily startled by the characteristic squeak of the leather releasing me from its grip. I stepped across the room to the trunk, which I had unthinkingly begun to use as a catchall for journals that I had meant to read and for all manner of other papers that seemed to have no immediate home. I steadied myself on the edge of the desk.

I knelt down slowly, placing the papers on the floor, thereby disturbing the thick layer of dust that had settled on the brown leather over the years and that the trip north had not entirely removed. As I began to search for a way to unfasten the tarnished black lock, my fingers involuntarily traced the engraved initials "B.R." Even in my drunken state, I realized that these were not Grandmama Cecelia's initials at all. Neither were they her mother Catherine's. Perhaps a male relative of whom I had no knowledge? Who *was* the original owner of this obviously one-time handsome piece? I was now caught by the mystery.

I examined it more closely still. It stood about eighteen inches high and three and a half feet long. As I rubbed away some of the years of dust, it was clear to me that this was a costly piece of imported leather that had probably set the owner back quite a penny. It was too small to be a steamer trunk and too large to be a lady's cosmetic trunk, or so I thought. My knowledge of women at that time in my life was confined to one-night stands, relationships lasting barely weeks and one brief live-in experience with a seriously young undergraduate, all based on a profound respect for lust. My fingers found their way back to the lock.

But my curiosity would have to wait a bit longer as the lock was fastened solidly, and in my current state, I could scarcely remember my name, let alone where I had stashed the key that had been in the Customs envelope attached to the trunk. I was, however, not to be deterred.

In a sudden burst of frenzied energy, I raced about the room in the semi-darkness, out the door and down the hall into my bedroom, where I commenced rifling through the contents of my junk drawer while my unmade bed screamed for me to descend upon it and sleep off this depression – and bender. I groped for a moment, and then I had it! I leapt back toward the den. I put the key in the lock.

I stopped, remembering something distant. A fragment of memory had just begun to surface. It occurred to me that I may have some knowledge of the possible owner of the initials. There had long been a rumour in my family that great-great-great-grandmother Bridget Ryan had taken her own life when she was seventy years old, which, by my calculations, would have been in about 1880 in the house in Baltimore. At that time, she was considered to be extremely elderly, most of her contemporaries having succumbed to one hysterical malady or other years before. By all accounts, Bridget was hale and hearty to the end, and her sudden death was shrouded in a cloud of mystery, her Victorian family presumably trying to keep the details as private as possible.

This mystery had often played upon my mind during my own darkest moments when, in despair, dying by my own hand had seemed preferable to living by someone else's. Although I had brooded, I had never had the courage to do it. Evidently, Bridget had more courage than I did.

I returned my thoughts to the present and to the lock. It was not easy to open, apparently wanting to keep its secrets just a bit longer. When I finally managed to loosen it, it was with shaking fingers that I raised the lid to expose the contents.

My hand first uncovered a small black, velvet-covered box. Its bronzed edges were old and marked, but it opened easily when I lifted the lid. Inside was an astonishingly beautiful piece of what appeared to be jewelry. Lifting it out of the box by its long gold chain, I was startled to discover a crystal scent bottle threaded upon it. I recognized it at once. During my doctoral research, I spent a great deal of time examining materials that had played a part in everyday life in America during Poe's era, and this object was clearly from that period. I wrestled the top off and held it up to my nose to determine whether a scent could last through the decades.

I was immediately assaulted by an unfamiliar and entirely foul odour emanating from the inner aspect of the delicate crystal. I threw my head back and coughed, quickly replacing the top to once again trap the malodorous material.

I turned the piece over and over in my shaking hand, feeling a slight chill make its way from my lower back up to my neck, where it settled in to prickle the hairs. I replaced the necklace in its box and continued my perusal.

Between two pieces of discoloured lace, I uncovered a small picture in a tarnished silver frame. It was a daguerreotype. My immediate reaction to the eyes in the portrait was strangely visceral. My stomach turned, and for a moment, I thought I might be sick, for I gazed upon what looked to be a genuine likeness of Edgar Allan Poe. I knew that few authentic portraits existed, and I had never seen this one before. The thought that I might hold yet another in my hand was overpowering. Perhaps this was the feeling psychics experienced when they held objects belonging to others. Where had it come from? Who had owned this trunk? Perhaps the next item that I put my hand on was to give me my answer.

It was a thick, leather-bound book – I could see that it was a diary. A private collection of another human being's thoughts and feelings. Private. I felt somewhat obscene as I dared to loosen the clasp and then turned to the first yellowed page written in flowing, romantic script. It was unmistakably the hand of a woman. A loose page that had been tucked inside the front of the journal fell free. Reaching down to pick it up, I noticed that my hand was shaking uncontrollably. I placed the page on the desk under my lamp, where it seemed to glow in the spotlight. All at once, I had the eerie feeling that I was no longer alone in the house.

What I read that night was a journal, painstakingly kept for fifty-some years by a woman ahead of her time in many ways. As I read, I could see her clearly in my mind's eye, and I began to see myself with new eyes.

The loose page began the story.

"Baltimore, Maryland, October 7, 1880

I am an old woman. Yet within me live the dreams and hopes, the needs and lusts of the young woman that I was. They are with me always, waking and sleeping. Beneath the leathered and deeply furrowed skin, beneath the coarse hair, the failing eyesight is the body of a lithe and vibrant woman. I am now ready to die. I have lived too long and perhaps too well. And yet I have lived not half long enough nor nearly well enough. At least if I could not live my life on my own terms, I shall die on my own terms..."

THREE

I could scarcely believe that the man I knew my father to be could be speaking these words.

"I have spoken to them," he said, clearly avoiding my eyes, "and they will not hear of it."

As I watched the words form and take shape to float across the room toward me, I felt faint with an unknown emotion. In that moment, for but the briefest of seconds, I hated my father for being a man. I hated all those men that he represented.

It was as if I were dreaming. He spoke, but I could not answer him. My throat refused to make a sound. Catching but a phrase here and there, my mind wandered to contemplate the source of these unaccustomed words.

"... not seemly for a woman, Bridget ... no women at the university ... men have the proper qualities for physicians ... other talents to pursue ..."

My mind began to fill so with whirling thoughts of what my life would become that I heard only snatches of his following comments. I felt my head swimming in a sea of disbelief. How could they deny me this opportunity? How could these men deny me my life? What gave them the right? And how could my father have allowed them to do so? I thought for the briefest of moments I might be sick.

"After all," I heard him saying calmly, "you are a young woman. Your education need not be quite so focused." He bent to pick up his pipe and placed it between his teeth. "There are other things –"

"Other things? What other things, Father?" I blurted out, almost against my conscious will. "Dancing? Cooking? Making lace?" I stopped a moment before

20

going on. "I am not a child nor a pet. I am a woman – I have a good mind – a mind worth more than those of many of those men the university sees fit to admit – and I want to learn. I want – no need – to live a life worth living." I was on the verge of tears, but I was constantly aware of Abigail's presence in the room, and I would not let down my guard while she listened.

She sat to the side of us, as on the periphery of the action, in the brocade chair that Mother had placed there lovingly so many years ago. She sat calmly tatting a length of lace, no doubt with which to adorn yet another useless linen handkerchief or prissy collar. Periodically, she nodded as if in agreement with Father but said nothing.

I could see now that Father was trying to make me, his bright, willful daughter, see the practical problems of my request. I did not want to hear them. All I had ever wanted in the world was to be like him – to be a physician, to use my knowledge, my skills, my hands, my mind and my heart to heal. I wanted to be independent. Father knew all these things. He had even encouraged me, but now he was failing me.

For some time now, I feared this might happen. At sixteen, you may believe that you will change the world, but the terrible fact is that the world will try mightily to change you first. It is simply a question of will against will. I knew that the medical college had never yet accepted a woman, that they firmly believed that this was men's work, that there were more genteel pursuits for young women. I believed in my father, though, and I had expected the impossible of him. Perhaps this was unfair of me, but I was willing to do the impossible. Could he do less? He had the power to help me take the first step, or so I had thought. It was over. I would not be admitted.

I felt all the years since Mother died enter into my consciousness and envelop me with sadness. I missed her desperately. I was barely five years old when she was taken from us in childbirth, and over the years since, I realized that I wanted to save mothers and children from this fate. I thought it was my destiny. I knew in my heart that Father had done his best both as a physician and a father for these past eleven years, but now I could see that he could not accomplish everything. It was a revelation that I would never forget.

It was quiet now. We all sat in our corners, awaiting the next round. Father was nodding at Abigail as she looked knowingly at him. I had never been a defiant daughter, but I could feel the beginning of a rebellion growing within me, a palpable presence in my chest.

"I will make some arrangements for you to go to stay with your Uncle Liam."

I looked up in bewilderment. At that moment, my father looked more uncomfortable than I had ever seen him. He cleared his throat and looked away from my eyes. Uncle Liam and his wife of recent months had taken up residence near the new University of Virginia, where, with his Oxford education, Liam was a professor of ancient languages. Grace, my new aunt, was a young woman, not many years my senior.

"You mean that I can study there?" For a moment, I allowed my hopes to rise.

"In a manner of speaking," Father said, clearing his throat again and biting down on his pipe as he gazed out the window. Father was almost six feet tall – I owed my height to him – but he now looked almost small of stature, so unsure of himself he seemed. It was an unusual and uncomfortable circumstance. "Women are not permitted to enroll at the university, as you well know, Bridget, but you can spend time on the campus and use the library facilities. Liam informs me that the library remains at least partially unfinished, but he assures me that more and more volumes arrive monthly. You will have Grace to chaperone you, of course. You will have access to many learned people and all the books that you could possibly wish for."

"All except what I really want to study," I said more to myself than to him. He was looking at Abigail and did not hear me anyway.

"You may go for a year," he said. "Your young Aunt Grace has been asking if you could spend some time with them, and I believe that the time has come. As you can imagine, she is some years younger than the wives of the other professors. While Liam does not believe that to be an impediment to worthiness for a professor's wife, her life can, of course, be lonely."

There were so many unspoken thoughts in that statement. But I knew, although I had not been told as yet in so many words, that Father planned to remarry and that I would be an obstacle. I had met my young Aunt Grace only twice before, but I knew well that she did not share my philosophy of life. She seemed charming but unlike me in so very many ways. She would, no doubt, be instructed to make a lady of me and turn my thoughts from books to young men. I had no particular objections to young men in my life if only they shared my intellectual curiosity and did not expect me to fetch and carry for them. I had already gained knowledge of young men's limitations in the carnal realm. That fact alone would have come as quite a shock to Father.

"Please think about it, Bridget," he said. "You know I only wish for you to be happy. But I worry about you. I blame myself sometimes. You do not seem to share the interests of other young women." He sighed. "I have done my best. I have tried, but being a physician is all I know. I should never have let you believe that you could do what I have done."

"Sean, there is no need for you to reprove yourself over this. No man could have done better on his own."

Abigail had dared to speak. The hair on the back of my neck bristled with every utterance, every syllable that emanated from her lips. She was speaking about me as if I were an inanimate object, as if I were not even in the room. I would not be subjected to this any longer. My father deserved better, so I chose to ignore rather than fight.

I looked at her as she sat upright in her chair. Her flaxen hair was held severely back from her rather pointed face, emphasizing the surprisingly steely aspect of her blue eyes. They always seemed icy and remote to my eyes. Father had told me on more than one occasion that it was a mere figment of my imagination, and if I would simply take the time to become better acquainted with her, I would see her more as he did. I knew it would never happen.

I raised myself to my full five feet and seven inches, four inches taller than Abigail. "I will think about this, Father. We shall speak at breakfast."

I walked slowly and deliberately, with as much dignity as I could muster, toward the archway leading from the parlour to the hall. I knew that I would be in view until the sweep of the staircase turned. As soon as I was past the turn, I ran to the top and down the hall to my room, where I furiously closed the door and began to sob uncontrollably.

I crumpled to the floor like a marionette that had suddenly lost its strings, then sobbed for what seemed like a very long time. The hot tears dropped silently onto the green satin of my dress, creating wild patterns that seemed to reflect my thoughts back at me. Suddenly, as quickly as the tears had begun, they stopped. I picked myself up from the floor and walked over to my desk, my father's indulgence of my interests. I had insisted that I preferred to have a desk rather than a dressing table, and, in his usual way, he had found a compromise that I could find acceptable. Beside my frilly dressing table stood the large oak desk. It was not a small lady's writing table; rather, it was a heavy desk with drawers to fill with books and notes and pens of all kinds. It was a heavy desk upon which to stack heavy books – a large surface upon which to spread out the pages and to make notes in a journal.

I sat down in the large leather-covered chair and opened the top drawer. From under a sheaf of papers, I withdrew a small volume that Father had given me as a gift at Christmas when I turned ten years old.

I turned the book over and over in my hands. Finally, I placed it on the desk in front of me. *American Lady's Preceptor* was the title on the cover. I opened it to the table of contents, and my finger moved downward from the top of the page. "The Value of Time," "Observations on Reading," then down to "An Essay on Women," "Studies Proper for Women," and my own personal favourite, "Religion, the Best Female Acquirement."

This book was Father's attempt to educate me. He had sent me to the convent school, where I had acquired a taste for education in most everything except religion. Oh, the nuns had tried as best they could to interest me in a religious vocation, but I would have none of it. As a motherless girl, I was a likely prospect in their eyes. Although I did not share their interest in the ecclesiastical life, I did appreciate that they had one thing that other women of my acquaintance did not possess. They had a real education – what I called book learning. What they lacked in knowledge of the flesh, they made up for in the wisdom gained from years of this book learning. I craved to share that with them.

I can yet see Sister Eulalia Marie standing before us, her class of fresh-faced, well-scrubbed, well-heeled nine-year-olds. "Ladies," she would say as she paced back and forth across the front of the room, her heels clicking rhythmically on the wood floor, each hand buried deep in the opposite black sleeve, "you must learn to read beyond the words you see before you. You must absorb the essence of the writer." She would turn and rap her yardstick forcefully on the desk. "There is where you will find the essence of yourself. There, and not in the arms of a man."

The class giggled nervously. Some reddened. I looked around at all the silly girls who did not understand what Sister was saying to them and never would. I already perceived that I was different. I knew what she wanted us to understand, and I meant to try to find myself that way. I meant to read everything that my hands could touch, and I meant to understand and read beyond the words on the pages.

Not that I did not like boys, though. Indeed, I found them almost as fascinating as my studies. But boys were a thing of mystery to the convent girls. We rarely saw any at all, except for those girls who had brothers whose friends came to call. As time went on, I did not care much about whether Father would let me meet the boys or not. I had learned the ways of the flesh, as Sister Eulalia called it, at the age of fourteen with one of those brothers. But there would be as much time as necessary for more of that after I realized my life's dream. It was then, at the age of fourteen, that I decided I would become a physician like my father. Then, I could save those mothers and babies as I had desired since my mother's death. I now knew that my father would have found it infinitely easier to have a daughter who would do what other daughters did. But he had instilled in me an early love of learning and helping, and as I approached my sixteenth birthday, I perceived that Father was finding this a difficult road. It was almost a betrayal, and the truth is I did, indeed, blame him for not working harder on my behalf to gain me entry into the medical college. I was devastated. And I was not prepared to give up my dream.

I placed the book in my hands back into the drawer and took up my pen. I dipped it into the ink, and I began to write.

"*Dear Uncle Liam,*
Father has conveyed to me your kind offer to have me stay with you in Charlottesville. I humbly accept this kindness and look forward to seeing the university. I understand that I am able to gain admission to the library, and this, for me, will be almost as agreeable as attending the university. Perhaps I may be permitted to sit in on one or two lectures on history and the ancient languages.
Please convey my gratitude for this offer to Aunt Grace. I know that I shall enjoy seeing her again.
Your loving niece,
Bridget Ryan."

I folded the page in four, thus creating a heavy square, and then addressed the outermost flap to Uncle Liam at the University of Virginia. I lit the candle on my desk and sat patiently as wax dripped onto the edge. When enough had accumulated, I ensured that the soft wax formed a seal on one edge. It was done. I would convey my decision to Father at breakfast.

It was at that moment that I knew with certainty my childhood was over.

FOUR

The flaxen-haired shrew was called Abigail Densmore, and I knew that Father meant to make her my stepmother. Her very presence in our home was as unwelcome as an icy rain on a summer's day, at least to me.

From the age of ten, I had conjured in my mind a complete picture of my mother, and Abigail was nothing like that image in my young mind. The reality of my mother was long buried under waves of emotion from which I cannot say that I ever really healed. From bits and pieces of real memories, now seen as through a veil, I recreated my mother in my mind. That image was as real to me as if she had read me stories every night, held my head in her lap when I felt unwell (which was very infrequently), shared with me all those Christmas mornings filled with glee, and became to me the friend in adolescence, the like I have never really experienced.

This, I know, was a tall order to fill in any human person, and Abigail could never hope to take that place in my heart. Not that she really wanted to.

Abigail Densmore was closer to my own age than my father's. I had recently begun to wonder at the behaviour of the Ryan men, who seemed to need to cultivate relationships with women young enough to be their daughters. Perhaps they believed that these young wives could bear them the children that their dead wives had found so difficult. Perhaps they were seeking to recover lost youth. Perhaps, and this I believed to be closer to the truth, women their own age were so old. They had turned into matrons before their own eyes. Surely, men longed for something more.

Whatever the case, Father and his brother Liam seemed to be taking similar steps. Thus, I realized very early on in my father's friendship with Abigail that she was likely to become my father's new wife. I fervently wished that there would be no children of the union, and I believed that to be unlikely anyway. You see, Abigail emerged from rather a different life than either my father or I had experienced.

She had been born and raised in New York City, a place I hoped only to myself to visit at some time in my future. My friends all said that New York was filled with rich, stylish men and women on one side and evil criminals on the other. Both seemed deliciously interesting to me from my sheltered existence. It seemed to me that there must be a constant, dark battle to see who would win out – good or evil. As far as I could see, there was little difference between the good and the evil.

Father had met Abigail exactly one year earlier when she had come to Boston to visit relatives. It had been the Christmas season, and Father usually turned to Holy activities. Although he had left regular Mass attendance immediately upon my mother's death, he had insisted that I learn what the church had to offer, and once a year, he would attend Mass with me.

It was midnight Mass, and the choir was particularly inspiring that night. The air was crisp, and light snow fell outside. Father and I had just arrived at the cathedral and seated ourselves in a pew. I was still upon bended knee, pretending for Father's sake that this was my usual church behaviour (that could not have been further from the truth as I, too, had lost faith), when several of his friends who were constantly attempting unsuccessfully to find him a female companion, took the seats in front of us. Abigail was with them that night.

After brief, whispered introductions, I spent the remainder of the Mass staring at the back of the black-coated figure swathed in foxtails. When we rose to join the choir in the chorus of *Adeste Fideles*, I noticed that she did not seem to be singing, and I wondered if she shared our religious faith. Every so often, the figure would turn her head slightly so that only Father could see her face. There was something about that tiny movement of her head that made me angry.

All during that season, Father seemed different. Perceptible only to me, his mood seemed slightly raised. Two days after Christmas, Father was invited to a party. Normally, he would refuse such an invitation, but this one he accepted. I watched him groom and prepare himself, all the while knowing that he must be anticipating a meeting with someone, likely Abigail. I had been correct, and her presence had become ever more frequent since that time. She had found a hundred different excuses to visit her relatives. Father had, on at least three occasions, found it necessary to travel to New York to hear a lecture from a visiting physician. He tried mightily to keep this all to himself, but I was well aware of the change in his mood. I suppose I ought to have been happy for him, but I could not bring myself to like this woman who spent much of her time in the pursuit of what I deemed trivialities. Indeed, I truly knew little of what might have occupied Abigail's days in New York and did not wish further illumination on the matter.

After making some discreet inquiries of my young friends and their mothers, I was able to ascertain that Abigail Densmore was well known in New York for hosting literary salons, where writers came to mingle and read from their works. As Abigail was evidently the daughter of a wealthy importer, it seemed to me that she had a great deal of money with which to play patron to the arts. I surmised that since she appeared to possess no artistic talent herself beyond tatting endless yards of lace, she needed to be around such people. She seemed to me to be a "watcher" rather than a "doer." Thus, she came to be in our home that Christmas. At least if I went to Charlottesville for a year, I would be spared her company.

After I placed the letter to Uncle Liam on the desk to let the wax dry, I changed into my nightgown. I poured some water into the pitcher by my bedside and washed my face slowly.

When I crawled into my bed, I fell into a fitful sleep, haunted by dreams of writers sticking their writing quills into me, laughing as I writhed. It was, however, painless writhing, and I thought it was very curious. But the images of the tormented eyes, ringed in darkness, remained with me for a very long time.

FIVE

CHARLOTTESVILLE, VIRGINIA, APRIL 1826

I arrived at the home of my Uncle Liam and Aunt Grace just as spring was in full flower. It was breathtaking. The University of Virginia was situated in Albemarle County in a verdant valley where the pitch of the mighty Alleghanies comes to rest in the gentle undulation of tree-topped slopes. Set at the confluence of several surrounding mountain ranges was the quadrangle of buildings and the library rotunda, which filled my undernourished scholar's soul with awe. Since I had spent many of my sixteen years within the confines of Boston, rarely had I encountered the opportunity to breathe in the freshness of the open air in spring. I promised myself to take full advantage of the sensual opportunities that were sure to be afforded to me in my exile.

The thought of the university was thrilling to me. Very new and fresh itself, this academy of higher learning had been the dream of President Jefferson. But that dream had taken almost half a century to be realized. Uncle Liam had come here less than a year earlier to take up his position in the new university as a Professor of Ancient Languages. How I envied him his hours among the grand tomes, full to brimming with Latin and Greek. I had learned much of these myself and craved another opportunity to enlarge my education. In my young head, I knew that any hope of ever entering a medical school to pursue my real dream was dashed, but in my heart, I could still not accept it. How long I must live with that incongruence, I did not know.

My leave-taking from Father was amiable enough. But it reminded me that I could no longer conjure up that feeling of being his little girl, loved and protected from the outside world. I clearly no longer shared the same place in his life as I had for so many years, and I knew deep within me that this was not entirely his fault, if it could be construed to be anyone's fault.

Abigail had wisely kept her distance in the weeks before my departure and had been absent for the actual leave-taking itself. As I hugged my father on that day, I felt grown up. I knew that the next time we kept company, he would be engaged to Abigail, and my life would be forever changed. I buried my face deeper into his shoulder, and I did not cry. I still blamed him for my failure to obtain a place in the medical school.

My Uncle Liam was a much younger brother to Father. As gregarious as Father was serious, Liam bore a striking resemblance to his older brother. He was tall and red-headed, but he was almost always smiling, in contrast to his older brother. I knew that Father was then about fifty years of age, some fifteen years or so older than Liam. Liam's new wife, Grace, however, was just past twenty. I had met her only once before, at her wedding to Uncle Liam the year before. Upon meeting her again at her home at the university, it was clear to me that she longed for the company of another young woman. She was pretty and vivacious, with auburn hair and hands that seemed to punctuate her every sentence. Her conversation was full of lace tablecloths, menus, and children, although, at the time, she had none. I feared that I would have little in common with her.

There were only eight professors at the university; most had been brought over from Europe, and most were unmarried. Those who were married had wives who spoke little, if any, English and seemed to have rather serious natures, at least according to Grace. Thus, she had languished here for months prior to my arrival.

I could see that my presence was as much for her as it was intended to be for me. Although we were different, I liked Grace, yet I fervently hoped that our activities would not divert me from my primary purpose of being here.

I tried to take in the details of the university as our carriage passed by on the way to Uncle Liam's home. The campus itself was incomplete. Construction was clearly still underway, and I would eventually become familiar with Uncle Liam's discussions with other professors about the overcrowding problems to which professors and students alike were subjected. Evidently, this overcrowding was even more problematic in the dormitories where the young men lived, and it seemed to play no small part in what I began to realize was a distinct problem with gambling and fighting among the student body. On more than one evening that spring, Uncle Liam was called out of his bed at night to deal, in his turn, with the pugnacious youths. I was appalled to learn of this violent turn of behaviour on the part of young academics. Did they not realize the value of the education they were receiving? Did they not feel privileged simply to have the opportunity which fully half of our population was being denied? I was not frightened by the thought of this atmosphere of wickedness, only angry that it happened at all.

Grace and I fell into some rather pleasant habits during that spring. As she was inclined to sleep rather late in the forenoon, I learned quickly that my best hours for poring over Uncle Liam's books and stealing out to stroll through the campus and the library without a chaperone were early. I could still hear my father's admonition about Grace as my chaperone ringing in my ears, but I chose to ignore it, and Grace did not seem the wiser. I knew that it was only a matter of time before reports of my morning activities made their way back to

Uncle Liam. But for the moment, I would enjoy a modicum of freedom.

By the time Grace had arisen and prepared herself for the day, I would have spent several happy hours soaking up as much from the pages of the books as my relatively unused mind could possibly accommodate. I had made a friend of Mr. Wertenbaker, the university librarian. It was easy. Like many men, he was clearly susceptible to feminine charms. Thus, although I should not have been permitted, he allowed me access to the library.

Always an observant child, I found that this developing skill was beginning to provide considerable fruit. I began the habit of making myself as inconspicuous as possible so that I could look, listen and learn. Doing so was frequently no easy feat as I was tall, not unattractive, and the only young, unmarried woman of reputable character near the campus. Many of my most interesting evenings were spent in the background as Uncle Liam and his colleagues shared a glass of brandy and discussed philosophy, life, literature and their students. On the one hand, I longed to take part in these discussions. On the other hand, I knew that I could learn more by listening unobtrusively – not that the professors would have welcomed a young woman into their discourse in any case.

These discussions, coupled with my own observations of the young men, created perhaps my only longing during those happy months. It now happened that I longed to learn more about men, not mere boys whose fumblings I had already encountered.

I was the only woman sitting among the dusty volumes, reading a Latin discourse on that fresh spring morning. In fact, I was, of course, the only woman in the building on most occasions. Grace had accompanied me to the rotunda (which always reminded me of the Roman Pantheon, drawings of which I had seen in one

35

of Father's books) when we heard that a shipment of books had arrived to fill the shelves that were yet bare. She had, however, taken her needlepoint outside, and as a result of her unusually early rise, she quickly fell asleep. I could see out a window that her head had nodded against a tree.

It was my custom to spend those solitary mornings in the company of a book of Latin, Art, Literature or History, and when I could charm Mr. Wertenbaker to allow it, with a book of anatomy or other science. These were, however, few and far between as sciences were not an option for these students at the time. Since I had only a year within which I could fulfill my desire for such an educational experience under my father's good graces, I considered it my duty to be as diligent as humanly possible. On this particular morning, I happened upon a book of herbal medicine and wondered if it had made its way to this library by some kind of mistake. I pounced upon it.

I was thus engaged when I spied the face of a young man who had become more familiar to me of late – at least from a distance. I had completed my Latin reading for the morning and had taken up the book on herbalism. As soon as I noticed this young man, I continued to pretend to read as I inspected him across the cavernous reading room. This was not the first time I had noticed him.

I had made discreet enquiries as to his identity, and Grace had been more than happy to fill in the details that had been missing from what I overheard from Uncle Liam's evening conversations with other professors. She had, with some glee, informed me that this compact, muscular, handsome young man with the dark, brooding eyes was one Edgar Poe. I had considered this name for some time as I lay awake these nights in my narrow bed and decided that this was not a pleasant name at all. It sounded too stuffy, too pompous. I had thus renamed him Ned, though we had yet to become acquainted in the flesh.

I knew that he was a student primarily of both ancient and modern languages and that he was known to be somewhat moody by times. Upon overhearing Uncle Liam declare that young Poe was not only a scholar but an expert in the gymnastic arts, I had made it my business to discreetly visit the university's new gymnasium on two occasions, where I had secretly observed his prowess. It was not easy to keep hidden, but I managed it. As was his habit, Uncle Liam was right in his assessment of the young man's skills. For my part, I had then decided that I would become more intimately acquainted with Ned Poe.

Under the guise of study, I now planned my encounter. My father had told me on many occasions that I had already cultivated the ability to do a great many things well. One of these, of which my father was wholly unaware, was that given the infrequent opportunity, I had become rather competent at charming men. But, much to my chagrin, there was something about the look in his eyes that compelled me as I had never felt compelled before. It was a sulky look, almost like an overindulged child, yet the shabbiness of his waistcoat, well-disguised by careful grooming, belied the spoiled attitude.

I arose from my study table and replaced the heavy Latin tome in its appointed place on the shelf, keeping the book on herbalism and two other smaller volumes with me. As it had been rather cool in the early morning when I took my leave from my uncle's lodgings, I had worn my favourite wrap, a Parisian-styled walking coat Father had given me just before I left home. My father had many friends among the Boston importers and thus had access to many costly and coveted European goods. The coat, an ankle-length pelisse, was buff-coloured and fastened down the front with braided loops and buttons.

One of the features I particularly liked was that its double-shoulder capes echoed the fashion of men's overcoats. It gave me a feeling of power when I stepped out with it around my slim shoulders.

I took my time as I donned the coat, knowing full well that the mid-day sunshine was likely to coax me to remove it presently. I did not, however, want to miss the opportunity to catch the eye of young Ned Poe across the room. With slow, deliberate motions, I fastened each loop over its corresponding button. I noted with disdain that two other young men had looked up from their books to gawk admiringly. I attempted to keep my indifference from becoming evident.

Finally, at the moment that I placed my hat upon my head, Ned Poe closed his book and stood up. I caught his eye, and instead of coyly smiling and looking immediately away as was customary, I held his gaze steadily for what seemed to me to be a lifetime. In reality, it was but a split second. Ned Poe was no doubt a popular young man with the ladies, but I would be no such conquest, of that he could be assured.

My heels clicked rhythmically along the stone floor as I entered the hall outside the reading room. I was aware of being followed and thus slowed my pace slightly as I turned to exit through the heavy oak doors. As I pushed against the door, I heard a voice behind me.

"Please, allow me," the voice said cheerfully.

Could this be the voice of one who is known to be so moody? I turned to take in my gentleman. It was indeed Ned Poe, but he was sporting a rather nasty-looking bruise below his right eye that had been hidden from me inside the library. I wondered momentarily at his part in the nightly fisticuffs.

"Thank you, sir," I said in my politest tone. "It seems you have already had one altercation too many this fine morning."

He smiled and lightly touched his bruise.

"I could say that I had encountered a door while assisting another beautiful young maiden, but that would be untrue on two counts."

"What, pray tell, sir, are those two counts?"

"The first count is that there is not another maiden as winsome as you in all of Albermarle County, I'll wager. The second count is that I would be lying about my face's contact with a door, a lie that you are likely to find out about when next you converse with your uncle, Miss Ryan."

I turned quickly to take in the set of his jaw. I was uncommonly impressed by his apparent prior interest in me as well. He gallantly took the three volumes from my hands, and we walked together across the now sunny quadrangle toward the building where I was to meet Grace. I fervently wished the distance to be greater.

"Please allow me to introduce myself formally. I am Edgar Allan Poe," he said with the flourish of a bow. "But, of course, you already know that."

"I believe it to be rather unseemly of you to bring that up, Mr. Poe," I said.

"Now, now, Miss Ryan. You are not going to become suddenly coy, are you? I rather like you the way you really are. Such false modesty does not seem to become you." He turned the books over in his hands. "And it does not seem to fit the deportment of a woman acquainted with such literature."

I flushed at his impertinence, profoundly hoping that he believed my reaction to be feminine wiles when, in reality, it heralded a lust I wanted yet to keep secret.

"Please call me Bridget," I said, "and I will call you Ned."

He ran a hand through his thick, dark hair and laughed. "You may call me anything you like, Bridget. I believe that we will find we have a great deal in common, you and I."

As we neared Grace's still dozing figure, he passed the volumes to me, bowed slightly and kissed my hand.

"I will see you again – soon," he said. His dark eyes seemed to be able to penetrate my thoughts, and it occurred to me that his statement was more an order than a request. He was, indeed, as I had hoped.

SIX

"You cannot know what it means for me to have become acquainted with you." Ned was lying under a tree, playing with a blade of grass. Stretched out below us were the valley and the university. We had climbed a gentle slope in an effort to put distance between ourselves and the university that lay below, glinting in the summer sunshine.

"Ned Poe," I said rather more abruptly than I had intended. "You have been saying that for the past month, since we have been keeping company regularly. For a poet, you are more than a little parsimonious with your words. It is about time you explained yourself. I know little of you yet."

Since our first chance encounter in the library, Ned and I had been stealing away from the campus several times a week to walk and converse. Neither Uncle Liam nor Grace (and thus Father) knew of this developing liaison, and it was my intention to keep it that way. This would be my secret.

Surprised to learn that he was just barely seventeen years of age, almost a full two years younger than his comrades, I judged him to be among the most truly intelligent of the young men I had met since coming to Charlottesville. Certainly, he was more intelligent than any of those I had met while suffering through my childhood in Boston.

He was a very adequate conversationalist, which is more than can be said for the rest of the silly men at the university, but most of our discourse had been confined to discussions regarding some portion or other of his studies or of my own exceedingly less formal

41

undertakings. I enjoyed these conversations greatly, but I felt that I did not know him as I wished. I had begun to suspect that Ned was hiding his true self from everyone, including me. I had heard that he bestowed upon his dormitory companions regular readings of the poetry that occupied his mind a great deal of the time. He had, however, not offered the same to me. Yet. Although up until that moment, I had been happy just to have his company, I now needed to know more about him.

I looked over at this broodingly handsome man whom I now counted among my few friends. I observed his thick, dark hair that curled so around his ears, his muscular body. He was barely taller than I was, yet he had a commanding presence. It was his eyes – something about those eyes pierced my being, perhaps even my soul if indeed I had one.

"Bride," he began, his dark eyes seemingly searching for the words. I was fond of the endearing name he called me, as it was his alone. "I might say the same of you. I have not heard much of your life in Boston with your father beyond simply that he is a surgeon and your mother is dead."

I drew a short breath. In spite of the fact that Mother had been dead for many years, a cold dread still crept up on me at the mention of her passing. I knew, however, that both of Ned's real parents had died in his early childhood, so I forgave him his transgression.

I took his hand in mine and felt a small thrill. I began to stroke it gently. "Tell me, my Ned, who you are. Tell me the darkest secrets that lurk behind those shadowy eyes." I continued stroking his hand. "There is a woman whose memory stays with you, is there not?"

He turned away from me and lay back on the grass, his hands behind his head. He stared up at the sky for a moment, and we sat in silence until he spoke.

"Do you dream, Bride?" he asked, turning to me abruptly.

"Yes, I do. What about you? What do you dream of, Ned?"

"Unspeakable things."

I waited a moment to see if he would continue. "Tell me of these things."

He hesitated only a moment, playing with the grass. "I have been in a burial vault when the stone doorway closes behind me with a magnificent crash." He smashed his fist into his other hand. "As a veil, the darkness keeps me from seeing the details of the grotesque that mark the corpses all around me. Then, I come upon a more recently stored corpse. It is a young woman, and I can see that she must have been a beautiful waif in her life. Just as I am observing the beginning of decay upon her brow and drink in the stench of the process, her hand reaches for my lapels and empty eyes implore me to help her. Her soul is not away. Her force is with the body still." As he spoke, his eyes widened, and I could observe a pulsation in his neck. The throbbing quickened. He clutched the grass on either side of him and was silent for a second.

"What else?" I said when finally he began to come back to himself.

"You are not frightened by me and my wild dreams?" He seemed incredulous.

"There is little that frightens me, Ned. My father is a surgeon, as you know, and I spent many a day with him on his rounds and in his surgery after Mother died." I hoped that he had not seen the flinch.

Ned sat up. "Tell me of the human dramas you have seen."

I lay back on the grass and stared up at the sky as I spoke. I had not told anyone else about these significant events that I had seen with my father. Even my father had never been privy to my thoughts about them. Our conversations had been confined to the details of the procedures, which, in themselves, fascinated me.

"I have seen the beginning and the end, Ned. I have seen the birthing of babies, difficult births and easy births, and I have seen death that has come peacefully and death that has rolled over its victim like the force of Mother Nature in all her anger and frustration. In the end, Ned, I suppose the bible might actually have the last word. 'Ashes to ashes, dust to dust.' But that is really all."

"Surely you don't truly believe that? That death really is the finality of being?" Ned sat up and looked down upon me.

"Actually, I do," I said. "Unless one has offspring to carry on at least some of the ideas of one's lifetime, I believe that when life is gone from the body, it is truly the end."

"You have neglected your religious studies, I believe, my Bride."

"Quite the contrary. My mind was filled with the teachings of the nuns, Ned. I have simply grown to realize that they were wrong in most cases." I turned on my elbow to look at him. "You are not put off by my Catholic upbringing?"

"Hardly," he said. "But I am concerned that you believe in the finality of death. It seems to me but a shadow."

He stopped abruptly as if he thought he had said too much. He rose and began to pace with his hands clasped behind his back. He seemed deeply troubled. Then he turned and smiled at me, but I could see the furrow of his brow yet.

"You are a most unusual young woman, Miss Bridget Ryan. I must confess I have not met anyone like you before."

I looked up at him as he stood above. He was no more than one inch taller than I, but he looked tall from this vantage. "What is it about me that is unusual?" I said, leaning back and shading my eyes with one hand.

"You seem so definite about all that you discuss. You are not given to vapours and hysteria as I have seen in many young, and even might I add, older women."

I smiled. "I truly do not plan to spend my life as other women have spent theirs. If I am to be denied my heart's desire one way, I am bound to find it another. I have sworn this to myself."

"I feel that anyone who stands in your way might come to no good," he said. Then he walked over to a nearby tree and leaned against it heavily.

I rose from the grass, brushing a few stray pieces from my frock, which I had hitched up in a most unladylike fashion. Sister Eulalia Marie would have gasped. I could see that the black cloud of despondency had once again wrapped itself around his countenance.

"What is it that troubles you so, Ned?" I took his arm, and we began to walk, falling into a rhythm as we made toward a stream that gurgled its midsummer happiness.

"I am afraid that I shall have to leave the university." His previous line of conversation seemed to have been left behind.

"It was my understanding that you were excelling in your chosen studies. What has happened?"

"Yes, of course, I am excelling, but it is my stepfather. He refuses to give me any more money, although he has a great deal. He arrived here earlier this week to attend to some business in Charlottesville. I am afraid that we have had rather a nasty fight."

I had heard rumours of a loud discussion that Ned was reported to have had. However, given the violent nature of the off-hours activities of many of the students, the encounter barely registered with those who may have overheard. Uncle Liam had mentioned it briefly over sherry only the evening before.

"Bride, you know I lost my parents at an early age. At least you still have your father. Both my parents perished during my fourth year. I was taken in by John and Fanny Allan. My stepmother is as wonderful a person as you could imagine." He smiled at the remembrance. "But she suffers ill health, and I fear for her. My stepfather holds tight to the purse strings. He does not know how dear it is to subsist at this university." His smile faded from his lips as quickly as the last of the evening sun slips over the horizon.

What I did know was that the University of Virginia was among the most costly educational institutions available and that most of Ned's classmates were products of wealthy families more prone to spending and gambling than to studying. I also knew that the professors were well looked after. Uncle Liam always contended that it was his due as he had studied at Oxford in England in preparation.

"How much money have you lost?" I said rather a bit sternly.

"Do you imply that I have been gambling away my allowance?" He feigned offence.

"Do you deny it?"

He was silent. It was clear to me that Ned was in much more profound trouble than he cared to admit to me or anyone else, least of all his stepfather.

"I have some money, Ned," I said. We had stopped walking, and I now bent down to pick a daisy that danced in the breeze.

"Bride, I could not take money from you. It would not be right."

"You are probably right." I twirled the daisy around and around. "But I am fully sixteen years old and swiftly becoming an adult. I have no intention of having my life ruled by what other people think is right. Besides, no one need know." I paused momentarily. "Is it your preference to leave the university prematurely?"

Well," he began, "there is one debt that is weighing particularly heavily on my mind. And I cannot bear the thought of yet more fisticuffs in the dormitory."

"It is done," I said with some finality. And so it began.

SEVEN

During the long afternoons that year in Charlottesville, Grace told me stories of her life. I was appalled when I learned that she had already had two husbands and was now just past her twenty-first birthday. Grace was petite and rather delicate to my eye. Although our views on life in general and women's potential, in particular, differed so very much, she was easy to like. When she talked of her life before Uncle Liam, I listened. Perhaps there were things I could learn from her after all.

The afternoon she told me about her past was the afternoon when I felt that I had truly made a friend. Prior to that time, no one had ever confided in me so.

We had decided to take a picnic out to the expansive lawn bordering the campus. The rays of September sunshine shone radiantly as if trying to fool us into thinking that winter might never come this year. But we knew better and thus wished to make the most of the warm weather.

"Tell me about your life, Grace. I know so little about you, and you know so much of me." I poured her a glass of cider and then watched her sip daintily on it for a moment.

"Bridget, it seems like a lifetime ago that I left Ireland. I was barely sixteen, all alone, and the voyage was horrendous. I was sick from the first day to the last, as was the case with almost everyone on board. It was such that upon every new morning, I wished for death. And then it was over as quickly as it started."

"You were alone?" I could not fathom such a situation.

"Yes. My family was in dire straits, and after Mother died, Father thought it best for me to make a new start. There were no prospects even for a young woman in my village. So, he made arrangements for me to work as a nanny in the home of a wealthy Boston importer."

"What must it have been like to be in a foreign land at such a young age?"

"If I am being honest, it was terrifying."

Shortly after taking her employment, according to Grace, the lady of the house took quite a liking to her and sought to find Grace a husband. Three days after her seventeenth birthday, she was wed to a young teacher at a boys' school, which one of her charges attended on a daily basis.

"Then the unthinkable happened," she said.

I knew what was coming as I had heard from my father the story from the time of her young husband's death. Grace's version of the story of her young husband's eventual untimely death indicated that his hunting rifle misfired one day. My father had been called to see the body. I had been but twelve years old at the time, and Father had decided that it would be unseemly for him to take me if it could be avoided. I remembered only too well spending the evening with old Mrs. Wannamaker in her dark, lilac-scented home next door to ours. I could barely breathe whenever I had to spend more than the briefest of moments in her doorway.

That night was especially memorable as Father had been gone far longer than he had intended. The hushed conversations I heard in the following days indicated that this young man had placed the muzzle of his shotgun to his mouth and pulled the trigger.

According to local rumour, Grace had been in the next room and rushed to find him in this state. From what I have come to learn about anatomy and violence, it could not have been a sight that she would want her mind to recall in later days, so she chose to see the death as purely accidental and put it out of her mind. Grace might have been sharing her story with me, but she chose not to convey any feeling about finding her dead husband. And I chose not to discuss the rumours, confirmed by Father, that it was anything but an accident.

She met Uncle Liam when she came to our home sometime later to thank Father for his assistance in her time of need. That was the first time I saw Grace from afar, although I did not meet her face-to-face until her wedding. She struck me at the time as a wisp of a girl, although she was older than I was by some five years. Although money had been tight in her household, she tended toward the fashions of the day rather strongly. Uncle Liam was home from England, where he was studying for a brief visit. He was in the drawing room, sharing a sherry with Father at the time of her arrival. They invited her in.

I was spying from behind a doorway as she met the two men. Her fashionable gown sported the newest in waistlines and sleeves, and her slight figure wore it well. Her light auburn hair was tucked into a neat knot at the back of her head, with tight curls arranged around her temple and forehead. I noted this carefully as it was in direct contrast to my own countenance. I always had considerable difficulty taming my unruly black tresses into anything that resembled a tidy knot. Her hair was, unfortunately, just about the only thing that did impress me about her at the time. As she offered her hand to each of them, she seemed to me to be too subservient, too obsequious. I quickly lost interest and went off to my bedroom to read.

I finally met Grace at her wedding. Although it was quite unseemly for a widow to marry in white with a veil and a train, Grace seemed to wash her life of any previous marriage and came to Uncle Liam as if a virgin. Perhaps it had been so.

Grace and I thus knew little of each other before that day I arrived in Charlottesville. We were both also in

50

unaccustomed roles – I, as the house guest, and she, as the chaperone. We would have to find our way. And so, we did. We grew closer weekly as we began to share our feelings and our lives.

One afternoon, as we sat together in her flat, the rain beating against the windows, she told me that she once again was not with child. It was clear to me that I knew more about these things than she did, given my experience with Father and his birthing mothers.

"I am sorry to mention this to you, Bridget," Grace said, flushing. "I forget sometimes that you are but a child and should not be forced to think of such adult things yet." She picked up her embroidery, which she had dropped in a basket beside her chair.

I bristled at the suggestion that I was a child, pretending to read for a moment before looking up.

"Why is it that having a child is so important to you? It seems to me your life could be quite complete without one," I said.

"It has little to do with having a child, really." Grace placed her embroidery in her lap and smoothed the folds of her skirt. "It is really about a husband. Having a child is what they want, you know. If a wife is unable to have a child, what is the use of her?"

"What is the use of her?" I said, my voice rising. "Is a woman on this earth only to have babies?"

"You speak as if it were not an important thing to have a child to continue the family name." Grace's eyes grew wide, showing me quite clearly that she was genuinely astonished that I failed to share her opinion of a woman's place in the world.

"I do believe that having a child is important, but it is not the only thing that a woman has to offer the world." I picked up the book from where I had placed it on the table beside me and held it up in front of me. "There is much to be learned from books and lectures. There seems to be so much to expand our world. So much to see and do and learn."

How could I make Father and Uncle Liam understand if Grace, being a woman herself, could not understand?

"Bridget, you are a very bright young lady, and I love you very much. But I fear for you and for your future, as I know your father does as well. You must seek your happiness where it is available to you. You cannot spend your life chasing dreams that will never come true."

I was determined that this would be the only time that Grace and I would converse about my lot in life. I refused to entertain the idea that my life would be dictated by anyone other than myself. I decided, however, to be charitable to Grace, as she and Uncle Liam had been to me. I did not discuss this with her again, but sought those topics where we could share ideas without fear of acrimony.

Grace was many good things – a good chaperone was not one of them. I believe that she found me rather more imperious than she was used to in her life, so she tended to let me go about my business alone or at least kept an eye from afar. She knew that I spent my mornings in the library, and she came to know that I spent some time with Ned Poe. How much time I spent, she did not know. But from time to time, she would ask me about him, and I would evade the issue as much as possible.

"You know that Liam is becoming aware of your friendship with Edgar Poe. He disapproves of your association with any of the students." Grace and I were setting the table for a late dinner. Uncle Liam was expected presently.

"What does he think I am doing when I converse with the young man?"

"Don't be impertinent, Bridget." Grace wiped a knife on her crisp, white apron and continued to place cutlery. We were expecting three other professors for dinner.

In truth, Ned and I had been seeing each other weekly. We discussed art and literature, and once he had finally read me a poem he had written. His melodious voice served him well in this endeavour, and the writing itself was not without its merits. I had noted that Ned tended toward the sombre; his poetic narrator was always alone and unhappy in his solitude but never able to do anything about it. I thought a great deal about Ned and his poetry.

Uncle Liam arrived home shortly after Grace had decided that I was impertinent. He was accompanied by two of the three guests we were expecting. Both were from Europe, and I looked forward to listening in on their conversations that evening. No one seemed to know the current whereabouts of the third guest, one Professor Blaettermann. Consequently, we sat down to dinner, expecting him to join us presently.

We had almost completed our main course when Professor Blaettermann burst through the door, breathless and accompanied by a member of the local constabulary. We were greatly excited to hear his story and forgot the remainder of the dinner that Grace and I had prepared.

Professor Blaettermann's usually wild, curly hair was wilder than usual, and his handsome face had its jaw set stiffly. It was clear that he was angry but exhilarated at the same time.

He proceeded to explain that he had been called into town to the residence of a local businessman, into whose home a number of students had apparently pushed themselves uninvited. They had been in search of a certain servant woman, and, unfortunately, they had found her. When Professor Blaettermann arrived, the woman was sobbing and pulling on her torn clothing, which she contended the students had ripped in the attack and roughly pulled from her body. Professor Blaettermann had been able to piece together a story told by onlookers. According to the witnesses, the students had been shouting "Whore! Whore!" in the belief that she had infected a number of students with a disease.

At the mention of such things, Uncle Liam looked at Grace, who nodded toward me to join her in the next room. I did not wish to leave. The story was fascinating, and it was not the first time that I had heard about such diseases. I recalled Father's description of a patient who had to be locked away to protect her family and friends from her madness. I had heard whisperings about her character. I knew, perhaps more than any of those in attendance at Uncle Liam's that night, about the disease of syphilis as I had gone to one of Father's books and looked it up to find how she had contracted such a villainous malady. I cringed as I recalled the description of such patients. Grace, however, followed Uncle Liam's lead and took me by the arm.

Once next door in the adjoining room, I ensconced myself by the door to listen for familiar names in connection with the episode. Grace tried to distract me, but in vain. For the next quarter of an hour or thereabouts, Professor Blaetterman described the episode in detail and listed off the names of students who were reputedly involved. I did not hear Ned's name mentioned. I knew that such activities were not to his liking, and I sat back, relieved that he would not be expelled. He had problems enough with his debts and his stepfather's stubbornness about money.

I fell asleep that night pondering the murky depths of madness.

EIGHT

My year had come to an end. I returned to Father's house in Boston, and although the house itself was much the same, I was different. It no longer felt like my home. It was spring, with its promise of newness and freshness, but my heart was as dark as the clouds that rumbled across the sky, mountainous and threatening. I was restless and untethered. I walked for hours through the streets I had come to know so well with Father on his rounds, wondering what would become of me. I had spent much of the past two months trying to keep myself busy with my studies, all the while aware that they seemed to be leading me nowhere.

Through the summer and fall in Virginia, I had relied on my weekly rendezvous with Ned as much as I knew that he had depended upon those assignations to help him deal with the social realities of such a tumultuous community of scholars. Thus, when he came to me in January to tell me that he was forced to abandon his studies, I refused to listen to him. His stepfather had, as threatened earlier, finally refused him any more monetary support, and he was returning to Richmond. He told me that he intended to stay there only as long as it took him to find a position elsewhere, but I also knew that he was drawn to military life. I believed that the structure and discipline, in stark contrast to the unsettling life of the university, appealed to him. I must admit that I turned on him when he told me of this interest. I accused him of not wanting to have to make decisions for himself, of being spineless. He took my barbs with good humour, as I believe he knew in his heart that I knew him only too well.

I wandered down on the docks, against the explicit directions of my father, who thought it a wholly inappropriate place for his daughter to stroll. But my year in Virginia had opened my eyes to a great many things, not the least of which was that I was a woman now and that Father would no longer control my life. I just had to find my own direction.

I watched as goods and people were loaded onto vessels that would ply the seas, heading for faraway places in the world – and, as I stood there in a dream-like trance, I imagined each of them to be mysterious and exotic. A thrill shivered momentarily down my spine as I considered what would happen if I boarded one of these vessels and headed to an unknown destiny. I dreamed of seeing London and Paris and of the South Seas. It had occurred to me that I might get a fairer hearing for my desire to seek a medical degree if I ventured abroad, where they had been training doctors for longer than we had in America. But these were dreams only.

I sighed as I watched a large ship weigh anchor. The passengers hung over the rails, waving frantically to the people below. I wondered what adventures lay ahead for them, and I, too, waved. The wind whipped raindrops around my head, so I turned my collar up to keep out the chill. My dream had vanished, and it was time to go home.

That evening, when I arrived home, Father was not there to question me about my activities. Instead, Mrs. Wimpole, our housekeeper, flitted about excitedly, clapping her hands and nervously clinking the silver and crystal onto the table. I noticed that the lace tablecloth adorned the large mahogany dining room table, and the silver tea service on the sideboard gleamed with a newly shined vibrancy. Four places, instead of the usual two, had been carefully set.

I tried to get Mrs. Wimpole to tell me what was going on, but she told me she was busy.

"Ask your father," she said, wiping her pudgy hands on her apron. She smiled conspiratorially and turned to go back into the kitchen. As she was about to push open the door, she turned back. "Perhaps Miss Bridget would like to dress for dinner." Then she disappeared.

"What is going on?" I called out to no avail. Picking up the hem of my skirt in a huff, I took the stairs two at a time in a very unladylike fashion.

We were having company for dinner. That much was clear. I expected that Abigail would be one of the guests, and I had resigned myself to the fact that she was a part of Father's life now. There had been no further explicit mention of marriage in the days since my return from Virginia, but it was clear that Father and Abigail had spent a great deal of time together during my absence. I loathed the way she looked at him so endearingly while he sipped his sherry from a crystal glass in the evening. I also loathed the fact that she joined us for dinner at least three times a week when she was not at her mysterious New York house. She was small and insignificant, I thought. But Father did not seem to hold that view.

I sat on the edge of my bed, my arms wrapped around the post that reached almost to the ceiling. I loved the way the ivory silken drapes hung from the canopy. Ever since I was a little girl, that bed represented solace, sanctuary — a place where I could distance myself from the realities of my little world. I had missed it while I was away. I was slowly beginning to realize, though, that I would soon have to leave this place forever. I sighed and dressed for dinner.

When the grandfather clock on the stair landing struck seven, I descended the stairs to the sounds of voices wafting from the parlour. The large, double oak doors were slightly ajar, and I could hear Father and Abigail laughing and tinkling glasses. The other (male) voice was unfamiliar.

I twisted the crystal scent bottle that hung from a gold chain around my neck. Father had given it to me when I turned sixteen, and it somehow made me feel much more like a woman. For some reason, I uncapped it and inhaled deeply of the exotic scent. I was immediately at ease. I opened the door and entered the parlour.

Father noticed me immediately and moved to welcome me into the room. The unfamiliar voice belonged to a tall, imposing gentleman who sported a small, dark goatee and an impeccable costume. I judged him to be somewhat younger than Father.

"Bridget," Father said, "here you are at last. Do come and meet our guest." He placed one hand squarely on my back, and I could feel a slight impatient push as I moved toward the visitor's outstretched hand.

"Please allow me to present my daughter, Bridget." Father turned to me. "Bridget, I would like you to meet Mr. Dalton Densmore from New York."

Before I had a chance to say anything, Abigail spoke. "He is my second cousin." She smiled broadly.

Dalton Densmore from New York City took my hand and kissed it. "Enchanted," he said.

I immediately knew that I did not share his enchantment. I thought I detected a slight leer as he looked up after brushing his lips lightly on my hand. He did not immediately let my hand go. I finally had to pull it from his grasp.

"I am pleased to meet you," I said, trying to fight the sudden urge to wipe my hand upon my silk skirt. I walked over to the fireplace, waiting for some explanation of why one of Abigail's relations should be spending an evening in my home.

"I understand that you have just spent a year in Virginia," Dalton said, moving toward the fireplace. He tapped his pipe out in a nearby ash basin and laid it on the table.

"Yes, I have," I said.

"Mr. Densmore runs a fleet of shipping vessels," Father said. "His business is very successful." He smiled at Abigail, who had turned her head away to sip her sherry.

"But I would trade all that success for the happiness of a family life, such as your father has here in this marvellous home." Dalton feigned a pout.

I was beginning to dislike him very much already. Fortunately, before the conversation could follow that line any further, Mrs. Wimpole announced dinner, and we adjourned to the dining room.

Though the dinner was one of Mrs. Wimpole's best and my favourites, turkey and cranberries, it was made less palatable by a constant serving of Dalton's successes and talents. Just as dessert was being served, the conversation, however, took an alarming turn. Father was focusing on my talents.

"Yes, Bridget is a fine seamstress. Her year in Virginia with her Aunt Grace has done her a world of good."

Dalton smiled at me.

"Father, I spent most of my year reading in the library and perfecting my Latin and Greek."

Dalton looked puzzled. "Latin and Greek? What possible use could that be to a young woman as beautiful as yourself?"

I placed my fork on my plate and turned to Dalton. "Yes, I suppose for a woman who makes it her life's work to tend to every whim and wish of a husband without thought to her own intellectual capacities, Latin and Greek and all the other interesting things that our world has to offer are of very little use." I went back to Mrs. Wimpole's very delicious pastry.

Dalton laughed. "You will give up these pursuits as you begin to take your proper place in the world." He pushed a large piece of pastry into his even larger mouth. Crumbs fell onto the pristine cream lace of the tablecloth. "You will certainly find them unnecessary impediments to your duties."

I heard a deep intake of breath from my father. He knew me well enough to know that a remark like that was likely to instigate a tirade from his young daughter. "Yes, yes," my father said quickly, dabbing his mouth genteelly with his linen napkin, "we all do find our place eventually, do we not, Abigail?"

Abigail had been looking at me with what I interpreted to be distaste, not an entirely unknown feeling for me to feel in her gaze.

I decided, for the sake of my father, that I would not pursue this line of discussion. "I met an interesting poet during my year at the University of Virginia," I said, trying to change the subject. "He had a very distinctive view of life and death. He believed that there was a very thin line between the two. What do you think?" I turned to Dalton.

"I try not to think about death at all," he said. "There is much money to be made and much life to make it in."

I shook my head and decided to abandon any further attempts at erudite discussion. The man was very clearly a Philistine, thus not worth my consideration. The after-dinner conversation was no more intriguing than that during dinner. But what had become evident to me was that Father had brought this man here to parade me before him as a potential mate. I should have guessed as much. It would be to Father's and Abigail's benefit to have me out of the way – looked after, as it were. I decided to forgive them for their transgression this time. But that night was to be the first of many.

Over the next few months, I was subjected to the company of several more just as unsuitable young and old men, all of whom were sorely in need of a wife to run their domestic affairs. I was determined not to be that woman. It was becoming clearer by the day that Father was becoming exasperated at me, and it culminated in an evening of rancour, which he and I had never experienced before.

"Bridget, I have tried. I have done my best, but none of these men seems to think that you would make them a suitable wife."

To say I was furious would be to say that a hurricane is a windy day.

"They do not think that *I* am suitable! I do not think that *they* are suitable. And I thought you would know better. I do not wish to be auctioned off like some piece of livestock." Father and I were alone that night. Mrs. Wimpole was visiting with her sister, as she did once a week, and Abigail was visiting her house in New York.

"I have tried my best, and I have waited patiently," Father said. "Now, I must go on with my own life." He turned to me and took me by the shoulders. "Bridget, Abigail and I are to be married one fortnight from today. I wish you to be there, but only if you can be civil. You must have known for some time that this announcement would be coming, but I had wished that you would be settled before that time. I must go ahead with my life."

I crumpled onto the sofa like a marionette whose puppeteer had inadvertently let go of the strings. I felt limp. Father was right. I *had* known that this would happen. But it still came as a blow. It was summer now — a beautiful time of year for a wedding. And so it happened.

On a beautiful summer day with the sun shimmering overhead and the seagull's song heard in the distance, Father and Abigail Densmore stood under an arbour in our back garden and took their vows. I stood close by, grasping my bouquet of lily-of-the-valley to my breast. Dalton Densmore stood close behind me, his new fiancée clinging to his arm. I marvelled at how some women would put up with even the most repugnant specimens of the male gender simply to secure a husband.

I thought about Father, more than fifty years old and Abigail, a mere twenty-six years old, and wondered what their lives would be like as husband and wife. As they pronounced that they would be together until death did them part, I was thinking about their wedding night. I could not see my father in that position at this point in his life, and I did not wish to see Abigail in that position. It was unthinkable.

What was more unthinkable, though, was the possible outcome of such a coupling. Surely, Father did not wish to have any more children. This possibility had not seriously occurred to me before, and I had never questioned him about his intentions.

I tried to put it out of my mind. Two months later, it was impossible for me not to think about it every day of my life.

NINE

I was elated. It was a beautiful September morning – the kind that makes one thank God for living in this part of the world. The leaves were just beginning to take on their fall colours, promising, like a teasing woman, to be more breathtaking this year than any before. "I am worth awaiting with some anticipation," Mother Nature seemed to be saying. Flocks of birds had begun amassing, and I took a moment to watch them from my window every morning.

I was beginning to become accustomed to the notion that Father was no longer mine alone. Although I yet failed to understand his attraction to Abigail completely, I had come to tolerate her existence – and, I wager, she mine. But my elation of this morning had little to do with either my truce with Abigail or the weather. This morning's post had brought a very welcome package. Immediately upon recognizing the handwriting, I tore to my room to be alone with its secrets. It was from Ned.

I had heard rumours that he had been in Boston briefly, and I had secretly hoped to see him, but that had not happened. I knew that this was his birthplace, but that he had spent little time here since the death of his parents many years ago. I supposed that it would be difficult for him to be here.

I turned the package over in my hands. Clearly, it was more than a letter. Instead of immediately tearing off the brown wrappers and the strings, though, I shook it and poked it like a child on Christmas morning. As I held it to my nose, I noted a slight scent of cigar smoke and tar. Then, I observed something unusual about the mailing stamp. It had originated in none other than Boston. Unable to wait another moment, I struggled with the string and tore open the wrapper. A book wrapped with a letter emerged. It was a slim volume of poetry. Upon its cover was the title "Tamerlane and Other Poems," but its author was listed only as "a Bostonian." Ned's first book!

I ran my hand across the cover, trying to feel his presence. Finally, I opened it and began reading even before looking at the letter. I recognized the lines at once. They were ones that Ned had shared with me beneath the trees during our long walks in Virginia. I breathed deeply and took up the letter that accompanied it. It was headed "Fort Independence, Boston Harbor." It read,

> *"My dearest Bride,*
>
> *It has been far too long since we have kept company, but I know that your family obligations keep you far too occupied to take the time for a lowly poet. So, it is with considerable humility that I present this little volume of my cherished poetry. I hope that you might regard it as a small gift from one lost soul to another. I often think of our friendship as I am mired in the mundaneness of living every day. It provides me with considerable strength when all seems bleak and dark.*
>
> *I have now been several months in the army, and I think often of your admonitions to me. Indeed, I do cherish the discipline of my newfound life. The regimen of the day keeps me from so many dreams of terror at nightfall. The details occupy my mind.*
>
> *I am so hesitant to broach this subject and tremble at the thought of your response. But I humbly wonder if you might consider taking a small portion of your time to see me before I am assigned (as I shall be in due course) to a station away from my beloved Boston. I long for the touch of your hand and remain ever your servant.*

I had spent the past months studying Father's medical textbooks and the volume on herbalism that I had charmed from Mr. Wertenbaker at the university library as a kind of going-away gift to me. I did not know where any of this would lead me, but I was sorely in need of a diversion. The thought of once again seeing Ned filled my heart with sunshine more glorious than that which blazed through my curtains, where I had pushed them back against Abigail's admonitions that I might thus be seen in my boudoir from the street. I cared not, as I longed for sunshine in my life.

At once, I sat down at my table and took pen in hand as I had that fateful night when Father had first crushed my very future. I replied to Ned that I, too, longed to see him. It was two weeks before we could make arrangements for a rendezvous. Those two weeks seemed interminable.

If it were humanly possible, Abigail was more tiresome than usual during that long wait, or so it seemed to me. She berated me for not practicing the piano, which I detested, and had to speak sharply to me as we sat one evening with several neighbour ladies, quilting. My mind was numb from the continual lack of challenge and intellectual intercourse. She was especially most waspish the morning I had conspired to see Ned. Matters were worsened by the fact that Father had left to see a patient some hours before, so we were alone in the breakfast room.

"Bridget," Abigail said, pouring coffee from the silver pot on the breakfast table, "your Father wishes you to attend the theatre with us on Friday next." She took a sip of coffee and quickly clinked the china cup back into its saucer. She raised her hand to cover her mouth. I had noticed that she was looking rather wan lately, but it was difficult to tell as she favoured the pallid fashion of the day. A lady did not take the sun on her face. She had told me this many times during the brightest days of the summer just past.

"Did you hear me?" she said sharply.

"Yes, I heard you," I said, biting into a thick piece of toast.

"What are your plans for today?" Abigail seemed to have regained her composure and was sitting straight up in her high-backed chair.

"I shall take a walk and do some reading. I thought that I might enjoy a few hours at the convent this morning. Sister Eulalia Marie has asked me to attend with her young students whenever I can."

It was true that I had rediscovered Sister Eulalia and had, on several occasions, spent a few hours with her charges. Father thought it a fitting replacement for my dream of a medical career. I could, perhaps, be a lay teacher at the convent school for a time. I did not dislike my work there, but it represented second best to me.

Abigail took an audible deep breath while she watched me slather another piece of toast with strawberry preserves. I licked the drops that began to fall off the edges in a most unladylike fashion.

"Excuse me," she said, fleeing from the dining room.

I shrugged my shoulders. "It must have been something I said."

Mrs. Wimpole turned from the sideboard where she had been setting out some eggs. "I know it is not my place, Miss Bridget," she said, "but you might consider how you treat Mrs. Abigail."

I got up and put my arms around her increasingly ample waist and laughed. "It certainly is your place. You've known me for so long, Wimpy. And I will give it some thought." I smiled at the thought of my upcoming day and, grabbing another bite of toast, I left to find my wrap.

Ned and I had made arrangements to meet at a small park not far from the waterfront. He had leave for several hours. Since the appointed place was not far from the convent, my story seemed plausible. I left the house, making my way toward the convent, my heels clicking gaily on the cobblestones. As I approached the familiar gray stone arches, I took a turn down a small street to the right, past the cathedral and the cemetery, to the park that abutted. As I passed by the black, wrought iron fence that enclosed the dead and separated them from the living, I spied the figure of a man standing over a newly dug gravesite. I recognized the black back at once. He stood with military erectness, his hands clasped behind his back as he gazed toward the pile of damp earth. Unseen, I stopped to watch.

The figure crouched down and picked up a handful of the dirt. As he rose and let the dirt fall from between his fingers, a cloud passed overhead, blocking out the sun. The sharp shadows that had, only moments before, provided a stark contrast between light and dark gave way to a blurring of boundaries. He could have been a ghost at that moment. I continued walking toward the park's gates as a woman passed by, leading a small dog that yelped at my skirts. Ned turned and, seeing me, walked toward the path.

His large gray eyes looked sombre, almost melancholy, as I approached him. As we came nearer to one another, he smiled and stretched out his arms to me.

"I had no idea that I would not be able to bear being away from you," he said as he fiercely encircled me with his arms. There was a ferocity in his embrace, such as I had not felt before.

"I, too, missed you, Ned."

Arm in arm, we walked. I had expected him to lead the way along the path. Instead, we walked among the graves.

We walked slowly and silently around the headstones, many of which were now quite old. I looked at those we passed and wondered why a child had died in infancy, why a woman no older than myself was taken, and where their souls, if we truly possessed souls, resided these many years after their passing. Ned seemed more troubled than usual, but I thought it was better to leave him in his shroud of silence until he was ready to loosen its bonds and speak.

We walked toward a dark spot deep within the cemetery. Two men, dirty and dripping with sweat, were working diligently to open a new grave. Ned walked toward the open pit and looked down at the man flinging soil.

"Mind you don't get yourself in the way," one of the men said as he dug his shovel deep into the soil. Then, ignoring our presence completely, the two men continued their work.

Ned stared down into the hole for a full minute. He took a deep breath and turned from the sight. "Have you ever wondered what it might be like to be beneath the ground? To feel the dark presence of the worms who will be your only companions as you cross that threshold into oblivion?"

I had not. "I do not suppose that one would be aware of such things. After all, thankfully, death takes away that consciousness."

"There have been many accounts of live burials. It is such occurrences that occupy my mind."

As the daughter of a physician who had seen her share of dead persons, I seriously doubted the accuracy of such reportage. Ned, however, seemed sorely troubled by this or something else. I thought it better for the present moment not to engage him in an argument.

We continued our walk in silence. When we reached the border of the park, we took a seat upon a bench. Once outside the residence of the dead, Ned seemed more relaxed.

"Bride, I am truly happy in the army. I have actually chosen well. I do, however, miss the intellectual discourse of the university and, of course, my times with you." He turned to face me directly. Taking my hand in his, he continued. "Bridget Ryan, you haunt my thoughts, waking and sleeping. Today is the first time I have felt well since we last encountered one another. I fail to understand my own physiology. I seem to feel the physical need more than for the poisons of alcohol, which I have forsaken for the time being."

I looked carefully at Ned's face to understand the meaning behind his words. Then, an odd thought struck me. Surely a proposal of marriage was too ludicrous to be a possibility? He was in no position to take on a wife, and although I truly believed that love was a part of our liaison, it was so much more than that. It was so much more than something to be confined within the boundaries of conventional life. Indeed, in any event, I believed myself to be entirely too headstrong and independent for his artistic temperament. What Ned and I would become to each other was but a murky thought in my mind, but I knew that it would not be husband and wife. I did, however, wonder at his evident desperate need for my presence.

He took my face between his two cold hands. I could feel them shaking as he looked deep into my eyes.

"Bridget," he said formally, "I ask you to pledge that I might be permitted from time to time from now until the end of this lifetime to see and touch your face and to speak with you. I believe that I cannot live should I be denied such."

I could see that he was serious. Although I failed to understand fully his meaning fully, I placed my hands on both of his and nodded. His entire being seemed to relax as if I had fixed a craving deep within him.

"It is done, then. I shall see your father quickly, and we will have it done before I am removed from Boston."

The breath caught in my throat, and I could feel a redness creeping up my neck. I had misunderstood.

"Ned, I … " I was momentarily at a loss for words. "Ned, you can't mean that you wish us to marry?"

Ned dropped my hands, which he was still holding in his own. He looked at me intensely with his melancholy eyes.

"But Bridget, I thought that I meant a great deal to you. I know that I cannot offer much at this juncture, but that will change. Surely you can see that. I have published a book. There will assuredly be more. You will not have to live in servitude to a husband but rather in companionship with a comrade who will share your life force."

I had to make him understand. I arose from the bench and walked toward a gnarled old tree across the path. "Ned, do you see this misshapen old tree?"

He nodded.

"It has been here for countless years. Spring after winter after autumn after summer, and so on. It has done its duty to protect the little gravesites from the wind and the earth from erosion, and what does it have to show for its selflessness? It is alone and withered, like a wizened old widow who has devoted her life to home and hearth, never moving, never experiencing life outside the confines of these fences. That is how I see marriage, Ned."

Ned began to speak, but I silenced him with my hand. "That is how I see marriage now. I do not doubt that those thoughts will change even as the rains change the face of a mountain over the centuries."

Ned was silent. I could see the hurt in his eyes, but I knew that I was unable to provide him with any more explanation. I walked back to the bench, and he followed me. We sat in silence for a few moments. I could hear the gravediggers in the distance and a seagull who had flown from the docks to scavenge along the city streets.

I drew a breath. There was one other thing that I knew I had to say before Ned walked out of my life again. I drew another breath for fortification.

"We need not take such public vows to enrich our friendship. I would become your lover." I looked straight ahead, avoiding his eyes and waited.

"Bride, I wish more of you than that."

He was silent again. Then, he reached for my hand. "Bride, I implore you to hold our friendship to your heart at all costs."

I promised him that I would while, to my horror, inside of my heart, I felt that something had been crushed. I did not, until that moment, realize how much I had hoped that we might become lovers and yet not husband and wife.

Finally, he spoke, and our previous conversation seemed to be all but forgotten.

"What will you do now, Bride?"

Until that second in time, I had not been aware that I had made a decision. "I will become a teacher. I plan to set out for the South Seas or to Africa. But first, I will visit England." As the words left my lips, I realized that my life was sealed.

Ned smiled. "I believe that you will do well." Then, just as quickly as the clouds had come to shield the sun, a veil of darkness covered his face. "When will you return so that I might see you as you have agreed?"

"You may stop worrying," I said, trying to sound light when I, too, was feeling the weight of my decision. "I shall return regularly to America, and we shall maintain our correspondence so that you will know."

Ned pulled out a battered gold pocket watch and clicked it open. At first, it failed to comply with his request, but after a moment of prying with his fingertip, it opened. "I must return." He clicked the watch shut and then returned it to his waistcoat. "Until next time." He stood, bent down where I was sitting on the bench and kissed me lightly on the lips.

I watched as he walked toward the gates of the cemetery, picking up speed as he went. I touched my fingertip to the place where the kiss still lingered and wondered when I should see him again.

TEN

As I arose from the bench, tiny drops of rain began falling. I drew my coat close to my neck as much as possible to keep out the melancholic feeling that was descending upon me and to keep out the stiff breeze that was beginning to pick up. I was sorely troubled by the conversation that had just passed between me and one whom I had come to consider my soul's mate. And that seemed to me to be the crucial part of the problem – I believed our souls to be mated and might be convinced to see our bodies mated; Ned believed our lives should be as well.

Before I could give conscious thought to where I was going, I found myself ringing the little bell outside the door at the convent school. Little Sister Ann Rose opened the door and peeked out through the crack, as was her way. When she spied me, her face broke into the broadest grin one could imagine, showing an abundance of large, rather crooked white teeth. She could not be more than fifteen, I thought, and although there were but two years between us, I felt that I was worlds older than the little postulant.

She gestured me into the foyer with its soaring ceiling. When the sun was shining at midday, glorious coloured light danced off the stone walls through the stained glass, creating a dome-like covering for the hall. The colours that thus played upon the walls had always made me think of myriad rainbows intertwining. It had always been this way from the first moment I had entered this grand room at the age of five. Today, there were no rainbows.

"Miss Bridget, we were not expecting you this morning," she said and then added quickly, "but we are always jubilant to see you."

She said "jubilant" like she really meant it. It was Sister Ann's current favourite word. Over the past months, this word had been preceded by such others as elated, exhilarating, and most recently, invigorated. It occurred to me that she seemed to be moving through them in alphabetical order. The little nun-in-training seemed to be reading the dictionary, perhaps more than her prayer book.

"I should like to see Sister Eulalia Marie if she is not with the children at the moment," I said as I undid the buttons on my coat.

"I shall take you to her office myself," Sister Ann said, almost skipping down the long corridor toward Sister Eulalia's office.

Sister Eulalia Marie was the second-in-command at the convent these days. Just as she had when I sat among her fourth-graders, she still taught her girls, as she called them. Recently, though, she had been spending more and more time doing what appeared to me to be administrative work. I believed that her loss from the classroom would leave a gaping hole in the education of the convent's charges, but I recognized that she was being groomed to move into a Mother Superior's role.

Sister Ann Rose left me at the doorway to Sister Eulalia's office. I knocked softly as if not wanting to disturb God.

"Enter," she said in a clear, strong voice.

As I stepped across the threshold, I regressed into a fourth-grader. I instinctively smoothed my coat, as I had done so many times in the past, and stood more erect, as Sister Eulalia had admonished us to do.

Sister Eulalia looked up from her desk, her reading glasses perched on the end of her nose. The light in the room was poor, with only one small window and a dim oil lamp at the desk where she worked. Her black habit was immaculate, as usual, and the white of the wimple framed her face like a portrait in a picture frame. I could not imagine having to wear such an outfit day after day.

"I hope I am not interrupting you, Sister," I said, extending my hand as to a friend.

"Bridget, it is always such a pleasure to see you." She placed her writing implement on the table, took my hand momentarily, and then folded her hands on the desk as if in anticipation. "I hope that you are here to tell me that you are now ready to take on a class of your own." She waved me into the seat across the desk from her.

I sat down in the bare wooden chair and cleared my throat. I was not at all certain that I did know what I was here to say. But when I opened my mouth, words did emerge.

"I have come to appeal to you for your help in accomplishing a goal I have set for myself." As I spoke, the idea took shape, and I gained confidence in my words. "I do wish to become a teacher under your auspices, but for a limited period of time. I shall work hard, and I shall learn all there is to being a teacher. Then, I ask that you send word to a sister convent in England and send me there as a lay teacher."

I looked at Sister Eulalia carefully to ascertain her reaction, but as usual, she was implacable. I would have to press on. "There is an opportunity for me to pursue my dream of becoming a physician in England, where they are considerably more enlightened. If I can make my way over, I can have a chance."

Sister was silent for a moment. When she finally spoke, it was softly. "And what does your father think of your plans and goals?"

"I have not revealed any of this to him."

"I thought not." Sister Eulalia arose from her chair and walked over to the window. It was not large, but it was elaborate. A high arch was filled with stained glass depicting the Madonna and child, while the lower square portion was transparent, letting in the only natural light in the room. She tucked each hand in the other sleeve and stood tall. She was several inches taller than even I was. "Bridget, I have long recognized that your life wishes were not like those of your classmates. In fact, once, when you were about twelve, your father and I had a long conversation about your future."

I must have looked startled at this revelation as she stopped momentarily and looked at me. I had indeed been unaware that Sister Eulalia and my father had discussed such things.

She continued. "I told him that you would not be content merely to be someone's wife. That is when he asked me to encourage you to a religious life, but I knew that you did not have a vocation."

She walked to the other side of the room, her black skirt flowing around her legs. The rosary falling from her belt clicked softly in time with her heels. She stopped close enough to where I was sitting so that I had to tilt my head to see her face as she continued.

"You have told me your dreams before you have broached the subject with your father because you know what he will say."

I could not deny it. I knew that my father would never agree to let his only daughter embark on such a risky expedition. He would certainly try to stop me.

"In fact, if he were agreeable to this, he could afford to place you on a boat and make the arrangements for your accommodation in London. I believe that he has friends and colleagues across the Atlantic, does he not?"

"Yes, Sister, but I do not want him to keep me, as it were."

She nodded. "I know this, Bridget. I know that your fondest dream is to be your own person." She paused as if considering whether to continue. "I, too, wished the same for myself. I chose the church as my way to a life of my choosing."

She walked back to the window and looked out into the quadrangle below as she continued. "It was after the third proposal of marriage that my father told me that I must choose one of the suitors or the convent. I chose the convent. At first, the Mother Superior believed that I was hiding away from my life and that I would never be a nun. But deep down, I had always known that the reason I refused the life that was my lot at the time was that I wished to devote my life to God."

I had not known any of this about Sister Eulalia. In a flash of revelation, I realized that I had thought of nuns as having been born in their habits. I had not considered that they had been young women with fathers and mothers and, of all things, beaus. Sister Eulalia with a man! I could not conceive of it.

She sat down again at her desk. "Bridget, I know that you do not share this latter experience with me – that you do not have a calling to serve the Lord in this way. So, society has made it difficult for you to pursue your life's work."

"Will you help me?" I asked.

"One thing at a time," she said, placing her glasses on the end of her nose once again. "Of course, you may begin teaching here on a regular basis. But first, I wish you to discuss this and your further plans with your father."

"What if he disagrees?'

"You know that he will disagree. He will not be able to understand his daughter's wishes. But he must be a part of her decisions."She looked at me for a long moment, seemingly able to read my mind. "Bridget, I promise that I will try to make him at least understand. I believe that this is as much as we can hope for."

As Sister Eulalia picked up the papers she had been reading when I entered the office, I began to rise from the chair. Before I could thank her, she said, "Bridget, is there anything else you wish to tell me today?"

I looked at her blankly.

"What person or event finally pushed you to the realization of your life decisions?"

She was a very astute woman, and I almost believed she could read my mind. I knew that there was no point in denying anything, but I was not yet ready to discuss my relationship with Ned with anyone.

"Perhaps I shall share it with you someday, Sister. And thank you."

As I let myself out, I could hear the lilting voices of the little girls as they rose in a familiar hymn whose words deserted me.

ELEVEN

My path was now clear to me. As I made my way back home, the clouds began to clear. The sun emerged from behind a cloud to shine down on me, casting long, clearly demarcated shadows. I had always loved the September sunshine. And now, I realized that this would be a winter of anticipation as I looked forward to beginning my life sometime in the spring or summer of the following year.

I slipped into the front door as quietly as I could. I still needed some time to myself—perhaps to make a few notes in my journal to collect my thoughts. I was hanging my coat on the hall stand when Mrs. Wimpole came quickly down the hall. Her increasing bulk made it difficult for her to move quickly, which she rarely did. I was surprised.

"Miss Bridget, your father has been waiting for you in the library. You must go to him at once." She wiped her hands on her apron as she spoke. Something in the tone of her voice seemed to herald something of great import.

"What is it now?"

I was imagining that the matter had something to do with Abigail and her cronies. I had been subjected to an increasing number of her New York acquaintances showing up at our doorstep, bag and baggage. I found most of them to be overly nonchalant. There seemed to be little concrete about them. The fact that most were writers made me wish to dismiss them out of hand, but on the other hand, Ned's literary proclivities made him all the more attractive to me. I could not determine the reason for this dichotomy. With this thought whirling about in my head, I made my way to the library to see Father.

Father was sitting in a brocade-covered wing-back chair to the side of the fireplace, his glass of sherry untouched on the mahogany table at his side. His head was back against the chair, and his face was ashen.

"Father?" I said gently as I entered the room. I was suddenly alarmed at the look of him and felt I should not disturb him too much.

He did not hear me at first; at least, he did not acknowledge that he had. I walked closer to the chair.

He looked up at me. "Bridget, we must talk."

I, too, felt that I had much to discuss with him, but his countenance indicated to me that it was a time for listening, not for speaking on my part.

"Father, is something wrong?" I sat down on the floor in front of him as I had so many times as a child. Mostly, these had been happy times when we would sit companionably in front of the fireplace, his hand resting on my head from time to time as he read his book and I mine. The feeling now was different.

"Something is wrong, Bridget. Something is quite wrong." He sighed heavily. "As you have probably noticed, Abigail has not felt well of late."

I thought about her antics at breakfast. She had seemed a bit off, but I had not really noticed it over a period of time. Indeed, I hardly paid much attention to her, caught up as I was in my own life.

"Abigail is with child."

I thought that I had not heard him correctly. Abigail to have a child? My own father to have another offspring? It was too horrible to contemplate. All the more reason for me to leave this house, and perhaps sooner than anticipated.

"Did you hear me?" he said.

"Yes, Father. I heard you," I said in a small voice.

"That, however, is not the whole story," he said, reaching for the crystal glass of sherry. "I would not be so concerned if that were the entire truth."

I looked up at the faraway look in his eyes. I arose from the floor, smoothed out the folds in my dress and took my place in the chair facing him across the fireplace. I was a grown-up now, after all.

"Tell me, Father," I said gently. I could see the pain in his eyes.

"Things are not going well."

I could feel my gentleness ebb away as I grew frustrated with the story's slowness. He had just informed me that I was to become – what? A half-sister to someone? This was quite enough information for me to take in at that moment, but I could see in his eyes that there was more. My impatient nature was beginning to take over, but I fought the urge to press him.

"Abigail is very ill." He sipped his sherry and did not look at me. "I fear she will die."

The silence in the distance between us filled the room with a heaviness – a thick fog that seemed almost impenetrable. I fought down an immediate impulse to be elated that she would no longer be a part of our lives. But I knew that her presence was important to Father. And he was clearly in deep anguish. My heart went out to him. My father, who had cared for me and loved me for so many years, needed my comfort and care. I knew that I must be there for him.

I arose from my chair and went to sit on the arm of his chair. I placed my arm around his neck and he leaned heavily into me.

"I shall be here for you, Father."

"Will you help me to care for her, Bridget?" He stopped a moment. "I know that it has not always been easy for you to have Abigail here with us and in my life. But I need you." He looked into my eyes. "We need you."

I could feel a kind of desperation in his voice. All at once, I knew that my grand plans, which had, only this day, become fully formed in my mind, would not be a present priority. I had a physical pain in my heart when I considered the possibility that they may never come to pass.

Later, alone in my bedroom, I considered the portentousness of my day. I took out my journal to try to write down the events and my feelings about them. I thought about Ned and his preposterous idea that we could ever be husband and wife. Putting down my writing implement, I walked over to my bed, sinking into its wonderful feather mattress with its matelassé coverlet. I ran my hand over the raised pattern as I had so many times as a little girl. The ivy pattern was thin with wear, but I still loved how it felt to my fingertips, yearning for stimulation.

"Tamerlane" stared at me from the bedside table. Considering it for a moment, I picked it up and turned it over in my hands. Once, when we had been walking in the hills above the university, Ned had recited several portions of this poetry to me. He told me then that he had written it when he was a lad of thirteen. I remembered being struck by the sadness of a young man who would be contemplating such words and committing them to paper. What kind of childhood must he have had? I thumbed through the pages – there were just over four hundred lines of deathbed confession of an Oriental conqueror. What kind of mind did he have to consider this at the age of thirteen? I held the small volume to my breast and lay back on the pillows.

I stared up at the canopy above and thought about Father and Abigail. The very idea that they should be having a baby was preposterous. Perhaps this was God's way of saying that it was not right. Perhaps it was God's way of telling me that I should give up my foolish idea of having a life of my own. But then, I did not believe in such a vengeful God. At that moment, I did not feel very charitable toward Abigail, Father, or even God. I was angry. I was sorely disappointed. Even more disturbing is that I was frightened – frightened of my own life that lay ahead.

I turned toward the wall, still clutching the book and cried. When next I opened my eyes, another September morning had dawned, and the rain was rushing against my windowpanes.

TWELVE

Boston, Winter, 1827-28

Autumn rain gave way to Indian summer with its golden, slanting rays of waning light. And quickly did the winds of winter blow into my life. That winter crept along, stealing my life force from me. I remember it more as a feeling than as a series of events, but it was those events that turned my life in a direction over which I initially felt I had little control. Powerlessness frightened me more than any other thing at that time in my life.

February blew in with a fury of windswept, freezing rain. The streets were so coated with ice for days at a time that we were all but confined to the house. Father ventured out to see his patients who dared not brave the elements to come to him in his office, and I could see that he was becoming worn out. Before my eyes, he seemed to have aged a lifetime, worrying about his wife and the baby, who seemed to be sapping her life.

Thus was I relegated to the confines of four walls and the care of a stepmother whom I liked little better now than when I had first met her. How childish of me, but I felt that she was responsible for my father's deterioration. Regardless, I knew that I must assist my father in any way possible, and that came down to caring for his wife, who, I believed, was dying.

Finally, and in my mind appropriately, in the midst of a snowstorm, Abigail was delivered of a scrawny little boy who appeared to have extraordinary difficulty breathing from the first moment he made his entry into the world. There was much confusion that night.

It began at noon with Abigail's piercing scream just as we were sitting down to lunch. The sun was shining for a change, yet another calm before a storm, and Father and I were enjoying a cup of tea as we watched the sun glint like so many diamonds on the mantle of snow which had fallen silently in the night.

The scream was so fearsome that Father dropped the delicate china cup he so loved to drink his tea from. As it crashed upon the lace of the tablecloth, it shattered, causing Mrs. Wimpole to run into the room.

"Send for Dr. Ryan," Father said to Mrs. Wimpole, his hand still shaking.

Mrs. Wimpole was, herself, quite overcome by the situation. "But, Dr. Ryan, *you* are Dr. Ryan."

"No, you fool."

I had never heard Father talk to Mrs. Wimpole that way, but she did not seem to notice.

"Dr. John Ryan, who visited us this week." He dug deep into his pocket and retrieved a small piece of much-wrinkled paper. "Here is where he is staying. Do it now."

Mrs. Wimpole took the piece of paper and then removed herself from the room as fast as her bulk would allow. I expected that she would ask the neighbour's son to fetch the man.

"Father?" I said. "Who is Dr. Ryan?" The weather that week had been unusually pleasant, and I had taken the rare opportunity to spend most of it at the convent school when not needed by Abigail. Evidently, I had missed much.

Abigail screamed again, and I knew that we must attend to her. I gathered my skirts and ran to the stairs. When I turned to see if Father was following me, he was just opening the whiskey bottle. I knew that he would be of little help today. I hoped that this other Dr. Ryan would be more useful. I had assisted Father in many births over the years, so they held little for me to fear, but I felt a profound dread about this one. Abigail had been confined to bed for the past months and I knew that the baby's movements had been few of late.

I ran up the stairs two at a time, my skirts about my waist, to find Abigail trying to get out of bed.

"I cannot do this," she screamed. "I must get out of here."

It was clear that she had taken leave of her senses, and I knew that it would be a long day.

The labour was prolonged and loud. I heard the clock strike three just as the knock came at the front door. After three hours of sitting with Abigail, Father was nowhere to be found, and I found myself praying that it would be Dr. Ryan. The relief that washed over me when he walked into the room and laid his large, black leather bag on the end of the bed must have been visible even to Dr. Ryan himself, and I was ashamed of my frailty.

Dr. Ryan was a tall man of about Father's age, although he looked younger. His red hair was streaked with gray, and it curled around his ears. His high collar made him seem regal somehow. Mrs. Wimpole had provided me with some details about him before his arrival. I had discovered that he was a distant cousin of my father's who was visiting the city temporarily to lecture at the medical college. He made his home in Baltimore.

He administered a small amount of laudanum to her, and she settled for a while. I wondered about the effects that the mixture might have upon her baby, but deep inside, I realized that it was probably more important to allow her to conserve her strength. It seemed that she would need it.

Mrs. Wimpole brought tea on a silver tray, which she placed on a little table by the door. Dr. Ryan suggested that I take a break, which I did so gladly. Taking a cup of tea and a biscuit with jam, I retired to my room for a brief rest. Within the hour, I heard the scream again, and I knew it was time. When I opened the door, Dr. Ryan beckoned me to help, and the next few hours were a nightmare as Abigail clawed and bit her way toward delivery.

Finally, the little child arrived. I wrapped him and held him to Abigail. Her eyes were glazed and seemed to be rolling uncontrollably around in her head, and she did not see. It was probably just as well: the child was having difficulty breathing. The next moments were, if anything, worse. I looked toward Dr. Ryan. A growing pool of blood surrounded him.

"I cannot stop it," he said calmly. "I need your help."

I opened the door to find Mrs. Wimpole standing in the hallway with Father, who appeared to be immobile. Thrusting the meagre bundle into his arms, I ran back into the room, carefully closing the door behind me. For the next hour, Dr. Ryan and I worked to save Abigail's very life, but it was not to be.

The clock struck four as Dr. Ryan pulled the sheet over Abigail's face and turned to look out the window for the first time that long night. The wind was howling, and the snow was lashing against the window. He seemed to collect his thoughts for a moment, as I had seen Father do when he had lost a patient. Finally, he turned to me.

"Fetch your father, Bridget."

I took a deep breath and looked down at the disarray and stains on my dress. Regardless of my feelings, I knew that Father would be devastated.

When the sun rose over the treetops and the world awoke to a new day, Father was a widower. Neither had the tiny boy been strong enough to breathe for very long. I retired to my room and wept. The years of anger and resentment over Mother's death came back to wash over me in a tidal wave of emotion. The profound sorrow and loss I had felt as a child were no longer buried. I knew that as an adult, I should feel for Father's loss, but I was too wrapped up in myself to take much notice.

What seemed like some hours later, a light knock came on my door. I was still crying and did not wish to see anyone.

"Bridget?" came the voice. "May I come in?"

It was Dr. Ryan. I did not wish to have him see me thusly, but I knew that I must let him in. I got up off my bed and briefly checked my face in the mirror over my dressing table. I was dishevelled, and my eyes were swollen. I quickly donned a satin robe that hung on a hook inside my door and opened it a crack.

"Dr. Ryan," I said, "please, come in."

The calmness and litheness of his movements belied the fact that he had just spent a horrendous time delivering a now-dead woman of a now-dead baby, powerless to do anything about it.

"I could hear you crying, Bridget. And I wanted to talk to you." He peered at me closely and took my hand. We sat together on the edge of my bed. "Will you be all right?"

I took a deep breath before speaking. I wanted desperately to talk to someone, but I hardly knew this man. "Yes, Dr. Ryan, I believe I will be."

"Bridget, please call me John. You make me feel so old." He seemed to hesitate before continuing. "I wanted to tell you how impressed I was with your medical abilities in assisting me tonight. Thank you."

I nodded.

"Bridget, I know of your desire to become a physician. Your father and I have discussed it at length over the past several years. In fact, I myself did speak to the admissions committee, but I fear I may not have been insistent enough. Until tonight, I did not realize what our profession would be missing to keep you out of the medical college. I cannot promise you anything, but I will do my best once again if you still wish to proceed."

For a moment, my hopes began to soar again. Perhaps I would realize my dream after all.

"I would be most grateful for any help you could afford me ... John," I said, choosing my words carefully so as not to reveal my true ecstasy.

"It is done then. I shall take your case once again to the authorities." He dropped my hand and arose from the bed. He walked over to the window, and I sensed that he had something else that he wished to say. He stopped beside the window and opened the drapes slightly to let in the light of day. "Bridget, I fear that your father is not well."

I looked up, a lump forming in my throat.

"I have been seeing him as his personal physician for the past year, when I have been in Boston from time to time. I have been concerned about his growing fatigue, and perhaps you, too, have noticed that his weight has dropped. I am afraid that this further burden of such a profound loss may be too much for him."

I felt ashamed. I had been so concerned about myself that I had failed to notice that my father might have a developing health concern. That my father was anything but hale and hearty was inconceivable to me. He had always been my rock, my immovable support, regardless of my own childish behaviour.

"I shall take my leave now," he said. "I promise to return tomorrow to see your father. If I can be of any help in the arrangements for the funeral, please send word. Mrs. Wimpole has the address where I am lodging while in Boston."

"When do you return to Baltimore?" I was finally able to collect my thoughts.

"I am required to lecture at the medical college for one more month, so we shall see one another from time to time.

"You will dine with us on Sunday?" I asked.

"It would be my pleasure," he said as he left me.

THIRTEEN

BOSTON, SPRING-SUMMER, 1828

John Ryan was true to his word. He was a great help to me and to Father as we dealt with the aftermath of the loss of Abigail and her baby. Indeed, there were times that I did not know how I would cope with Father without John to assist in even the simplest of ways. By the time John was required to return to his medical practice and his teaching in Baltimore at the end of March, we had weathered what I thought was the worst. We still had not, however, read Abigail's will.

Father had told me little about Abigail's New York life; he seemed to have a trifling interest in it. All I really knew was that after she moved into our Boston home, she had continued to maintain her lodgings in New York. I had heard vague references to some kind of family business, but as Father seemed to have little interest in it, it held little concern for me.

On a dull, foggy April morning, Father and I made our way to the offices of "Willard Willard and O'Connell, Solicitors." Surprisingly, to me, at least, no other members of Abigail's family were present.

One of the Willards began the reading of the will.

"I, Abigail Densmore Ryan, being of sound mind, do hereby ..."

My mind drifted off to John Ryan and the task he had promised to carry out for me. I had once again allowed myself to fantasize about my possible acceptance to the medical college. I was two years older now, and John had seen firsthand my dedication and potential.

"... bequeath to my husband, Dr. Edward Ryan, all assets of my estate, including my house in New York, my interest in the Euro-America Import/Export Company and my cash assets."

I snapped to attention. I had been wholly unaware that Abigail had any such assets, but the news did not seem to surprise Father. I wondered now why he had failed to tell me about it. It occurred to me that perhaps Abigail had cautioned him against it.

"It seems, Dr. Ryan," Mr. Willard was saying to my father, "that you are left a very wealthy man." He stopped, seeming to notice Father's discomfiture. "Dr. Ryan, you seem to be surprised about the extent of the late Mrs. Ryan's assets."

"Yes," Father said slowly. "I mean, no. I knew of Abigail's assets but took no interest in them. She was much more important to me than money ever could be."

I, for my part, was stunned at the recognition that Abigail had left Father hundreds of thousands of dollars, not to mention her controlling interest in what the solicitor explained was a successful import/export business headquartered in New York City. I had been under the obviously misguided impression that it was her father, not Abigail, who owned a business.

"What shall I do with a business such as that?" Father said to Mr. Willard. He seemed to be much in a state of confusion.

"Perhaps you should take some time to contemplate this," Mr. Willard said wisely. "Perhaps visit New York. See the house, consider the business. Just take your time." He closed the folder in front of him and pushed his chair back. The reading of the will was over.

Father and I discussed the acquisitions at some length. We determined that someone ought to go to New York, but Father's health was not good, and I was needed to care for him. Thus, we decided to put it off for a while. Father contacted someone at the business, and we forgot about it for some months. Spring gave way to the delights of summer, and Father's mental state seemed to rally.

On a beautiful day in June, John Ryan walked up our front steps and pulled the bell. It was a pleasant surprise, indeed.

His news was equally as pleasant; one might even refer to it as exciting.

"They wish to speak with you in person," he said.

"Who?" I asked, not quite comprehending the import of his words.

"The admissions committee at the college."

I was ecstatic.

"Bridget, calm down for a moment. You must be in Baltimore the week after next." He handed me a piece of paper with a name and address on it. "This is the person with whom you must speak. Can you get away?"

I took the paper and looked at it as if it were my future in my hands. I held it to my breast. "I will be there, John. Father is quite well at the moment."

For the next week, I read as many of Father's medical books as I could. I considered what to wear, what to say, and the impression that I must make on these powerful men. Yet in the back of my mind, I resented that they had this power to control my very future. At least this time, I would be permitted to confront them in person.

Two days before I was scheduled to depart for Baltimore, Father called me to his bedroom early in the day.

"Bridget, my dear, I am not feeling well today. Could you please ask Mrs. Wimpole to bring me breakfast on a tray?" He looked at my face, which must have displayed considerable apprehension. "No need to look so, child. It is nothing. Just an ageing man feeling his age, no doubt."

I looked at my father and realized how much weight he had lost over the past months since Abigail's death. How could this have gone unnoticed by a daughter who professed to love him so much? I felt wretched.

I stayed by his side that day, and by the next morning, it was clear I would have to send for one of his colleagues. I was so afraid. My formerly strong and powerful father –

at least in the eyes of a young daughter – was wasting away. Deep in my heart, I knew that he had some kind of wasting disease that the doctors would be able to do little about. Thankfully, his decline was rapid.

On the day that I was scheduled to be received by the admissions committee at the medical college, Father died. I knew that my hopes of ever gaining entrance to medical school were buried alongside him in the bleak cemetery where Ned had proposed to me what seemed like such a long time ago.

A month after Father's death, when all the activities that death and society demand had been completed, I found myself in Sister Eulalia's office once again.

"I understand that you are a now-wealthy woman, Bridget," she said from behind her desk.

"Sister, I do not know what it is I should do."

"Take your time, my child. Your wounds are fresh. But this is the time to beware. Men will fall upon you as the desert traveller falls upon an oasis. Guard yourself and your integrity carefully."

"I do not need a man, Sister," I said with more vehemence than I had intended.

Sister Eulalia looked at me contemplatively. "Are you so certain? Have you examined your world lately? I, of all people, understand your compulsions, but we still live in a man's world. Perhaps you might be well off to find an appropriate husband."

"How does one define an 'appropriate husband,' Sister?"

Sister Eulalia arose from her desk. She walked regally across the small room to the window. Before answering, she gazed out the small portion of the window that did not contain stained glass as if deeply contemplating the answer to my question. It was, however, a question to which I did wish to have a response, so I did not interrupt her meditation.

After what seemed like some moments, Sister Eulalia turned to me.

"Bridget, my child, that is a question that women have pondered since the institution of marriage was created to provide refuge for the family. It seems that the definition of an 'appropriate husband' is as elusive as is the exact definition of the absolute truth of God." She placed her hands inside her cuffs as was her habit and walked toward me. "An appropriate husband, after all, is a companion who holds a wife's values as dear as his own, who respects her, who allows her to be as much her own person as he is his own person."

I thought about that for a moment, considering Ned and his preposterous proposal. Then I reviewed in my mind the gentlemen that Father had presented to me as potential life companions. None of these measured up to Sister Eulalia's definition. I thanked her for her insights and gathered my things to leave.

"Be patient, my child," she said as I reached for the doorknob. "God's will is revealed all in good time. He will not forsake you." She smiled that slightly devilish smile that I remembered so well. "Or perhaps *she* will not forsake you."

Even I had to smile.

As I walked the short distance back to the house, I decided that now was the time to make a trip to New York City. I truly needed a change of circumstances, and this seemed to offer the perfect foil. I shivered with both excitement and a bit of trepidation at the prospect. It was a delicious picture I had developed of New York, with what I perceived as its refinements on the one hand and its vulgar aspects on the other. I wanted to experience both.

I informed Mrs. Wimpole of my decision, and she was sore afraid for me. She was vehemently opposed to my solitary leave-taking and made me promise to tell Uncle Liam of my plans. Thus, as a slightly older, married woman, Aunt Grace was called upon to be my chaperone, and together we travelled to New York City, den of iniquity, at least that is how Wimpy couched it. It occurred to me that Uncle Liam was having difficulty maintaining Grace's interest in the academic community and yearned for a change of scenery for her. What more immoderate change could she have than to accompany her rash, young niece to such a place? Besides, I looked forward to spending some time with Grace.

Thus, the two of us made our way to New York with excitement building as we neared the city. Our carriage took us to the address provided by Mr. Willard at the reading of Abigail's will and stopped in a very pleasant neighbourhood.

The servants at Abigail's house, which was now my house, had been kept on indefinitely after Abigail's death. Neither Father nor I had wished to see them out on the streets, nor did we relish the thoughts of what might happen to the house if left unattended for a period of time. Thus, when Grace and I arrived on the doorstep of the imposing New York brownstone, they were prepared for our arrival.

The house was impressive to see. Within its gated walkway was a small front garden that rivalled any I had seen in the country. It was a controlled riot of colours filled with shasta daisies, purple foxgloves, and myriad others I was too ignorant of botany to recognize. Even in late summer, the garden was still at its height. Grace was quite taken with the display. I had not thought her a gardener. There was much about Grace that was unknown to me, I reckoned.

Before I could pull the bell beside the impressive mahogany door, it was opened by a severe-looking woman in an impeccable maid's uniform. She was slim and carried herself with considerable grace and what I perceived to be austerity. I was vaguely pleased to note that she was slightly shorter than I in stature. She curtsied briefly.

"Miss Ryan," she said. "Welcome to your home."

I thought I detected a slight scowl as she said the word "your," but perhaps I was being overly sensitive. After all, this house had belonged to Abigail for some years, and they had worked for her even after Abigail had married Father. I knew that Father had been here several times himself.

Grace and I entered the front hall. It was much larger than one might have expected from looking at the house from the outside, and it was even more impressive. The tiles of the marble floor were arranged in an attractive swirling design, slightly obscured by the vividly coloured oriental rug in the center of the circle. On the rug was a large, round, mahogany hall table holding the largest display of fresh flowers I had ever seen. Above the arrangement hung a massive crystal chandelier whose fobs were also arranged in swirls. I heard Grace gasp as she looked up. I endeavoured to maintain my decorum. I was beginning to remove my gloves, as it was a warm afternoon, when four other servants entered the hall.

The introductions began. The housekeeper who had answered the door was Mrs. Cameron, who was doubtless in charge. I hoped fervently that she did not expect to be in charge of me. She introduced the cook, the upstairs maid, the gardener and the seamstress. I wondered at the need to have one's own seamstress, but I did not know anything about New York society. Perhaps it was de rigueur for those who could afford it. Lord knows I could have afforded just about anything my heart desired at that time. I just did not know what I desired.

The house ran on a schedule to which Grace and I were clearly expected to adapt. For the first time, I began to consider what it must have been like for Abigail to enter into the household that Father and I and Mrs. Wimpole had created for ourselves. We were clearly far looser in our household arrangements. It also occurred to me that Abigail must have found it extraordinarily difficult when she was used to such regimentation. I actually felt compassion for her for the first time and wished that I had known her better.

We had been in the city for but two days when invitations began to arrive. Sitting in the morning room sipping coffee, I read several invitations while Grace was already at work in the back garden, which was more impressive than the front. There were two from Father's former colleagues, and one I had been seriously considering from the manager of the Euro-American Import/Export Company, when I heard a ruckus at the front door.

Mrs. Cameron arrived at the door of the breakfast room looking slightly flustered.

"Miss Ryan," she said. "You have a caller."

A caller, I thought. How exciting. Who would call upon me here, and why was she so unsettled? Before I had an opportunity to ponder these questions aloud, they were answered.

Pushing his way past Mrs. Cameron was one Dalton Densmore, Abigail's insufferable cousin.

"Well, well, well," he said, his gaze moving from my person to the table and back to me. "Aren't you the lady of the manor now?" He flicked his hat off his head with his walking stick, neither of which Mrs. Cameron had taken from him at the door, and it landed on the center of the table.

"Mr. Densmore," I said, extending my hand. "How kind of you to call upon me."

He took my hand. "Not kind at all, as you shall see, cousin." He planted a kiss on my hand. "I may call you cousin, may I not?" He feigned a pout.

I truly did not wish this smarmy man to call me his cousin or to be in the same room with me, for that matter, but I knew I must be polite to my late stepmother's cousin.

Dalton moved his face closer to me. I fought the urge to turn my face away when I smelled upon his breath the foul odour of liquor at such an early hour in the day.

Perhaps that would, however, explain his erratic behaviour.

"Cousin, will you not invite me to take coffee with you this autumn morn?" He slid into the chair beside me at the table and began poking at the toast on the plate. He then stuck a finger into the jam pot, causing Mrs. Cameron, who had been standing all the while at the door, to move toward him. He looked her squarely in the eye while ceremoniously placing the finger into his mouth. He seemed to savour her discomfiture for a moment and then moved his finger back toward the pot as if to take another finger full. I heard Mrs. Cameron's intake of breath, and I feared she might strike him should he repeat his vulgar act, which, it appeared, he knew to be repulsive to her. His finger hovered above the open pot for a brief interval, then he smiled and picked up a white linen napkin to wipe his lips and hands.

"Don't worry about your precious china and crockery, Mrs. Cameron," he said, folding the napkin and replacing it on the table. "I promise not to throw any this time."

I looked quizzically at Mrs. Cameron, who said nothing but moved back to her position near the door.

Dalton leaned toward me and, *sotto voce,* said, "I mean to have what I am due, cousin. Mark my words."

For a moment, I thought about the absurdity of Father trying to marry me off to this odious man and wondered if it was me to whom he referred. I sat straighter in my chair, thinking that indeed he should not have me. But then I realized my miscalculation. It was not me he believed to be his due, but my surroundings. He had received very little from his cousin's estate, and I had been too busy to contemplate why this had occurred.

Before I could respond to him in any way, he had placed his hat back upon his head, nodded to Mrs. Cameron as he made a hasty departure and was gone.

I absently raised my china cup to my lips and was greeted by stone-cold coffee. I grimaced and placed the cup back on the table.

FOURTEEN

NEW YORK CITY, FALL 1828

Despite the melancholy circumstances that had given rise to this visit to New York City, my youthfulness betrayed me by providing me with a thrilling feeling every time I thought about this cosmopolitan city, which seemed to have a personality all its own. Even the scorching Indian summer heat that had descended upon the metropolis – which seemed to make everyone except me testy and short-tempered – could not dampen my enthusiasm.

Grace and I had strolled along Fifth Avenue only the day before, revelling in the stylishness of both the men and women. Then, as we took a wrong turn, we found all of this juxtaposed with terrible poverty, as we spied a small, dirty child begging in the street, his mother watching from across the alley. Upon our return to the house, when I had mentioned this to Mrs. Cameron, she deplored that we should ever venture out into the city unchaperoned. When I informed her that Grace was my chaperone, she cast an evil-looking eye upon me and pronounced, "You will come to no good in this city if you cannot learn to protect yourself."

I ignored her and went about the business of my day. The city did not frighten me. I still felt a thrill when I thought of the steamy underbelly that must exist just beyond our imaginations.

Later, when I left the morning room in search of Mrs. Cameron, I could see through the window that Grace was still occupied in the garden. I had completed my task of examining the invitations and one request to call. The request was for that afternoon and was from one Dr.

Nicholas Stanbury, evidently a contemporary of my father's and a physician in Richmond, Virginia. He was visiting friends in New York and had heard of my father's death and my arrival in the city. Could he come by to pay his respects? I would send word that I would be expecting him at four.

I found Mrs. Cameron in the kitchen preparing menus for the following week. After seeing that she had dispatched the appropriate message to Dr. Stanbury, I confronted her about the incident we had endured earlier that morning. I was curious to divine the source of several of Dalton's comments, most specifically the reference to the broken china.

Mrs. Cameron was reluctant in the extreme to discuss this with me. There seemed to be some veiled reference to drinking and a falling out that Dalton had had with Abigail prior to her death. I recalled the final time that Abigail had ventured to her house in New York. It had been some six months prior to her death before she had been confined to bed with her growing pregnancy. Indeed, it had been the last time she had ventured beyond the walls of our home and upon her return, she had been particularly distressed. I put this off to the usual female fallibilities to which I did not succumb. Evidently, her emotional state had been precipitated by her encounter with her drunken cousin.

I walked slowly outside into the back garden, contemplating this turn of events. It seemed I would have to deal with this situation before I could move forward with any plans. One of those first plans was to invite the manager of the Euro-American Import/Export Company to tea. We should discuss the future.

Later that afternoon, as I prepared to receive Dr. Stanbury, I heard Mrs. Cameron receive someone at the door. When I descended the staircase to the foyer, I was greeted by a crate whose contents were a mystery but whose destination was clear. It was for me.

With some assistance, I broke into the crate to discover a brown leather-covered trunk. Smaller than a steamer trunk and larger than a toiletries trunk, it had brass corners and a brass lock and was lined with deep burgundy velvet. Most stunning of all were the letters "B.R.," which were engraved on a brass plate near the lock. There was a small, folded letter inside.

The heading on the letter was of the Euro-American Import/Export Company. It read as follows:

"Dear Miss Ryan,

Please accept this trunk as a token of our esteem. It arrived from London by steamer just three days ago, and I thought of you, so I took the liberty of having your initials engraved on it. As the new owner of such an import/export business, I thought that you might have need for such a charming piece.

I look forward to meeting you and remain your faithful servant.

Samuel T. Bowness, Manager"

The piece was, indeed, charming, and Mr. Samuel T. Bowness was clearly a clever man. I would look forward to my first encounter with such a person. The trunk was a lovely piece. It occurred to me that I might get a great deal of use from it in my as-yet-undiscovered new life.

I had little time to consider this, however, as the clock struck four in the afternoon, and the bell rang. Dr. Stanbury had arrived.

A nondescript man of approximately Father's age, Dr. Stanbury looked every bit the physician – confident and imposing. I considered how my life seemed to be full of medical men. He accepted my offer of sherry, and we retired to the parlour to chat. I still felt a bit uncomfortable in this parlour surrounded as I was with so many items that spoke to me of the minutiae of another person's life. I had yet to decide what I should do with any of them.

He began his conversation with the usual condolences about Father's death, after which I related to him the details of Father's marriage and subsequent widowhood. Dr. Stanbury seemed to have some notion of that occurrence, but few details. Then he mentioned that he had recently become acquainted with Uncle Liam when he was called to the University of Virginia to consult on an unusual case of a contagious illness among the students. He did not elaborate on it, although I would have enjoyed the medical conversation. I had not realized how much I was missing that part of my life. I began to feel a physical ache of loss.

"I did have occasion to meet a young friend of yours, Miss Ryan," he said, sipping his sherry. "I believe you are acquainted with a young man by the name of Edgar Poe, are you not? At least your uncle indicated this to me."

I felt a sharp pang and realized that not only had I missed my medical discussions, but I had also missed Ned. The feeling took me entirely by surprise.

"Yes," I said finally, "yes, I am acquainted with Mr. Poe. How did you come upon him? I do not believe that he studies at the university any longer." I was trying mightily to remain nonchalant about the whole issue and fervently hoped that Dr. Stanbury had not noticed my excitement at the mention of Ned's name.

"Quite so. No, I did not meet him at the university. I had occasion to attend his stepmother's death last winter. February, I believe it was."

"Mrs. Allan is dead?" I said, unable to comprehend that I had not been aware of this occurrence.

"Yes, she had been sick for a very long time," he said. "Were you acquainted with her, then?"

"No, not personally, that is," I said, choosing my words carefully. "Mr. Poe had mentioned her on many occasions, and I understood that they were close. Mr. Poe must have been devastated."

I was more than sorry about her death. I was fearful for Ned. I remembered some of our final conversations when we had finally opened up to one another. He had loved his foster mother to the same extent as his foster father had loathed him. I recognized that Ned's life would have changed dramatically upon the death of such a beloved person. I had no doubt that his current position in life would find him in considerably lower circumstances.

Dr. Stanbury took out his pipe and nodded to ask if I would permit it. I did not like smoke of any kind around me, but I wished him to continue with his story and nodded my permission.

"It was a most peculiar thing," he said, lighting his pipe and shaking his head at the same time. "Most peculiar, indeed."

"How so?" I said, not wishing to sound overly anxious, but at the same time hoping that he would get on with the story.

"It seems Mr. Allan left it until too late to get word to young Poe that his stepmother would not recover." Dr. Stanbury inhaled deeply of the pungent tobacco smoke in his pipe, then continued thoughtfully. "I had wondered if he had not done it purposely." He stopped to puff momentarily. "In any case, young Poe arrived in Richmond the day after her passing. In fact, I met him at the funeral. But that was not the most bizarre thing. No, it happened the following day." He took another long puff of his pipe and then settled back into the chair as if the inhalation of such a foul substance might have relaxed him.

"What happened?" I said softly, nudging him onward in his story.

"Well," he continued, "I happened to be passing Shockoe Hill Cemetery the following day. It was raining, and I had just come from attending a difficult birth. I remember the patient vividly, although I had never seen her before or since. A woman of ill repute," he looked at me directly. "Oh, I am sorry, Miss Ryan, I should not speak of such people in your presence. A lady such as yourself."

"Dr. Stanbury, there is no need to apologize. I have seen and assisted my father in caring for many such women in my short life. They are persons, just as are we. Please continue with your story."

"Yes. Well, I was walking past Shockoe Hill Cemetery when I noticed a dark figure near the new grave where we had buried Mrs. Allan only the day before. I stopped momentarily and noticed that it was young Poe. Just as I was about to call out to him, as I believed that he might need some assistance, he began pounding on the grave and clawing at the earth. It seemed to me that he was acting in a very deranged manner. Deranged persons can be expected to act in these bizarre ways, you know." He cleared his throat.

I was becoming increasingly agitated at his digressions, but did not wish to appear either rude or anxious. "Please go on," I said gently.

"Yes, of course." He cleared his throat again and continued. "I called out to him, but he failed to hear me. So I entered the cemetery and went to him. He was severely disturbed, evidently overwhelmed by grief. I was able to ascertain that he had been there the whole of the night before and all that day, keeping vigil over her grave. He was mumbling something about her not being able to get out of the coffin on her own. Frankly, I found him particularly disturbing." Dr. Stanbury reached for his sherry glass and raised it to his lips as if to wash away an offensive taste.

"What happened to Mr. Poe?"

"I don't know, really," he said. "He told me he needed to be alone, so I left him. I believe he reconciled with his father for a time, but I have heard a rumour that he may be in Baltimore. I seem to have quite lost touch since I no longer have Mrs. Allan for whom to care."

I could now hardly wait for Dr. Stanbury to take his leave. I had to find Ned. The rest of our conversation was but a blur. I tried to concentrate on what Dr. Stanbury was saying, but my mind was racing as I formulated a plan to find Ned. He would surely be in need of consoling.

I was then taken by an idea. I would contact John Ryan. He would likely be happy to assist me in discovering the whereabouts of a lost friend. I knew that John was back home in Baltimore and would have his finger on the pulse of the city. Perhaps Ned was employed with one of the new literary journals I had been hearing about. One thing was clear. It was time to return to Boston and get on with my life. I would meet with Mr. Samuel Bowness of the (my) import/export business and attend to that detail, but then I would leave immediately.

FIFTEEN

Mr. Samuel T. Bowness arrived precisely at one p.m. the following day in response to the message I sent to his offices immediately upon Dr. Stanbury leaving me. The ornate, gold-plated mantle clock struck the hour just as Mrs. Cameron let him in the front door while I awaited him in the parlour.

As he entered with an outstretched hand and condolences for the death of Abigail and my father, I took in his countenance. Mr. Bowness was a tall, rather lanky man sporting a balding head of graying hair and a full beard of the same colour. I placed his age to be about fifty. He seemed nervous and a bit high-strung to my eye, with his collar so tight I thought that his eyes might bulge out at any moment. When I shook his hand, it was cool and just the slightest bit clammy. I wondered how a man of his stature in the business community might be so nervous in the presence of one such as me – unschooled in business and clearly young enough to be his daughter.

"Miss Ryan," he began, taking a handkerchief out of his breast pocket and mopping his brow as he took the chair I offered to him. "I am pleased to meet you. I have been looking forward to this for some months. There is much about the business that we need to discuss."

I was a bit puzzled at his apparent need for my counsel. "Mr. Bowness, it was my understanding from Abigail's solicitors that my involvement in the business would be in name only and that it would continue as it had always done."

"Yes, well," he said, his nervousness ever increasing. "It is that 'name' that I'm concerned about."

I was becoming increasingly puzzled. As I was about to speak, Mrs. Cameron rapped on the door and entered with a tray of lemonade. Mr. Bowness seemed inordinately grateful for the distraction and took up a crystal glass with alacrity. He gulped in a rather ungentlemanly fashion. I also took a glass as Mrs. Cameron laid the tray on the table between us and left immediately.

"I am a bit puzzled, Mr. Bowness. Perhaps you could explain."

"Explain. Yes, explain. I should do that," he said, taking another large sip of his lemonade.

I waited as patiently as I could, stopping myself from tapping on the crystal. I placed the glass on the table to avoid appearing rude or irritable.

Mr. Bowness cleared his throat and mopped his brow again before continuing. "Miss Ryan, it is about your cousin."

I must have looked puzzled.

"Mr. Densmore. Mr. Dalton Densmore."

"Yes, yes," I said, "I know Mr. Densmore. He is not actually my cousin but my late stepmother's cousin. But what does he have to do with the business?"

At that moment, I had a sudden but somewhat murky flash, as if there were something buried in the back of my mind, something that I should know but that I was failing to access. What was it about Dalton and the import/export business that I should know? Then, I recalled a tiny snatch of conversation at the dinner table upon our first meeting. Abigail had introduced him as an importer/exporter from New York. Surely, she did not mean that she was in business with him! It was too horrifying a thought to even put into words.

"As you know, Mr. Densmore is a part-owner of Miss Abigail's," he looked at me as if suddenly apologetic, "I mean your company."

Using all the self-control I possessed, I tried to speak as if I had, in fact, known that tiny detail. "Please remind me," I said. "Just how much of a part does he own?"

"He is a quarter owner," Mr. Bowness said. "But he seems to think that he owns the whole thing now. I was told by the solicitors that upon Miss Abigail's death, her shares went to her husband. Then, upon her husband's death," he looked at me, "I am sorry to bring that up, Miss Ryan, but upon her husband's death, the shares were left with all of his estate to his daughter. That means you."

So that was what Dalton had been talking about. His due. He felt that he should have received the remaining shares of the company, thus making him the owner, free and clear. I felt a sudden angry flash – how dare he?

Mr. Bowness took his handkerchief from his breast pocket again, mopping his brow as if continuing would require some effort on his part.

"Miss Ryan," he continued, "Mr. Densmore has been rather...How might I put this? Unpleasant, I should say, about the entire matter. Of course, it is not his business but yours."

He seemed relieved now that he had told me what he evidently considered to be a bit of unpleasant business. He relaxed a bit into his chair and slowly sipped his lemonade this time rather than taking such large gulps.

As my anger ebbed slightly, it occurred to me that the best course of events might be to simply let Dalton have the whole thing. What did I know of business anyway? I was not a businesswoman. I had little interest in importing and exporting goods, and it seemed that I would certainly have enough money without the added burden of a business.

"Perhaps he should have it, then," I said finally.

To say Mr. Bowness looked stricken would be a great understatement. He appeared as if one might look when shot through the heart. His eyes bulged out even more, and a vein in his neck began to throb quite noticeably. Then he choked, ever so slightly, on his mouthful of lemonade. Placing the glass back on the table with some effort, he tried to compose himself.

"Do you mean the business? Miss Ryan, please. You are joking, of course."

Indeed, I was not joking, but I thought better of saying that at this juncture, given Mr. Bowness's response to my first thought. I did not relish the thought of his apoplectic form decorating the oriental carpet.

"Well, Mr. Bowness, perhaps you could tell me just exactly what you mean by 'unpleasant.' What is it about Mr. Densmore's behaviour that has been unpleasant?" From my rather limited experience of him, I knew full well that Dalton's mere presence was unpleasant. But I recognized that Mr. Bowness had considerably more familiarity with this objectionable individual.

Mr. Bowness was looking uncomfortable again. No doubt, he would not like to speak unkindly of one of Abigail's relatives, no matter how odious. Feeling completely out of my depth on these business matters, I nevertheless wished to appear helpful, as Mr. Bowness was so clearly in need of assistance of one sort or another.

"Unpleasant, yes, I did say that, did I not? Well," Mr. Bowness cleared his throat a bit more loudly than I thought seemly, but he was clearly having difficulty with our interview. "Mr. Densmore is given to– how should I say it? Drink. There, I've said it." With that pronouncement, he sat back as if he had unburdened himself – as if it were now someone else's problem. My problem.

When I asked him for further particulars, Mr. Bowness provided me with sordid details of Dalton's final encounter with Abigail, some six months before her death. I remembered her return from New York on that occasion. She had seemed agitated and had chosen not to speak of her trip. Previous trips had been followed by days of stories about the salons she hosted, the literati of the moment keeping company and the shopping excursions. That last time had been different, and there had been no more talk of New York as Abigail concentrated on her pregnancy and became increasingly ill.

"I knew only what had transpired at the offices," Mr. Bowness said. "Heaven knows what went on after they left."

He rolled his eyes heavenward. "Mr. Densmore evidently had not liked a decision that Miss Abigail had made, although if you ask me, she was the businessman of the two – if you will be so kind as to pardon the reference. In any case, he had imbibed far too much of the whiskey he keeps in his office and staggered out to greet her when she arrived. He never liked it when she arrived from Boston. The staff loved her so much, you see." He stopped and looked at me as if to gauge my reaction.

"As much as they dislike him?" I asked.

"You, too, seem to have a certain common sense about you," Mr. Bowness said. "I do believe that women are wasted in the kitchen and nursery, if you will pardon me." He sipped his glass dry and placed it back on the table.

It was clear to me that I would be expected to do something about Dalton. Just what that ought to be escaped me at that time. I would, however, write him a letter via my solicitor and assure him that we would discuss our relative positions in due course. Beyond that, I knew I was in somewhat over my head. I made a firm decision to discuss this with John Ryan and perhaps even Sister Eulalia. She was the most sensible woman I knew and always had insights that were just slightly beyond the rest of us.

As I bid Mr. Bowness goodbye, I realized just how much had come to bear on my head. Perhaps those learned men were right not to accept me into the medical school. Despite the staff and Grace keeping me company and the beautiful surroundings, I felt ever more alone. I knew I must return to Boston at once and set about finding Ned wherever he might have set himself up in Baltimore.

That evening at dinner, I informed both Grace and Mrs. Cameron that we would return to Boston within the week. We dispatched word to Mrs. Wimpole and to Dr. John Ryan in Baltimore.

SIXTEEN

BOSTON, FALL, 1828

Both Mrs. Wimpole and John Ryan were waiting at the top of the steps as Grace and I alighted from our carriage a week later. I was surprised, but pleasantly so, to see John back in Boston, and I had a momentary thought that I wished he would stay awhile. I flushed at my own impertinence and thought that I should consider myself to be important in his life.

I knew that John's solicitude was genuine; ever the physician concerned about the physical and mental state of his late cousin's daughter. I welcomed his deep concern as I was feeling more and more that I belonged nowhere any longer. New York was fascinating, but it was clearly not my home. Boston, too, however, although I had spent many happy childhood years here, was becoming less familiar to me. Without Father, it hardly seemed welcoming any longer.

I believe John sensed this about me. After dinner on that first night back, Grace retired early to her room in preparation for Uncle Liam's arrival the following morning. They would return to the university, where Grace still clung to the hope that she would become a mother in due course. Mrs. Wimpole, clearly delighted at our return, brought port and cheese and then left us to our discourse.

I told John about the problem concerning Dalton and his presence in the business. John demurred his ignorance of all but medical matters, but seemed uncommonly felicitous of my decision to put Dalton off for the time being.

"You have been through a lot, my dear," he said, getting up to check the fire. It was yet early autumn, but the weather had turned, and the evenings were becoming slightly cool. He had helped Mrs. Wimpole to set a small fire in the parlour so that I would not become chilled. I smiled to myself when I considered his care. But, I reasoned, he was a physician. I was merely a duty.

Then, I told him about my desire to seek Ned's whereabouts.

"This young man – he is a close friend of yours?" He seemed to be looking at me knowingly.

"Yes, a friend," I said. "But a friend who is usually sorely in need of his friends. And he has recently lost his beloved foster mother."

"And you have recently lost your beloved father," he reminded me.

I thought about this for a moment in silence, then said, "John, I believe that I am better equipped to deal with such occurrences than my friend. Would you consider assisting me in ascertaining his whereabouts in Baltimore?"

"If it means that much to you, then I cannot refuse," he said finally.

I had considerable faith in John and his ability to find Ned for me. He would stay with us for two more days, completing some work with the local medical establishment, and then return to Baltimore.

The mantle clock was striking eleven when I arose, suddenly exhausted after our long train ride. As I took my leave, John caught my hand and kissed it gently.

"Sleep well, my dear," he said, holding my hand for just a moment longer.

I looked at him fondly and bid him goodnight. When, at last, I was tucked up well in my bed, I cried silently. I was an orphan now, and tomorrow was my twentieth birthday. Perhaps I would seek out Sister Eulalia Marie. She could be of help.

The following day dawned dark and dreary, with an unrelenting rain pelting against the windows. Liam arrived at the appointed time and chose not to stay, insisting that the weather would make their return to the campus rather longer than he had anticipated. Classes would resume in several days, and he could not be delayed. Neither he nor

Grace mentioned my birthday, and I was unaccountably grateful for this omission.

By the time I took my lunch, Liam and Grace had left, and the rain had all but stopped. Brief glimpses of the sun could be seen between the clouds that scudded across a gray sky. John was staying in Father's old room, having helped Mrs. Wimpole to clean it and determining that I would not be offended. I knew that Father would have wished it. But, according to Mrs. Wimpole, John had left the house early in the morning with no word of when he might return. I was missing his company.

As I sipped my coffee and read the newspaper that Mrs. Wimpole had left for me, I heard the doorbell chime. In a moment, John was standing at the door, and Mrs. Wimpole was retiring to the kitchen.

Suddenly, John produced an enormous bouquet of red roses and freesias from behind his back. "Happy Birthday, Bridget," he said, presenting them to me.

Astonished, I could scarcely speak. I was embarrassingly pleased with this turn of events. "How did you know?" I asked.

He nodded toward the kitchen.

"Wimpy. Of course, I should have known."

Mrs. Wimple took that moment to emerge from the kitchen with a large white cake, adorned with what could only be twenty candles, proclaiming what I considered to be my adulthood.

I threw my arms around her. "Thank you so much," I said, suddenly overcome by gratitude for these people who were as loyal as I could hope anyone to be.

Mrs. Wimpole cut large slices of the cake for us and set about putting the flowers into my favourite crystal vase, decorated with a Chinese etching. They were stunning in the middle of the table. With that, she withdrew again, leaving me alone with John to savour our cake and the sunshine that was now timidly peeking through the sheer lace of the curtains.

"Bridget, I should like to speak with you before I leave."

He seemed so very solemn. I wondered if he had more bad news for me.

"Of course, we should speak. Is there something wrong? You are not ill, are you?" It suddenly occurred to me that he looked a bit off-colour.

"Ill? Me? No. No, of course, I'm not ill," he said. "I didn't mean that kind of thing."

He seemed to hesitate. It was not like him. John generally seemed to be in control and in charge of every occasion.

"What is it? We can talk now if you desire it."

"Bridget, I realize that this may not be the time to discuss this, but I feel that I must say my piece before I return to Baltimore."

I nodded for him to go on.

"Since the moment I came to tend your stepmother, I have observed you and grown to respect you in very many ways. I realize that I am old enough to be your father, and this may come as a considerable shock to you, but I realize that I have grown very fond of you." He hesitated, looking carefully at me. Then he spoke very quickly. "I believe that I love you and wish you to consider doing me the honour of becoming my wife."

He seemed to interpret my lack of immediate response as astonishment.

"I realize that this may come as a shock to you," he repeated. "And I do not expect your answer at this very moment. I also realize that, since I have never been married, you may consider this a deterrent. Still, I assure you that the only reason I have yet to take a wife is that, until I met you, I had never met anyone with whom I considered sharing my life. Now, I know that you have this friend, Ned Poe, and I do not know what you mean to each other, but he cannot possibly love you as I do. Of course, you would need to consider moving to Baltimore. Would that be a problem?"

He seemed to have run out of air. I could not help myself; I began to laugh. John, however, was mortified by my reaction, so I had to explain quickly that I was only laughing at the rapidity of his delivery and hoped that he did not speak that quickly when he lectured to his medical students. Then, he smiled and began to laugh with me. When we finally calmed down, I considered what I might say to him at this juncture.

"John, this may come as something of a shock to you, but this does not astonish me as much as you might think. I believe I may have harboured some feelings for you as well. But I do need to consider the extent of these feelings and all of the occurrences in my life of late. Will you permit me a bit of time before I respond?"

John seemed clearly relieved. "Of course. Take as much time as you need. I must return to my colleague's offices now, but I shall see you at dinner – I hope."

With that, we took our leave, and I was left to consider all that had happened. I went upstairs to find my handbag and then left the house, heading toward the convent.

SEVENTEEN

It had been some time since I had last darkened Sister Eulalia's doorstep, and much had happened in my life. But I knew instinctively that she would not turn me away. Our connection, forged so many years ago, would withstand the separation.

As I again stood before the imposing door separating mere mortals from those who shared their daily lives with the divine, I briefly thought that Sister Ann Rose might open the door. I looked forward to her happy demeanour and wondered at her newest word. But, of course, she did not bid me in. She would have moved along to the novitiate by now – or perhaps even decided against such a vocation. It happened often.

Instead, when finally my bell pull was answered, I was greeted by a tall, severe-looking but unfamiliar woman. As Sister Ann Rose had done, she wore the garb of a postulant. But this woman seemed rather old to be taking on such a vocation. I briefly wondered at her life to this point.

"May I help you?" she asked rather more suspiciously than I believed my appearance enjoined.

"Hello. My name is Bridget Ryan. I am a friend of Sister Eulalia Marie's. I had hoped to have a brief audience with her today."

With that, the nun stood up even straighter. "You are an acquaintance of Mother Superior's?"

It was my turn to be surprised. So, in fact, Sister Eulalia had been so elevated. It had been her goal, if nuns were permitted goals. I knew that she would make an excellent Mother Superior. I was pleased for her.

The new greeter finally introduced herself as Sister Maria Xavier, recently arrived from Baltimore. She told me that the Mother Superior was in an interview and would be finished presently and then bid me to wait in the chapel.

I pushed open the door of the chapel where I had attended daily mass for many years when I was a young student at the school. We had stood in line giggling as we attached small, round doilies of crocheted lace to cover our heads. I had always considered this rather a useless convention, but I found myself instinctively touching my hair and bowing my head ever so slightly, aware of the fact that I had not thought to wear a hat on this warm day. Sister Maria Xavier did not seem to notice as she hurried away to announce my presence. I observed a distinct limp in the tall postulant as her heels clicked away along the stone corridor.

Not only had I not been in this chapel for these many years, but it had also been some years now since I had even been to mass on a Sunday. As I looked around, I realized that it was considerably smaller than how I remembered it. As a small child, such an edifice can, indeed, seem overpowering. Now, it seemed an intimate space. I genuflected out of habit, then sat down in a pew, crossing myself and kneeling for a moment as had been the custom for so many years, and I tried to determine when I had stopped believing, if ever I had believed.

The chapel was dark, with deeply stained oak walls and high, stained glass windows. Just as when I was a child sitting here, listening to the increasingly more familiar Latin words, I had often felt enclosed, and not pleasantly so. I wanted to tell them to replace the windows with clear glass to let in the sunshine and the light – in fact, I remembered telling Sister Eulalia exactly that on one occasion when I was about eight years old – but I knew that there was little likelihood that anyone would listen to one such as I. And now I felt that same feeling creep into my bones. I shivered as I gazed upon the image of Christ on the cross, blood dripping from every wound.

I arose and walked toward the bank of candles lit in memory of someone or as an entreaty for something and watched the flickering light for a moment. I reached into my bag for a coin, which I placed in the receptacle to the side. I then reached for a long wooden taper and lit the end with one of the candles. I then lit a small candle on the back of the farthest row and blew out the taper. Replacing the taper in its stand, I knelt before the candles and clasped my hands together in prayer. But what should I say?

I thought of conversations Ned and I had had on the subject of God and the hereafter. He had been particularly convinced that death was not a finality. As for me, I still contended that "ashes to ashes and dust to dust" was all that there was. Now, I knelt before the God of my youth and could think of no prayer. Perhaps I should consider something that Sister Eulalia had said to her young charges many years ago. "Stop talking to God when you pray, but listen instead."

God, are you there? I am listening now.

Just as this thought crossed my mind, Sister Maria Xavier returned to fetch me.

"Mother Superior will see you now," she said. Her demeanour had softened somewhat, as I had hoped it might do when she saw Sister Eulalia's response to hearing my name.

We exited the chapel together and then proceeded down the long corridor lined with oak door after oak door. We turned the corner just in time to see Sister Eulalia bid farewell to a young woman and what were so clearly her doting parents. She must have been having an interview prior to entering the convent, I thought. I sighed and considered how easy life might have been for me had I accepted a call to God. But truly, there was no call.

Then Sister Eulalia turned to me. "Bridget," she said, extending her hand, "it is so good to see you after all this time." She took my hand warmly into hers and, to Sister Maria's obvious surprise, we retreated arm-in-arm into the Mother Superior's office.

The new office was larger and more ornate than that which Sister Eulalia had occupied for so many years. The walls were panelled in the same dark oak as in the chapel, and the ceiling was a kind of fresco. It had several large, stained-glass windows and one clear one. I looked at the clear one delightedly, realizing it looked down into the quadrangle where the schoolgirls played, and the nuns took their morning air. I smiled as I remembered my own impertinence so many years ago, suggesting to Sister that the chapel ought to have more sunshine. Sister saw me smiling.

"Yes, Bridget," she said, taking her place behind her large, ornate oak desk. "I, too, remember your need for sunshine and light. When I first occupied this office, I told the workers to replace one of the windows, ostensibly so I could keep an eye on everything that happened in the courtyard. With that one act, everyone believed me to be an indisputably vigilant Mother Superior, one not to be crossed, I am told. Truly, it was in remembrance of a little girl's longing for light – a longing that, truth be told, I often share."

I was inordinately gratified to hear Sister make such a comment. That I should have had any influence on her at all was a great compliment.

"Sister... Mother, it is so wonderful to see you," I said, fumbling over her new title as I took the chair across the desk from her. It was clear to me that this was where she belonged. She was so good at being in charge of things, and she would be a great asset to this convent.

"Much has happened to you since last we talked, Bridget. I have heard the sad news of the deaths in your family, but I have also heard a rumour that you are now a wealthy woman. Please, tell me how you are holding up under all of these changes."

"Sister...Mother, this is precisely why I am in search of your counsel." I was suddenly flustered with the recognition that I always seemed to seek out this good friend only when I needed something from her. "Which I seem always to be requiring," I said, continuing.

"Bridget, this is why we are friends. Of that, I have no doubt. It is as it should be."

A sudden thought entered my mind, and I blurted it out. "I would like to donate a sum of money to the convent school."

Sister Eulalia smiled. "I knew that you would get to that, but that is not why you are here, is it?"

I flushed slightly. "You know me too well, Mother."

I stood up and walked back toward the window. There were no children in the quadrangle as it was late on a Saturday afternoon. Soon enough, they would return to fill the space, taking their fresh air in the middle of the day.

"How might I be of service to you, my dear?" she said, folding her hands in front of her on the desk.

I took a breath and tried to catch the thoughts that were swirling about inside my head like a whirling dervish. Just when I thought I had captured one, another pushed it out and took its place. Another breath, and I caught one.

"Mother, you recall my tenacious intention to pursue a medical career?"

She nodded but did not interrupt me.

"Of necessity, I have forgone that dream – at least for the present."

I could see a small smile forming at the corners of the Mother Superior's mouth. She knew me only too well. That I should completely let go of such a dream, she would know was difficult for me. I continued.

"I am left a wealthy woman, and now I find myself with a proposal of marriage."

Judging from her expression, this was not what she had been expecting, but she said nothing.

"It is John Ryan. Dr. John Ryan. He is a distant cousin to my late father, and he attended both the death of my stepmother and of my father."

"Hardly a good track record," Sister Eulalia said softly.

I had not thought in that light. Then I realized that she was joking in her wry way. Had she not been a nun, Sister Eulalia would have made a formidable businesswoman.

"What is he like, Bridget?"

I tried to describe him to her and realized that I had not given him much thought in this way. He was almost, dare I say, a father figure to me now as I explained it to my old friend. But I realized that he was more than that. I respected him and found his company most desirable.

"Do you love him?" she asked.

It seemed a most sensible question. Still, I had not thought much about its answer. She could see that I hesitated.

"Bridget, do you love him?"

"It is not so much that I do not love him – in fact, I believe I could. It is more that I have had little opportunity to explore that aspect of our relationship."

There, I had uncovered the truth inside my mind."I believe that he and I share a respect that is not often seen in such marital couplings."

"Have you discussed this with him?"

I felt foolish now that I realized I should have been more transparent to my suitor – that he and I should have spent more time together. But then, that had been impossible. Then she asked if I had doubts because of how attractive and eligible a young, wealthy woman might appear.

The answer to that question was much clearer to me. I had no concerns that John Ryan was after my perceived money. As I passed the thought through my mind, I realized with a certainty that he may, in fact, be the only person, save Ned, of course, who might not see the money before the person.

Sister Eulalia and I talked some more, interrupted only by Sister Maria Xavier's arrival with tea and biscuits on a silver tray, which she placed decorously on the desk between us, then poured two cups of honey-coloured liquid into the porcelain cups, which I observed were painted all over with tiny, pink flowers. I accepted the proffered tea gratefully.

I sipped my tea and continued thoughtfully. "I shall have to move to Baltimore," I said, almost as if to myself.

"Baltimore is a wonderful city," Sister said. "I was brought up there, you know."

I did not know. I realized that every time we met, I became privy to yet another previously obscure piece of information about this remarkable woman. I believe we tend to think of nuns as being not quite mortal.

We spent the next quarter-hour discussing relocation to new surroundings in an agreeable city such as Baltimore, when Sister asked me a most unusual question.

"What about the other man in your life? Does he know you are considering this proposal?"

I was taken aback, as I was unaware that we had ever discussed Ned; I had supposed that was the man to whom she referred. She continued.

"No, you have never told me about him in so many words, Bridget." She arose and tucked each hand in the opposite cuff, as was her habit, and walked to the window. "When you returned from your year in Charlottesville, I was acutely aware that there was something – or indeed someone – on your mind. You did not, however, choose to share this with me. I am now wondering if this deeply felt relationship is somehow behind you – both physically and in your mind."

For the first time in my life, I lied directly to Sister Eulalia Marie. "It is completely behind me, Mother," I said resolutely.

She looked at me, and I knew that she was not convinced of my authenticity. She did not remark upon it, however.

As I took my leave, I asked the Mother Superior if I might be married in the convent chapel, where I had spent so much of my youth. With that simple request, I knew that my mind was made up. I would marry Dr. John Ryan and follow my life wherever it led me. But I was in no particular hurry to get to this new life.

EIGHTEEN

BOSTON, WINTER-SPRING 1828-29

By the time autumn had wafted in with crisp days and crackling leaves falling underfoot, then blown out with a gust of December wind sending fingers of ice down unprotected necks, I had made my decision. On the first Sunday in December, I told John that it would be my privilege to become his wife. We spent many hours that night discussing our future, and it was clear to me that John would support any decision I made about my purpose in life. Twenty-five years my senior, John was not considering having children. Unlike my Aunt Grace, I had no particular desire to procreate – not now, and I suspected not ever.

I had kept in constant touch with Mr. Bowness throughout the autumn, and he was encouraged by how the business was growing. Even Dalton had not made a nuisance of himself as yet. According to Mr. Bowness's most recent letter, Dalton's domestic situation seemed to take up a great deal of his time and energy at this point.

It seemed that his new wife had given birth to twins rather earlier than his family might have liked, and both she and this new family were demanding much of his time. I was pleased and hoped that this was a harbinger of things to come.

With John's assistance, I found other positions for all the staff at the New York house, and the house was sold again, without comment from Dalton, to a physician who had recently immigrated from England. I had not realized how burdened I felt with the property until it was no longer an encumbrance.

Encumbrances were the last things that I needed at that point in my life. I was still vaguely unhappy about my lot in life and had yet to figure out what I ought to be doing. I knew only that this marriage to John would never be a conventional one, at least from my point of view. And I believed that John felt the same. But I did harbour a gnawing feeling that I must pursue some more noble calling. I had almost made peace with the conclusion that I would not be able to follow my life's dream and become the physician I knew I had the capability of becoming. I would marry John, move to Baltimore, oversee the New York business from a distance and seek my true path.

It was this very thought I was considering over my coffee the second Monday morning in December when Mrs. Wimpole entered the room carrying a small package.

"A piece of mail for you, Miss Bridget," she said, setting the package on the table before me. She noticed that my cup was nearly empty and, knowing I preferred several cups in the morning, poured another for me.

"What is it, Wimpy?" I said, buttering a small scone.

She looked at me as if I were a small, simple child. Of course, she could not know.

"Well," she said as if to placate me, "it is marked from Baltimore. Perhaps a little gift from your husband-to-be."

I smiled. John's solicitude had not gone unnoticed by Mrs. Wimpole nor by me. He was generous to a fault and seemed in no way interested in the money that I seemed to have in abundance. He had even encouraged me to donate sums to charities that I felt worthy of such support. I had done so for the convent school and was considering other options.

I sipped my coffee as I took the package up for closer scrutiny. It was not large, nor was it heavy. I peered closely at my name and the handwriting. The penmanship was unmistakable. I was familiar with that elegant, curly flourish on the capital "B" and "R." The hair on the back of my neck stood on end, and I began to flush. To hide such a state from Mrs. Wimpole, I coughed and took a napkin to my face. She looked at me as if concerned, then left when she realized that I was fine.

The package was from Ned. In the past months, I had all but forgotten my desire to see him and now felt guilty at my lack of manners at the very least. I had yet to send my condolences for the loss of Mrs. Allan, now dead more than a year. And what would Ned say when he heard the news of my impending nuptials? Something in me wanted to keep that news from him, while another voice told me to break away from him once and for all.

I opened the package with shaking hands, not knowing why I shook nor how to control the shaking. I only knew that I was touching something that Ned had touched only days ago. I removed the string and then the brown paper to reveal a small book. Ned's second book! I was thrilled.

A plain but attractive cover proclaimed the book to be called "Al Aaraaf, Tamerlane and Minor Poems by Edgar A. Poe." This time, he had his name on the cover. It felt odd to see it in print, as his first book had kept him anonymous. I fanned the pages, noting the texture of the paper. The book was slender, with some seventy thin, almost onion-skin-like pages. I had a momentary thought that it could be more substantial, this work of Ned's, but it was Ned's work nonetheless, and I was delighted to see it. As I opened the front cover, a single page fell to the table. It was a letter. It was dated some months earlier, and I wondered how it was the package had taken so long to reach me.

> "My Dear Bride,
> I hope this letter finds you well and that you will again accept a minuscule token of my regard for you. Even in your absence, you continue to be a constant inspiration. I hold you dear in my heart and await the time when next I may be permitted to gaze upon your countenance, and the months of separation will vanish in a second.
> I was released from the Army in April of this year by being able to provide for them a suitable

replacement for myself. I now await admission to West Point in the hope of enhancing my discipline and serving my country further.

Should you have the occasion to visit Baltimore, I may be reached at the above address and would welcome you more than you can ever know.

My stepmother has now passed beyond this life to where I cannot see her excepting for in my heart, and I continue to behold her in my dreams at night. I shall forever hold her in this barren heart of mine, and I know that she and my mother look down upon us.

I have heard nothing of you and sorely wish to know of your current circumstances.

I remain forever,

Your Ned"

I gazed at the letter for a very long time, or so it seemed, wondering just what it was I felt for this dear, tortured and talented man. In just a month, I was to leave for Baltimore to view a house that John wished to buy for our matrimonial home, but that he would not finalize without my comment. Could I see Ned while there? Could I tell John about this meeting? I had chosen to tell John little of my friendship with Ned. I did not know how he would react, but more importantly to me, I wished to keep Ned all to myself. It seemed to me that there was very little to tell in any case. John had made it clear to me that he recognized that, even in marriage, he would not own me, a sentiment for which I was extremely grateful and one which sent Aunt Grace in spasms when we discussed it. Yes, I would attempt to see Ned while in Baltimore, but I would guard my privacy. I remembered Sister Eulalia's admonitions about the men in my life, but was as yet unprepared to act on her advice. So, I harboured my secret.

I did not believe it to be auspicious for a wife to keep secrets from her husband, but I was torn by the idea that there were aspects of me that perhaps were private, to which no one, even a husband, ought to be privy. That much independence I would maintain. Surely, it could cause no harm. I secreted the book away in the back of a large drawer in my oak desk with the other.

As the months went on and spring began to show the promise of summer ahead, I turned my attention to a December wedding. Mrs. Wimpole assured me that it was never too early to begin planning.

Wimpy proved herself a Godsend, as usual, engineering as she did the minutiae of details. The move to Baltimore would be the most stressful and yet exhilarating part of the whole process. I believe that she was more excited than I was to be moving. I had worried that she would not want to leave her friends in Boston, but she was adamant that what she really needed at this point in her life (I believed she was about 50 years old) was a change. She had not felt the same about the house and her work since Father had died, and I knew that she held many memories dear to her heart. Perhaps she and I shared that need to put some things behind us.

NINETEEN

BALTIMORE, SUMMER 1829

I stood on the walkway gazing at the house before me. John paced nervously. Such nervousness was a side of him I had not yet seen. I concluded that my approval was of paramount importance to him.

He had already this hot and humid morning, taken me down to the harbour to see its magnificence, then toured me through streets where the city's 80,000 inhabitants lived and worked. I could see that it was a fine city and said as much to John, who appeared immeasurably relieved.

Now, as I stood before the house that would be my home if I but said the word, I considered what life might be like there. The house itself was passable. Indeed, it was more than passable, truth be told. It had just been completed for a colleague of John's whose wife had fallen ill, and they had relocated to New York. Thus, it was available to us. It looked large to me, with its red brick facade and its grand entrance. At least it looked grand to me. It did look like most of the other houses on the street, with a rather small front yard and a gated walkway leading to the front door.

We entered the front door and were greeted by a sweeping staircase, much like the one in my home in Boston. The railing, as was everything else in the house, was more ornate, and the windows all boasted panes of stained glass in their upper portions. I believed I could make it my home and told John as much.

"Are you certain?" he asked when we finally completed our tour.

"Indeed, it is a fine house, John," I said, looking at the oak panelling on the walls of the study. "I believe we shall be very happy here."

John wrapped his arms around me, an unaccustomed gesture but not an unwelcome one. I smiled to myself and eased into his embrace. He kissed me gently on the cheek and seemed to relax. The house had passed the test. Perhaps he thought he had passed the test as well.

"I am sorry to say this, my dear," he said, breaking away from me, "but I shall have to leave you at the hotel for the afternoon. I have patients to attend to. I do wish that Mrs. Wimpole had been able to accompany you. You would have been glad of the company."

"John, I am quite able to amuse myself for several hours."

"I'm afraid it may be more than a few. I shall have to have a very late dinner tonight. There is a difficult case that I may be required to have moved to the hospital this afternoon. Will you be quite comfortable in the hotel?"

"Of course." I replaced my gloves, which I had removed earlier, to feel the texture of the woodwork. "It will be pleasant to have a few quiet hours after all the commotion at home these past few weeks."

Knowing that I was referring to the recent visit of Grace and Liam, John smiled, and we made our way back to the hotel, where, as he had promised, he left me alone.

I removed Ned's letter from my bag and unfolded it carefully. I looked again at the address where he indicated he could be reached and approached the concierge for directions. When he read the address, he frowned.

"Madam," he said, "are you certain that this is where you wish to go?"

"Is there some problem, sir?" I asked, puzzled by his reaction.

"I believe it may be a boarding house in an area of the city that is perhaps not conducive to visits by refined young women."

"Nevertheless," I said, rather more haughtily than was probably necessary, "this is where I need to go. An old friend of mine is staying there. Are you able to oblige with directions?"

"If I may be so bold, Madam, I will provide you with an escort and transportation."

I nodded, somewhat relieved, I must admit. It had occurred to me that the death of Ned's stepmother may have left him in even more dire straits than those he had experienced at the university. His stepfather, Mr. Allan, was not likely to have changed his colours so easily. All the more reason that I must see him and help if at all possible.

The concierge had been correct in his assessment of the potential crudeness of the situation. As the carriage he had arranged for me turned into the street, in spite of the heat, I pulled the lap blanket farther up toward my shoulders, almost burrowing down so as not to be seen. I was glad of the sunshine, as I would not have wanted to visit such a place at candlelighting or under the cover of darkness. I wondered what John would think of his bride-to-be now.

The carriage stopped in front of a run-down-looking wooden building, which was, indeed, a boarding house. As I sat there looking out at the facade, rain began falling, first in large, plopping drops, and then, almost immediately, it became torrential. The various neighbours, who were sitting on the stoops of the adjoining buildings smoking and talking, quickly vacated their spaces. I was grateful for the lack of a welcoming committee.

When the rain subsided for a moment, I walked up the three steps to the door, holding my cloak tightly around me. Perhaps I was not quite as brave as I made myself out to be. I knocked and was soon greeted by a woman I took to be over sixty years old, dressed in a house dress that had perhaps seen better days. Her feet were bare, and the hem of her dress was unravelling. Her wiry grey hair was dishevelled, and she smelled slightly like what I had taken to be gin.

"What?" she said as she eyed me up and down.

"I am sorry to bother you," I began. "I am in search of a man by the name of Edgar Poe. Would he happen to be among your tenants at present?"

She seemed to brighten a bit. "Mr. Poe? The writer? Is he a friend of yours? You a publisher type?"

"Actually, we are old friends," I said as she looked past me to the carriage at the curb. The driver had alighted and was tending to the horse.

She looked at me suspiciously again. "Friends, are you?"

I nodded and smiled slightly.

"He's not within at the moment, but you can wait in his room if you like."

I had a moment of panic, wondering when Ned should return and how long I dared wait. "Do you know when he is expected to return?"

"Usually comes back for tea," she said, ushering me into the dark, narrow corridor.

I followed her up the steep staircase in the increasingly stifling heat, noticing the peeling plaster and deeply scuffed floors. My heart went out to Ned, having to live like this.

When, at last, I found myself alone in Ned's room, I stood in the centre, almost fearing to move. I quickly took in the Spartan furnishings and the small window covered by a thin curtain. There was a small stove in the corner. With little to see and the heat beginning to become oppressive, I removed my cloak and loosened the neck of my dress. I finally sat down on the narrow bed and waited.

It seemed that hours had passed, but it was likely only minutes when I heard footsteps and voices in the hall. The doorknob turned, and Ned entered the room carrying a sheaf of papers under his arm. When he saw me sitting on the bed, he dropped his bundle, causing paper to strew itself all over the floor. He choked slightly.

"Bride!" he cried. "It is you!"

I stood up and straightened my skirts as Ned reached for me and threw his arms around me. It seemed a bit out of character for him to make such a bold gesture, but I supposed he must be very glad of a friend.

"I had no idea it was you who waited herein. My landlady indicated only that someone awaited me. She did not even suggest that it was a woman. I feared it might be someone else."

"A bill collector, perhaps, Ned?" I said, narrowing my eyes to take in his countenance.

He looked tired, with deep furrows etched in his young brow. His eyes were ringed in dark hollows, and his clothes bespoke a difficult existence.

"Are you not as glad of the sight of me as I am of you?" he asked, somewhat reprovingly.

I was apologetic. "Ned, I am surely as glad of the sight of you. I am but chagrined at the sight of your abode."

"I do not apologize, Bride," he said, gathering the papers he had dropped on the floor. He managed to place them on a small table beneath the window, which he proceeded to attempt to open. There was not a breath of air in the room, and I wondered how he worked or even lived in such a space. After what appeared to be a significant effort on his part, he was finally able to lift the window slightly, and I could now see a faint breeze moving the flimsy curtains. Then he seemed to be looking for something.

He finally found a bottle, which he retrieved from under the bed, then offered me a drink, which I accepted.

"How did you find me?"

I pulled his letter from my bag and showed him the address on the top.

"Of course," he said. "But you have taken great pains to come to this place. I am hardly worthy of such effort."

"Ned," I said, rising from my chair and coming to sit beside him on the narrow bed, "you are worth every effort. I want to help if I can."

He looked at me knowingly. "Bride, I realize that your first thought is to be of financial assistance to one such as myself. And I remember your help in the past."

I decided to change the subject for the moment and extended my condolences to Ned on the death of Fanny Allan. It was clear that even after all this time, he was still devastated by the thought of her demise. Indeed, I had been correct in assuming that his stepfather would have become even more problematic if that were possible. Ned had been all but disowned. All of this led back to his money problems.

"I must say I was pleased that one such as you, with such talent, had chosen to leave the army," I said finally.

"Yes," he said, "but I await my acceptance into West Point."

"So you said in your letter – but West Point?" I cried. "Why ever would you do such a thing as to enter another military life?"

Ned said nothing but looked at me with such longing in his eyes that it was palpable in the air between us.

"You are avoiding your destiny, Ned Poe," I said finally.

He sighed. "I do not believe that one can avoid one's destiny, Bride. Do you really believe one can?" He looked carefully into my face as if searching for a reaction.

It was my turn to be silent. I considered his words carefully and knew that it was not his destiny but mine to which he referred.

"Tell me, my Bride, what is it you are doing in Baltimore this hot summer day? You did not come all this way just to see an old friend."

I had considered this moment all the way from the hotel in the carriage. What would I tell Ned of my upcoming marriage to John? And why did this seem such a problem for me? In the end, after much consternation, I told him I was to be married.

He looked at me sadly, and I wondered if he had thought I might have reconsidered his own proposition of so long ago. "So, you will be a physician's wife," he said at last after I informed him about John. He arose from his place on the bed and walked to the window to try to thrust it open farther. Finally, he sat down in the chair beside the stove and put his face in his hands as if to cry.

"No, not just a physician's wife. I will find my way. I have a business in New York, you know. It was left to me by my father upon his death." I did not know why I thought to tell him this.

Ned looked up, puzzled. "A business? What kind of business?"

I tried to explain the details to him, but he was so clearly distraught by my announcement. And he seemed distraught on so many levels.

Finally, I noticed that the sun was setting and that I would have to leave presently. I had no idea that it had become that late. When I arose to go, Ned came over to me and threw his arms around my neck again. Then he kissed me for a long time. As the tears began forming in my eyes, I knew that I must leave at once.

I did not know when we should meet again. I only knew that I was troubled by our leave-taking and the feelings that it evoked deep within me. It was as if on every encounter with Ned, I held up a mirror to myself. We lived and moved in different worlds, but somehow, we were the mirrors of one another's innermost feelings. We were connected.

When I returned to the hotel, I drew a bath and tried to wash off a feeling of slight unease. I knew that I should discuss this with John, but I also knew that I would not.

It was very late when John returned, missing dinner. But I cared little. I went to bed and slept a dreamless sleep, putting all thought of the rendezvous behind me.

TWENTY

And so I was married. But what is there to tell of this? The ceremony took place as planned in the chapel at the convent, with Sister Eulalia acting *in loco parentis* for me on that day. I wore my mother's wedding gown, although the dressmaker had to add several inches to the hem, since I would have towered over my mother had she lived to see me in the fullness of adulthood, which is how I felt when I became a wife.

Just before we left the convent to take a small supper with friends at the house, Sister Eulalia called me aside, and we spent a few private moments in her office. It felt peculiar in the extreme to be standing here in my wedding dress, clutching my bouquet of white roses as snow fell softly outside the window in the quadrangle.

"I have something for you, Bridget," she said, going to the cabinet in the corner and opening it with a key that she withdrew from somewhere deep in the folds of her habit. She removed a small leather pouch from the cabinet and locked the door again before returning to me as I stood near the window.

As Sister Eulalia placed the pouch in my hand, I saw tears form in her eyes, a sight I had never before beheld. I placed my bouquet on the low table near the window so that I could turn the pouch over in my hands. It was fashioned in fine, black leather, soft and supple, with a thong of leather drawing it closed at the top. Finally, I loosened the drawstring and poured the contents into my hand.

It was the most beautiful rosary I had ever seen. "Sister, where did you get this?" I said, almost gasping at the beauty. The beads were of the finest crystal, and the crucifix of solid gold. It almost glowed.

Mother Superior sat down behind her desk and folded her hands before her. "Bridget, I have had that rosary for many years, locked away for this very day. It belonged to your mother."

I looked at her, puzzling over her words.

"Before her death, it had been her fondest wish that you would be educated here at the convent, and so you were. Upon her death, your father asked me to take this rosary, her special one, for safekeeping and that I should return it to him on your wedding day so that you might feel your mother's presence with you on this special day. I have taken the liberty of taking his place in this endeavour and present you with your mother's love."

The tears that were now beginning to spill down Sister Eulalia's cheeks, so unlike her stern demeanour, seemed to be contagious. I, too, could feel the tears, hot and salty, making their way down my cheeks and onto my mother's dress. I could not speak yet.

"Bridget, I know that you do not hold as strongly to your faith as you did in years gone by. I recognize the need within you to question what is taught and the outcomes in your life. I respect that, and I know that it is unlikely that you will go down upon your knees and say your rosary each day as you might. But, if I may be permitted a word of advice." She stopped for a moment and withdrew a handkerchief from her sleeve with which to dab her eyes before continuing.

I sat down in the chair opposite her desk and stared down at the glowing crystals in my lap.

"My advice is this. Set sacred intention each day," she said softly.

I looked up at her, not comprehending what she was trying to say to me.

"Listen to your innermost voices, and put aside a moment each day to connect with that part of you that tells you how to stay upon your own path. God will always be with you."

For the first time in my adult life, I believed that I understood something of God and the church. Sister Eulalia Marie, in her wisdom born of many years of listening to her own inner voices and of dealing, on the bodily level, with so many of her charges, deeply understood that I would never return to mother church. But her words etched themselves deep in my soul, and I knew that this sacred intention of which she spoke might help me in finding my way with John and beyond. I embraced her as I might have embraced my mother on my wedding day, then took my leave, the rosary, safe in its pouch, clutched within my palm.

The wedding behind us, John and I could settle into our new lives in Baltimore. After a month of cold, dreary weather and little to do in the new house, with everything settled, I was beginning to feel a restlessness overtake me and wondered at the wisdom of my decisions of late.

Late one Friday evening, early in February, with the snow whirling around the candlelighters outside on their rounds yet again, John rushed up the steps and flung open the front door. In his haste to find me, he had neglected to remove his outerwear, and snow began to fall off him onto the rug in the drawing-room.

"John, whatever is the matter?" I asked, rising from my chair by the fire where I had been patiently awaiting his return for our evening meal.

"Bridget, I need your help," he said, breathlessly. "Please come with me."

It did not occur to me to ask the nature of the help he required; I only knew that I felt a sudden, overwhelming sense of worth, the like of which I had not felt in some time. I quickly donned my overcoat, gloves and a hat, and followed John to the carriage waiting at the end of the walkway.

We pulled away and were rattling over the ice-covered street for a time before he caught his breath enough to tell me of our destination.

"Bridget, I have a patient who is having continuous seizures and cannot be moved. But that is not the whole of the matter."

I knew this could not be the situation for which John had requested my presence, as it was a common one for him in his duties as a physician.

"The disturbance caused by this in the household has resulted in his wife's going into labour, and she is but seven months along in her pregnancy. I cannot handle this alone, and my partner is busy with a surgery this night."

I had not attended at a birth since that night when Father became a widower, but I remembered everything he had ever taught me and everything I had ever read. I would be John's right arm this night.

I could not have foretold the scene into which we were plunged when we arrived at our destination. The house was in a working-class part of Baltimore, near the docks. It was slightly shabby, from what I could see in the darkness, but even more alarming was the number of children who seemed to be underfoot at every turn. We entered the narrow hall that led to the parlour, where a man lay upon the settee, gasping for air. It seemed he was between convulsions at this moment, so John and I followed a young woman whom John had introduced as the eldest daughter, Siobhan. Appearing to my eye to be about seventeen years old, Siobhan was a strikingly beautiful auburn-haired creature whose beauty was marred only by a small, ragged scar along the right-hand side of her face. She led us to a small bedroom at the top of the first landing.

Once inside the room, lit only by two small candles, I could make out the shuddering form of a woman who lay in labour upon the bed. Despite the chill in the room, she had kicked off the covers and had flung her arms across her face as if to keep out the spectacle of her own confinement. Just as I stepped beside the bed and introduced myself, there came a mighty roar from downstairs, and John quickly left to attend to his first patient.

I removed my coat and asked Siobhan to bring a basin of water for me to wash my hands. She was puzzled by my request.

"No doctors never asked to wash before. You'll just get yourself dirty, Miss," she said in an Irish lilt.

"Nevertheless, I would ask you to comply. I will also require fresh, clean wrappings," I said, beginning my assessment of the woman who seemed to be in the late second stage of labour. Judging from the number of children to whom she had already given birth, I suspected that this would not take but another quarter of an hour.

"Who," the woman asked, catching hold of my arm, "who are you? Where is Dr. John?"

"I am Bridget, John's wife," I said. "What is your name?"

"I am Kate," she said.

She no sooner had the words out of her mouth when another contraction racked her body. I could see that she was trying mightily not to scream.

I placed my hand on her swollen belly and counted. The hardness finally subsided, and I judged the contractions to be moving her swiftly toward birth.

"Dr. Bridget," she said when finally there was a break in the pain. "Dr. Bridget, I have birthed eight babies and never has one felt the like of this. Something is not right." She grabbed my arm. "Please help my baby."

At that moment, Siobhan entered the room with a basin of cold water, no doubt the best she could do, and some wrappings that, to my eye, did not look particularly clean. But they would have to do.

I rolled up my sleeves and went to work. It was quickly clear that it was not the baby's head that was presenting itself. Kate was, indeed, right. This was not quite normal. I tried not to panic. I had seen my father successfully deliver a breech baby before. I had also seen a breech baby suffocate before it was delivered. I took in a deep breath and thought about Sister Eulalia's advice. Set sacred

141

intention, she had said. Listen to your inner voices. Another breath and I was listening.

Kate could control her pain and fear no longer. She began to wail seemingly uncontrollably. I directed Siobhan to her mother's side to hold her hand and talk to her. It was clear that Siobhan had never considered herself in this role before and had some difficulty soothing her mother. Nevertheless, after several awkward minutes, I had them breathing together, and I was now able to gently manipulate the feet and legs as they came out. I said a silent prayer of thanks that the baby was coming early, as it would be a small thing.

When the legs finally appeared in full, I noted that it was a girl, but I could not interrupt my concentration to inform the mother of this. I implored her to pant so as to stop pushing. I worked quickly as I knew that the moment was upon us when the baby could live or die. I would not let her die.

Finally, the slimy little head pushed its way out, and I adeptly removed the cord that was wrapped partly around the neck. I lifted her by her tiny ankles to let the fluid drain out and the air in. A gasp and a cry. She was tiny but alive. I quickly wrapped her so that she would not be cold and wondered at the stage of gestation. It seemed to me that the child was further along in pregnancy than that, an observation I shared with Kate as I set the baby in her arms at last.

Siobhan, who now seemed happy to have been a part of the excitement, answered for her mother. "Oh, Dad was away until seven months ago. This one's only a seven-monther, that's for sure."

Kate looked at me and said nothing. I nodded to her and noted the unmistakable gratitude in her eyes. I would keep her secret.

"Thank you, Dr. Bridget. I'm forever grateful to you for your help with this one," Kate said.

I began to correct her in her salutation, but thought better of it. To remind her that I was "just the doctor's wife" would not have been helpful at this moment. Besides, I was unlikely to ever see her again. I left it at that and went down the stairs to find the other doctor.

TWENTY-ONE

BALTIMORE, FALL 1830

It had started innocently enough. I had no intention, at least consciously, of becoming the women's doctor of Baltimore, but we oftentimes allow ourselves to be propelled by events – fate, perhaps.

It was September again. The leaves were beginning to take on that golden touch of autumn that I loved so dearly. I had just sat down to enjoy my morning coffee when I heard Wimpy, who had grown to love her new home, receive a guest at the door. As I had not been expecting anyone, and so loving a surprise as I did, I put down my cup and arose to see for myself.

The voice at the door was loud and seemed urgent – it also seemed familiar to me.

"Mrs. Ryan is busy just now," I heard Mrs. Wimpole saying to the visitor.

"Please, missus," came the obviously young, female voice in response. "She's needed sorely. Please. I have to have a wee word."

"Siobhan," I said as I came into the hallway.

She heaved a deep sigh of what seemed akin to relief and took a bold step inside the door.

"It is fine, Mrs. Wimpole. I know this young woman," I said upon spying the alarm in Wimpy's face.

I knew what Wimpy must be thinking. Here was a young woman whose world-weary clothing belied the fire in her Irish eyes. Both her youth and her evident impecuniousness placed her in a class of persons whose presence rarely graced our halls – not that I would have objected. But Wimpy would have found her out of place.

"How is your mother, Siobhan?" I had often wondered about Kate and her "seven-monther," and whether her husband had ever noticed. I knew that men in these classes

144

could be very jealous and suspicious. Perhaps these were not traits confined to the lower classes, but I had little experience of that.

"Ma – she's fine. 'Tis my friend I'm here about."

"Please, come in." I gestured toward the parlour

Siobhan looked uncomfortable. "Oh, no, I couldn't. Please, Dr. Bridget, I need you to come with me. Please say you will."

"Siobhan, I am not really a doctor. If you need a doctor –"

She took my hand. "We want no one but you. You know about these women's things. You can birth babies. I saw you. We know you can help us now."

"Is someone having a baby?"

Siobhan looked down. "No," she said quietly. "Not a baby exactly."

I realized that I would receive little more information from her unless I accompanied her to wherever she asked. I reached for my cloak, then considered that, if it would be of much help, I might need to take some supplies. John's extra bag of medical paraphernalia was kept under the front stairs.

"Mrs. Wimpole, please ask Samuel to bring around the carriage." I looked at her face. "Do not worry. I know this girl. I shall be safe. If Dr. Ryan returns presently, please tell him I shan't be long."

When we were finally ensconced in the carriage on the way to an address that was unknown to me, Siobhan sat back and appeared to relax slightly.

"She's bleeding something fierce, Ma'am."

"Siobhan," I began gently, not wanting to scare her, "if I am to help you, you will need to provide me with several more details. Who is bleeding and why?"

"It's Patsy O'Toole, Ma'am. She's only eighteen, and already she has three babies. She can't take one more baby now. She'll die of old age before she's twenty, she will." She seemed to shudder at the thought. "But he won't leave her

145

alone. And when she used that bit I gave her, he only got in a fury and hit her. Now she's gone and tried to get rid of it herself..."

Siobhan was babbling so fast I could hardly take in her words. But a picture was emerging in my head.

"Ma'am, you understand, don't you? You being a woman and all. I don't mean that you'd ever have to do these things, but you do understand."

It was clear that she was pleading with me – with someone – to understand their plight. And, somehow, even with my own limited experience of life, I did understand. And I felt her pain.

I pressed her hand, which, clad in its threadbare gloves, was lying in her lap, her fist clenched. "I do understand. At least enough to help if I can."

The house was one of many, one connected to another, lined along the narrow street. Despite the cold air this morning, children played with a stick and a ball in the street.

"These children should be in school," I said more to myself than to Siobhan. She did not hear me in any case, as she peered toward our destination.

"It's here, Ma'am. Tell him to stop here."

As I stepped down from my carriage, I was greeted by a gaggle of curious children. They were not what one could call clean, but they had a certain spirit that seemed to set each of them apart as an individual. Their Irish lilts, as they poured over the carriage, were unmistakable.

"How many of these children live here?" I asked Siobhan as she picked her way through the flock and made her way up the dilapidated porch stairs.

"Most," she said, intent it seemed on getting to our patient.

I had thought I would be prepared for just about anything after all those years with my father. But the sight that awaited my eyes was more wretched than I could imagine.

When we entered the house, Siobhan found Patsy, crawling, dragging herself through the kitchen in a vain attempt to feed a wailing baby while a slightly older child played with a ragged dog on the floor. There was a meagre fire upon the kitchen hearth, and the cold seemed to draw all the good from a body. Her nightgown was soiled with both old and new blood stains, and she was clearly crying along with her pitiful child.

Siobhan quickly took charge, getting Patsy to her small bedroom that she and her husband clearly shared with several children. Then she left to see to the children while I took charge of the patient.

As I examined the young, obviously terrified mother, and spoke quietly to her, it was clear to me that her mental state was far worse than her physical state. After a brief time, she told me of her horror at finding herself pregnant for the fourth time in almost as many years, her feeling of helplessness and her husband, who believed completely in his conjugal rights.

"He says the church requires it of a wife," Patsy said miserably.

"What do you think?" The moment the question passed my lips, I knew how absurd and unthinking it must seem to such a woman. Of course, she would be in no position to argue with either her husband or the church.

Thus she had decided to take action herself. With the help of a much older neighbour woman, and without a word about the baby to her husband, Patsy and made her way to the office of a "doctor" who said that he could get her out of this situation. She had scraped together money from her friends who deeply understood her situation. But all had not gone well. The doctor had evidently wanted more than money from this young woman who, I could clearly see, would be a very beautiful girl when cleaned up and smiling – if that were ever permitted to happen in her life again.

As she told her appalling story, I found my fury rising within me. Who was this despicable, so-called doctor? And, more importantly, what could I do about it?

As she told the story, I realized that the worst of her predicament was yet to come. She gripped my hand tightly as a wave of cramping overtook her small body. She had tried to end the pregnancy herself with the help of an implement provided to her by another of her neighbours and had taken some kind of tea, designed to bring on labour. It was awful to see.

I could do little. I, too, felt helpless as I stayed on while she bled and bled. Finally, it seemed to be over, and my worst fears were behind me. I believed that she had passed all of the necessary tissue at this point in her pregnancy and felt that she would recover. Truth be told, I knew that there was still a possibility that some of the tissue may have remained behind. I only fervently hoped it had not. The most pressing problem at this juncture seemed to be how to prevent such a thing from happening again in the future.

Although I felt I had done little for Patsy O'Toole that might not have happened without my intervention, Siobhan and Patsy evidently felt differently.

Later that night at dinner, when I told John about my day's activities, he was concerned for my welfare, travelling as I had been in the more disreputable parts of the city. But I was not to be dissuaded.

"You know, my dear," John said as he placed his teacup on the table and wiped his mouth, "there are those in the medical profession who believe that it is not right for women to procure abortions."

"But it is legal prior to quickening, is it not?" I asked, knowing full well that I was right.

"Quite," he said, "but I fear that this may change. And be mindful that preventing conception is not legal at present." He peered at me closely. "Why are you so

148

interested in these women and their plight? It can have little to do with you."

I was not certain how I truly felt about it all. I did feel a pull from somewhere deep within me that seemed to connect me to these wretched women. But I did not know its source – I only knew that they had more to do with me than was evident on the surface of it all.

"Perhaps you are feeling a bit lost here in Baltimore. You need something more to fill your time," he continued.

"Please, John, I just need to think about all of this for a time."

I knew that John must feel an internal conflict between his desire to let me be my own person and his upbringing that instilled a desire for a conventional wife. But I had discussed this with him, and he knew who I was.

We did not discuss the matter again for some time. After that fateful day in Patsy O'Toole's home, word spread quickly among the working-class women that there was a woman "doctor" who knew about women's issues. As loath as they were to let men see those parts of them, and as common as male midwives were becoming, the women welcomed one of their own into their lying-in chambers and into their homes. With John's blessing, I attended several of these births through the winter as a kind of lay midwife. The women continued to call me Dr. Bridget and I finally realized what I must do.

TWENTY-TWO

SPRING- SUMMER 1831

By May of 1831, Siobhan had become to me like a sister and a work companion: she proved herself a young woman quick of wit and with a keen and open mind. On the eve of her seventeenth birthday in March of that year – the first day of spring to be precise – I presented her with a copy of one of my favourite books John had acquired within the past several years. I had discovered, much to my surprise, that Siobhan could read. She had timidly, and with pride, told me that she often visited the nuns who had taught her rudimentary literacy skills. She had worked on learning more on her own with the books they provided.

I knew that it might be a bit of a risk to provide a girl such as Siobhan with such a book. And a risk on so many levels. First and foremost, of course, I had initially been unaware of her level of literacy. It was not a foregone conclusion that a young woman of her state in life would have been provided with even the most rudimentary of educations. Now, her growing interest in all things medical and surgical reminded me of my own youthful passion for the subject.

I had discussed this with John; however, since he had known the family in his medical practice for some years. After all, it was his visit to Siobhan's seizing father that had drawn me into their lives at all.

"Yes, I believe that Siobhan can read if that is what you mean," he said one morning as I broached the subject with him before approaching Siobhan. "But why on earth would you ask such a peculiar question?"

I explained to him that since I had come to know the women of what I now knew to be referred to as "mechanics row" on Wilks Street, I recognized in Siobhan a kind of kindred spirit, as it were. Upon hearing of this, John tried

150

in his quiet way to dissuade me from my course, for all the reasons that I, too, knew I ought to be careful of providing Siobhan with further inducement to a life that was outside her reach.

Despite his misgivings, John did provide me with the information that, as far as he knew, Siobhan did, indeed, have the requisite literacy skills, which she later confirmed. He even agreed to procure a copy of "The Anatomy and Physiology of the Human Body" by John Bell for me. Since it had been published in London, it was not necessarily available quickly. Consequently, he agreed that she should have his copy, which I had been voraciously devouring since it had arrived.

The other misgivings that I had about such a gift were much the same as those John harboured. What would she be able to do with this knowledge? I had a half-formed idea, but was not yet prepared to share it with John.

When the day of her birthday was upon us, I visited Siobhan in her home, where she was assisting not only her own mother but also Patsy O'Toole and several other mothers in the care of their young children.

It was complete tumult in the house that day, but in Siobhan's hands, it always seemed to be a controlled pandemonium. She was able to avoid having the children swarm me during our visit. That was a blessing, indeed.

When I handed her the parcel with all good tidings for her birthday, it seemed clear to me that she had rarely received gifts in her young life. She was taken aback by the gesture.

"Oh, I cannot take it, Ma'am," she said, trying to push it away.

"You most certainly can," I said, thrusting it into her hands and placing her fingers around the edges. "And, have I not admonished you on more than one occasion to call me Bridget?" I took off my gloves and sat down by the window. "You make me feel so old, and I am all of twenty-one."

"You're so smart, you are. I sometimes forget you're but a young woman not unlike myself," she said, giggling now.

With that, she put herself to the task of unearthing her treasure. As she pulled off the paper and gazed upon its contents, she said nothing. I thought she must be disappointed. I too remained silent, and when Siobhan looked up, I could see the brightness of eyes on the verge of tears. She was overcome with emotion.

She dropped the book on the table and threw her arms around my neck, taking me by complete surprise. I could do nothing but laugh. In moments, we were laughing together and were thus in this state when Kate, Siobhan's mother, rounded the doorway.

"I don't know what I can say to you, I don't," she said, wiping her eyes. "It's the most beautiful thing anyone has ever given me. I'll study it day and night – if you'll say I can be your official assistant."

That was not quite what I had been expecting, at least not in so many words. But there it was. I would now have to proceed with the next part of my plan. But that would have to wait. Kate, it seemed, needed me.

"I am so heartened to see you here today, Dr. Bridget," she said, setting her provisions on the floor. "We have a neighbour whose young daughter is ill. She is loath to see the doctor – no offence to your dear husband, you understand. But... could you be so kind?"

"Is it some kind of women's problem? A pregnancy, perhaps?"

"Oh, no. Nothing like that. She's a wee, young thing. But she's sore afraid of doctors, she is. Been sick a lot, you know. She'd like you, and Mrs. Clemm – that's her mom – asked specific for your help. Will you come?"

"Where does she live?" I said, rising and retrieving my gloves.

Kate smiled and led me several doors down the street and up a narrow stairway to the top flat. We were greeted by a solid, homely woman whom Kate introduced as Maria Clemm, a widow. She wore a crisp, white cap, the kind I had never fathomed on women inside houses. Grace had worn them from time to time, and I had often laughed at her for such a useless garment. Mrs. Clemm had also wrapped her ample body with a fringed shawl. I judged her to be in her early forties and wondered how young this child could be. She had more the appearance of a grandmother than the mother of a "wee" one, as Kate had indicated.

I looked around at the tiny home, tidy but threadbare. Contained within several baskets on the floor, I could see sewing implements and articles of clothing. Maria evidently took in sewing.

"It's my Virginia," Maria said. "She's not well."

Maria led me into the tiny bedroom that adjoined the small parlour. It was just as tidy as the parlour and even smaller. I did not see her at first; she was so small and seemingly insignificant. Virginia was lying upon one of the two small beds in the cramped room, a thin coverlet upon her fragile body.

As Maria brought me to the bedside, the child sat up, peering at me over her coverlet with two penetrating violet eyes. She was not a particularly attractive child, with her dark brown hair hanging lank bout her small face, but her expression was soft and delicate. I judged her to be about seven.

"Hello," I said, sitting down on the edge of the bed. I was greeted in response by a miserable cough that racked her tiny body. "My name is Bridget. How old are you, Virginia?"

"Nine," her mother responded from the doorway.

I was surprised at this. She had the aspect of a much younger child. I placed my hand upon the child's chest and could feel the crackling as her breath passed in and out. I opened John's bag that had accompanied me and retrieved his stethoscope with which to listen to these crackles more carefully. While doing so, I noted that the child had a dreadful catarrh. I wondered how long she had been in this state.

In response to my question, Maria informed me that Virginia often succumbed to one malady or another. "She has always been sickly," she said.

I had seen Virginia's symptoms on many occasions when I visited sick rooms with my father. Knowing what to do and recognizing that if I did nothing, the child would likely not receive any treatment at all, I felt confident in my ability to provide a remedy.

I discussed with Maria the need for Virginia to take fresh air daily, even when she felt unwell. Then I retrieved from John's bag a bottle of quinine and prescribed for her a two-grain dose three times a day and a small dose of laudanum to help her sleep. I had always believed strongly in the restorative value of slumber.

"Take care with the laudanum," I said to Maria as I donned my gloves. "Too much is not good for anyone." I glanced at the tiny figure on the bed. "It is especially problematic for such a small body as Virginia has."

Maria thanked me in her awkward way and inquired after the cost of my visit. I refused to consider taking anything from this poor widow.

"You'll be blessed, Ma'am," she said as I made my way down the stairs, where Kate awaited me in front of the house.

I thought little more about this incident in the ensuing weeks. Siobhan continued to read and study, and I continued to make my way into her neighbourhood on a weekly basis to see women who were in need of some minor health care, all the while concocting my idea – my idea for a kind of clinic. After all, I thought, I have the money. Surely this is a good thing.

Without telling John anything as yet, I began searching for a suitable building close enough to my "patients'" homes for them to access it easily, but far enough from where they lived that their husbands would not become curious. It was a brazen idea, I knew. There was no such thing as this. But if women could not become doctors, perhaps we could band together to help one another. I had a bit of knowledge and a whole lot of money to offer into the bargain.

One evening in early July, when the gauze curtains in the parlour rippled pleasantly with a summer breeze, John and I sat down in companionable silence, sipping a pre-dinner sherry from crystal glasses I had brought from my father's home in Boston. I was peering closely at the glass, remembering my childhood with Father, when John interrupted my reverie.

"I understand you have been making real estate inquiries."

I came back to the moment, leaving my meditation behind. I sensed from the tone of John's voice that this was not a rhetorical statement. He would be expecting a response.

"Yes," I said carefully, not knowing why I felt it necessary to be so cautious.

John said nothing, waiting, it seemed, for a more detailed response. I sipped my sherry as nonchalantly as I could muster before providing him with a more elaborate explanation of my recent clandestine behaviour, or so it must have seemed to him.

"I am considering purchasing a small house – a building – to use as a kind of clinic. For women."

"And who will treat these women?" he said slowly.

"We will look after one another."

John seemed to give this some considerable thought. "Do they believe you to be a doctor?"

"The women I see do not seem to care that I am not what the establishment would call a doctor. Indeed, it seems to me that I have as much education and training as many of the revered surgeons in this city. All I lack is the education of the physician."

I was referring, of course, to the fact that surgeons apprenticed, learning their craft through their own experience and that of others. Physicians, like John, had attended a medical college and possessed a degree, the education and subsequent recognition that I had been denied as a consequence of nothing more trivial than my sex.

"Be careful, Bridget," he said finally. And he said no more on the subject at that time.

I was careful – careful not to let those selling buildings know that I, a mere woman, was making this purchase without the overseeing eye of a husband. I had carefully ensured my anonymity as it were. I was in regular contact with Mr. Bowness, who advised me that the business was functioning well, even without my presence, not that my presence and lack of business acumen, as I saw it, would have been of any help. He regularly took the opportunity to tell me that Dalton's behaviour had been under control for some time and that he continued to do his work for the company as his percentage ownership allowed and required.

When I wrote to Mr. Bowness for the money to purchase a building, without so much as a single question about its intended use, he transferred the funds to a Baltimore bank. He also placed a local solicitor at my disposal. It was this solicitor through whom I intended to conduct all business dealings, thus ensuring that anyone with whom I did business was not put off in any way by a woman taking such matters into her own hands.

With these arrangements in place, I continued my search.

Late in August, I believed that I had found the perfect building. It was located in the centre of the city, just far enough from Wilks Street and its surrounds to be outside the neighbourhood, but close enough for my patients to have easy access. I took the carriage to pick up Siobhan, who was fast becoming indispensable to me. She would manage the facility for me, and I wanted her support for this purchase.

When I arrived in front of her home that morning, she burst out the door, a large smile on her pretty face. She was flushed with barely contained excitement, or so it seemed to me.

"You must meet him," she said as she arranged her skirts around her.

I gave the signal for us to proceed and turned my attention to her obvious exhilaration.

"Who is he? And why must I meet him?" I said, enjoying this previously hidden dimension of my friend.

"He is Maria Clemm's nephew, and he has come from Richmond to live with her. He is the most romantic man I've ever met, he is." Her eyes shone with an emotion that I wondered if she had ever felt before.

Richmond, I thought. The thought took me to a reflection on the only person in my acquaintance who lived there for any length of time – Ned Poe. I realized with an uncomfortable start that it had been a long time since his name and the face it conjured had even crossed my mind. I wondered if this treasure of manhood to which Siobhan referred might know anything of Ned and his family.

"Well then," I said, my own excitement growing at the prospect of perhaps learning about Ned, "I shall have to meet this phenomenon at the earliest opportunity."

That opportunity presented itself in short order.

When Siobhan and I returned to her house after viewing the potential clinic building (which we had determined to be as close to perfect as we were likely to find), we were greeted by Kate, a baby under her arm, telling us that Maria Clemm was wondering if I might see to Virginia again.

This time, accompanied by my new assistant Siobhan, I climbed the narrow staircase to the top of the stairs to find Maria Clemm sitting on a hard chair sewing as if her life depended upon it – which it probably did. It seemed that Virginia was unwell again, but Maria was convinced that all she needed was some encouragement from a "doctor." I said that I would do my best.

Indeed, I found Virginia to be not as unwell as Maria might have imagined. She seemed very glad to see me and proceeded to ask me questions about my patients when I sat down upon her bed.

"Virginia," I said, "how often do you take some fresh air?"

"Fresh air, Ma'am?" She looked a bit puzzled. Then suddenly, she pointed to the window, "There, Ma'am, I open the window whenever it feels stuffy in here."

That was precisely what I had thought. Virginia was suffering from an overprotective mother, a situation to which I would have to give thought to correcting.

"Have you met my cousin, Ma'am?" she said, sitting up brightly.

"No, I have yet to have the pleasure. But I do understand from Siobhan that he is quite a gentleman."

"Oh, indeed." Virginia's eyes were bright and open now, and she looked more the picture of health than I had ever before seen her.

As I leaned over my bag to ensure that I would not leave anything behind, Virginia shrieked and quickly covered her mouth and drew the covers to her neck, her eyes smiling.

"Oh, he's here!"

I looked toward the door, and there he stood – Virginia's cousin, Maria's nephew, Siobhan's paragon. The thumping in my ears was my own heartbeat.

TWENTY-THREE

My own Ned. Standing in the doorway.

I could scarcely believe my eyes, and it seemed clear from the look on Ned's brooding face that he could barely believe the vision he beheld either. I arose quickly.

"Ned," I began.

He took one step inside the door of the tiny room and was quite nearly upon me.

"Ned?" Virginia said, clearly confused at my use of this endearment. "But Dr. Bridget, this is my cousin Edgar, the one I told you about. He's Edgar Poe, the poet. Perhaps you've read some of his work." For nine years old she suddenly seemed very grown-up. Her violet eyes lit up as she gazed with obvious pride at her cousin.

"My own darling Virginia," Ned said, taking her hand, "Dr. Bridget, as you call her, is an old friend of mine. We have been acquainted some five years, is it not, Bridget?" He turned to me, still holding onto Virginia's frail hand.

"Indeed, I suppose it is. How time does get away from one." I looked at Ned carefully, taking in the curve of his forehead, the dark hair curling around his ears, the cravat he wore even on this summer day. Even the melancholy look about his gray eyes had changed little and was perhaps even more pronounced. And I wondered at my own reaction to seeing him after all this time, remembering our last encounter.

"I would like to catch up with my old friend, Virginia. Could you please excuse us?" He seemed to speak with her as if she were an equal to him, this little child.

I followed him out through the parlour where Maria Clemm waited. He briefly explained to her that we were old acquaintances and would return presently. He lightly took hold of my hand as we made our way down the narrow stairway.

When we emerged into the street below, Siobhan, awaiting my return, was dumfounded to be informed that, indeed, Mr. Poe and I were old friends. She was quite flustered with her introduction to this man whom she seemed to find darkly attractive – at least she had given me that impression in earlier discussion.

It seemed quite natural that Ned and I should fall into step side by side along this narrow street. I even found myself taking his arm; this was a gesture that he did not seem to mind in the least. When we got to the end, we turned toward the park and I took in the usual shabbiness of his garments and how he seemed to be unsettled. He told me of his experiences at West Point and how he had been court-martialed. He seemed dismissive of this, perhaps even light-hearted. For my part, this news startled and disturbed me. How could this have happened?

"Allegations of neglect of duty," he said with a wave of his hand as if it could be of no import.

"What kind of duties?

"Failing to appear at parade and the like – church for example," he said.

I was trying to understand why Ned had even gone to West Point in the first place after his previous experience in the army, but it seemed he still retained a kind of romantic notion of the wandering life of the soldier. His current discourse even seemed to me to imply that he had not altogether given up the notion of such a life.

Ned told me of his foster father John Allan remarrying a much younger woman, and of being completely disregarded at his time of financial and other need. According to Ned, he had spent several dreary months in New York before deciding to join his aunt and cousin in Baltimore. While he tried to give the impression that he had come to assist them in their time of need, I knew only too well that it was more likely his time of need that took precedence.

"I am closer to my brother now, in any event," he said.

160

He was referring to his brother Henry from whom he had been separated since they were children. He had spoken of Henry on several occasions to me, and I knew that despite their geographical disparateness, Ned considered them to yet be close. There was more good news in that Ned had evidently published yet another volume of poetry while in New York. I was pleased for him and told him so.

"I shall have a volume sent to your home if you would be so kind as to provide me with an address."

I was happy to provide him with this detail and then proceeded to tell him of my own news of recent months. I chose my words carefully when I began to tell Ned about John and our life together. We came to a bench in the park and sat down side by side. I noted that he failed to watch my face when my marriage became the topic of conversation. Try as I might, I could not catch his eye. I knew him to be a jealous man but thought that enough time had passed since his outrageous proposal that he might have gotten over it. I was perhaps wrong.

"So, do you love this man, this John Ryan?" he said when I stopped speaking.

"I suppose, in my way, I do love him," I said, realizing that this was perhaps not as convincing as John himself might have wanted it to sound.

"He is much your elder," Ned said standing and pacing back and forth in front of the bench.

"Please sit down beside me Ned. I have missed you much through these years. Sad, is it not, that our lives should run in a kind of parallel, almost touching, but never quite crossing?"

He sat down finally. "That, my dear Bride, is entirely your doing if you recall. I should have liked nothing better than to spend my days – and nights – with you." He hesitated for a moment, as if not knowing whether or not to continue. "I believe that we were meant to be together, Bride. And further, I believe that you hold this conviction

161

deep within your own heart as surely as do I. Please do not attempt to deny it."

I was at a loss for words. In truth, I did not know how I felt at that moment. I recalled, with a deep glow in the crevasses of my soul, and my body, that I had loved this man – this brooding man with the mind that harboured the darkest, most mysterious, often malignant thoughts I had ever heard. I had loved him with the wild heart of the young. And yet, my life had changed and I had moved on; at least I thought that I had moved on. I supposed that one's life can change without the yearnings and longings underlying it changing. Indeed, neither Ned's corporeal life nor its deepest underpinnings seemed to have changed very much.

When we returned to my carriage still waiting in Wilks Street, Siobhan seemed a bit more reserved than her usual gregarious self. I had thought that she would be thrilled to be introduced to this treasure of a man, but instead, she seemed a bit aloof. Could she be jealous? That, of course, would be nonsense; she and I would have to sort it out.

I took my leave, however, as John and I had a theatre engagement that evening. We would be joining friends of his and I had a great deal to consider from this day. The first consideration was whether or not I would tell John of my encounter with Ned. I had, of course told John of my acquaintance with Edgar Poe, the poet, at the University of Virginia, but I had chosen not to tell him of our last encounter, and would not likely tell him of this one. Something for my own heart, I thought.

John was in good spirits when I arrived home. It was a welcome change. Of late I had found him to be almost a bit detached from me in certain ways. I had also observed that this distance from me seemed ever more marked whenever I related to him any of the progress toward the development of my clinic. I would put all of that out of my mind tonight as I dressed for the theatre which was a particular love of mine at the time.

I sat before my dressing table in the large upper bedroom I shared with my husband, trying in vain to tame my wild hair. It is not easy to contain something as riotous as my heavy, curling tresses, but I loved them nonetheless.

My attire for this evening would be a plum-coloured frock of a wonderful silk with a plunging neckline and sleeves that ballooned from the elbow to the shoulder. They were the latest fashion and I believed them to be quite charming in an evening ensemble. What I liked most about this dress, however, was the tightness of the waistline below which fell the skirt in soft folds. I believed that it suited my slim figure providing me with more of an hour-glass look. Sometimes I baffled even myself with my deep dedication to the plight of poor women set as it were against my penchant for appearing desirable. The two passions were coexisting quite nicely, however.

When finally I completed my ablutions and descended into the parlour where John was waiting, looking handsome himself in his tailcoat, I noted with considerable satisfaction his reaction to my appearance. He was more than pleased. So, in this frame of mind, we donned our cloaks and ventured out into the night.

The Baltimore Theatre was a glistening building, at least to my eyes, and that night it shone with newly installed gas lights glinting off carriages and the silks and satins of the ladies' dresses. There was a welcoming buzz about the scene that night.

We met several of John's friends and their wives on the portico of the theatre then entered the lobby together. I liked these friends of John's despite not really finding that any of the women shared my interests. There was David and Amelia Ralston – parents of some seven young children, as well as Graham and Anna Robinson whose three children were older. David too was a physician whereas Graham was a businessman. Both of the women were – well, they were wives. The conversations tended to run to discussions of children and households. I liked these women but felt little comradeship with them. Indeed, I much preferred to partake in the male-oriented discussions of local business and politics. I always found that I could learn bits of information that could prove useful to my professional aspirations. Tonight, however, I was more interested in enjoying the theatre company's presentation of Shakespeare's *Hamlet*, a particular favourite of mine.

I lost myself in the play that night, forgetting for a few hours my concerns about the women in my care and of seeing Ned. More importantly, I forgot about the fact that it was likely that I would see him from time to time, whether I desired it or not now that he was ensconced in Wilks Street, at least for the time being. His itinerant past led me to believe that this arrangement too would be temporary.

And I found that I looked forward to the thought of seeing him regularly in spite of my misgivings. Ned was on my mind far more than was proper for a married woman such as myself. But there was little I could do to stop my reeling thoughts as I lay in bed those nights that hot summer. I should have been thinking about my own dear husband. Instead I found my mind wandering to the "what ifs."

What if I had just run off with Ned? What if I had married him? Was I not a rich woman in my own right? Could I not have taken care of him, nurturing perhaps a great poet? Could that not have been my contribution to this world?

No matter how often I went over the practicalities of my situation as well as the less pragmatic aspects, it all came down to the same thing: Ned and I would not have made a wholesome combination. We both had a kind of hidden wild streak and with Ned's preoccupation with death, as it were, this could only have come to a corrupt end. Nevertheless, as I tossed and turned in my bed those nights, I thought of Ned in that squalid flat in Wilks Street, surrounded by people who could never appreciate his gift, and I considered how I might most decorously assist him in his time of need.

The other apprehension that I had yet been unable to solve in these several weeks since Ned had returned to my life, was Siobhan. I had tried to talk to her about Ned and my past friendship with him, but she did not care to discuss it. Indeed, I believed that she was jealous and thus resentful of my relationship. This particular vexation might prove to be more of a problem for me in the end.

TWENTY-FOUR

BALTIMORE, AUGUST 1831

"I understand you have been seeing Edgar Poe."

It was a hot, early August evening, and I was trying to read, holding my book with one hand and a fan with the other. I had a glass of lemonade on the table beside me and had noted that even it had succumbed to the soaring temperature.

"I am sorry, John, I do not think I heard you." A feeling of discomfort made its way down the back of my neck, settling in my shoulders.

"Edgar Poe. Your poet friend from Virginia. I understand you and he have been keeping company for a few weeks. I do not seem to recall you mentioning him to me recently."

"Had I not? It must have slipped my mind." I picked up my glass and slowly sipped the now-warm lemonade.

"Yes, I suppose. In any case, were you aware that his brother has expired?"

I closed my book and placed it on the embroidered ottoman by my chair.

"How do you know this?" I said, trying my utmost not to sound overly interested.

"I attended at his deathbed not two days ago. William Henry Poe, I believe, was his name. In fact," he said, looking carefully at my face, "I met your young poet. An unusual man, if I may be permitted an opinion."

"I am so sorry about Henry," I said, trying to conceive of how this might have affected Ned. "What was the nature of his ailment?"

"A bit difficult to say," John said, lighting his pipe. "My best guess would be cholera. But he seemed a sickly young man in any case. His regular physician was unavailable, and I was asked to visit with him. Edgar arrived just as

Henry was breathing his last. Strangest behaviour I had ever seen. He draped his body over his brother's and placed his ear to the chest. Then he acted as if he himself were stricken. Was he always thus?"

I fanned myself and arose from the chair to open a window for a bit more of a breath of air. "He has an unconventional view of death, as I recall. Even his writing shows this confusion about the line between life and the hereafter – if you believe in such things."

Indeed, it had been only a few weeks since Ned's arrival at Maria Clemm's home, but John was correct; we had spent some time together on several occasions. Several times, we had walked arm in arm through the park, then sat on a bench talking for an hour at a time. I had, however, neglected to tell my dear husband about any of these encounters. I realized only too well that John must be curious about my friendship with Ned, but I could offer no further information at that time, nor did he pursue the matter, for which I was very grateful. Based on this conversation with my husband, I thought it better that I not attend Henry's funeral.

Ten or so days after this discussion, I made my way to Wilks Street with the specific intention of finding out about Ned's condition, especially his state of mind. I knew how much he had counted upon his brother's companionship since the death of his beloved foster mother and the inhuman wickedness and ignominy he had suffered at the hands of his foster father.

When I arrived at the Clemm household, Virginia, more vigorous and merry than I had seen her yet, greeted me at the door. She seemed pleased to see me.

"Dr. Bridget, please come in. Eddy will be so glad of your arrival. He is sorely beset with grief."

"Where is your cousin, Virginia?" I said, entering the small room that was stifling in the late August heat.

"He is attending the gravesite."

"Oh, dear," I said softly. I knew how such things affected Ned's thoughts. His mind would be filled with whirling images of death and near-death. His misery would know no bounds. I considered the possibility of making my way to the cemetery to find him and bring him home, but reconsidered.

"Dr. Bridget," Virginia said, lifting what appeared to be a publication of some sort from the table, "here is a story Eddy has written." She looked at me shyly as she extended it toward me. "I thought that you might read this. Oh, Dr. Bridget, he is so despondent."

Virginia was no longer as happy as she had been upon my arrival. Clearly, she was happy for the company, but simultaneously at a loss about her beloved cousin.

I took the publication from her and examined the cover. It was the *Saturday Evening Post* dated August 13, 1831. I puzzled over it for a moment until Virginia came to my rescue and pointed out a particular piece within its covers.

"A Dream" was the title of the piece, and the author was given as "P." and nothing more. When I began to read this morose piece, it was appallingly clear that Ned was the author. When I arrived at the portion that said, "...I saw the grave worm twining itself amongst the matted locks which in part covered the rotten skull," I realized just how crazed Ned must be by this inopportune and distressing death in his family.

I stayed with Virginia for a while and, just as I arose to take my leave, I heard footsteps on the stairs. Ned emerged into the room like a phantom coming forth from its haunt, his pale, sullen face as white as the new-fallen snow, but with great hollows of melancholy where bright eyes should have been.

He breathed heavily when he saw me and sank into a chair near the window.

"Where is Muddy?" This endearment referred to his his Aunt Maria.

"She has taken some sewing pieces to our neighbour," Virginia said.

"Ned," I began, trying to find the appropriate words. "Are you all right?"

"I am not," he said, dropping his head into his hands.

"I am so sorry for your loss."

"You did not attend the funeral. I looked to see if you were there. You were not."

"I thought better of it," I said, restraining myself from going forward and taking him into my arms. "Funerals are a family affair."

"I have no wish to live another hour."

Ned was close to the breaking point, and I could see from the terror on Virginia's face that she was frightened for his very life. I, however, had heard Ned talk like this before, and although I recognized that he was indeed bereft to the core of his soul, I felt that his talk of ending his life would not become a reality. It was a fiction that he lived out in the innermost corners of his mind.

"Write about it, Ned. Take pen in hand and put your thoughts on paper." I was well acquainted with this method of purging one's mind of inescapable thoughts and knew that Ned could expunge his suicidal contemplations with such an activity. He did as he was bidden and I took my leave.

TWENTY-FIVE

New York, December 1831

The plans for my clinic had progressed well. I procured the building, and Siobhan seemed to have forgiven me for my close acquaintance with Ned, at least for the moment, and we had begun to welcome our patients on a daily basis. I could tell that John still harboured a certain skepticism about my ability to take on such a project, and I had invited him onto the premises several times. He had declined. I hoped fervently that he might reconsider before too much more time went by.

I saw Ned regularly, and we had recaptured much of our earlier closeness. We talked for as long as my schedule would permit. He had recovered somewhat from the death of his brother, but his work had been going poorly. He was finding it increasingly difficult to provide for either himself or for his aunt and cousin. I had helped out on several occasions, but he would not consider any deeper subsidization. I told him that I considered it to be a patronage of the arts. To this he did not object, occasionally taking my proffered assistance with something akin to enthusiasm. But I believed that as a consequence, he felt the need to prove himself to me. I looked forward to the fruits of his literary labour.

Things had been going smoothly for me and for my women, when I received an urgent letter from Mr. Bowness imploring my presence in New York. According to him, the business had encountered a problem that only I could deal with.

It was a particularly cold December, and we were making our Christmas preparations. I had even consented to attend midnight mass with John, and thus he was dubious about such an excursion to New York, but in the end did agree that I should go to deal with the business matter. Since the house had been sold, I would be required

170

to stay in a hotel, a situation that was not deemed appropriate for a woman alone. Thus, John agreed to accompany me. Indeed, he insisted on doing so.

I had loved New York from that very first visit, which seemed such a long time ago. Truly, it had been only two years since that first visit, and I had returned but once more in the intervening time. But so much had happened in my life in such a short time; I sometimes felt I needed to stop and breathe. A visit to New York was just the breath I required.

There was an energy about the place that defied description. The women were dressed well (at least in the places that we went), and there seemed to be a constant bustling of people with places to go. I felt energized here.

Travelling, however, was such a tiring prospect. As novel and astonishing as the train seemed to me and many others at the time, it was uncomfortable, noisy and smelly. Ashes rained from the smokestacks constantly, and upon disembarkation, it was impossible not to be soiled by such a hail of cinders that one might actually catch fire. Or so it seemed.

Such an experience required a degree of recuperation upon arrival at one's destination. Thus, when we finally arrived in the city, John and I settled into a hotel room and took dinner in the dining room with great enthusiasm. The room was panelled in dark oak, and the walls were hung with elaborate tapestries in deep burgundy and green. At the windows hung heavy silk draperies that kept out the chill of the December night. I felt like a grand lady as I sat at my lace-covered table being waited upon by several attentive staff members. While I was enjoying this interlude of pampering, I noted with some concern that John did not appear as relaxed and pleased as did I.

"John, whatever is the matter with you? Are you ill?"

"No, my dear, I am not ill. At least not yet."

"Are you not enjoying your roast lamb?" I said, eyeing his plate that had hardly been touched.

"It is difficult to do so, Bridget," he said, placing his napkin on the table beside the china plate.

"Why would it be difficult? Is it something that the staff has done? Something I have done, perhaps?"

"Not exactly," John said, looking more discomfited than I had seen him. "Perhaps we do need to talk a bit."

I waited for him to continue, not really wanting to stop my enjoyment of my delicious roasted chicken, but recognizing his seriousness.

"Bridget, I feel very uncomfortable here." He waved his hand at nothing in particular. "Here in this grand hotel with a rich wife. Most physicians will never be able to experience this."

"Oh," I said, realizing for the first time the circumstance within which John must find himself. John was a proud man, and I had a good deal of respect for him. He was, however, correct in his assessment. It was a reflection of what I had long thought about physicians: they had never been accorded the place in society that I deemed was their due. Perhaps the day would come, but it had not as yet.

"I believe I understand you, John." I placed my hand over his as it rested on the table. "But can you not enjoy your good fortune? What I have is yours as well."

"I have never tried to control your life or your money, Bridget," he said, clearly misunderstanding my meaning.

I tried to make him understand that what I had was his to share in equal parts with me. He seemed a bit appeased by this exchange, and I felt that he had been holding this notion in his head for some time. Perhaps it explained his reluctance to visit my clinic. I asked him about this.

"No, Bridget, that is not the reason," he said finally. "And I prefer not to discuss that with you at this time."

I was perplexed but chose not to pursue the matter. We would return to it at a more felicitous time.

We finished our meal and slept well, snuggled on the large feather bed, insulated from the world.

When we awoke the next morning, the streets were blanketed with a carpet of fresh snow, but this did little to subdue the constant buzz of activity that greeted us when we stepped outside the hotel.

We arrived at the front door of the Euro-American Import/Export Company at precisely nine o'clock. I had expected to be greeted by my erstwhile business partner, Dalton, but the feeling of expectation was laced with a certain amount of trepidation; I did not like Dalton Densmore any more now than I had when I first laid my eyes upon him in my father's parlour. Mr. Bowness, however, turned out to be our greeter.

I could see from the look on his face that he believed this meeting to be of a serious nature. He had, after all, summoned us most precipitously, and here we were.

"I trust you are well, Mrs. Ryan," Mr. Bowness began when we were settled into the small boardroom. He cleared his throat uncomfortably and forced a weak smile. "You find New York to be a pleasant departure, I hope."

Mr. Bowness seemed to be making small talk, and I wondered if he was procrastinating, so I requested that we proceed. I thought to take advantage of the opportunity to put him out of his misery. At the very least, he could share his burden with me.

"By the way," I said before he was permitted to get on with it, "where is Mr. Densmore this morning? I had expected to see him here."

Mr. Bowness's eyes seemed to almost bulge out of their place in his face. I seemed to have touched a nerve. He cleared his throat again.

"Well, Mrs. Ryan, actually, it seems that..." he cleared his throat yet again.

I offered him water, which he gratefully accepted. I feared that he might choke if he did not get his secret out at once.

"It seems that Mr. Densmore is the, uh, reason for, well, for my request for your presence." There, he had it out.

We were sitting at the table such that I could see directly into Mr. Bowness' face. He held his hands in front of him on the table, his fingers intertwined so hard together that I could see, even as we spoke, he threatened to cut off his own circulation.

"Where is Mr. Densmore this morning?" John asked, evidently trying to be helpful.

"Well, I thought better of extending an invitation, you see." Mr. Bowness was, if anything, even more uncomfortable.

I could feel my patience slowly ebbing away. "Mr. Bowness, if there is something important that you wish to say to me, please do so. Procrastinating any longer can only make the news more difficult. I am presuming that the news is not of the favourable sort."

"This is very difficult for me, you must know, before I can really begin."

Mr. Bowness looked at me with his watery eyes, and I could read sincerity in them. I knew that he had been a good and loyal employee, managing the day-to-day activities of this evidently flourishing business with little guidance.

"Please, Mr. Bowness, I am certainly ready to listen to whatever it is you have to say."

"I do not wish to speak ill of your cousin – Mr. Densmore."

"He is not my cousin, only the relation of my late stepmother. Do go on." I was trying as hard as I could to be patient.

"There have been some irregularities. In the books."

"Irregularities?" John asked, leaning forward to better hear Mr. Bowness, whose tone had become quieter now that he seemed to be getting to the heart of the matter.

"I dared not write to you about this. Indeed, I have been watching it occur for some time now."

"What have you been watching?" I said.

"Money seems to be missing."

"Seems to be missing?" said John. "Is it missing or is it not?

"It is missing." Mr. Bowness turned back to me. "Mrs. Ryan, I have kept meticulous books ever since I came to work for Miss Abigail's father over twenty years ago. There has never been a penny that could not be accounted for. I am stricken."

Indeed, he had gone quite white. He took a handkerchief out of his breast pocket and mopped his brow.

"How much money is unaccounted for?" I asked, trying to be as gentle as I could, but fighting a rising panic. The implication was becoming too clear.

"It is tens of thousands of dollars, Mrs. Ryan."

I gasped. John sat back in his chair and whistled quietly.

"How long have you known about this? I asked when I finally caught my breath. "I first noticed a small irregularity about six months ago. Of course, I went straight to Mr. Densmore. He explained it all to me. I could not quite understand his figures, but I felt in no position to argue with him. He is, after all, one of the owners. But when it happened again last month and for a much larger sum of money, I thought to write to you immediately."

"Have you also spoken to Mr. Densmore about this?" John asked.

"No, sir, I have not." This was Mr. Bowness's first emphatic statement in this exchange. "And I did not inform him of my plan to write to Mrs. Ryan, and he does not know that you are here today." With that, he sat back and reached for a large ledger book that he had obviously stowed under the table.

It was large and dog-eared, with a black leather cover. Embossed on the front cover in gold lettering was the name "Euro-American Import/Export Company, est. 1806."

Mr. Bowness opened the very large pages, and I could see row upon row of meticulously inscribed figures. As I watched him turn to the pages he wished us to see, I noted that he seemed to treat it as if it were a prized possession. It, no doubt, represented for him a lifetime of work.

"Here, Mrs. Ryan." Mr. Bowness pointed to a row of figures. "This is where I first noted the discrepancy." He turned forward several pages and pointed to another row. "And this is where I began noticing it again." He sat back and mopped his brow again with his handkerchief, which I noted was embroidered with his initials. I wondered momentarily if there was a Mrs. Bowness who possessed such fine embroidery skills. I ought to have been more interested in his life than I had been in the past.

John and I studied the figures for some minutes. As far as I could understand (and I feared that my own understanding had serious limitations), Mr. Bowness was correct: there were, indeed, sums of money that seemed to have disappeared. When I asked him where he believed the money had gone, if it was possible, he looked even more uncomfortable.

"I have investigated this," he said. "It is my belief that Mr. Densmore has been making unauthorized withdrawals."

John took in an audible breath and said, "That is a serious allegation, Mr. Bowness."

"Serious, indeed, Dr. Ryan. But I have completed what I consider to be a very exhaustive inquiry. I did not dare to suggest such a thing without first ensuring that I was looking in the right direction. I have a friend who is a banker locally and knows Mr. Densmore's finances."

I must have looked startled at the implications of this disclosure. Mr. Bowness sought to convince me of his ethics in this situation, and I was mollified.

"Should this carry on much longer," he continued, "the company will almost certainly cease to be profitable. We will be out of business."

"Embezzlement," I said, mostly to myself, trying to contemplate the gravity of the situation. Worse, what was I to do about it? I did not relish the thought of confronting Dalton. I disliked him at the best of times and, truth be told, he frightened me. This would be most unpleasant and perhaps even dangerous.

I thought about that morning in the breakfast room when he burst in unbidden with his assurance to me that he would get what he was due in his estimation. Perhaps this was his way of ensuring that he got his due. Perhaps it would be better if I did not try to do anything about it. I suggested such an approach to Mr. Bowness, who was horrified, to say the least.

"What he has done to you is more than reprehensible," he said. "It is illegal."

"Are you suggesting that I contact the local constabulary? Have him incarcerated?"

Mr. Bowness did not reply and took his meaning to be that he cared little for Dalton, cared less about what happened to him.

John and I decided to return to the hotel to discuss the situation and promised Mr. Bowness that we would return the following day with a decision. The more I thought about Dalton and his antics, the angrier I became. It was John's view that we should contact the police immediately, but I implored him to allow me to bide my time for a while longer. Further, I was becoming a bit fractious regarding John's role in this matter. It was my company, after all. This attitude did nothing to enhance our relationship that night, and thus I returned alone to the offices the next morning while John visited with some colleagues.

Mr. Bowness introduced me to a number of the employees in the office that morning. They seemed a pleasant and, more importantly, loyal group of people whose livelihoods depended entirely on their ability to maintain their positions here at the Euro-American Import/Export Company. The more I spoke with them, the clearer it became to me that Dalton's immoral and illegal behaviour could not be permitted to curtail their employment, nor would it be permitted to continue one more day. Although I had made that decision, I had yet to formulate a plan with which to implement that decision.

Mr. Bowness and I were sitting in his office taking tea when, true to form, Dalton burst into the room smelling again of liquor.

"Well, well, well. Look at the two of you," he said, leaning into my face.

I turned away from him as his hot breath wafted fumes of what I took to be gin into my nasal passages.

"Is it not a bit early for a libation, Dalton?"

"Is that all you can say to me, cousin? And while you sit here and plot my downfall. May I join you?" he said, slithering into a seat directly opposite me.

I was grateful for the distance between the two of us. I feared I might have to slap him, should he place his face in front of mine again. I asked Mr. Bowness to leave us alone, and he was very hesitant to do so. I assured him that I would be quite well and that I would call him when Mr. Densmore and I had completed our business.

Mr. Bowness closed the door behind him, and Dalton and I were finally alone in the room. I began with some niceties about his wife and twin daughters, and told him about Christmas preparations in Baltimore. I offered him a cup of tea, which he accepted, and I noted that he was beginning to relax.

I arose from my seat and went to the side table where the tea tray was laid out. While I fiddled with the teacups, my back to him, Dalton continued to talk about inconsequential affairs such as the weather and the condition of the New York streets.

"Tell me about your work here lately, Dalton," I said in as congenial a manner as I could manage. I turned back to the table and set the teacup before him, taking my own seat, this time at the head of the table. I clasped my hands together, placed them on the table in front of me and looked at him carefully.

Dalton had aged greatly since we last spoke. His face was lined deeply, and upon closer inspection, it looked as if he might have slept in his clothes. I wondered how often he was in an inebriated state so early in the day.

Sipping his tea with relish, he began telling me about the company and how he saw it in the future – at least to the extent that he could think coherently. We were in that room together for what must have been close to an hour. I could just imagine Mr. Bowness and the other employees waiting breathlessly for our dialogue to be finished and to ascertain the outcome as it affected them.

Finally, and without warning, Dalton collapsed. I moved toward him quickly and found him breathing only very shallowly. I arose, smoothed my dress and went to the door. When I was ready, I flung it open forcefully. "Come quickly. Mr. Densmore seems to have suffered a collapse."

Pandemonium followed as Mr. Bowness and several of the other men rushed into the room, only to find Dalton fighting for breath. I dispatched one of the young boys who ran errands for the company to the hotel to search for John, then made arrangements for Dalton to be moved to the hospital.

There was much confusion. Several hours later, when we had finally located John, he and I travelled to the hospital only to be told that they were very sorry, but Mr. Densmore had expired. Drank himself to death, was, I believe, the exact way they put it.

TWENTY-SIX

BALTIMORE, SPRING 1834

John had not asked me much about that morning in New York City when Dalton Densmore ceased to be a problem for my company and its employees – and for me. Indeed, we had returned to Baltimore feeling much more light-hearted than we had in some time. John returned to his patients, and I to mine. Although I knew there were issues regarding the latter that John had yet to make his opinion known on, we carried on as if a burden had been lifted.

We – Siobhan and I – called the clinic "The Hildegard Hospice." I had settled upon that name after remembering a book I had read many years ago, when under the tutelage of Sister Eulalia Marie. Since moving to Baltimore, I had often wondered after her well-being and connecting the name of this clinic – so dear to my heart – with my mentor seemed to draw me closer to her. Sister Eulalia had offered me a book she thought I might find inspiring. It was a rather unusual book, as it told the stories of interesting women in the history of the Catholic Church. This was most unusual, and I inferred from Sister that it was the only one of its type. It described a medieval nun, Hildegard, whose fame encompassed both mysticism and healing. I thought that quite appropriate and would look to her as our patron.

By late spring, the clinic was well-established, and we were gaining something of a reputation among the working-class women of Baltimore. Unbeknownst to me, but increasingly well-known to John, it seemed, we were also garnering something of a reputation among the medical establishment of Baltimore.

One Sunday evening, as we sat together reading companionably in our parlour, John put down his book and lit his pipe thoughtfully. I could feel his eyes upon me across the room as he gazed in my direction. For a moment,

I pretended not to notice. Finally, I could stand it no more. It was clear that he had something he wished to share with me.

"You can tell me now," I said.

"Tell you what?"

"Whatever it is that has you staring with such fierce intensity and that seems to have been bothering you for some time." I put my book down so as to attend to him more directly.

"Well, my dear, as a matter of fact, there is something I've been meaning to discuss with you." He puffed gently on his pipe and blew the pale smoke lightly toward the ceiling. It smelled a bit like sweet grass in the summer.

"I am certainly listening." I looked at his face and at the lines that were ever more pronounced on his brow and around his mouth. Perhaps he ought to stop smoking a pipe, I thought, but felt it better not to bring the matter into the conversation at this point.

"I have heard some mumblings," he said. "It seems people are talking about your hospice."

"Well, what is being said and by whom?"

"Several of my colleagues have mentioned that they are unsure what exactly is going on at this hospice or clinic of yours. Indeed, there is a rumour about that you are providing some kind of information to these women – illicit information."

"Illicit? What exactly do you mean by illicit?"

John arose from his chair and walked over to the window. Rain was tapping gently against the pane. He turned to look at me from this higher vantage point – a gesture that was not lost on me. "Are you familiar with the work of a Dr. Robert Owen? A Dr. Charles Knowlton?"

"I believe I am." I had wondered how long it would be before we had this conversation. As many times as I had considered how I might respond to it, I had yet to fully determine a correct approach. There was nothing like the real thing to propel one toward a decision.

"Have you ever met either of them?"

"I have not."

"Are you in possession of any of their published work?"

I took in a large breath of air to calm the annoyance that was rising within me. "Am I under interrogation as a result of some crime? This sounds as if I should have a lawyer and a jury present."

"Well, my dear, perhaps you ought to be. Not that I have any particular opinions on the subject, but I have no doubt but that you are well aware you may be treading perilously close to a legal precipice. Have you been providing copies of a pamphlet called 'Moral Physiology' to women at your establishment?"

It had taken me over a year, but I had finally procured a copy of this famous pamphlet to which John referred. I had, indeed, been providing it to my patients to read and consider. Dr. Owen was a pioneer in the area of controlling the number of children that a couple brought into the world. While I did not necessarily believe that his recommendation of *coitus interruptus* was likely the most efficacious technique that one might employ, his information was of considerable use to my women. I wondered if John also knew that we provided a kind of prophylactic to our patients who were able to convince their husbands that it would prevent conception of yet another child. And, indeed, I was very well aware that what we were doing was not strictly legal. It was, however, in my opinion, the only ethical thing for us to do. And it was so desperately needed. I was not in the slightest ashamed of what we were doing.

"I have been providing such a pamphlet to women who request such information." I sat with my hands in my lap, looking directly at John, defying him to suggest that what we were doing was wrong.

He sagged back into his chair, deflated, it seemed. "I was afraid it would come to this. Bridget, you cannot go on doing this. I cannot defend you against allegations from my own profession. And make no mistake, I have been doing this. Indeed, if they decide to make a report, you could very easily go to jail. I must now insist that you cease these actions."

I stood up and smoothed out the folds in my skirt. "I will not."

Memories of that fateful day in my father's house when he informed me that I would not be permitted to enter the medical school to pursue my life's dream seeped into my consciousness. The feelings of loss resurfaced, but mostly I was angry. How dare they? I was no longer the young girl who had little choice but to do her father's bidding. I was a mature woman now, and I knew in my heart that what I was doing was so fundamentally right. What right did this group of men have to try to control women's bodies?

"Do you have any idea how desperate these women are? Do any of those hypocritical, self-serving physicians know – or even wish to know? They claim to be working for the good of society, but all they really want to do is force their own value systems on others. Well, they have no idea what it is like to be a woman and especially no idea what it is to be a woman whose husband forces himself on you time after time, with little regard for the outcome. And it is their bodies that must contend with the consequences. No, I will not stop."

Moving quickly toward the door and out into the foyer, I picked up my wrap and let myself out the front door into the rain. I knew I must find Siobhan and prepare her for what might happen next.

By the time I arrived at the clinic, the rain was pummeling the steps leading up to the veranda, bouncing back to re-soak anything in its way. I knew that despite the hour and the fact that it was Sunday evening, Siobhan would most likely be here. I was actually beginning to worry about her, as she seemed to spend all her time here, when I believed she should begin to develop a social life.

However, I also knew that my counsel could hardly be considered credible on such matters: my own life seemed to lack such a balance. Had it not been for my marriage to John, I should likely have joined Siobhan here on these evenings myself.

Despite the worrying circumstances under which I now entered the front hall, I was, just as I was each time I stepped across the threshold, astonished at what we, a group of mere women, had been able to accomplish.

The house looked like any other on the street. It blended seamlessly into the neighbourhood, and we had no need for signage. Our clients came to us by word of mouth, entering through the large, heavy front door in anticipation of being cared for and considered in all their undertakings with us. As you entered the doorway, you were faced with an inner door which then opened onto a foyer with a large staircase going straight up to a landing and then turned for several more steps to the second floor.

To the right of the rather narrow foyer, in what was originally intended to be the parlour, was the office I occupied, where I saw and spoke with the women who sought a bit of medicinal advice. It was kept warm in the winter and these damp spring days and evenings by a large parlour stove in the corner and oriental rugs that I had scattered on the floor. I had a large oak roll-top desk that Mr. Bowness had kindly found for me in one of his shipments, and a wing-back chair upholstered in dark blue silk. Locked in the desk were my own medical implements, and we locked our other supplies in a large armoire beside the stove. Facing the desk from the other wall was a blue settee upon which my patients sat to tell me of their problems. Anyone entering the room would find it a challenge to determine just what the nature of our business was, as it were.

Across the hall from my office, Siobhan and the other women who worked here from time to time had their own space. They helped new mothers to learn to care for their babies and often had groups of women laughing and talking about their husbands and their lives. Upstairs, Siobhan had fitted out a kind of nursery where our ladies could leave their children to be cared for when they were seeing me or taking part in the discussions in Siobhan's room. Occasionally, when one of them was in a desperate situation, one of them would ask to leave her children for the day while she took care of other matters. It occurred to me that such facilities ought to have been widely available for mothers whose very existence relied on their ability to bring home what money they could. There was a feeling of deep camaraderie and ease here within these walls. It seemed safe.

My conversation with John, however, had left me feeling more vulnerable than I had in some years. Indeed, I felt that the clinic was now vulnerable. In truth, I was not really surprised by this turn of events; I had been expecting it to happen at some point. If there was one thing that they could not say about me, it was that I was a fool who did not understand the consequences of her own behaviour. I most assuredly did know exactly what I was doing and how certain people might react. I only needed to prepare a defence.

I found Siobhan on the second floor preparing the nursery room for the morning when we expected to greet our clients. I bid her good evening and asked her to come downstairs to talk to me when she had finished.

"Is there something wrong, Dr. Bridget?"

I had asked her to drop the "Dr." as we were friends and I was not a physician, but she found that difficult.

"I do not believe there is anything wrong, Siobhan, but there is an important matter we need to discuss." I left her to her activity and returned to my office.

On the floor beside the desk, I kept the trunk that Mr. Bowness had sent to me as a welcoming gift when I first visited New York several years ago. It seemed like a lifetime ago, and I had hoped to be using the trunk for world travels. But now it was to have an even more important duty.

I removed the key to the desk from my bag, whose drawstring I had fastened around my wrist and unlocked the desk. Rolling back the cover, I was doing an inventory of the items I needed to place in the trunk. First the pamphlets, then the prophylactic devices. Some of them were locked in the armoire, which I also unlocked.

By the time Siobhan had completed her tasks and come downstairs, I had filled the trunk and pulled back several of the oriental carpets on the floor, revealing a loosened floorboard. I had taken this precaution myself when we first moved into the hospice. I had realized that there might come a time when we needed to be somewhat more clandestine about our activities.

"Whatever are you doing?" Siobhan said as she came through the door and discovered me on all fours, my skirts hiked up, determining if the trunk would fit into the space beneath the boards. I stood up.

"Siobhan, there is something we need to talk about."

When I finished relating the details of my conversation with John to her, she was enraged.

"How can what we do be illegal? How can it be wrong to help these poor women? What we're doing is right."

She possessed all the self-righteousness of a young idealist – and I supposed I, too, still maintained a degree of idealism myself.

"What we are doing is not wrong, Siobhan. I do not want to hear you even contemplate such a thing. However, what we are doing is not, strictly speaking, legal. We can help women to terminate those unwanted pregnancies, but we are not really permitted to prevent them from occurring in the first place. I, for one, believe that the authorities are entirely wrong about this, and we must not permit the beliefs of a group of ill-informed, small-minded males to overshadow the very bodies of these women. We must continue to do what we can to help them. One of the most important things we can do, however, is to ensure that when they come to examine the premises..."

Siobhan's hand flew to her mouth to suppress a kind of frightened cry at this thought. I continued.

"... and they *will* come to examine the premises, of that you can be certain."

"Who will come?"

"Very likely a group of local doctors, perhaps a politician. There is little John can do to stop them. And I cannot ask him to try. Consequently, we shall hide our contentious materials."

Siobhan understood completely and moved quickly to assist me in our endeavours. As we completed replacing the carpets, I wondered how long it would be before we were graced by some kind of inspection. As I gathered up my belongings, I heard a commotion at the front door. Peeking my head into the foyer, I heard Ned's voice, clear, but slurred as he stumbled into the building.

"John Allan has died," he said.

I did not know if this was happy news or yet another misfortune in his life.

TWENTY-SEVEN

Ned babbled almost incoherently all the way back to his lodgings with his aunt and cousin. With Siobhan on one side of him and me on the other, we managed together to propel him homeward.

When we arrived at the flat, Mrs. Clemm was extraordinarily surprised to see Ned at all, much less to see him in our company. It seemed that he had been away for several days and had come directly to the hospice upon his return.

"Where exactly have you been, Ned?" I asked when we had finally calmed him enough to sit down in Mrs. Clemm's parlour.

"I have just returned from Richmond, and he was gone. Gone for several weeks, and no one thought to contact me. Louisa was there, with the baby. I cannot bear to go on." He was babbling. He buried his face in his hands and sobbed.

Siobhan appeared to be horribly unnerved by this display of male despair and very confused about his visit to Richmond and his mention of Louisa. I explained quietly to her that Louisa was his foster father, John Allan's new wife.

"I cannot conceive of him failing me with such finality. He has had his way to the end and beyond the grave even." Ned was almost wailing.

Virginia appeared at the door, looking puzzled by the commotion. I suggested to Siobhan that she keep Virginia company in the bedroom while Mrs. Clemm and I sorted this out. Siobhan was not happy about this arrangement, wishing instead to stay, but did my bidding anyway.

Mrs. Clemm brought us tea after which I was able determine several things about Ned's expedition to Richmond. Evidently, he had felt so despondent about his financial situation that he had gone to Richmond to beseech John Allan yet again for pecuniary consideration,

188

only to be told upon his arrival that John Allan was, in fact, dead. Furthermore, the will had already been read, and Ned was given no consideration whatsoever. Mr. Allan's considerable estate had been left to Louisa and her sons in its entirety, nor did she feel any obligation, even of the moral nature, to provide even a penny to Ned as John Allan's long-time foster child, once so well-loved by the first Mrs. Allan.

Siobhan returned to the room, clearly having listened to this exchange. She sat down beside Ned and, in a most congenial manner and placed her arm around his shoulders. He leaned against her, and I felt a pang of what I could only later describe as jealousy. To my mind, it was a most unwelcome and incomprehensible sensation. I had not realized that Siobhan and Ned had become such good friends in recent months.

Siobhan took her leave and bid me good evening. As she did so, I thought I could detect a tiny self-satisfied smile playing about her lips. Surely I must be mistaken!

I sat with Ned just a bit longer.

"Bride," he began, "you have been such a good friend to me through the years." He looked over at his aunt, who was sitting in a rocker by the window, sewing and continued *sotto voce*. "I have loved you from the first day I saw you. I fear that my life on this earth will end before I am granted my life's only real wish."

He arose and walked to the door of the bedroom without illuminating me further about this life's wish. "I must sleep now," he said and was gone.

Virginia returned to the parlour. "Is Eddy going to be all right? Is he sick?"

"No, Virginia, he is not sick. Only sick at heart, it seems," I said. "He will be fine. He has simply experienced a rather large kind of shock. He will recover presently."

She smiled. "I am so glad that Siobhan was here."

I must have looked puzzled.

Virginia giggled and put her hand over her mouth. "Oh, Dr. Bridget, perhaps you did not know."

"What is it that I should have known?" I almost did not wish to ask the question as I perhaps did not wish to hear the answer.

"I have been taking little notes to Siobhan from Eddy for some time now. He writes her a little letter, and I am dispatched to deliver it to her hand. It is all quite romantic."

"Virginia," Mrs. Clemm said from her corner, "perhaps Edgar does not wish for you to be telling such things. Some things are private."

"But Dr. Bridget is an old friend of his. Surely he would not wish to keep such a thing secret from his good friend. Love is such a sweet thing. I wish it for myself someday." Virginia clasped her hands together; her eyes had that starry look of a smitten young woman.

I did not know quite how to react to this news. I should have been very happy to know that two people, both of whom I loved dearly, were finding a relationship that they could perhaps cherish. But I did wonder why neither of them had thought to mention such good fortune. And, indeed, I truly did believe that, given his predilections and lack of financial support, Ned would not make a good match for Siobhan – or perhaps for any woman, come to that.

When I returned home, John was waiting for me.

"It is late, Bridget, and I have been worried about you."

I told him that I had found it necessary to discuss our conversation regarding the clinic work with Siobhan.

"I hope that you have taken my counsel to heart. I have no wish to see my wife incarcerated for such a misdemeanour. Come to bed."

As I readied myself for sleep, I told him about Ned's sad story and about his apparent infatuation with Siobhan. John found this latter quite amusing. I did not, however, tell him of the trunk nor what Siobhan and I had done with it.

Indeed, I thought little about the trunk again for several weeks. But on a bright, clear Friday morning in late May, I could think of nothing else.

TWENTY-EIGHT

They arrived as a group on the front steps of the hospice at ten o'clock in the morning. There were four of them, all dressed in black suits and carrying portfolios. Siobhan answered their knock, and when she came to find me, she was very distraught at the prospect of letting four men onto the premises unannounced, much less letting in members of the medical establishment who had taken it upon themselves to scrutinize our activities. I told her to bid them wait in the foyer while I slipped out the back door of my office and up the stairs to tell the other women that there were men about.

When I came down the main stairs to greet our visitors, I was very composed and felt quite in control of the situation.

"Good morning, gentlemen," I said, extending my hand to the obvious leader of the group. "How might I help you, gentlemen, this fine morning?"

The leader of the group shook my hand and smiled, a bit patronizingly, I thought. He looked around and removed his hat.

"Mrs. Ryan, is it not?" he said.

"Yes," I said, "I am Mrs. Ryan, and this is my hospice. I believe that you are Dr. King and," I said, turning to the man on his left, "I believe I recognize Dr. Morse. How is Mrs. Morse these days? It seems an age since I have seen her." I extended my hand to him as well.

He shook it and, seeming to my mind to be a bit uncomfortable, said, "She is well, thank you, Mrs. Ryan. I hope that we are not intruding in any way."

"Of course not. I have looked forward to showing off my premises to members of the medical establishment at some point." I turned to the remaining two men who brought up the rear. "I do not believe I have had the pleasure of your acquaintance, sirs."

Dr. King introduced me to the remaining two as Drs. Murphy and Watson. I shook their hands, and when I shook Dr. Watson's hand, I felt a slight chill as he seemed to look me up and down. He was the tallest of the lot, in his early forties, I would have said, with a shock of dark blonde hair falling almost over his forehead and curling around the back of his neck. He bore that slight paunch of a man who is ageing before his very eyes and a look of hunger about his hazel eyes. I wondered about the object of his hunger. I sincerely hoped it was not vengeance against women running healthcare clinics for other women.

"It is a pleasure I have looked forward to," he said, his hand holding mine for just a moment too long in my view. I did not quite believe the sincerity of his words.

I glimpsed Siobhan peeking out the door from the room across from my office. Her eyes were growing large with what appeared to me to be naked fear. Then she ducked back quickly as Dr. Watson looked around.

"This is a rather pleasant building, Mrs. Ryan. What exactly is it you do in this dwelling?"

I ushered them into my office and sat down behind my desk, bidding them all to take a seat. I told them about the work we had been doing to help women prepare for motherhood and care for their children when they needed to go to work.

"I understand that you are regarded as something of a doctor, Mrs. Ryan," Dr. King said, as he removed a small leather-bound notebook from his portfolio.

"You flatter me, Dr. King," I said. "I am no doctor, and all who come to the hospice are aware of this. I simply use my knowledge to assist these poor, disaffected women in pursuing better health. When they bring their illnesses to our humble setting here, I assist them to find appropriate care – from a doctor or a hospital."

"Is your husband involved at all in this enterprise?" Dr. Watson, who had remained standing in the corner, removed a pipe from his breast pocket.

193

"No, he is not. I have money of my own that was left to me by my father, and have chosen to use it for the benefit of these women." I noted that he was about to light his pipe. "I am so sorry, Dr. Watson. I do not permit smoking materials of any kind on the premises."

"Whyever not, woman?"

"I believe that it is rather unhealthy to breathe smoke from such materials. I have noted the children coughing more whenever they are around smoking pipes or cigars."

He certainly did not look convinced, but chose to follow my rule. After chatting for a few more minutes, I invited them to tour the premises with me.

"Yes, of course, Mrs. Ryan, we would be delighted."

I took them on a brief tour, introducing them to Siobhan and several other women who were present that morning. Siobhan seemed to shrink from the introductions.

"I must speak with you a moment, Dr. Bridget," she whispered, while they looked around the room housing the children.

"When these men have left," I whispered in response.

When we had returned to my office, I asked them if there was anything else.

"Well, to be honest," Dr. King cleared his throat uncomfortably, "there is one more matter we needs must discuss with you. It is the actual reason for our attendance with you today."

"Well, let us get on with it, man," Dr. Watson said from where he had perched on the windowsill.

I looked at him disapprovingly and then turned back to Dr. King. "Please, Dr. King. Whatever it is, I am certain we can deal with it." I smiled, and it took all of my composure to maintain it and not to scream, for I knew with a certainty what he was about to say. I sat down at my desk and gazed at the floor for a moment.

"Yes, well, I shall get directly to the point, then," he said. "You see, we have heard rumours about your activities. It seems that there is a belief that you are providing these women with more than support for motherhood. Shall I say there are rumours that you are providing them with support for non-motherhood?"

I sat still, my hands folded on my lap, maintaining my forbearance and self-control. I would not help him with this; rather, I would force him to be clear and specific.

"Yes, well, I am certain you understand what I am saying," he said.

"No, Dr. King, I am sorry, but I do not understand. Perhaps you could be more specific."

"He means you are providing these women with information on how to prevent conception." Dr. Watson stood up and crossed his arms.

Drs. Morse and Murphy maintained their silence but seemed to look on with heightened interest.

"Mrs. Ryan," Dr. King said, "are you familiar with a Dr. Charles Knowlton?"

I worked very hard at maintaining an implacable face to present to these men. I knew only too well the famous – or perhaps infamous – Dr. Knowlton's work, and I admired it greatly. Indeed, a copy of his book "The Private Companion of Married People" lay only inches below the very feet of the vexatious Dr. Watson as he stood upon the red and blue wool rug in the middle of the floor. I glanced toward his feet and then into Dr. King's eyes.

"I know of his reputation," I said calmly.

"Are you then aware of the fact that he was imprisoned for three months' hard labour in the House of Correction for trumpeting his own views on the desirability of birth control?"

"Indeed? Was he? It seems a shame to silence discussion of such an issue as that one."

"Have you personal knowledge of his views, Mrs. Ryan?" Dr. Watson moved closer to me and leaned toward me, bringing his face close to mine. "What do you think of his opinion on this subject?"

I knew that I would be able to contain my outrage for only a very short time longer, but I knew that should I fail to maintain my composure, such a reaction could have devastating repercussions upon our ability to continue our enterprise here. How I longed to put these sanctimonious men in their place – these men with their self-righteous views on how women ought to live their lives.

"Well, gentlemen," I said, rising to face them and thus forcing Dr. Watson to step back, "I was unaware that opinions kept to oneself were in any way illicit or, for that matter, the business of any particular individuals who choose to insinuate themselves into other people's places of work. I believe that I am entitled to maintain silence on the matter of my opinions. Have you seen any explicit evidence of such activity?" I unlocked the top of my desk and rolled it back to display the tidy contents.

They were silent, but I noted that all four of them leaned in to get a better look at my desk.

"Of course you have not, and unless there is anything further, I shall bid you good day." I walked toward the door.

"Perhaps you could unlock that armoire, for us to have a look," Dr. Watson said, running his hands over its surface.

"Do you wish to bring the police in here to look as well?" I could feel my anger surfacing. "I will unlock it for you to look, but I warn you not to harass me in this manner, for I have nothing to hide."

I unlocked the cabinet, and they looked inside. There was no incriminating evidence in view. I locked it up again and showed them the door.

Finally, they took their leave, and I was much relieved to see their backs. As soon as the door had closed behind them, Siobhan came bounding out into the foyer. Her hair was in disarray, and she seemed agitated. Relations between us had been rather strained since I discovered that she and Ned had developed a friendship, although I could scarcely understand my own emotions on the topic.

I made a note to remember to smooth things over with her. But now she seemed in a state.

"Dr. Bridget," she said, wide-eyed and almost breathless, "what I was trying to say to you when those gentlemen were here – one of them, the tall one with the blonde hair?"

"Yes, Siobhan, Dr. Watson. What about him?"

"You remember my friend, Patsy? The one with all the babies? The one who got rid of one on her own? You remember?"

"I remember, Siobhan. Go on."

"He's the doctor, he is." She put her hand firmly on my arm, trying desperately to make me understand.

"The doctor? Yes, I know he is a doctor."

"No. You don't understand. He's the one. The one who tried to have his way with Patsy in exchange for getting rid of the baby."

I thought back to that fateful day when Siobhan had taken me to visit her friend, Patsy, bleeding from a self-inflicted abortion. Patsy told me that she went to see a doctor who would take care of these things. She also told me that she did not stay for the desperately required procedure since he had made it clear to her that he wanted more from her than her money.

I looked toward the door over which threshold he had just stepped. I understood.

TWENTY-NINE

SUMMER, 1834

How I loved the summers! The trees in full bloom held their boughs to the sky in earnest tribute to the god-like aspects of the sun and the warm rain. The breeze blowing in through the open window of my office smelled of lilac, then lavender, and finally more earthy fragrances as the season wore on.

When I told John of the spring visit of the auspicious medical representatives, he said little but admonished me to be careful and not to involve him. I was disappointed in his reaction, and in him, truth be told. Although he did seem to share some of my sensibilities about the plight of these women, his sympathy fell short of actually wanting to be involved or even associated in any way with such activities. I believe he was frightened, and I had not thought him to have such little strength of character. I had little understanding of the growing brotherhood of the local medical establishment.

Siobhan and I had settled any differences that may have developed between us, and we were closer than ever, at least as I saw it. Oddly enough, our reconciliation had actually been of Ned's doing – though he had not planned it nor did he ever realize that it had occurred.

It happened one evening early in July. Siobhan had been at home with her mother and younger siblings when Ned had burst through the door demanding to see her and have her hand (when Siobhan told me of this later, I was green). He was, however, evidently intoxicated beyond what Siobhan had ever seen in a man – even on her father's worst benders. A bitter argument ensued; she was left crying and angry at having let her heart be broken. Her mother had encouraged her to go immediately to visit me at my home, which she had reluctantly done. Siobhan continued to harbour a feeling that we were of two different classes of person, despite my assurances that, as far as I was concerned, we were simply two women who were friends and colleagues.

I welcomed her into my home as I always was wont to do, and we talked long into the night. I was much relieved to have my friend back, but I felt another, more disagreeable emotion that I did not admire in myself. Somewhere deep inside of me, I felt relieved that Ned no longer paid his attentions to Siobhan – or anyone else, for that matter. Why could I not let this go?

Siobhan and I returned to our amicable working relationship, and because she had worked so hard for all these months, I provided her with a rise in salary. She was astounded, but she too recognized her own talents. Indeed, she had begun a small school of sorts in a back room on the first floor. I had heard her reading with the little children and was astonished at her ability to encourage even the four and five-year-olds to read. She drew pictures on a tiny chalkboard we had bought and made up stories. Occasionally, I would stand outside while she related such a story to a wide-eyed and rapt group of little ones. On one such occasion, I had suggested to her that she ought to write down these stories. That simply made her laugh at what she considered to be the absurdity of the remark.

I continued to provide what assistance I could for as many of the women who wished it, and we were not bothered any longer by the medical establishment, at least for the time being. On several occasions, however, Dr. Watson's name did enter into our conversations. Several of my patients had experienced similar encounters as that related to me by Patsy O'Toole. Each of these discourses I filed into the back of my brain, only to be used *in extremis*, I thought.

As I continued to attend at births and to welcome women into my office when they so desired it, I concluded that there were three distinct kinds of women who came to us at The Hildegard Hospice. First, there were those who truly required the services of the local hospital. How I recognized the need for such immediate attention that was beyond our limited capabilities at the hospice was sometimes not as concrete as I would have liked. It was more an intuitive sense that I seemed to be developing and that I trusted more and more as my judgments proved valid.

The second distinct group of patients was those whose complaints concerned the birthing of their babies or other such minor ailments that could be dispatched quite easily with a small dose of calomel or other of our limited medications.

The third group, however, comprised those women for whom I believe we were able to do the most real good – and this was the largest group, it should be noted. These were the ones who appeared here each day, timid and reluctant, but arriving anyway on the advice of a friend, or sister, or aunt. They had minor complaints, often of an aching in their heads, or minor soreness in the stomach, or other comparable malady. After a time of conversation and demonstration to them that we cared about them as people, it usually became clear that the source of their trouble was not within their bodies, rather it was within their spirits. Hardship and troubles within the family seemed to be at the root of many of these afflictions. These women worked hard and put up with situations that were to my mind, intolerable, but I had never been required to live in that world. Even now, I was but a peripheral player in their lives. In any case, as time went on, I became ever stronger in my belief that this was our main mission – to show these women that someone cared about their lives. I thought about Sister Eulalia's admonition to me to set sacred intention each day and was truly convinced that this work I had taken on was doing just that. I thought that she would be proud of her protégé and vowed to write to her immediately.

One afternoon, as I sat with several of these women and we took tea together, Siobhan knocked on the door rather more urgently than usual.

"Dr. Bridget," she said, using the honorary title only when we were in the company of our patients, "I must talk with you straight away."

Her eyes showed a fear that I had not seen in some time as she had learned to relax into her role here at the hospice and became more confident in her abilities and gifts. I excused myself and went out into the foyer, closing the office door behind me.

"Bridget, it has happened again, "Siobhan said, looking around to ensure our privacy.

"What has happened again?"

"I told her to come here to speak with you – that you knew a way to perhaps stop the babies from coming every year. But she would not listen. I fear it's my fault. I ought to have tried harder." Her eyes began to glisten with coming tears.

I put my arm around her and tried to calm her down, as I was having difficulty determining exactly what it was she was talking about. Soon, however, it became horrifyingly clear. Her neighbour, in a desperate attempt to avoid yet another mouth to feed, adding to her current brood of six, had taken the family's savings and gone to procure an abortion. The doctor had, according to Siobhan, had his way with her, assuring the terrified woman that it was part of preparing her body for the procedure. I felt sick – so sick in fact that I had to cover my mouth for fear I would vomit on the floor.

As much as I feared that I already knew the answer, I asked the question. "Who was it, Siobhan? Who was this despicable man?" I could not bear to call him a doctor.

She was crying now.

"It was Dr. Watson, was it not?" I said, trying to help her through this.

She nodded.

I swallowed hard and stood up straight, smoothing out the folds in my skirt. I brushed a stray curl from my forehead and took a deep breath.

"I have work to do," I said finally.

Three days later, I was prepared to carry out my work.

"Where are you off to this morning looking so lovely?" John asked as I donned my cape at the front door. "Not going to your hospice this morning?"

"Yes," I said, smiling sweetly, "as a matter of fact, I am going to the hospice today, but I wanted to feel especially cheerful today, and this frock puts me in a good mood."

John smiled admiringly at me, and the glow of his attention warmed me – something that seemed to be more and more lacking lately. Perhaps I had been too busy for him. I would pay more attention to him when I returned home this evening.

I did not go directly to the hospice that morning. I had a stop to make on my way, a stop about which I could hardly be expected to tell my husband. Since it was a lovely morning, I walked the ten blocks to the address that I found easily. The house was large and imposing, with a wrought iron gate leading to an impressive oak door. The brass nameplate was well-polished so that I could see my reflection as I walked by. I walked up the front steps with a sense of purpose, my mission well planned.

I pulled the bell, and while I waited for the door to be answered, I smiled at the sight of a ruby-throated hummingbird as it drank sweet nectar from the pink clematis tumbling down the trellis beside the porch.

THIRTY

To say that Dr. Watson was surprised to see me on his doorstep would have been a considerable understatement. His countenance immediately revealed to me his astonishment.

"Good morning, Dr. Watson," I said, extending my hand to him. "I had not expected to be greeted by you personally; rather, I had expected a maid – or a wife, perhaps?"

He took my hand and seemed to gather his senses about him, recovering from the apparent shock of seeing me on his doorstep. He kissed my hand and bid me enter.

"Mrs. Ryan, what a pleasant surprise this is." He stepped aside to allow me to precede him into the hall. "My wife is visiting with her mother in Boston. Alas, I am alone today."

Of course, I already knew all of this. I had made it my business to know that we would be alone when I called on him. I looked around the foyer and found it to be dark and masculine in look, with dark wood everywhere and a lack of softness. I wondered at his wife's opinion on the matter of the decor. Or perhaps she was not permitted such an opinion.

"I am sorry for the intrusion," I said, smiling as coyly as I could, having little experience with such ploys. "I was hoping that you might be able to help me."

He ran his fingers through his unruly hair as if to improve its disarray and became more serious, concerned for my welfare, perhaps?

"Please, Mrs. Ryan," he said, opening what was evidently his office door, "come in and tell me how I might help you."

I followed him into an office which was furnished in very business-like furnishings – a dark desk, several chairs, a metal cabinet with glass doors containing what appeared to be a selection of medicines and instruments, and a large screen at one end which appeared, to my eye at least, to be hiding something. I longed to look behind the screen to see exactly what implements he had in his office. I noted the heavy draperies that hung at the two high windows, ensuring complete privacy within these four walls and the one very unbusinesslike piece of furniture – an overstuffed settee, upholstered in a most gaudy shade of red silk.

He sat down at the desk and bade me sit across the expanse of dark wood to face him. I adjusted my skirt around me and removed my gloves, holding them in my lap. I kept my eyes downcast while I prepared myself for this encounter. My heart was racing, and I hoped that it was not evident to him. On the other hand, perhaps that physical involvement might add to the authenticity of my story.

"Dr. Watson," I began, looking at him through my eyelashes, "I understand that you and I may have some business to discuss."

I watched his face carefully. Although it remained impassive, he leaned slightly forward in his chair as if to hear me better.

"Mrs. Ryan, I would be delighted to work with you in any way I could. Indeed, I have been hoping that we might encounter one another again. Would you care to take tea with me while we discuss this?"

The very last person in the world with whom I would have liked to take tea was this smarmy man who now smiled at me with a smile that had an element of expectation to it – or so I thought. The outrage that had led me to take this rather unusual step of visiting with this doctor was an almost palpable knot in my stomach and my heart. It was all I could do to prevent myself from striking out at him, slapping him as hard as I could across that silly grin. No, what I really held within my breast was a murderous feeling that seemed to be counter to everything I had ever believed about human beings. I could not remember having ever come face-to-face with such an embodiment of evil, which is how I had begun to think of him since hearing stories of his exploits with my women.

In any event, I agreed to tea, grateful for a moment alone to compose myself. When he had gone to attend to the tea, I quietly arose from my chair and walked over to the screen. As I peeked around the corner, I was greeted by a bed, raised on blocks, with a contraption over it that resembled a small canopy. Hanging from the canopy were leather straps. At the foot of the bed was a metal table on which had been placed a series of instruments of increasing size. On the floor between the bed and the table were a small stool and a shiny metal bucket. I quickly took my seat again, lest Dr. Watson should return and find me prying into his business.

Presently, he returned to the office carrying a small tea tray which he placed on a low cabinet beside the door. As he began to pour the tea, I went over to him immediately.

"Please, Dr. Watson, allow me to serve you. I feel somewhat as if I have barged in on you today. Let me make it up to you." I smiled at him sweetly.

Both his smile back at me and the hand he then placed on my shoulder made me shiver. He did, however, allow me to serve him his tea. He sat down once more at his desk while I busied myself with the milk and sugar, stirring both cups well. The spoon tinkled almost gaily off the sides of the fine china cups he had brought out for the occasion.

"When do you expect your next patient this morning?" I asked as I passed him his teacup.

"Oh, not for an hour or more. We have ample time to become acquainted and to discuss any business you might consider appropriate, Bridget. In private, of course."

I cringed slightly at this familiarity, but was heartened by the time available to us. I did relax and sat back, taking a sip of the strong tea, watching him as he did so. He told me how happy he was to see me and apologized for his part in the intrusion at the hospice.

"Our information must have been mistaken. I saw no evidence that you were doing anything wrong at your women's hospice," he said.

I smiled charmingly and warmed to my morning's activity. We were just beginning our true conversation when I heard the creaking of the front door. Dr. Watson looked puzzled as he, too, tuned in to the sound.

"I thought that you were expecting no one," I said, placing my cup back in its saucer, which sat in my lap.

Dr. Watson had taken a seat beside me on the settee, and before he had the opportunity to rise to ascertain the identity of our intruder, the office door opened, and the entire frame of the door was filled by the menacing form of a woman whose expression quickly shifted from surprise to displeasure. I thought this must be the housekeeper arriving early to do her day's chores. I was mistaken.

Dr. Watson rose quickly and placed his cup on the desk. "My darling Emmaline," he said, much to my incredulity.

How could this tall, hulking form of a woman with her coarse features and snarling mouth possibly be married to a "pretty boy" such as Dr. Watson?

"This is a sorry picture, Lowell."

Her voice was as unrefined as her features – raspy and low. I felt a slight trepidation at the sight and sound of such a woman who was clearly as surprised by her husband's activity as he was at her appearing so unexpectedly. Exactly what she surmised we were doing was a mystery to me. Still, I thought that I had better inform her of the innocent nature of our encounter before she drew any unfortunate conclusions. What surprised me, however, was the way that Dr. Watson seemed to almost cower before her. I had to suppress a giggle at this interesting turn of events.

I stood and extended the hand that was not holding the teacup and saucer. "Mrs. Watson, I am Bridget Ryan, wife of a colleague of your husband's."

She looked down at my hand and sniffed. "I know who you are, Mrs. Ryan. Women the like of you are not welcome in my home."

I wondered what kind of woman I appeared to her to be.

The proprietary nature of the comment about her house, coupled with the incongruousness of her appearance, led me to wonder at their relationship. I did not, however, have time to wonder for long. It was clear that I should leave immediately, which I did.

THIRTY-ONE

SPRING, 1835

"My Dearest Bride,

I have been much occupied of late with the business of my writing that I fear I have neglected my friendship with you, my dearest love. I thought to put this right by writing to you with news of what has so absorbed my time and my energy.

I have been making inquiries of a magazine newly published in Richmond that has agreeably published a piece or two of my work. I do not in any way wish to presume your interest, but based on our past discourse, I believe you may enjoy my writing. Consequently, I humbly enclose several of the self-same pages for your perusal, and I hope to be able to discuss these with you when next I have the pleasure of your company.

Virginia has been telling me of her visits to your hospice and highly praises both the work you are doing there and your person as well. She holds you in the highest regard and admires you and looks up to you. My cousin is such a sweet girl.

I still lie awake at night, Bride, and consider our devotion to one another, and not to wish him ill, but should your husband meet with some untimely end, perhaps you will reconsider our discussion that is never far from my mind.

I await word from you so that we may meet to renew our friendship.

I remain forever,
Your devoted Ned"

How Ned's proclamations of undying love now seemed preposterous, perhaps even lunatic! After his display of undying affection for Siobhan (and who knew who else might have been the recipient of such pronouncements?), I wondered at his understanding of women – or even of himself. I was at once exasperated and yet maddeningly welcoming of his attentions.

In truth, I felt a bit guilty about not having kept company with him as often as he (and to be sure, I) might have wished it. In my position as a married woman, and despite my protestations about my right to my own life, I recognized that I need not make life difficult for John. Indeed, I did have respect for the institution of marriage and wished to remain faithful.

I was folding Ned's letter to put it in the drawer of my writing desk when John opened the door of the den, which we shared, and entered with a silver tray holding a decanter and two crystal glasses so full of sherry that they threatened to spill everywhere.

I laughed. "Has Wimpy gone to bed that you were forced to pour the sherry yourself?"

John smiled a kind of half-smile. "Indeed, I am not so good at pouring sherry as I am at being a doctor."

He placed one glass in front of me and placed the tray with the remaining glass on a small table next to a chair close to the hearth. He sat down and raised the glass to his lips.

"Bridget, there is something I have put off discussing with you, but now I feel it pressing upon me and must open it to the air."

I got up from the desk and, carefully picking up my own glass, I took a small sip, then sat down in the chair facing him on the opposite side of the blazing fire. "I have felt for some time that there may be some unspoken thoughts between us. Please, do not hesitate to tell me of your concerns."

He began. "It is about an incident that occurred some months ago. It seems that you visited the premises of a certain Dr. Watson, and I do not believe that you ever mentioned it to me."

"Yes," I said, sipping my sherry thoughtfully. "He was among the group of doctors who visited the clinic one day in a vain search for illicit materials. I had not thought it important enough to detail the identities of all the men."

"There has been some talk about you and Dr. Watson."

"Talk? What manner of talk?" I asked, truly dumbfounded by such a revelation.

"Among the medical community. Dr. Watson has a reputation of sorts, about which I believe you know."

"Yes," I said carefully, "if you are referring to the nature of his medical practice, then yes, of course, I know. Some of my own women have been the unfortunate recipients of his brand of care."

"Then, Bridget, it is my duty as your husband to inquire as to the nature of your discussion with this man in his office."

For a moment, I was puzzled by his serious tone, and then, of course, his meaning struck me with a force such as I have never felt. "John, if you are asking if I had been to see this man to procure an abortion, you are terribly wrong. I simply wished to discuss with him some issues that concern us both. Indeed, I even had the occasion to meet his rather peculiar wife that morning. An odd couple if ever I saw one." I shook my head at the incomprehensible nature of the union.

John said nothing. He simply looked at me for a long moment, then took his final sip, placing the crystal glass firmly back on the silver tray. He arose from his chair, and I noted that he was looking tired, perhaps even old. He came over to my chair and raised my hand to his lips and whispered, "Thank God." He kissed my hand and turned to leave the room.

Before he reached the door, I arose. "John, did you seriously believe that I would do such a thing? That I would not wish to carry your child?" I was closer to tears than I had been in some years.

He turned, his hand on the door handle. "I did not know what to think. You see, Bridget, there is something that I have never told you." He looked down at the expanse of rug between the two of us.

"You can tell me anything, John. I thought you knew this."

"You see, my dear, I am unable to father children. I should have told you. I am so ashamed of all the things I have been thinking about you in recent months."

I wanted to go to him and tell him that it was all right, but something stopped me. This man, whom I believed held me in such high regard, had thought that I was perhaps keeping company with another man. I could not endure it. He had his own demons, too. He left the room, closing the door behind him.

I returned to my chair by the fire and poured myself another sherry from the decanter on the tray. I looked thoughtfully into the fire as if I could find some answers there.

It seemed to me that, for all my strengths, I would never understand men as long as I lived. Those I had known in my life had acted in the most unpredictable ways. First, my father, who was as close to me as I thought a human being ever could be, had taken a wife I would never have considered appropriate for him. I never did come to terms with the attraction between the two of them. I had considered the possibility that I was simply jealous, but had rejected that explanation as preposterous. I knew I would have welcomed a new stepmother into my life if she had been someone whose presence would have added to our household. No, I could not have been jealous.

Then there was Ned. What was there to say about Ned in my life? Our friendship was very difficult to comprehend. While we shared a love of literature, there was little else we had in common. He was, indeed, handsome, but then there were so many other handsome men in the world. But there was something about him – about the way he looked deeply into my eyes, about the way I knew that in the depths of his mind he was in torment of sorts – that made him almost bewitching. Indeed, he seemed to mesmerize most of the women with whom he had contact.

And now there was John. He clearly kept things deep within him – things that he was loath to share even with me. We seemed to have a kind of mutual respect, and this was an aspect of our relationship that I cherished intensely, but he, too, seemed to hold deep within him certain agonies that he could not bear to share even with the one closest to him. How could one come to know another if he failed to divulge significant aspects of his very soul?

No, I thought, I did not really understand men, but I would continue to try to do so. It seemed the least I could do.

I had hardly recovered from my contemplation about the peculiarities of men when I faced the distinct possibility that I knew precious little more about women, at least about certain kinds of women.

We were conducting a group discussion about the practicalities of motherhood (I, of course, was merely the hostess, knowing as little as I did about motherhood) when there came an insistent knock on the front door of the hospice one afternoon early in May.

When I opened the door, I smiled at the sight of three women who had never before entered into our milieu, but my delight at seeing new people was quickly overshadowed by my recognition of the woman who stood face to face with me. Well, perhaps I was more correctly face-to-neck, given her considerable height. It was, of course, the peculiar Emmaline Watson.

"Mrs. Ryan," she began, staring beyond me into the hallway, "we have come to talk with you about your work here in this – what do you call it? Hospice?"

I bid them enter and welcomed them into my office. I was certainly puzzled by this queer and sudden interest. They sat, and declining my offer of tea, began to ask me questions about the nature of our work with the women of the neighbourhood. It soon became clear that this was not a sudden interest. Evidently, my work had been the topic of conversation among the more genteel women of Baltimore for some time. And indeed, it was not necessarily looked upon as the most suitable occupation for a woman of my means. Naturally, as the conversation progressed, I noted myself becoming more and more fractious. That one ought to consider a leisurely life more appropriate than devoting one's life to a charitable occupation was unacceptable to me. That perspective, however, did not seem to really capture their motives.

"Mrs. Ryan," said Mrs. Watson, "you seem to believe that what you are doing here is a step forward for these women and for women in general. I must say that you must have a very different view of women than do we." She gestured toward the other women. "We have come to serve notice to you that we will be watching you with a keen eye. Should you be found to be doing anything immoral or illegal, the proper authorities shall step in. This I promise you."

I was dumbstruck. It was infuriating enough to be visited by representatives of the local medical establishment, but it was equally, if not more, repulsive to be visited by members of my own sex who were, as far as I could see, nothing more than appendages to their husbands – not exactly what I deemed to be an occupation to engender pride. I quickly gathered my thoughts so as to respond in as forceful a way as I could.

"Mrs. Watson," I said, rising so that I would be taller than she this time, "first, you have no business to come here, into my place of business, and tell me that you will be watching me. You have no business to pass judgment on me at all, in any activity in which I might participate. Your

213

opinion on the matter of what I am doing here is of no consequence to me. And, who do you believe yourself to be to come in here and tell me what is moral or immoral? The very thought of you taking the higher moral ground on this issue is repugnant and contemptible. Perhaps you should consider having this discussion with your own husband."

Fearing that I may have said too much, I moved to the door and opened it, then stood aside to allow them ample room to pass. "When you can prove to me that you have something better to offer these women, then I shall listen to you. Until then, I wish you good day and ask that you do not darken my doorstep again. Am I clear?"

"It is now my turn to ask you, Mrs. Ryan, who you think you are to be standing there pretending to be – what is it that these ignorant women call you? Dr. Bridget? As far as I can see, you are impersonating a physician, and I shall see that all appropriate consequences visit themselves upon your sorry head." She arose and pulled herself up to her considerable height, filling the room with her bulk as she did so.

I noted with some satisfaction that she sported a large, black mole on the side of her cheek, adding to her unbecoming countenance. It seemed appropriate somehow.

"Our group has ways of finding out who is spreading the godless gospel of controlling motherhood."

Our group? What did she mean by this? Was she some kind of crusader for a religious-based morality squad? I shivered at the thought, but thought better of engaging her further in conversation about any matter at all.

They filed past me, with me having to move out of the way to let Mrs. Watson through. When they were gone, and I had shut the door firmly behind them, I leaned against the door frame for a moment, contemplating our odd discussion. It seemed a very natural thing for me that women who were in a position to be of service should do so to help the plight of those less fortunate. Was I really such an oddity?

THIRTY-TWO

AUGUST 1835

I next saw Ned one drizzly summer afternoon in August. He had sent a letter to me via Virginia asking me to meet him. Telling no one of my plans, I set out from the hospice to the cemetery where he was waiting on a bench under a tree.

As I approached him, I noted that despite the humidity and heat of this damp summer day, Ned was dressed completely in black, his cravat wrapped around his neck as if to keep out the dampness. Lost as he seemed to be in his thoughts, he did not see me until I was very nearly upon him. I called out to him, but he failed to hear. When he finally looked up, I thought I could discern worry in his eyes, but he quickly smiled when he spied me. Again, I wondered about the innermost workings of this poet's mind.

He arose and greeted me warmly, kissing my hand and then my cheek. I returned his affection and he bid me sit beside him on the damp bench. I did so.

"Bride, I am so gladdened by your presence. I have things to discuss with you that are of great significance to my life. I could not leave without speaking to you for what might be the last time in a very long time at least – perhaps even forever."

I was alarmed and wondered if he were sick. "But where are you going, Ned?"

He took my hand in his as he spoke. "I have been honoured with a position in Richmond."

"You are returning home?"

It was as if a dark cloud had moved across his face. "I am a Bostonian. Richmond is not my home."

I had not realized the full extent of his great sensitivity to the issue of his home. In spite of having spent his childhood in Richmond with the Allans, I believed it was his unpleasant experiences with his foster father that did not allow him to think of it as his home.

"But why Richmond, then?"

"I have been given a position as editor – actually assistant editor, but for all intents and purposes, I shall be the editor – with the *Southern Literary Messenger*. A Mr. Thomas White, the magazine's publisher, has recognized the extent to which I might be able to contribute to the success of his endeavour. He is, after all, a mere printer. I, on the other hand, am a man of letters. Together, perhaps we can make a go of his enterprise." He smiled, looking proud of himself.

"But what do you know about being an editor, Ned Poe?" I knew I was likely reacting in a more churlish manner than I would have liked to be evident, but I was feeling uncomfortable with this turn of events.

He dropped my hand. "I had thought that you might be at least happy for me at this modicum of success that has finally entered my life."

"Oh, Ned, of course I am. It is just that I see you as a poet. Poets are not editors."

"I am much more than a poet, Bride. I have had several pieces already published in this publication and intend on becoming a great asset to the critical literary field in America."

I arose from the bench and walked across the path. I picked a stray daisy weighted down by a mantle of raindrops. Thunder roared in the distance, and I wondered how long it would be before we were drenched.

"Then you must go, of course," I said finally.

Ned arose from the bench and walked over to where I was now pretending to sniff the pathetic little flower. He put his arm around my shoulders, and we walked slowly down the path together.

"There is one other thing that I have yet to divulge to you, Bride."

He stopped walking and dropped his arm from my shoulder. Leaving the path, he wended his way between the headstones that marked the resting places of so many fallen human beings. He crouched down beside a newly-filled grave and took in his hand a clump of damp earth. He seemed deeply lost in thought as he squeezed the mud out between his fingers.

I stood still on the path, my arms crossed upon my chest, waiting for him to ready himself for what had all the makings of a confession. Finally, Ned wiped the mud from his hand onto the grass adjoining the grave and stood.

Without actually looking at me, he tucked his right hand into the low neckline of his jacket and began. "It is close to ten years that you and I have known one another, is it not? Yes, I have come to love you well over those years, despite the abyss that separates us. Indeed, I do believe that you have greater depth of knowledge of my soul than even I do – certainly than any other living person. I fight my demons nightly, Bride, and it is only thoughts of you that keep me away from the brandy most nights. I have lived in hope for many years that you and I would marry one day. But you have moved on in your life, and I in mine. How far on I have moved, I have yet to tell you." He looked at my face for the first time since he had begun his speech. "What I am trying so awkwardly to tell you is that I am truly, deeply and irrevocably in love."

I opened my mouth to protest when he continued quickly.

"I am planning to marry Virginia."

The words hung in the air like a tiny bird caught on a stiff gust of wind in a winter storm. Virginia? Surely I had heard him wrong. Surely this grown man, as old as I, could not be telling me that he was in love with a child. It was grotesque – more grotesque even than any plot he could concoct for his poems or stories. Perhaps he had finally lost sight of where the fantasies of his mind stopped, and the reality of this world began. I decided to maintain a composed approach to this incongruous conversation.

"I thought I heard you say that you said that you are in love with Virginia," I said finally. "Since such a thing is impossible, perhaps you could correct this clear misunderstanding."

He walked over toward me and took my arm. "You do not misunderstand, Bride. I resolve to make Virginia my wife. And she is as deeply in love with me as I am with her."

"Virginia in love? She is thirteen years old, Ned." I shook off his arm and walked ahead of him. Turning around again to face him, I said, "And she is your cousin, in case that fact had slipped your mind. It is unseemly."

"I am surprised at you, Bride. You, of all people, who care little for what the world thinks of you. How can you stand there and judge me because something is 'unseemly' according to an arbitrary set of conventions? I had never thought of you as conventional in any way."

I took a deep breath and stood my ground. "The age gap between the two of you is unacceptable."

"Unacceptable? To whom? Surely not to you, one who is so much younger than her husband? Surely not to the woman who refuted my proposal all those years ago? Surely not to the woman who professes to love me through all these years, and yet has never allowed much more than a chaste kiss to pass between us? Surely it cannot be unacceptable to you, Bridget Ryan." His voice rose with emotion as I had never heard from Ned before in all the years of our acquaintance.

I collapsed on the nearest bench just as a clap of thunder roared overhead, and the heavens finally opened. A flash of lightning illuminated Ned's face for the briefest of seconds, permitting me to see the determination on it. I shook my head. I could not fathom his reasoning.

He sat down beside me and tried to shield me from the rain. His wrath seemed to have washed away with the first large splashes of rain.

"Please understand. I had no control over my deepening love for Virginia, nor she over her love for me."

"Have you told Siobhan?"

He took in a breath that I could hear quite plainly. "I have not. I had hoped that you might tell her of this. I have not had the face to confront her on any matter – much less one of this nature – since we fell out."

I shook my head in exasperation with this man, whom I believed to be acting in a completely childish manner. Perhaps he and Virginia were, indeed, suited for one another!

"When will you be married?"

Ned went on to explain to me that they had no concrete plans as yet. He would leave within a fortnight for Richmond and settle himself. Then, after finding suitable accommodation, he would send for Virginia and Maria – Muddy, he called her. He would write to me.

I had a feeling of deep foreboding about this pending move and the upcoming nuptials, but Ned was right after all. I was hardly in a position to pass judgment on his behaviour. He was right – I rarely cared what other people thought of my own actions; I should not play judge and jury to his decisions.

I was unsure what to say to him at this juncture. I knew that he might be correct in that this might, indeed, be our final encounter. Only God knew where he would end up.

Finally, I kissed him passionately full on the mouth, and he was dumbstruck and perhaps a bit bewildered even as I left him sitting there on the bench, the rain dripping mercilessly from his nose and tendrils of hair.

That night I slept well – better than I had in some time. I did not ruminate about the activities of the day, as was my usual condition. I thought briefly about Ned and the preposterous life he had set up for himself, and about young, naïve Virginia, who had always been in love with her dashing cousin, or so it had always appeared to me. I did wish them well.

I slept the sleep of the dead.

THIRTY-THREE

SEPTEMBER 1835

It was the darkest year I had known since the death of my dear father. I could take joy in nothing. So deep was my despondency that some mornings, it was more than I could cope with to even leave my bed. Indeed, it seemed hardly surprising to me that I should feel somewhat discouraged, as the hospice had been subjected to weekly visits – or should I say inspections – from one Emmaline Watson or one of her associates. The harassment was approaching monumental proportions in my mind.

When Mrs. Watson first returned to the hospice some four weeks after the first visit, I thought it would be my best approach to be as accommodating as I could. As much as I had the overwhelming urge to smack her haughty face, I held myself back and offered her tea. I did not know until after several more weeks of constant visits that her group of "righteous women," as she liked to call them (frequently), had taken me on as a kind of project. It was their mission in life, it seemed, to ensure that I did nothing to challenge their view of morality in the world. As angry as this made me, I realized that if I took them on and began a war of sorts, I would jeopardize my ability to continue providing much-needed services to people who had come to depend on the clinic.

After this second inspection, Siobhan and I sat down to discuss our options. She was becoming as militant as I was in her need to see that the right thing was properly acknowledged and allowed. I cautioned her about the necessity of being ready to fight if a fight were in the offing. We were not, however, ready yet. So, our approach, for now, would be to smile and cooperate, as if we welcomed their presence.

My feelings of sadness and discouragement, however, seemed to me to be disproportionate even to these events. I had always been able to cope with setbacks before, but now I had lost interest even in some of the activities at the clinic. I delegated more and more authority to Siobhan, who herself seemed to be thriving in her new position. I had trouble concentrating and began to question the wisdom of almost everything that I had done or had planned to do.

When I tossed and turned at night – night after night – John's concern began to grow. He suggested that we take a vacation to the seaside, but I declined. At any other time in my life, I would have jumped at the chance to walk along a beach and sink my feet into the cool, wet sand, letting all my cares flow out with each receding wave. But I had not the energy to even contemplate preparing for such a trip. Thus, for several months, I wallowed in my own depression and could not see that light at the end.

If I had thought myself at a low point through the summer, I did not know that I would receive a letter mid-September – a letter that would first sink me even deeper before I hit that bottom and began to bounce back up.

I was feeling a bit better that morning when Wimpy, elated at this seemingly positive turn in my mental health, brought the letter to me in the breakfast room. I was actually enjoying my coffee for the first time in months and savoured the last drop before unfolding the large wad of paper.

"September 1, 1836
Richmond, Virginia

My Dearest Bride,
There are so many things I long to talk over with you, my dearest friend. I find my position here in Richmond provides me with a great improvement in my circumstances, and I believe that I am well-suited for

this kind of editorial occupation. Thomas White has taken a rare interest in me, as I believe I have contributed greatly to his publication. He also has a ravishing daughter – a graceful, blue-eyed creature called Eliza. She and I have become friends.

With all of this to be grateful for, I was despondent beyond comprehension when I received a letter from Muddy telling me of her intention to consider the offer of one Neilson Poe, my learned cousin, to provide lodging and even education for my darling Virginia and a home for her. This cannot happen! I should never be allowed to gaze upon Virginia again. Like you, Neilson disapproves of my marrying Virginia, but I must have her as my little wifey and bring her and Muddy to live with me here in Richmond.

They have cruelly torn away my last grasp on life. I have no more desire to live. And I will not.

Console me quickly, my dearest Bride, or perhaps it will be too late. I return to Baltimore forthwith to consecrate a marriage with my cousin. I hope that you will see your way clear to provide succour to me in my time of need. I shall send word of the wedding to you through Siobhan.

I remain your loving friend,
Ned"

I could not bear it. Ned asking for my help in his pursuit of such folly! Perhaps it would be for the best if he actually followed through with his occasional threats to end his life. I threw the offending letter across the room and got up from my chair. As I walked past the buffet, laid out with my morning coffee, I noticed my reflection in the glass. It stopped me in my tracks. I had taken little of my usual interest in my appearance in recent months, and the mirror told the tale. I had aged almost beyond my ability to recognize myself. My eyes were ringed by dark shadows, and my hair was wilder than was usual even for me. Even my dress was dishevelled. How could I have allowed this to happen? More to the point, how could I reverse it?

I immediately returned to my room and washed my face. I sat before the mirror at my dressing table to take stock. I looked deeply into that reflection in the glass. Something inside my mind – and more importantly, I believe inside my heart – thudded to a reality I had not noticed before. I was a grown woman and totally responsible for my own life. I could let circumstances overpower what might happen in my life, or I could remain in control of how I respond to them. In that moment, I made a decision to change my responses. No matter what happened, the whirling circumstances of the world would no longer control me.

When John returned home that evening, it seemed he had expected to dine alone, as I had been spending more and more time in my room and less time dining with him of late. When he walked into the parlour, and I offered him a sherry, I could see by the look on his face that he was astonished to see me thus.

"Bridget," he said, taking the proffered glass, "you look wonderful. You seem to be feeling better."

"Much," I said, sipping my own sherry. "I have decided to burden you no more with a wife who is wasting away. I am born anew as it were."

"To what do we owe this sudden change in circumstance?"

"Well, I do not believe that it is a change in circumstance at all," I said, taking my usual chair by the fire. "I believe – no, I know – that it is rather a change in how I am choosing to see my situation."

"I am very glad that you are feeling that way, my dear." John placed his glass on the table beside his chair and removed a letter from his breast pocket before sitting down opposite me. "This came today, and I wondered at the wisdom of even telling you about it." He did not immediately offer it to me. "I believe that you may be able to help."

He passed me the sheaf of pages, which I unfolded to find two letters enclosed. The first was from my Uncle Liam to John.

"September 2, 1836
University of Virginia

Dear John,

I hope that this letter finds you and Bridget well and happy in your home in Baltimore. I dearly wish that I could say the same of Grace and myself as we continue our residency at the university. My work has been as fulfilling as it has been frustrating for the past decade, but I am unhappy to tell you that Grace does not share my enthusiasm for the academic life. This is why I am writing.

As Bridget may have told you, Grace has longed for a child with whom we could share our lives. I, too, have wished it, but it had not happened. Then, some months ago, it came to our attention that Grace was, after all these years, with child. We were elated. Then the problems began. I will not regale you with a full accounting of these women's problems, but we feared that she might lose the child. Now she is confined to bed on the advice of her physician. She, however, wishes to have Bridget with her.

She has written the enclosed letter to Bridget, to which I fear Bridget might feel obligated to respond by immediately leaving you and her work behind to minister to my wife. While I would welcome Bridget's assistance in this matter (more than you can ever imagine), I have no wish to cause problems for you in your life in Baltimore.

226

I am asking only that you yourself make the decision whether or not to show this letter to Bridget so that the decision can be a calculated one. If you choose not to convey this information to Bridget, I shall understand and shall convey Bridget's apologies to Grace. Should Bridget agree to come, and you support her in that decision, Grace and I should be most grateful.

We await with anticipation your response in due course.

Yours respectfully,
Liam Ryan, Professor"

I contemplated the words between the lines and truly did not know whether to be pleased that Grace thought so highly of me or to be angry that Liam thought that my husband ought to make such a decision for me rather than me making it for myself. I recognized, however, that John would not have chosen to make such a decision for me himself, and that is why he was showing me Liam's letter without preface.

I unfolded Grace's letter enclosed within her husband's. "My dear sister in heart, Bridget," it began.

Tears welled up in my eyes as I read her pathetic words. It was not so much what she said, but the feeling conveyed therein. Liam had been right: I felt compelled to immediately leave everything behind here in Baltimore and go to my dear aunt – and friend – in her time of need. I felt strongly that she might not succeed in being delivered of a healthy baby if I did not provide any assistance I could.

I passed the letter to John. He drew his glasses from his breast pocket and read the short piece quickly. He looked at me and nodded. He knew what I must do.

THIRTY-FOUR

CHARLOTTESVILLE, VIRGINIA, AUTUMN, 1835

It was not quite ten years since I had last seen the campus of the University of Virginia. Much had changed, and yet the ambience of a place of higher learning still held for me the same kind of nostalgia. It was a reminiscence of something lost, but yet never really grasped either.

I had taken the train to Richmond and the coach to Charlottesville, where Uncle Liam met me in the town. It had been a very long and jarring trip, and yet I was buoyed by the prospect of seeing almost-forgotten places once again and remembering a time in my life that I had thought I might never be permitted to revisit. When first I laid my eyes upon Uncle Liam, I thought that I was seeing a ghost – the spirit of my father. As he had aged these few years, Uncle Liam resembled ever more closely his older brother. I embraced him with extra fervour, and it was clear to me he was much relieved by my arrival. It was not so much what he said, although he did speak; it was more his demeanour. The furrow in his brow that I noted the moment I spied him seemed to soften ever so slightly as we made our way to his home and rekindled our friendship. We took a kind of tour through the streets of Charlottesville and out around the university on our way to see Grace, who awaited us at home. I was riveted to the scenery every inch of the way, never realizing just how much that year in Charlottesville had meant to me.

The university buildings that had been under construction those years ago were all finished now. The grand rotunda of the library was even grander in its completed state than I could have imagined, and all of the buildings around the quadrangle now boasted grand columns and facades that were stately yet hospitable.

According to Uncle Liam, the university library also boasted a fine and very large collection of volumes on every subject. I was green with envy.

Uncle Liam and Grace had moved to a fine house off the campus. The student body had grown in size, and thus the more senior professors were no longer required to patrol the campus during the night, breaking up fights and meting out discipline to unruly and often drunken students. Evidently, things had improved greatly since my own brush with higher learning.

I was uncertain what would await me at their home. Uncle Liam said little about Grace during our journey except that she would be delighted to see me. I asked only how she was, to which he responded simply, "She will be much better now that you are here."

We soon arrived in front of a pleasant, white clapboard house surrounded by a picket fence that enclosed a magnificent garden. I remembered Grace's interest in the garden at the house in New York and smiled at the reminiscence. Although the garden was past its prime for this year, it was easy to see that at the height of summer, it must be magnificent. The unseasonably warm weather, however, had nurtured the roses just a little longer this year, and fat, pink blossoms dripped from the climbing bush that adorned the arbour marking the entrance to the front garden.

As we moved closer to the door, I could see that a few weeds had taken over parts of the herbaceous border edging the walkway. Uncle Liam, noticing where my eyes had fallen, apologized for his lack of horticultural aptitude. It seems that, as a result of Grace's recent confinement, it had fallen to him to tend to the gardens, a task he completed with some trepidation regarding his own proficiency.

While their home was smaller than my own in Baltimore, it was indeed a handsome and welcoming abode. Grace's style had developed into a kind of comfortable, yet sophisticated country charm.

Uncle Liam led me up the wide staircase to the second floor to settle me in their guest room. The room was all in white, a colour (or non-colour depending upon one's own eye) that dominated the entire house. The canopy adorning the large bed was white, as was the coverlet and the filmy curtains at the window. Even the wood was white. It conjured a brief picture of a snowy day.

I quickly settled my things in the room, as I was anxious to see Grace. Uncle Liam had gone to see if she might be awake and prepared for my arrival. He returned presently to tell me that Grace was waiting anxiously to see me. I smoothed my dress, checked my wayward curls in the glass and followed him down the hall.

Unlike the rooms I had seen up until now, the room where Grace had taken up occupancy was not white, rather a study in yellow. Even the wallpaper bore tiny yellow flowers. And amid the profusion of yellow pillows and coverlets on the large bed sat my young Aunt Grace, who, by my reckoning, had aged more than what might have been expected. However, I was heartened to find that her countenance bore little of the hopelessness that she had conveyed in her letter to me. She seemed genuinely happy to see me, and an animation took over her face the minute we locked eyes.

I went to her bedside and threw my arms around her neck. I had not realized the extent to which I had missed our friendship. Although we had corresponded, I had not seen Grace in several years.

"Bridget, I am so heartened to see you at last. I have heard of your work in Baltimore and knew that only you would be able to assist me in this important time of need." She hugged me tightly.

When finally she loosened her grip on my neck, I sat back on the side of the bed and looked at her.

"I, too, am delighted to be here to help if I can. And I am very happy to see you." I looked around the room and the drapes that were drawn across the window. "How long is it since you have taken to your bed, Grace?"

"The doctor put me to bed – I do not remember." She turned to Liam, who was still standing near the door, watching us. "Liam, how long is it that I have been confined thus?"

Uncle Liam thought for a moment, then said, "I believe it is two months now, Grace."

Grace was pale, and ominous circles darkened her usually lovely eyes. She bore a pallor the colour of old snow in March. After Uncle Liam took his leave and we were alone, I began to question Grace in a most clinical way about her health and the health of this growing baby.

It seemed that she was, by my calculations, some six months along in her pregnancy and had suffered nothing more than continued vapours and a tiny spotting to cause the doctor to put her to bed. Now, she was bored and sore. She had not left the house in some two months and had hardly left this room. Her doctor had suggested she maintain semi-darkness and a regular dose of calomel to "keep things moving" inside her, according to how Grace interpreted her doctor.

I examined Grace as I would any woman who came to me six months along. The baby's heart sounded strong, and to my hands, the position seemed normal. I asked her to get up.

A frightened look stole over her face like a cloud across the sun. With encouragement, I helped her walk around the room once, then back to bed. I opened the curtains to let in the sunshine and even opened the window.

"Things are about to change around here, Grace."

She looked a bit hesitant, but I believe I detected a kind of hopefulness as well. And things did, indeed, change.

By the time I had been there one week, Grace had been out of bed every day and joined us for dinner for the first time. By the end of the third week, she took all her meals with us, and we were planning a drive out into the country.

Alone in my room at night, I wrote to John to tell him of Grace's condition, and to Siobhan to ensure that she kept me abreast of activities at the hospice. I had received one letter from her regaling me with stories of the women, including one visit from Mrs. Watson's contingent. I was worried about what kind of action Mrs. Watson might take against my clinic now that I was absent from my duties (and, truth be told, about the care that must be taken with some of our materials). Still, in her letter, Siobhan assured me not to worry and that she was quite capable of handling such situations. Nevertheless, I was troubled. I did not know how long I ought to stay away, yet I was unsure how I could leave before the birth of Grace's baby, nor did I truly *want* to leave before her confinement. I decided to leave that issue for a time and come back to consider my options in a week or two.

The day of the planned trip to the country dawned bright and crisp. The autumn sun was slanting deeply, giving the sky and everything it illuminated a kind of golden glow. We had decided to take a picnic lunch with us and brave the cool breezes on a blanket.

I had forgotten how much I had loved this place. Since I spent most of my life in cities, a trip like this into the country was a stimulation to the senses. I breathed in the fresh air and took in the visual marvels of the Blue Ridge Mountains, a sight that I never had a chance to behold in Baltimore.

Grace insisted that we tour the campus again so that she and I could reminisce about the times she had tried to chaperone me, only to fall asleep under a shady tree in the quadrangle. As we neared the university setting, she turned to me.

"Bridget, whatever happened to that mysterious young man with whom you kept company that year? Did he make a career in the military?"

I had wondered how long it would be until Grace brought up Ned and my relationship with him. "No, he did not," I said. "He has assumed a career as a literary editor, as far as I know."

"Did he marry?"

I believe I may have snorted in reply, but neither Grace nor Liam, who was maneuvering the carriage around a dog who had chosen the middle of the road to bask in the sun, seemed to notice.

"Not as yet," I said.

"Do you hear of him regularly, then?" Grace continued her probing.

"As a matter of fact, his aunt and cousin are women to whom I have ministered from time to time. So, yes, I do hear of him."

Grace turned in her seat, adjusted her lap throw and looked at me carefully. "Do I detect a bit of reticence in talking about this man? Is he the one whom you let get away, Bridget?"

"Could we talk of other matters, Grace? I find any conversation about Ned to be somewhat tiresome."

She ignored my protestations. "I remember him as quite a bright young man. And a handsome one."

"As I recall," said Uncle Liam, "he was also quite a poet. Has he published any poetry?"

I resigned myself to continuing this line of conversation and told them of his books of poetry, avoiding the topic of his impending nuptials. I feared that my response might give away more of my feelings than even I was sure of at this point. When we arrived at the campus, Grace insisted on taking me on a walking tour of the new structures as well as a walk down memory lane.

I had the strangest sensation as I followed my own footsteps of what now seemed so many years ago – a lifetime ago. So much had changed since those days when I thought that the world had done me wrong. I believed I had grown up significantly, but now that I was reliving a part of my past, I felt emotions I had buried deep within me. I felt a kind of emptiness when I thought of Ned and wondered if I had truly loved him – if I truly did still love him.

I shook off the momentary melancholy, returned to the present, and gave due consideration to what kind of a life I might have had in Ned's company. Indeed, though he liked to drink and was prone to hopelessness and dire unhappiness, I somehow believed that much of this was the result of his penniless existence. This would not have happened in my company. I could have provided for him. I could have been a kind of literary sponsor. Perhaps I had been cheated out of such a role. None of this could I share with Grace or Uncle Liam, so I pondered such questions alone within my thoughts.

We found a lovely spot beside the river in the sunshine, whose warmth we did need this day. As Grace's bulk was beginning to impede her movement, I helped Uncle Liam to set out the picnic things.

When we had set out the basket and the implements, Uncle Liam and I assisted Grace to a comfortable position on the blanket. I opened the basket and spread the food out in front of us. We were dining on cured ham and roast duck, accompanied by pickled beets and cornbread. For dessert, there was pound cake.

The sun was high now, and I appreciated its warmth. As I helped myself to another pickled beet, I again considered how long I would stay here and determined that I had no choice but to remain until after the birth. That would mean that I would be spending Christmas here in Charlottesville. I would have to write to John to see how he felt about this.

In due course, I received a letter from John, agreeing wholeheartedly that I must stay and that he would join us for Christmas. I was terribly happy to read this, as I had not realized how much I would miss him. Uncle Liam and Grace were delighted that they would have a family house full for Christmas.

And so the fall turned into winter, and Grace and I prepared the house for a Christmas celebration. We gathered pine boughs from the back garden and holly berries from the large bushes along the fence. When we had completed festooning the mantle in the parlour and the balustrade, the house began to feel – and to smell– like Christmases buried deep within my memory. I had but a vague recollection of my mother doing just such activities that Father had not continued after her death. I was at once happy and sad at the memory.

Just as he had promised to do, John arrived on Christmas Eve, weary from his journey but, I believe, happy to see me. He told me that the house was not the same without my presence.

We celebrated in style that year. Surrounded by relatives in the persons of Uncle Liam and an ever-changing multitude of their friends from the university, we ate and drank happily. I even accompanied Uncle Liam, Grace and John for midnight mass on Christmas Eve and was once again swept back into my childhood memories. I had not even been inside a church since my father's funeral, much less attended mass. When I happened to mention this fact, Grace clucked at me, and Uncle Liam wisely kept his silence.

The turkey had just been removed from the table. Christmas dinner was drawing to a close when Grace suddenly shrieked and placed both her hands on her belly. It was time.

I was very grateful that evening for John's presence, as it was not an easy birth, and Grace was neither a good nor willing patient. It fell to me to comfort her and keep her focused so that John could actually deliver the little child. And little it was.

When the twenty-four-hour ordeal was over, Grace had been delivered of a scrawny little girl whom she and Uncle Liam immediately named Mary Catherine Bridget Ryan. As I looked at her with her tiny face screwed up into a frown and her tuft of dark hair, I tried to comprehend what it must be like to long for something as Grace had longed for a child. I, on the other hand, did not long for a child, a fact that, through our conversations this fall, Grace had not yet accepted as the truth of my feelings. I did not have any desire to be a mother and was grateful that as long as I was married to John, this would not likely happen.

John returned to Baltimore three days after the birth. I stayed on for another fortnight to help Grace find the appropriate help and to provide her with moral support, although such support did not seem needed. As unprepared as she had seemed for the actual birth, she seemed to take to the maternal role extremely well. She was a born mother, and it was very nice to see.

When I finally had to bid her farewell, I was torn between wanting to return to my normal life in Baltimore and not wanting to leave this little enclave of family happiness. In spite of Mary Catherine's high-pitched crying, I had become very fond of the little one, and I had come to depend on my relationship with Grace. But I knew that this was not the reality of my life, and I had to leave.

I retraced my steps from earlier in the fall, taking the coach to Richmond and the train from Richmond to home. I had several hours to wait at the station in Richmond before my train was scheduled to leave (although the schedules tended to be somewhat erratic, to say the least), so I decided to take tea at a restaurant I knew to be next door to the station. I did not like the station as it was drafty and damp, with hard benches and not much else.

I threw my muffler around my neck and picked up my bags. As I reached the door, I was startled by the door opening in front of me. The black-clad man held the door

236

for me, his head bowed to protect it from the considerable wind.

"Excuse me," I said as he held the door for me to exit.

"Bride?" Came the familiar voice.

I dropped my case in astonishment: it was Ned himself. And he seemed thrilled to see me.

He stooped to pick up my fallen case and then ushered me back inside the building. "What are you doing in Richmond?" He said, his hand still on my back.

I told him about Grace and her baby. "And Ned, whatever are you doing here at the train station?"

"I am going back to Baltimore to get Virginia and Muddy."

"Are they coming to live with you here in Richmond?" I asked, not really wanting to know the answer.

"I fervently wish it to be so," he said. "Please, Bride, will you not sit with me for a while so that we might catch one another up on our lives of late?"

I considered this request. Again, I was torn – I truly did wish to spend some time with Ned, but wondered at the prudence of such a gesture. Finally, I asked him to join me at the hotel next door for tea, as I was chilled to the bone by this time and did not relish the thought of sitting here on a cold, hard bench for any length of time, even to catch up with an old friend. He agreed to join me.

When we were settled at a table in the hotel dining room, I began to ask him about his editing job.

"I am sad to say that I am no longer in the employ of the *Southern Literary Messenger*, but I hope that when I return with Virginia and Muddy, Mr. White will see fit to restore me to my position. I have been very good for his circulation." He seemed proud of such an accomplishment.

"Are you so certain that Virginia and Muddy will wish to move to Richmond? After all, Baltimore is their home."

Just as I had feared, Ned planned to bring Virginia back with him as his wife. We had been through this before, and he knew well how I felt about such a liaison. I was suddenly angry again and did not want to sit there talking with him any longer, but my manners dictated that we should finish our tea and return to the platform together. Unfortunately, Ned also wished to spend the entire trip sitting with me on the train, which he did.

When the trip was finally over and the train pulled into the station in Baltimore, I could see through the window that John was waiting for me on the platform. As I stepped down from the car, smiling at John, he was looking past me with a kind of scowl on his face. I turned slightly, and it was clear. His eyes were locked on Ned's.

THIRTY-FIVE

BALTIMORE, MAY 1836

Since my return from Richmond early in the new year, I had taken the habit of going less and less frequently to the clinic. Upon my return, it became increasingly clear to me that this phase of my work was complete. Siobhan had cemented herself firmly as the matron in charge of the hospice. She had been able, in her calm way, to ensure that Mrs. Watson's ladies were placated in their search for contraband literature on preventing conception. I felt like excess baggage.

I continued to provide the funding necessary to keep such an enterprise going, but confined my own work to visiting patients in their homes and delivering babies.

It was my habit to keep meticulous records of every baby I delivered, and I spent a good deal of my time sitting at my desk in the breakfast room completing my ledgers. I was thus occupied one bright May morning when Mrs. Wimpole announced Siobhan's arrival at the front door. I bid her show my friend in.

Siobhan's rosy cheeks were rosier than ever if that were possible, and her eyes sparkled. She clutched in her hand a large wad of paper, folded as if it were a letter. I bid her take a seat and poured her some coffee. She grimaced as she took a sip, being a tea drinker herself.

"You are looking well this morning, Siobhan," I said, taking another scone and applying raspberry jam in a meticulous circle.

"Yes, yes indeed, I am well this morning," she said, reaching for a scone. She began plucking raisins out of the scone before buttering it. "I suppose you're wondering why I've come so early, I'll wager." She smiled conspiratorially.

"What is going on?" I could not help but smile. She must have good news. A new beau, perhaps?

She took a bite of the scone and then unfolded the wad of paper. "Bridget, you'll never be able to guess what is written on these papers, you will not. Never, even if you should live to be a hundred!"

"An awful thought in itself," I said, intrigued by her coyness. "Tell me of your news. It is obviously of a happy nature.

"Here on these papers, it says that a publisher wants to publish some of those stories of mine. You know the ones, Bridget. You were always telling me that I should write them down. Well," she said proudly, "I took your advice. And here's what's happened!"

I took the papers that she offered for my viewing. It was indeed an offer to print the stories she had submitted – children's stories. I was astonished and proud of her.

"Tell me everything. How did this come about?" I asked.

Siobhan settled back in the dining chair and took off her hat and gloves to prepare for the telling. It seems that my absence from Baltimore in the fall had had some unexpected outcomes, to say the least.

When Ned had returned from Richmond to take Muddy and Virginia with him, he had stopped by the hospice to see Siobhan. According to Siobhan, they had mended any rift that may have fallen between the two, and Ned was as gracious and congenial as he ever was in his best times. They had spent an afternoon taking tea together, during which time Siobhan told him of her passion for telling stories. Like me, Ned encouraged her to write them down. Then, he generously offered to take them back to Richmond to see if Mr. White had any friends in the publishing business who might be interested in such stories.

I was puzzled by this unusual turn of events. It seemed to me to be quite out of character for Ned to be offering to see another writer's success in the face of his failure. Perhaps I had judged him too harshly.

In any case, Mr. White had indeed had a friend whose new publishing venture was very interested in the potential for selling children's books. They were quite taken by her stories, although they were insisting that she publish them under her initial only so that no one would know that she was a woman doing this work. This did not seem to bother her at all. It caused the hairs on my neck to bristle, but it was not really my business.

"Oh, Bridget, this is the best thing that ever happened to me, it is!" She suddenly looked stricken. "Oh, I don't mean that working for you at the hospice is any less good!"

I was not bothered by her evident excitement over her good fortune; I did, however, wonder if she would continue her work with me. She assured me that she would and that the money associated with such an endeavour as writing was inconsequential. I doubted that, in her case at least.

"I've been in contact with Edgar to tell him of my good fortune, and he has written me back with good news of his own," she said, picking up a de-raisined scone from her china plate and slathering it with butter.

I put down the coffee cup that I had just lifted to my lips.

"Mr. White has taken him back on as editor. Isn't that wonderful? Now he'll not be penniless again." She bit into the scone with obvious pleasure and was quickly forced to wipe excess butter from her lips that oozed from the fragrant morsel.

I nodded, pleased for Ned and took a sip of my coffee. I believed that Ned was truly keen to continue developing his reputation as an editor, though I worried that it might interfere with his more creative endeavours. I nibbled at my scone.

"And," she continued, "Virginia has become his wife. Just two weeks ago. Isn't that wonderful?"

I choked.

PART 2

"And all I loved, I loved alone."
~ Edgar Allan Edgar

ONE

PHILADELPHIA, FEBRUARY-MARCH 1842

I heard little of Ned after his unlikely marriage to Virginia. Something deep within me snapped on that day when I heard of his nuptials. It was as if that long connection through so many years had broken under the weight of his commitment to another woman – if one could truly call a thirteen-year-old girl a woman. Why this disruption had not happened when I married John, I did not understand. I knew only that my relationship with Ned and his mind, so full of grotesque images, would never be the same.

True to his word, he had indeed moved Virginia and Maria to Richmond with him, and for six years, I received a total of three communiqués from him. His first missive was prompted by his move from Richmond to New York in 1837.

Knowing that I possessed a business interest in Gotham, Ned implored me to visit the city forthwith, as Virginia was longing to see me. Naturally, I did not oblige, feeling that, in spite of my inexplicable feelings for this brooding man, it was better that our relationship die out in this way.

The second of the three communiqués from him during those years came to me from yet another address of the Poe household just over a year later. Ned had moved Virginia and Maria again, this time to Philadelphia. Again, he beseeched me to visit as Virginia was in need of the companionship of an old friend. Again, I demurred, wondering at his audacity to even inquire.

The third letter came in June of 1841. In the letter, he included a printed copy of a story he had written. Entitled "The Murders on the Rue Morgue", it was included in an

April 1841 issue of *Graham's Magazine*. I read the story with interest and realized that this kind of murder mystery was unlike any ever written. I found it intriguing, and for a moment I felt again that connection with Ned – but only for a moment. His discourse on the analytical power, which prefaced the actual story, I found to be ponderous and yet pointed.

"The analytical power should not be confounded with simple ingenuity," it read, "for while the analyst is necessarily ingenious, the ingenious man is often remarkably incapable of analysis." These words he had underlined in the copy he had sent to me, and I presumed for my reading that the word "man" could equally refer to a "woman."

I had thought about this for a very long time before replying to his letter, only very briefly, thanking him for the story and assuring him of my well-being.

In fact, at the time of the letter's arrival, I had been in the process of selling the company that had, for so many years, kept both John and me in a manner to which we had become very accustomed. Indeed, the income it continuously provided was well appreciated in our household as John had given up his medical practice and was now spending his days at home by the fire, ageing by the minute as far as I could see. Mr. Bowness's recent death had given me pause to consider the future, and I concluded that an era was over.

It had been less difficult than I had imagined to find an appropriate buyer for such a thriving business. I had been required to visit New York only once to finalize the details, and while in the city, I wondered about Ned's sojourn there. Indeed, I was under the impression that he and his little family still resided in the city. During the four days that the business deliberations kept me there, I was ever mindful of his potential presence. Every time I rounded a corner, I almost expected to come face to face with him, but it was not to be.

After these three letters through the years, I had come to expect them from time to time. Thus, I was not surprised when, in February of 1842, another letter duly arrived from Ned. I had just begun reading its contents, noting an unusually morbid and sombre tone – even from one such as Ned. He was held in the stultifying grip of agony over an apparent illness that Virginia had suffered and was, to all appearances, still suffering.

He wistfully described her sitting beautifully at the piano on a January day when, abruptly and without warning, she had begun to bleed from her mouth.

> *"...the blood bubbled from her mouth – I was certain that she had ruptured something inside that should yet be sound in a woman so young. She fell to the floor, and I, in my horror, beheld her blank stare. I thought for a moment that she was – dead. I kissed her mouth. I heard a piteous wailing and realized that it was emanating from my own lips. When Muddy entered, she found us thus.*
>
> *Since that time, Sissy has not awakened. I am sorely frightened and plead, no beg of you to come to our assistance. I know that if Sissy could hear a medical voice she trusts, it would do her inner voice a world of good – I know that she would open her eyes and look upon me once again.*
>
> *Please take pity on me – or at least on Virginia, who has been your ever respectful friend – and make the trip to her bedside. I, too, would benefit greatly from your presence.*
>
> *As always, your loving servant,*
> *Ned"*

I looked for a long time at the words upon the page. Ned needed me. But deep inside of me, I sensed an unwelcome feeling. I could not quite put my finger on it, as it seemed vague and elusive. I felt almost heady in the knowledge that his marriage to Virginia had not been without its considerable difficulties, just as I thought it would. I had not, however, thought that this was the kind of difficulty he would see as a result and did not wish upon him such distress.

The first person to whom I turned for advice was Siobhan. Over the past years, she had published several books, taken over my duties at the hospice and found herself a wonderful husband whom we all loved dearly. His name was James, and he loved her deeply. They had acquired a modest home some distance from Siobhan's old neighbourhood, and without thinking much about it, I found myself at her door – this time it was I who was seeking advice.

Siobhan was at once sympathetic to Ned's predicament and cautious about any involvement on my part.

"You know how dependent he can be on you," she said as she prepared tea for me in her small, bright kitchen.

"But what about Virginia?" I said, staring at the intricate detailing on the embroidered cloth on her kitchen table. I knew that it was her own handiwork, so diversely talented she seemed to be.

"Yes," she said, sitting with me at the table for a moment. "That is quite a different matter. Virginia was always a lovely little thing – but fragile, at least to my mind. How old would she be now?"

I thought for a moment about her age at the time of their marriage and put her at all of nineteen years by this time. The next thought that entered my head did so unbidden – I wondered if the marriage had ever been consummated. I shook my head as if to loosen the thought from my consciousness and buried it among a whirl of interconnected images of Ned and Virginia and the life that must be their lot.

"I believe she would be nineteen," I said finally.

Siobhan got up to bring the teapot to the table, which she had already set with cups and saucers and pieces of pound cake, which was her particular specialty. She sat down and began to pour the tea. "Nineteen! Is that all? It seems that they have been married for so many years that she ought to be much older, don't you know?"

I did know exactly what Siobhan meant.

"Why would you want to go?" she asked.

"I do not know what you mean. To help, of course."

She looked at me with a kind of knowing look as much as to say that she knew that there was more to my story, which, of course, there was.

"You're curious, you are." She took a large bite of the pound cake and chewed as if most satisfied with it.

"I suppose I am. Is that so wrong? And I might be of some real help to them."

"What can you do that can't be done for them by a local doctor?" she said.

"I believe I can offer a kind of moral support to them in their time of need. Perhaps Virginia does need to hear a familiar voice – see a friend's face. I am certain that she associates me with a pleasant time in her life here in Richmond."

"I can see that you have already made up your mind," Siobhan said, draining her cup. "How does John feel about this?"

How did John feel? I had not yet told him and had, myself, wondered at his likely response. Indeed, he was not well himself and needed me, but perhaps I could be absent for only a short time. Wimpy, although she was old now, too, was still a great asset to our household. She would provide for his needs in my absence, and I would only be gone a short time.

Siobhan had come to know me well over the years of our association, and indeed her role had evolved from that of an apprentice to a friend and confidante, and now even to an adviser from time to time. We had naturally had our

249

difficulties and disagreements over time; the most onerous, perhaps, was the one concerning Ned and his attentions, but we had overcome even jealousy and anger to reach a new level of understanding. As we both took a longer view of Ned and his proclivities, we were able to share our insights rather than hoard them, enabling us to understand one another and our relationships with Ned.

Now, Siobhan was right. I did have every intention of going to Ned as he requested. She wished me well, then bid me provide her with details of his circumstances upon my return.

John was not quite so understanding. He behaved as if he were suspicious of my motives and even my relationship with Ned, although he had no real reason to think we were anything other than old friends. He could not comprehend my decision to go to him (or to his wife, as I put it to him). I finally had to leave him in a sulk as I wrote to Ned of my pending arrival and prepared for my journey.

Within a week, I was ready and set out on the long expedition.

The minute my coach finally neared Ned's home in Philadelphia, I feared that I had made a grave mistake in coming. The house itself was slightly more prosperous-looking than any of Ned's previous abodes – at least those that I had known – and in itself was not cause for me to have such misgivings about my arrival. It was an unprepossessing three-story row house, faced in brick, with white shutters on the windows of the first and second floors. There was a small picket fence enclosing the tiny yard; both the shutters and the fence were in serious need of a coat of paint. None of this surprised me. It was just that a sense of apprehension seemed to be wending its way down my spine from somewhere around my neck, where the hairs began to stand on end as I gazed on Ned's home.

My arrival at the door found Muddy ministering to Virginia, who, although not comatose any longer, was confined to bed and clearly still gravely ill. Ned was not at home but at the magazine where he worked as editor. I was unaccountably relieved that I did not have to face him yet.

Ned had been right on at least one count: Virginia was greatly happy to see me. It seems she had not been able to cultivate any friendships since their arrival in Philadelphia, which was several years ago, and she was lonely and sick.

Indeed, she looked very sick to my eyes. As I sat on the side of her bed and squeezed her hand tightly, I could see that her pallor had deepened over the years, and her usually beautiful violet eyes were sunken in their sockets. She was skin and bones.

Worse, though, was the cough. The minute she began, I knew that she would have difficulty stopping. The cough seemed to start in the deepest part of her chest and soon involved her entire body. Her entire body was wracked with this coughing, and I noted blood on the handkerchief that she put to her mouth. There was no doubt in my mind of her diagnosis: she was suffering from consumption, and with the general state of her health prior to the disease taking hold, I knew in my heart that it would take her life. I wondered how Ned would take this news – or if, indeed, he had already come to terms with it. Surely the local doctor must have told him this.

I left Virginia sleeping fitfully, then made my way down the narrow staircase to the kitchen at the back of the house, where Maria, Ned's Muddy as he called her, was preparing dinner. It seemed that Ned must, indeed, be doing rather better financially than he had been in Baltimore. Although the house was not opulent in any way, it was much larger than Maria's lodgings in Wilks Street, and they seemed to have more amenities – or at least more rooms.

The kitchen, where Maria bent over a pot on the woodstove, was small but adequate as far as I could see. Unfortunately, Maria's bulk made the kitchen seem even smaller as she filled a room.

"Maria," I said as I stood in the doorway, "what did the doctor say about Virginia's condition?"

"Her condition? He said little except that she was very sick," she said, putting her hands on her back as if to stretch it out from all the stooping she was doing.

"Did he treat her in any way?"

"Treat? Yes, oh yes, he did treat her."

I waited for her to continue, and when it became clear she would need prodding for information, I continued. "What was the nature of the treatment?" Even as I asked, after my examination of Virginia, I feared that I already knew. I was in total disagreement with the current approaches to treating consumption.

"The nature of the treatment – yes, the treatment," she said as if trying to collect her thoughts. "A purging medicine, I believe." She thought for a moment. "Oh, yes, also bloodletting, but only the once. You see," she said, lowering her bulky frame gently into the chair by the stove, "Eddy became frantic when he saw her blood. He seemed to think her life was flowing out with every drop." She shook her head. "It was almost frightening to see."

Just as I had feared, I did not believe that either of these approaches to treatment would help her in the least. Perhaps Ned's hysteria at seeing the blood was not as irrational as it seemed to Maria.

"Maria," I said slowly, taking the seat on the far side of the table against the wall opposite the stove, "when the doctor was telling you how sick Virginia is, did Edgar really understand the gravity?"

"Gravity? Oh, I hardly think there was a chance. Eddy drove the doctor out the door soon after the blood episode. He wrote to you in great haste after that. There has been no doctor since."

"How has Edgar's own well-being been of late?"

Maria looked away from me for just a moment. "He takes a drink again whenever Virginia is quite bad."

I shuddered. I knew what "taking a drink" meant for Ned. He could ill hold his liquor, becoming inebriated from a very small amount. A drunken husband is not what Virginia ought to experience in her time of need – and as far as I could figure it, not what Maria needed either.

Just then, we heard the front door of the house open and close, and then footsteps coming toward the kitchen. Ned was home.

Maria stood. "You go see Eddy now, Dr. Bridget. You need to talk to him alone. I'll be along presently with tea in the parlour."

I got up and went out the kitchen door just as Ned looked up from where he was hanging his black hat on a hook outside the door. His eyes were large and tired, and he looked much older than when last we met. When his eyes met mine, a spark of life seemed to flicker for a moment.

"Bride, is it really you? Have you come at last?"

He held out his arms to me, and I went to him. His embrace was full of unspoken emotion. As for my own emotions, I could not begin to decipher my thoughts yet.

We went into the parlour and sat down on a settee upholstered in threadbare burgundy velvet. The room had dark wood walls and heavy drapes, and reminded me of the last time I had made a visit to a funeral parlour. I shivered.

Ned kept a hold of my hand as we talked. I wanted to move immediately to a conversation about the seriousness of Virginia's condition, but he wanted to catch up with me on my life, so I obliged. Finally, I could wait no longer. After all, Virginia was the reason for my visit. I put thoughts of Ned and Virginia as man and wife out of my head for a moment, then forced the conversation in the direction of Virginia's health. When I enquired as to Ned's understanding of the gravity of the situation, he dropped my hand and arose from the settee. He thrust his hands deep into his pockets as he walked over to the sideboard, where I noted an empty liquor bottle and several glasses. He did not look at me.

"She will recover," he said, "now that you are here."

I looked at my hands in my lap for a moment, preparing my thoughts. "Ned," I began finally, "I can work no miracles. Virginia is extremely ill with consumption. She may die."

I was unprepared for his reaction. His face contorted as he pounded his fist dramatically on the sideboard. The next thing I knew, he had flung his arm across its top, upsetting the bottle and glasses and sending them in a frenzy of shattering glass onto the floor. He bent down and picked up a shard of glass, examining its jagged features as he did so. Having no experience of this side of Ned's nature, I held my breath and waited for his next move.

To my utter relief, he placed the piece of glass on the sideboard and turned to me.

"I apologize most sincerely for that outburst. You, of all people, should not have been subjected to my wrath. You are here at my behest, and for that I am grateful. But you must understand something." His fists were clenched at his sides. "Virginia will recover. She will." He stopped for a moment to gaze toward the door where Maria was now standing, evidently having heard the commotion. "She must."

With that, he seemed to crumple as if his body had disintegrated within its clothes. He came back over to the settee and melted into it. Maria disappeared from the doorway, leaving us alone again.

"Ned, you must listen." I knew I was pushing the issue, but I felt that he had to come to terms with this situation. "First, Virginia may be able to recover a little if her treatment changes."

He looked up at me and smiled. "I knew that you would attend to us with your knowledge and skill. You are better than any doctor whose services I could have engaged."

He took up my hand again and kissed it before gently placing it down in my lap again.

"Bride, whatsoever you might tell us to do, we shall do with alacrity. I am your humble servant and ever grateful for your ministrations to my little wifey." He once again kissed my hand.

I shuddered at his use of the term "little wifey" and wondered at the character of their relationship. I knew, however, that I would do all that was in my power to help, but somehow I had to make him understand that there were no guarantees as to the final outcome for Virginia's health.

I stayed in Philadelphia for some ten days. Each day, I would leave my lodgings by my carriage and arrive at the Poe house to take up my duty as caregiver to young Virginia. Day by day, she improved. I moved her bed to the window and bid her take some fresh air.

I spent a morning in the kitchen teaching Maria how to prepare a decoction of anise and caraway seeds to assist Virginia in managing her cough. When we finally had the tea prepared and Virginia was able to sip it, the results were amazing. Within a day, her cough had improved greatly, and we, Ned included, were all heartened by the effects.

When Virginia was feeling up to it, I instructed her in the preparation of her own bath of a combination of rosemary and lavender. This she enjoyed greatly, and the bath filled the house with an amazing and inviting fragrance. Such was not the case with my third medicinal approach.

I had found suppliers in Philadelphia for the anise, the caraway, the lavender and the rosemary. The final medicine, however, would be more difficult to supply. I had brought a small quantity of the seeds of the fenugreek plant. A native of Asia, the plant was cultivated in other parts of the world and brought in from time to time on ships that plied the world's waters. I had acquired these seeds from a colleague of John's who had also lent me the books from which I had learned about herbal treatments. I had not told Ned that, for much of the past few years after Siobhan had taken over my duties at the clinic, I had spent as much time as possible teaching myself about herbal medicine. The seeds were difficult to find, and I had not had reason to use them before. They were, however, highly recommended for use in consumption, but the mucilaginous seeds that were the mainstay of their medicinal properties gave off a pungent and unpleasant odour. Indeed, when Ned returned home the day Maria and I were preparing the seeds on the stove, he let out a whoop of derision as he entered the house, and the smell filled his nostrils.

"What monstrous and noxious stench fills my nostrils? Must I be subjected to such miasma in my own home?" came his voice from the hallway.

I knew his contempt for the odours that filled his house was flimsy, however, since I knew he recognized the extent to which my concoctions had assisted Virginia in her recovery. And his gratitude was evident in his every word, every gesture, every glance toward me. Further, I knew that her recovery was likely to be but a remission of her symptoms. I had not yet found a way to convince Ned of the likelihood of an exacerbation, and I despaired of doing so before my departure.

When I donned my coat and hat for the final time as I departed the house, Ned implored me to stay on for yet a bit. I felt strongly that I had stayed away from John and Baltimore for far too long and bid him farewell.

"When shall I see you again?" Ned said, standing on the stoop as I embarked into the carriage.

Before I had a chance to contemplate an answer, Virginia burst out of the house, eyes bright, feet bare, her gown floating behind her. "Bridget, Bridget, you must not leave without taking this with you."

She reached me, totally breathless and gasping for life itself, with Ned flying behind her no doubt to see to her well-being. She thrust a sheaf of papers into my hands.

"Virginia," Ned said, appearing embarrassed. "I had not yet decided to show these to Bridget."

He apologized to me and told me that they were the manuscripts of stories he had written of late – several had been published. Virginia perceived that I was an aficionado of Ned's work and believed that I inspired his writing by my association with medicine and death. I was unsure how she had developed such a notion, but accepted the sheaf gratefully.

I knew not when I should see Ned again – if ever. But our life paths did seem to cross from time to time. When last I looked upon the house, Ned was sweeping Virginia off her feet and into the house. I said a silent prayer as much for Ned's capacity to endure the inevitability of Virginia's illness as for Virginia's ability to endure the ravages of the illness itself, for I knew in my heart that I would never again see Virginia in this life.

TWO

BALTIMORE, AUTUMN, 1842

By the time I had completed the exhausting and time-consuming trip back to Baltimore that spring and found my life there to be all but in a shambles, I had forgotten entirely about Ned and his problems. The summer found me ministering yet again to a critically ill individual – this time it was John.

More than a year earlier, John had begun experiencing pain in his chest and arms whenever he exerted himself. Prompting his early retirement from the practice of medicine, the pains had grown worse, not better, since that time in spite of his less busy life. When I returned from my very brief junket to Philadelphia, I found him to be in constant pain and all but confined to his bed. The extent of his deterioration in the space of a fortnight was shocking to me, and I felt pangs of guilt at my absence.

That summer was an unending stream of days whose features were all so alike they were but a blur to my mind. For two months, I did not have the energy or inclination even to visit the hospice. Siobhan, bless her, came to the house every week to tell me of the activities. Her school had grown, and she had engaged another young woman to assist her in caring for the children whose mothers toiled as maids and cooks in the houses of the more genteel class. I provided her with money to continue the work.

By August, it was clear to me that Wimpy, my connection to my father and my childhood, the one person who knew me better than anyone in the world, would be able to work no longer. Her own health had made it difficult for her to manage the stairs, although she continued to cook as well as ever. On one of the saddest days I had experienced since my father's death, Wimpy's niece arrived from Boston to take her aunt home to be with her family. I could see the unspoken thoughts in her niece's eyes – they were taking her home to die.

When they had finally left, I walked through the house, which seemed suddenly empty and lonely. I knew that I would require help now that John was so ill, but I could not clear my thoughts enough to proceed with such mundane tasks. For the first time in my life, I felt totally out of control. Even my earlier depression had not had the same effect on me. My carefully constructed reality was crumbling like a house of cards, and I was helpless to stop the disintegration. I curled up in a ball on my bed and cried until I could cry no more.

In early October, John called me to his bedside one morning. It was a Thursday, a particularly enchanting day. John now slept in his own room and managed to get out of bed only occasionally and with great exertion. He had begun coughing so profusely and expectorating such copious amounts of phlegm that it would have been impossible for me to attempt to stay with him. As I opened his drapes to let in the golden rays of the autumn sun, he began hacking and spitting.

"Please, John, will you not permit me now to provide you with an expectorant?"

All summer, I had been trying in vain to convince him that my herbal remedies had the potential to make him feel considerably better. He had little respect for such approaches to healing and told me time and again that I would come to no good if I continued to meddle with such substances. He was convinced that a daily dose of laudanum was sufficient to assist him with his condition, and I noted that day by day the haze in which he now lived deepened. When I failed to provide his daily dose of laudanum, he became agitated and pugilistic – a side of John that was, until now, well hidden. I chose to blame it entirely on the effects of the drug.

On this day, when finally he was able to catch enough breath to speak, he said simply, "I want to die...and you must help me."

I was certain I had not heard him correctly, and yet it was the clearest his speech had been in some months. When I turned from the window, he was sitting full up in bed, his great mound of pillows that propped him up to ease his breathing, untouched behind him. His face was flushed, his eyes bright, and I felt a sudden wave of affection for this man whose respect and love I had cherished all these years.

I went over to the side of his bed and sat down gently. "I am certain I did not hear you correctly, my darling. Tell me again."

He looked at me the way he used to when I was so much younger and he so much older and wiser. I had not seen that look in some years.

"Bridget," he said, another coughing fit overtaking him. He reached for another clean handkerchief on the bedside table before continuing. "Bridget, I will not recover. You and I both know this. I can hear the fluid in my chest, and I can feel it with every breath. I do not wish any longer to live like this confined to bed within these four walls that are as much a prison as any with such a name. I am begging for your help."

I sighed deeply, and John took my hand gently.

"We have not been as man and wife for some time now." He took a breath with some difficulty. "You are still a young woman and should marry again. My presence is now unnecessary on this earth."

I shook my head, trying to place the thoughts in less of a jumble. "I do not know, John. You ask too much, I fear."

He lay back on the pillows and coughed again. "No, Bridget, I do not ask too much. Indeed, over the years," he stopped to cough again, "I have not asked quite enough, I fear."

I looked at him quizzically, not knowing of what he spoke. He closed his eyes for a moment, and I waited. He opened his eyes again and looked at me silently.

"What have you not asked enough about?"

"In the main," he said with some difficulty, "your poet friend. I have not asked you enough about your poet friend."

"Are you interested in his work? If so, I could provide you with –"

He waved his hand to stop me from continuing. "You know that – is not – what I speak of," he said, catching his breath on every word. "I have wondered – about you – about you and this Edgar Poe."

For all the years I had been married to John, the one thing about which we – or at least I – had been unable to speak, was my relationship with Ned. John had intimated from time to time through the years that he would welcome some more information, but I always managed to put him off. Perhaps we needed to clear the air before I lost him altogether. But what could I say to him? That we were merely friends? That was a lie, and I now knew this. Ned and I were certainly more than friends, and yet we were not lovers – at least not in this life. Had I considered that possibility, though? I had. I had considered it even through the years of my marriage to John. Was that adultery in itself? Could one be accused of infidelity in one's mind? I thought not, but a husband might think differently. In the end, how could I describe my feelings for Ned? I had thought about this often since our first encounter in the library at the University of Virginia. Still, I had yet to find the right words to describe this emotion adequately, even to myself. I certainly could not describe it to another. I believed, though, that for John, the facts would suffice.

"We have been friends for many years, as you know."

John looked at me and sighed deeply as if he were a spent man. "Even now, you cannot tell me the truth."

I arose from the side of the bed where I had been sitting and went to look out the window. I could feel what

261

seemed like anger begin to well up from within me. I turned back toward him and could feel my fists clenched tightly at my sides as I spoke. "I have always spoken the truth to you. We are friends. Beyond that, I cannot even put words to it for myself. We have never been lovers." I crossed my arms across my chest and turned away from him toward the window so that I could not gauge his reaction.

Moments passed. "You must help me die," came his words finally. The moment had passed, and we were moving on.

I turned back to him and noted his utter deflation. He had given up his fight for life and was begging his wife to do him one last caring act.

"I will leave you now, John, and I will think about your request. Rest now."

I walked slowly down the stairs, holding on to the railing for support. When I reached the bottom landing, although I knew I should not leave him alone in the house, I slowly draped my coat over my shoulders and walked out the front door.

I walked and walked. I had no direction, no ambition, no purpose. I was just walking. I could not even think, so I let my thoughts evaporate and watched them curl away from me as the steam on my coffee curls away and is gone. I listened to the wind blow past my ears, working feverishly to dislodge my carefully crafted chignon. Soon, long tendrils of hair were whipping about my face, adding, I am certain, to the figure of feverish movement that I must have been making along mile after mile of Baltimore streets.

I walked through familiar areas and then into alien territory, or so it seemed. The sky changed from blue to steel gray, and I felt a drop of rain on my face. I cared not. I kept walking.

Finally, I had arrived at the water's edge and could walk no farther. I gazed out upon the harbour and at the ships that were alongside. It was afternoon now, and the docks were busy with cargo being unloaded and piled up on the docks. The men's voices rang out as they called to one another to be careful. Their faces glistened with sweat, and their muscles, long honed by a lifetime of constant physical labour, bulged through the flimsy shirts they wore today.

The sights, the sounds and the smells of tar and rope and sea air transported me back to that day on the Boston pier when I planned my life – when I made the firm decision to take control of where I went and what I did. How I had longed that day to get aboard one of those ships bound for Europe. As I looked at these ships below me on the pier, I reckoned that they would be heading south when they were ready – heading for the islands of the Caribbean – and I longed to steal aboard, leaving my life and all it had become, behind forever.

My dreams had seemed too strong, as if nothing could shatter them. But I had been wrong, and the world had worked hard to change the direction of my life's path. So, here I stood, not wanting to take stock of my life, yet knowing I had reached another kind of watershed. The stream fell away in several directions, and I was fated to select one, for if I failed to choose, it would be chosen for me.

The sun was now so obscured by a layer of thick, gray clouds that I was unable to judge the time. I knew that I had been gone a long time and ought to return to my duties at the house. John would again be in need of me, and I was failing him.

Wrapping my coat more tightly around me, I turned my back on the scene below and returned to my life.

I cared lovingly for John. In spite of my ministrations, his condition worsened by the day. It was as if I could see the life ebbing from his body as the hours ticked by. For a month, I endured this.

One evening, John had settled – I had acquiesced to his begging and increased his dose of laudanum. As I rummaged through my bureau for a nightgown, I happened upon a sheaf of papers that had found their way into the bottom, as if I had hidden them. At first, I did not recognize them, but as soon as I unfolded them, I remembered Virginia thrusting them at me as I left the Poe house in Philadelphia. In the throes of domestic turmoil over these months, I had not read them. Indeed, I had thought of Ned from time to time, but not about his writing.

I sat down on the edge of my bed and began to read. The first story I turned to was titled "The Masque of the Red Death" and was, as was to be expected, a macabre tale. It told of a Prince whose kingdom was ravaged by a kind of plague called the red death. "Blood was its Avatar and its seal – the redness and horror of blood," it read, and I remembered Maria telling me of Ned's abhorrence of the blood-letting the doctor had attempted, and I wondered when he had written this story. By the time I arrived at the end of the story, I knew something more of the man's mind, and I knew something of my own.

"And Darkness and Decay of the Red Death held illimitable dominion over all."

It was clear.

THREE

November 1842

It is time," he said, catching just enough breath to speak these three words.

I looked up from the side table, where I was pouring water from the pitcher into the bowl, to begin helping John wash his face. I looked up, but I did not look at him – yet.

"It has been a month," he continued.

"Yes," I said slowly. "It has been a month." I still did not turn to him as I did not wish for him to see the tears that had welled up unbidden in my eyes and that now threatened to push me toward emotions I had been trying mightily to quash.

I wiped my hands on the apron I was wearing, opened the heavy door and slipped into the hallway. A rush of cold air hit me as I left the warmth of the stove in the corner of John's room.

I made my way quickly to the kitchen, where the stove kept it warm and inviting. Although I had engaged a new housekeeper, she did not live with us, as Wimpy had, and had completed her day's work, leaving me alone in the house with my husband.

I went immediately to my locked cupboard in the pantry. Selecting a small, silver key from the chatelaine I now wore on my waist, I opened the small door with steady hands. The cupboard had three shelves, all full of small vials and tiny burlap bags with drawstrings. They held the herbs and plants that I had been using for several years to assist the women at the clinic with various medical complaints, and which I had taken with me when I visited Virginia.

The bottom shelf held a special item. I reached into the cupboard to remove a small black, velvet-covered box. Its bronze edges gleamed as I held it near the candle that lit the space in front of the cupboard. I removed the top and looked inside. There it was, nestled in the black velvet interior, exactly as I had left it.

The box contained my crystal scent bottle – the one that my father had given to me so long ago. Its long gold chain was wound gently beneath it on the velvet. I had not worn the piece since my father died, and it had stayed in my jewelry case in my bedroom for a very long time. Some time ago, when I was searching for a safe place to keep a very special substance, it had occurred to me that this would be ideal.

As I removed the piece from the security of its box and pondered its contents, I thought of Socrates and felt a kind of bridge through time. For within the crystal that was made to contain scent, to enhance a woman's allure, I had placed an ounce of the fluid extract of the leaves of *conium maculatum* – hemlock.

I went to the parlour to fetch a bottle of brandy and two glasses. Placing the decanter, the crystal glasses and the scent bottle on a silver tray, I returned to John, who was now dozing, propped as usual, on his pillows.

I placed the tray on the table beside the pitcher and bowl I had been using earlier and poured two glasses of brandy. Into one of them, I poured most of the contents of the scent bottle. As I poured, I was assailed by the repugnant odour that I hoped would be somewhat masked by the brandy. Then I placed this glass on John's nightstand. Pulling a chair over beside his bed, I took up the other glass and sat down to wait for him to awaken.

As I sat there in the semi-darkness, I thought about my marriage to John and how he had come to me at a time when I needed him so much. Now he needed me.

By the time he roused, I had drained my brandy glass and was feeling slightly light-headed. He opened his eyes and looked at me. Glancing toward his nightstand, his eyes rested momentarily on the brandy glass. As he turned back to me, I detected a slight smile, the first I had seen in a very long time. He was ready.

I poured myself another glass of brandy, then I assisted him to take the brandy as he spoke a bit about his love for me. Between bouts of coughing, John, grimacing only slightly at what must have been a most objectionable taste in spite of the brandy, drained his glass while I sipped at mine. After a while, his coughing stopped, and he lay back, more peaceful than I had seen him since his illness had begun. He smiled at me and said simply, "Thank you."

I held his hand and felt the effects of the substance take over his muscles. As the night went on, I could feel his breath become more and more shallow. Finally, it ceased.

I covered him up to his neck while I proceeded with cleaning up the room. First, I removed the glasses and the brandy and took all the contents of the tray to the kitchen. I washed and replaced the glasses in the parlour. After finishing washing out the scent bottle, I went upstairs to my room to wash my face and change my clothes. I went to my dressing table and took up the crystal bottle containing my jasmine oil. I placed two drops on a clean handkerchief, edged with tatting that I remembered Abigail had done. Breathing deeply of the exotic, oddly calming scent, I poured half of the jasmine into my scent bottle on the gold chain and placed it around my neck. I took a moment to admire it in the glass before I went on to face the light of day.

FOUR

The day of John's funeral dawned bright and cold. The late November wind whipped the fallen leaves about my ankles, forcing me to clutch my coat around me for warmth and protection. Siobhan and James had come to escort me to the funeral, and I realized that over the years, I had made many acquaintances but few friends. I counted Siobhan among that paltry number.

To my surprise, the church was filled to capacity and beyond. It seemed that every person associated in any way with the medical profession in Baltimore and everyone else with whom we had associated over the years had come to pay their respects. Indeed, even Uncle Liam and Grace had made the long journey to be with me at what they perceived to be a most difficult time in the life of a still young woman. Or so Grace had said upon her arrival at the house.

I had been astounded at the extent to which Grace had grown into maturity since becoming a mother. She seemed less like a friend now and more like a maternal figure to me. She seemed to relish this newfound perspicacity that came with age and life experience. She bid me return to Charlottesville with them after the funeral, but I declined.

As I sat in the large church, one whose threshold I had not crossed except on special occasions over the years, I looked out through the black veil and considered John's life. I felt strongly that he was smiling down on me now, thanking me for his deliverance from hell on earth. As I listened to the priest talk of heaven and earth and life after death, my mind wandered to Ned and his almost demented vision of the murky line between life and death. My thoughts also took me back to Boston and to Sister Eulalia whom I had not heard of in a very long time. At that moment, I considered a trip to Boston to visit my old mentor.

Finally, the interminable mass was over. As I walked back down the aisle flanked by Grace and Uncle Liam, I looked out through my black veil to the assembled masses. Smiling back at me with that kind of odd expression that people place as masks on their faces when confronted with another's grief, were many familiar faces, but also a substantial number of unfamiliar ones. For a brief moment I thought that I saw Ned sitting at the back, nodding in recognition. He would, however, have no way of knowing that John had even died.

Later, I was forced to endure a ritual that I have always considered to be unnecessarily distressing for grieving families – the post-funeral gathering at the house. I just wanted everyone to leave. I wanted them to take their flowers with them and close the door firmly behind them. My grief was private – but any chance for solitary contemplation would have to wait.

I felt very detached as I watched people, some of whom I barely recognized, milled about the house, stopping their conversations to replace their masks each time I approached a group. Frustrated, I took refuge in the breakfast room with a glass of wine. It seemed to be the only place in the house, save my own bedroom, to which I could hardly flee – at least not yet – that no one had discovered yet. My back to the door, I was gazing out the window at the snow flurries that were swirling around the dead plants when an unfamiliar voice interrupted me.

"Oh, I am sorry," it said. "I had no idea that you were in here."

I turned and was greeted by the sight of a young man, whom I placed at about my own age or slightly younger, with unruly blonde curls, a square jaw, and only slightly dishevelled clothes of a gentleman. Something about him made me want to smile. Perhaps it was the obviously unmanageable hair, a trait I shared with this stranger. Indeed, what was he doing at my husband's funeral?

"It is quite all right," I said, turning my chair back around to face the table. "I am Bridget Ryan."

"Yes," he said coming forward to shake my hand. "Yes, I know." His handshake was strong, not the sort a woman usually received from a man who somehow thought women could not quite handle their strength. "Oh, I am sorry. How thoughtless of me. Please allow me to introduce myself. I am Timothy Robinson."

"Well, Timothy Robinson, how do you come to be in my house on this day? I presume you were acquainted with my late husband."

"Indeed," he said. "I am sorry again for my apparent lack of manners." He gestured toward a chair across from me. "May I sit down?"

"Certainly."

"I have known John since I was very young. He and my parents were great friends. I believe you know them – Graham and Anna Robinson."

Indeed, I did know them. Though it had been some time since I had last seen them, given John's lengthy illness, they had been regular companions of ours at the theatre and to dinner, and although I had perceived them to be slightly older than John even, I had no idea that they would have a son so apparently close to my own age. Graham was the owner of Robinson's Dry Goods, a thriving Baltimore fixture.

"I have seen you many times, you know," he said, leaning his head toward me. "I have seen you at the theatre with John on numerous occasions. I have seen you in our store. You are hard to miss, you know."

I was unsure what he meant by that.

Perhaps noting my discomfiture, he continued, "Oh, I am sorry again. That must have sounded boorish. I did not mean it to be. I only meant that you are a beautiful woman and in a city like Baltimore, you stand out for both your beauty as well as your intellect."

I was unaware that I was beautiful, nor was I aware that anyone might be driven to notice such things about me. It was a new and not entirely unwelcome notion.

Timothy cleared his throat and arose. "Mrs. Ryan, please accept my sincerest condolences on the loss of your husband. He was a very good man. I have taken up enough of your time today, and I can see that you had wished for a moment of solitude."

Before I had even the chance to utter a sound, he was gone, the door closed gently behind him. And I was left wondering what had just happened.

I felt peculiar, and in an odd kind of way, exhilarated – a feeling that one ought not to be feeling at one's husband's funeral, I suspected. Timothy Robinson was a very unusual young man and one whom I should, under other circumstances, have very much liked to get to know better. Turning back toward the window, I sighed and sipped my wine.

As I turned, I noticed out of the corner of my eye that my mail had been placed on a silver tray on a small table just inside the door. Perhaps my new housekeeper had thought that it would be a good place to accumulate letters of condolence. The table was short and round, covered in a cloth of ivory jacquard silk that hung to the floor. On it usually sat a bouquet of fresh flowers. Today, the flowers were not there (the house was otherwise filled with the scent of roses and other fragrances, all of which reminded me of death), but in their place was this silver tray. With all that had happened this week, I wondered how long those letters had been there, unnoticed by me.

My curiosity and desire to avoid the crowd for as long as possible lured me to the table. I picked up several letters, then noted the familiar handwriting on the outside of the second one from the bottom. It was from Ned. I unfolded the heavy paper and began to read.

"Philadelphia

October 31, 1842

My dearest Bride,
My dear little wife improves by the week and then by the week falls back into that fitful grip of illness that so vexes me. You must know that your ministrations were so welcome and so successful that I shall be forever in your debt as if I have never been before. We are bound together you and I, or so it seems.

As you had shown considerable concern for Sissy's cramped and dank accommodation, we have taken up a new residence in the hope of improving her condition.

I have also found it necessary to leave my job at Graham's. You realize, of course, that it would be my hope to continue to write and make my way in the world as a writer. To that end, I made the journey to New York in the hope of selling my work. I am sorry to recount to you that I was influenced by comrades to imbibe considerably more than I (and you, I have no doubt) would consider prudent had I been more in control of my own behaviour. Alas, much of the trip is but a blur to me now.

I leave you now with the thought that you are missed dearly by myself as well as Muddy and my little Sissy. I await the time when again we shall meet, and circumstances allow me to provide recompense to you for all you have done through the years.

I remain forever,
Your Ned"

To say I was exasperated at Ned and his tomfoolery would be an understatement. Would the man never grow up? Would he never take responsibility for his own life? What was he thinking, leaving a position that provided the necessities of life for both himself and his family? I could no longer feel sorry for Edgar Poe – my Ned. He was a fool who drank too much and failed to see that he was in control, but simply chose that life and failed to apply himself to anything other than creating his stories. A formidable writer without question, he seemed singularly unable to put that talent to good use for any length of time. What would history say about this man-child with his peculiar opinions about death and life? What would future generations say about his failure to accept that death and life were not one and the same and that death was final?

As these previously unacknowledged thoughts whirled around in my head, I realized that the letters on the page in front of me were beginning to form puddles of blue ink, blotches that looked so much like dark rain clouds. My tears were streaming onto the page and, for the first time since John had died, I cried. I cried for John's death, for his dying, for his life lost. But I cried mostly for myself.

In such a state Grace and Siobhan found me, my head upon the tablecloth, the letter no longer discernible. They stayed with me for hours, until all had departed and I was left alone again to plan the rest of my life.

FIVE

John's death had provided me the opportunity to look yet more closely at what I ought to be doing with my life. Recognizing that I would never have the life of a wife and mother that was the lot of so many other women, and being quite certain that I was not meant to languish in my boudoir as the lonely widow, I turned my attention to my study of herbal medicine. While Siobhan and James increased their family (by the summer of 1845, they had already produced three sons), Siobhan continued to provide day-to-day leadership for the hospice. She took her little sons with her each day, and they played happily with those of the women whose needs we continued to serve. This left me free to study and to assist as many women as I could without having to concern myself about administrative matters.

In my decision to refuse to be the lonely widow, after some eight months of intermittent pleading on the part of Timothy Robinson, I had agreed to an evening at the theatre with him. I found his company to be charming and exhilarating. Younger than John by a generation, Timothy was at once light-hearted as well as hard-working. He took his work seriously, but not himself. I found in him a breath of fresh air after years of conversation about dying patients with John and dying everyone else with Ned. We had become regular companions, Timothy and I.

Ned – I had heard less and less from my old friend. Indeed, his correspondence had been increasingly cryptic, and I was frequently unable to divine his meaning. He had begun with letters detailing Virginia's clearly deteriorating condition, then moved on to lamentations about his unacknowledged work. His apparent desire for

274

recognition and accolades seemed to have outstripped even his desire for pecuniary success.

Thus, when a package arrived from him toward the end of August, it was with mixed emotions that I untied the string and unwrapped the heavy brown paper. I do not know what I expected to find, but this was not it. I looked at the pages of poetry, not being able to make heads nor tails of it. But it was the enclosed object that provided me with the most puzzle. For within the pages torn from the likes of the *New York Tribune*, the *Broadway Journal* and the *Southern Literary Messenger* was a black feather wrapped in a single sheet of paper. On the paper, in Ned's distinctive hand, were the words, "The plume return from whence it came, nevermore to be the spear within my heart." I spent hours, my head bent over upon this bizarre package. And it was thus that Timothy found me one rainy autumn evening.

"Bridget," came the voice as if from a great distance. "Bridget?"

The voice seemed closer still, and yet I could not seem to tear myself away from staring at the objects in front of me.

A hand upon my arm, and I awoke, it seemed.

"Bridget, are you all right?"

I looked up into Timothy's handsome face and realized that I had been as if in a trance. I smiled at him and realized that I had missed him. "How was New York?" I asked when at last I had regained my senses.

"New York was New York," he said, sitting down beside me. "The question is, how are you? What is it that has you so entranced that you have not the wits to greet a dear friend?"

He was smiling as he said this, and I was almost smitten. I showed him the torn sheets and the feather. He had no explanation for the latter but was much impressed at my acquaintance with Edgar Poe. I had told him of it, but it seemed even more interesting to him at this juncture.

"Ah, 'The Raven,'" he said. "Everyone in New York seems to be talking about it. Even the old businessmen with whom I was forced most evenings to dine seemed to have an opinion about it."

I was much interested that Ned should finally have some recognition, for the pages of the newspapers and magazines that he had sent to me all were published versions of this poem, "The Raven." I was perhaps just as intrigued by Timothy's obvious familiarity with it.

"Tell me," I said, "what are they saying of my old friend and his poem?"

"It seems that it has reached such a level of appeal that children follow him through the streets until he turns, raises his arms and shouts, 'Nevermore!' to disperse them." Timothy shook his head. "He seems a rather peculiar man. Not exactly the sort I would have reckoned to be the close friend of a woman such as you."

This last remark bothered me. I thought of myself as the sort of woman who would and did have a wide variety of friends and/or acquaintances. It vexed me to think that people were beginning to see me as the sort of woman who might not have such wide interests. Indeed, I was sorely bothered by Timothy holding this opinion.

I had been aware of the fact that Ned had moved to New York more than a year earlier. Indeed, the last correspondence I had received from him had been shortly after that move. I was not aware that he was beginning to receive such renown. Perhaps his wish was coming true. None of this, however, helped determine exactly what message he was sending me.

Timothy mulled over the text of the poem and held the feather up to the light to see it more clearly.

"A raven's feather?" he said finally.

I was unsure, but I surmised that, at the very least, Ned had meant for it to symbolize such. I shrugged in response.

"Well," Timothy continued, "it seems quite clear. You have told me a little of your relationship with this eccentric man, who, by the way, has something of a reputation as a drunk in New York – and thus I would conclude that you are the raven – his bird of ill omen."

"Me? An ill omen?" I was astonished at this interpretation. "Why would that be?"

"Simple, my dear Bridget. He was – and perhaps still is – in love with you. You have been the beak in his heart for these years while he has stood by and watched you live a life away from him, and while his own wife dies slowly before his very eyes."

My head was spinning. Ill omen? I was the harbinger of bad luck for Ned? If Timothy were right, then my occasional unkind thoughts of Ned and his victim mentality may have been closer to the truth than I dared to imagine. It was true: Ned did indeed often blame others for his misfortunes. He had blamed John Allan; he blamed editors for whom he had worked. He even blamed his own mother for dying and leaving him an orphan. In spite of all this, there was little doubt that he was a brilliant writer to whom history would no doubt owe a debt of gratitude for his contribution. Perhaps this victimization was a condition of the creative process. Whatever meaning all of this had, which I failed to fully understand, it was absolutely necessary for me to find out how Ned thought of me.

Was he still in love with me? I would find out.

SIX

BALTIMORE, JUNE 1846

Life goes on. And at the age of thirty-six, I was quite certain that I had grown up and matured as much as I was likely to. How naïve we can be! If I had really grown up, I wouldn't have begun noticing things I'd never seen before.

Ravens, ravens! I had never noticed them before, and now I seemed to see them everywhere, but mostly near the docks when I walked to meditate. At first, I mistook every black bird for a raven until I sought out Mr. Marvin Peabody, a local bird expert of sorts.

Visiting Mr. Peabody was a kind of enchantment I had not experienced since childhood. Passionate about birds, he was delighted that anyone should wish to visit with him and learn more about the loves of his life.

His home was on the outskirts of the city, down a narrow road overgrown with trees of every imaginable variety. It was, however, the tall conifers that raised their heads majestically to the sky that impressed me the most. The rows of age-old firs and pine trees led the way to the large, unusual house at the end of the lane.

Mr. Peabody was evidently unmarried but was attended to by a rather severe housekeeper whose frown indicated that she did not wish to be interrupted in the course of her housekeeping duties. She did, however, show me into the parlour where I waited several minutes for my host.

I took advantage of the opportunity to examine my surroundings. A large room, it had none of the delicate touches one might expect of a room decorated by a woman. In place of feminine touches, there were deep colours and straight lines. The drapes were of heavy gold damask, and the settee was large and deep, a very unusual piece, or so I thought. The tables were of dark wood, mahogany perhaps, covered with carvings and pottery figurines and framed pictures on stands – all of birds. There were even two taxidermy specimens. I shuddered at these. On the walls were yet more pictures and again all of our feathered friends, although I must say that not all looked very friendly to my eye.

My eye was drawn to a very large picture over the mantle. I arose from my place on the settee to examine it more closely. It was an oil painting, and something about it drew me to touch it. The paint was thick, and the tactile sensation was not unlike that I expected one would feel if confronted by the real bird itself. It was a likeness of a large black bird in full flight, its beak wide open as if in song. I believed it was a raven.

Just then, Mr. Peabody himself entered.

"Oh, I see you have found one of my ravens, my dear."

I turned to take in the owner of the rather high-pitched voice and found myself confronted with a very rotund, jolly looking man about six inches shorter than I was. The top of his bald head shone in the light of day, and the hair left around the lower portion of his head was gray and curling. He wore a pair of spectacles that continually slid down his nose, and he was forced to push them up again and again throughout our conversation.

"Please forgive me for my audacity. Mr. Peabody, I presume?" I held out my hand as he walked toward me.

"Oh, no audacity at all," he said, embracing my hand warmly as if he and I were old friends. "Anyone with an interest in my birds is welcome any time. Mrs. Ryan, isn't it?"

I told him of my particular interest in learning more about ravens, and he bid me join him in his study, where, he said, he kept his books and most important specimens.

The study was at the back of the house with a clear view of more bird feeders and obviously happy birds than I had ever beheld in my life up to this time. The desk was a very large oak one covered two feet high with papers and books. How he could ever find anything there was a mystery to me!

As I turned from the desk to take in the whole of the room, I was startled to find myself nose to beak with a very large black bird on a brass perch. I gasped. Its black plumage had a kind of purple and green iridescence that gave it an otherworldly cast.

Mr. Peabody chuckled. "She does that to most everyone who comes in here. She will not bite."

I must have looked startled. He laughed. "Athena is stuffed," he said quite unnecessarily I thought.

He sat down behind the desk, bade me take the seat across and pushed his glasses up onto the bridge of his nose. He adeptly removed a book that was buried beneath a formidable pile – but he seemed to know the exact location of everything.

"Mrs. Ryan," he began as he opened up the large, black leather cover, "I understand that you are interested in the raven. I would be most happy to assist you in your quest for knowledge, but before we begin, if it is not too impertinent of me, I should be most pleased to know the reason for this interest."

I shifted slightly in my seat and clutched my bag and gloves further into my lap. "I have a friend," I began, "for whom the raven is an important creature. I was hoping to better understand his preoccupation with ravens."

"Oh, yes, well," he said. "Of course. And I shall help you all that I am able. Where should we begin?"

"Well," I said, "what is so special about ravens?"

He clasped his hands on top of the open book. "Oh, they are special. Very special indeed. They are the most intelligent of all birds, you know. And their eyesight and hearing are unmatched among birds."

I considered this revelation. Intelligent, sharp senses. To be compared with such a creature may not be so bad.

"Please continue," I said.

"They are skillful fliers. Oh yes, they can soar to great heights, and can imitate a variety of sounds – including the human voice." He looked at me over the top of his spectacles. "Mrs. Ryan, if I might, is there anything specific about ravens that you need to know?"

I had thought that a man possessed as he seemed to be by birds might not be as sharp and astute as he now displayed himself to be.

"Do they have any symbolic meaning of which you are aware?" I said quietly.

"Yes, yes indeed," he said, his eyes lighting up. He turned the pages of the book until he came to what he obviously had been seeking. "They are trusted messengers between the world of the living and the world of the spirits, you know." He looked up at me. "They are sacred to many peoples of the world. Do you remember your bible stories, Mrs. Ryan?

I shook my head, failing to recall even one instance where a raven had been mentioned.

"You know the story of Noah? Noah sent out a raven to test the floodwaters." He got up from the desk and went to a large case filled with imposing-looking volumes. He ran his finger along the spines of these books until he came to a slim one which he removed carefully and brought back to his desk.

"This is a book of Irish medieval magic, my dear. In it, there is a list of several dozen prophecies that were made based on raven behaviour – and that came to pass, I might add."

I was distracted from this for a while as Mr. Peabody's housekeeper brought tea. He poured me a cup, and we talked a bit more about the so-called magical powers of ravens. But it was this myth of their connection between life and death that captured my attention, for it was Ned's preoccupation with that murky place between the two worlds that so fascinated me.

I had learned far more about ravens than I had ever thought I would that day. Indeed, I believe I even learned more about Ned and his writing.

I had pondered long about Ned's meaning. When, many months after I had received the peculiar feather and his poem, I received another missive from him, I made a firm determination that I would visit him in yet another new abode. For his main reason for writing (or so he said in so many words) was that he had moved his family to a little farmhouse in Fordham, near New York. I sent him off a letter telling him of my intention to visit.

Thus, when next Timothy was required by his business to attend meetings in New York, I accompanied him. And so I found myself sitting in a carriage outside Ned's cottage one fine June morning.

SEVEN

NEW YORK, JUNE 1846

I sat for what seemed a very long time, just looking at the house. I sat for so long that the driver eventually came to me to inquire if this was, indeed, the correct location. I bid him return to his seat and that I would alight presently.

I was thinking about the peculiarity of the situation. Ned and I had been friends – if that be the appropriate label – for what seemed a very long time now. Again, I thought about how odd it was that our lives ran in parallel, coming closer for a time and never really crossing, so that one path truly changed the other. It occurred to me that this might never happen.

I looked carefully at the little cottage that now housed the family of my itinerant friend. Located on the top of Fordham Hill, the cottage was small but not altogether unhappy-looking. Indeed, I could picture a happy family having many congenial experiences in this petite abode. But no such family lived here. For beyond that homey porch which extended along the entire front of the house I knew dwelled much distress – distress of a man who had devoted his life to an almost unacknowledged talent, taking to intoxicants whenever unable to face the reality of his life; a woman whose young life was ebbing ever closer to death even as I gazed upon her dwelling; and a woman who had devoted her life to both of these forsaking any ambition of her own. The little trio that made up the Poe family was indeed sad to me.

Finally, I could wait no longer. I alighted from the carriage, gathering my skirts around me as I picked up the satchel I carried. Within that satchel, I had stowed some remedies I believed might soothe Virginia in her affliction, as well as some articles for both Ned and Maria.

I approached the porch slowly, taking in the open feeling that surrounded this cottage. It was very different from any place Ned had lived before. Like me, Ned had grown to adulthood in the city, the sights and sounds and smells of the urban landscape always filling our senses. His choice of this pastoral backdrop – if indeed it had been his choice – for his work and his family must have come as a bit of a jolt to his senses. However, I had to admit that the clean air and open space would have been exactly what I would have prescribed for Virginia and her condition. I wondered how often she actually had the chance to leave the confines of the cottage.

I walked slowly up the three steps to the porch, pausing for a moment to look back toward the road before knocking. I was surprised that no one had yet realized that my carriage had pulled up in front. Surely they could not have much regular traffic up here.

I knocked and waited. Finally, the door opened, and Ned's face changed from deeply troubled to beaming with delight in the split second it took him to realize that I had arrived. Before he said a word, he drew me into his arms. The embrace was strong, almost fierce, as if he needed something from me.

When finally he pulled himself away from me, he stood there, his arms still on my shoulders, tears in his eyes.

"Bride, you cannot know how jubilant I am to see you here in my home. It has been so long, and I am in great need of you." He stood back to let me enter.

The hallway was narrow and dark with a small staircase winding to the rooms above. Having seen the outside of the cottage, I judged the upper rooms to be small, indeed. Ned led me into the main room and bade me make myself at home while he went to fetch Maria and a cup of tea for me. When I enquired after Virginia, his eyes darkened again as he told me she was asleep at present, but that as soon as she was awake, he would take me to her.

I took off my gloves and looked around the room. It struck me as bright and even cheerful. It had two windows that looked out onto the porch, and between them, against the wall, stood a table littered with what appeared to be Ned's writing paraphernalia. I walked over to it and ran my hands over the various papers and books. There was a candle that had burned down almost to its end, giving the impression of a diligent writer working at his craft long into the night. On top of a pile of books was a dog-eared copy of *The Broadway Journal's* January 3 issue. I picked it up and noted with some unexpected pride that the editor (and publisher) was listed as one E.A. Poe.

"Muddy will be along presently with our tea," Ned said as he returned to the room. "Now, you must tell me everything. I need to know everything." He stopped for a moment as he noticed the magazine in my hand.

"I see you have found me out." He took the copy from me and began to leaf through it before replacing it on the writing table.

"You must be very proud of how far you have come, Ned," I said, smiling.

But Ned did not seem to share my happiness at his obvious good luck. "Proud no more," he said, sitting down on the settee with a sigh.

I sat beside him. "What is it, Ned? Is there a problem with the journal?"

"That issue that you have examined is, I dread to tell you, the last. It ceased publication months ago."

Now I understood as I watched him hang his head and put his face in his hands. Then, as quickly as the melancholy had settled upon him, it lifted as he looked up, ran his fingers through his still dark, curling hair and looked at me. He took my two hands in his and said, "Now, Bride. You must tell me everything about your life. What excitement have I missed?"

As I told him of my current life in Baltimore, he seemed like a man thirsty for word of the outside world.

285

But when I mentioned Timothy, it was as if a cloud had again passed over the sunshine of his face. His eyes took on a kind of menacing shadow which did not lift until I had left the subject of Timothy. When I began to ask about Virginia, his happiness at speaking of her was eclipsed by a kind of melancholy, and although he would not for a moment yet admit that she was dying, it occurred to me that his denial was simply an attempt to conceal the depth of his feeling. At that moment, I believed, for the first time, that he did truly love that young woman. What kind of marriage it could have been through the years, I could not begin to imagine, but that he loved her, I now had no doubt.

When Maria finally appeared, laden with her tea tray, she placed it on a table and then turned to embrace me warmly. I was taken slightly aback by this display of affection because, although we had been friends for some years now, I had never known Ned's rather stoic aunt to be openly affectionate. I wondered what hardships had led to this change in behaviour.

"Virginia will be so happy to see you, Dr. Bridget," she said as she offered me a cup of tea.

"I will share in that happiness." I placed my cup on the table and opened my bag, which was on the floor near my feet. "I have brought along some medicinals that I believe might be of assistance to Virginia."

"We are eternally grateful, Bride," Ned said, brightening again. "Sissy and I have long believed that you are the only medical person who has the wherewithal to prevent any further deterioration of her condition. Indeed, you are our saviour."

I was alarmed at Ned's interpretation of my capabilities. His apparently firm conviction that I could save Virginia from what I believed was an inevitably terminal illness was very distressing. I knew that I could no more save Virginia's life than I could cure Ned of his condition, where one glass of wine seemed to turn him from an angel to a kind of demon who could not stop imbibing. I would have to find a way to explain this to him before I left.

When I had finished catching him up with my own activities, I turned my attention to Virginia. It seemed to me that he was avoiding the topic of her condition.

"Ned, I should be delighted to see Virginia now. Could you see if she is awake?"

He left for a brief moment and returned to beckon me across the hall.

He opened the door to a little bedroom where Virginia languished upon a narrow bed under a sloping roof. I noted that its little window looked out on the front porch and must have provided her with at least a bit of diversion.

She was small and wan, yet smiled as I entered her chamber. She even reached out her hand to me, which I grasped warmly and affectionately, for I did indeed like this young woman. Her violet eyes were sunken, and her skin dry and pale. Even her hair seemed lifeless and desiccated, and her cough was incessant.

I bid Ned leave us alone, then spent an hour talking to Virginia and assisting her to take some of the herbal preparation I had brought for her. After a time, it did seem to quell her cough, for which I was very grateful. Finally, Virginia was very sleepy, and I left her to what I hoped would be an easier sleep than she had been able to get, and made my way out of the room, eager for more space. Maria peeked out of the parlour and indicated that Ned was upstairs "in his chamber," she said, motioning me to go up.

The staircase was narrow and steep, leading to Ned's attic space. When I arrived at the top of the stairs, I noted that it was, indeed, an attic, and Ned was at work at a table in the center of the room. The slope of the roof was so pronounced that at my height, I could barely stand without hitting my head on the peak. There were several tiny windows whose panes let in but a meagre amount of light.

"Welcome to my library," Ned said, looking up from his work.

"Ned," I began, "we must talk. You need to understand some things about Virginia's condition."

He brightened immediately. "I can no longer hear her coughing downstairs. It is a sound that accompanies my daily activities, but I would gladly become accustomed to the silence." He smiled. "You have done it, Bride, as we knew you would."

"It is temporary, Ned. I believe that in your heart you know this. Virginia is seriously ill, and there is little I can do, save assist her in dealing with the symptoms. Neither I nor anyone else have the power to cure what causes this grave disease. Perhaps one day someone will cure it, but not today."

Ned would not hear of it, and thus our conversation continued. Presently, it was time for me to leave. I could hear from outside that the carriage had returned as I had bid the driver to do. It was time for me to take my leave.

Both Ned and Maria embraced me on the porch as I stood there wishing I could do more for this pathetic little family. But it was not within my power.

I felt like a used dishrag as I sank into the carriage seat and we pulled away from the cottage on Fordham Hill. I could not shake the feeling that I ought to be doing more – I just had no idea what that might be, short of providing pecuniary consideration for Ned. I did manage to press a small amount of cash into his hands, but he would take no more.

I returned to the hotel in New York, bathed and donned a stylish green silk dress to meet Timothy for dinner. We dined sumptuously that night, and for the remainder of my sojourn in New York, I tried to put Ned and his plight out of my mind. Indeed, Timothy's company was of great assistance in this endeavour.

We returned to Baltimore, and I continued with my previous activities at the hospice, spending as much of my social time with Timothy as was possible.

Time passed, and I heard no more from Ned. Eight months later, my housekeeper answered the door one snowy afternoon. I entered the hallway to be greeted by a wild-eyed Ned.

"Why did you let her die?" he said, just before collapsing onto my oriental rug.

EIGHT

BOSTON, JUNE 1847

It had been many years since I was last in Boston. I stepped down from the train and was immediately assaulted by noise and commotion. Looking for the carriage I had hired, I walked past a newsstand to purchase a copy of the newspaper that would perhaps acclimatize me to my old haunts. Finally, I found the driver who assisted me with my luggage, which was still waiting on the platform. Then I settled into the seat.

As I looked around at the streets, the people, and the bustle from the safety of my carriage, I felt that it had been a lifetime since I had last visited my childhood home. I had meant to visit Sister Eulalia on several occasions over the past years, but it had never come to pass.

Now, in the wake of so much pain and misery that had been visited upon me in the past few months, I found myself anxiously responding to the first telegram I had ever received in my life. Such a tremendous innovation! How communication would now change, I thought. If not for this new breakthrough Sister Eulalia might well have been dead before I would be able to reach her bedside. For the telegram which was delivered to my door only two days earlier had graciously, but urgently, requested my presence at the Mother Superior's bedside as she lay dying – or at least that was the implication as I read between the lines. It was signed by a "Sister Agnes Mary Francis, Assistant to the Mother Superior."

Ned's unexpected and unwelcome visit in February had gone poorly. He had been drunk and demonic to my mind. Virginia had died and he had evidently somehow held me responsible for not saving her.

It had been very difficult to get the details of her passing from him in his state, but my housekeeper and I managed to learn that she had died in late January and that he seemed to have been in a kind of dream-world during the ensuing month. Not believing that she was really gone, he had evidently visited her tomb daily during the following weeks in the hope that her burial might have been premature. I found his reaction irrational and deranged to the point where my own feelings about Virginia's death and its effect on my friend were unexpectedly unemotional. I felt little, save distaste for this man. I should have been compassionate, sympathetic, indulgent even, but all I felt was an emptiness. He left as precipitously as he arrived. His departure left me with a sinking feeling that his life was lost to us. Virginia's death seemed Ned's passing as well.

Then, a month later, while visiting a warehouse near the docks, Timothy was struck in the head by a falling barrel. He had remained comatose for several days before breathing his last, with me at his bedside. This I found devastating. I had not realized the depth of my affection for this kind, handsome man. Indeed, I was even considering responding positively to his latest proposal of marriage. For months he had been badgering me to become his wife and for some reason, thoughts of Ned kept me from answering him. After Ned's appearance at my home I had given serious thought to a life with Timothy. Now that was gone, too.

So, here I was, on my way to another death of another person. I sighed loudly and picked up the newspaper that I had placed on the seat beside me. My eyes filled with tears as I read a small headline: "Woman Admitted to Geneva Medical College." As I read the story of Elizabeth Blackwell's controversial admission, I was once again filled with the fury and profound disappointment that had surrounded me in Boston when last I strode its streets. It had been too soon for me. I silently wished her well and as the carriage pulled up in front of the convent, it seemed appropriate to say a tiny prayer for her.

291

I felt a lump rising from the pit of my stomach as I stepped down from the carriage and took in the stone walls of this imposing structure. I had been a little girl inside those walls and I had been a woman. I had even been a bride. Now I was – what? I did not even know.

I reached for the brass knocker and rapped it three times on the imposing oak door. I waited for but a moment before the door was opened by yet another young postulant. Evidently, I had been expected.

As I stepped inside the foyer that had once soared so high and wide over my young head, I felt as if it had diminished somewhat – although I knew that to be impossible. The ceiling seemed lower, the stained glass less vibrant. I sensed a kind of dullness about the place.

I waited a few more moments in the foyer while the little postulant who giggled and held her hand over her mouth when she told me her name was "Sister Mary Elizabeth" went to fetch Sister Agnes, the Mother Superior's assistant whose telegram I had received.

Presently, Sister Agnes appeared. She was tall and slender, not unlike Sister Eulalia had always been, but she had none of Sister Eulalia's equanimity. Indeed, Sister Agnes seemed to exude a kind of hurried anxiety such that I wondered at Sister Eulalia's condition. I was frightened.

"Mrs. Ryan, it was so good of you to come," Sister Agnes said as she gestured me down the hall. "Mother Superior speaks of you often and when she asked if I would enquire after you, I was only too happy to do so for her."

"I was glad to come. Is the Mother Superior very ill?"

Sister Agnes looked at me oddly. "How did you know that she was ill? I do not recall saying anything of that matter in my telegram."

"I simply presumed so, Sister," I said, scrambling to keep up with her as she hurried toward Sister Eulalia's office.

I thought this was peculiar, as I expected to be taken to her bedchamber.

"Please do not say anything such as that to the Mother Superior. No one is supposed to know."

I was puzzled. No one was supposed to know what? That she was ill? That she was not ill? Before I had a chance to enquire, we had reached the door, and Sister Agnes bade me wait outside as she announced me.

Finally, I was allowed to enter. I do not know what I expected to see, but I did not expect to see the Mother Superior standing in front of the little fireplace, beaming at me as I walked in the door.

"Bridget," she said, extending her arms to me.

I went to her immediately and was enveloped in a warm embrace. I felt as if my mother was embracing me – and perhaps in a way, I was.

I stepped back and went down on one knee. She reached down for me and bade me rise.

"Bridget, you are not one of my postulants." She smiled. "You do not belong on your knees before the Mother Superior."

"Mother, it is so good to see you." I could feel tears forming in my eyes, and somehow I did not care about this sudden, usually unwelcome display of emotion. Sister Eulalia was a friend, perhaps my dearest friend in all the world.

"I am equally as pleased to see you, Bridget – after all these years."

I felt a bit as if she were scolding me. "I know that it has been far too long. But I am here now and in desperate need of knowing if you are seriously ill."

She narrowed her eyes for a moment. "Did Sister Agnes tell you that?'

"No," I said quickly. "I surmised it for myself. Is it true?"

"Sit," she said, beckoning me to a small chair beside the fire. She sat down in the one on the other side of the fire, and I noted that she had some slight difficulty moving into that position. I had an impulse to assist her, but thought better of it.

"I am dying, Bridget."

I started to speak, but she waved me to be silent.

"I am dying," she repeated. "Sister Agnes knows this and is inordinately apprehensive about it. Indeed, she is apprehensive about most everything," she said dryly. "However, I did not request your presence at a funeral. I have no intention of dying while you are here. But I felt a strong call – from God perhaps?"

I believe she winked at me.

"The strong feeling told me that I needed to see you. No, that is not quite right. More like you needed to see me. And I knew that I needed to see you before it was too late."

I swallowed hard. "Oh, Mother, I am sorely in need of a friend."

"Perhaps you are in need of more than a friend." She looked at me closely. "Tell me, Bridget, do you still make time for your spiritual self?"

I shook my head. "No, Mother, I have not been to church in many years."

"That is not what I asked." She waited just a moment. "Now, my child, tell me everything. Start at the beginning and do not leave out even the smallest detail."

So, I began pouring my story and my heart out to this peaceful, kind, and surprisingly understanding woman. For the first time in my life, I felt that my mother had not really abandoned me in death, but that she lived through this woman who listened, did not judge and provided a serene presence that one could almost touch.

When I had come to the end of my chronological story, ending with Timothy's death, she looked at me, then leaning forward to take my hand across the distance between us, said, "Now tell me how you feel, Bridget. Especially about Ned Poe."

How I felt? I did not like to visit that part of myself if I could avoid it. It was apparent that I could not avoid it any longer in the presence of this woman, my mother and God.

As I spoke, telling her of Ned's Raven poem, with which she was familiar, I realized that I was mining the depths of my consciousness, finding little nuggets of emotion and thoughts that had been buried under layers of logic and rationality.

My feelings about Ned were the most irrational of all that I held deep within me, and yet they were perhaps the most important. He had been a friend, a confidante, a protégé of sorts.

"A lover?" she said as I rhymed off the aspects of our relationship.

"No," I said firmly.

"In your thoughts?"

I knew that I need not answer this question for her.

"Bridget, you must deal with this relationship, you know. It must come full circle."

I had a vague feeling of unease about the situation – the relationship –, and I had harboured it for a very long time. But I did not know what "coming full circle" would mean to Ned and to me.

Sister Eulalia coughed quietly, and it occurred to me that she was in some discomfort. She would, however, not allow me in any way to comfort her. It was clear that she felt her role was to somehow guide me in my time of need. I was unused to this position as the receiver of care. It was very uncomfortable.

She looked at me for a long time, it seemed. "Bridget," she said finally, "do you remember my advice to you about setting sacred intention each day of your life?"

I looked at her lined face framed by her elaborate wimple and wondered what colour her hair was.

"Bridget?" she said again.

I was brought back to the present moment and considered her question. "I do not believe that I ever really understood what you meant, Mother." That was the simple truth.

"I thought not," she said, coughing again slightly. "You have accomplished a great deal in your life, my child."

I began to dispute her opinion, but she silenced me quickly.

"Whether you believe it or not, it is true. And, indeed, you have been given much in the material world. Not one of us ever uses all of our gifts as wisely as we might, but you have done well. These material gifts, however, require a kind of spiritual foundation, as I see it. A moment of spiritual connection each day is all it really takes to help us see our true paths. I do not believe that you have really seen your true path through your haze of disappointment, that it did not take the direction that you intended it to when you were a mere girl of sixteen. It is our duty to seek that path and to prepare ourselves to walk upon it. It is not our role to prepare a path for ourselves."

I was unsure where this was leading. Indeed, it occurred to me that Sister Eulalia's mind might now be not quite as sharp and focused as it had been. Then, as if she could read my mind...

"Bridget, you do not believe that I am thinking quite clearly, do you? You can either choose to listen to an old woman or you can choose not to. It is completely in your hands. However, your choice will not change the way things are. Your life is neither good nor bad, but it simply is what it is. You must look deeply through the mist of your disappointment and sorrow to see where the markers are. You must return to your poet to complete that connection. And you must do it with a firm foundation that is found beyond your material world."

She arose with some difficulty and walked over to her desk. She sat down in her chair, taking her place as the matriarch of the convent, and in her role as my adviser. The sun streamed in through the small window, and for the first time in a very long time, I believed that I knew what I should do.

NINE

Upon my return to Baltimore, I was greeted by the most
fragrant of summers. The profusion of blooms in my
garden, I seemed to have never noticed before. And the
colours! How the colours assaulted my eyes when I took
morning coffee on the back stoop. It felt like a kind of
rebirth.

On the third day after my return, a letter arrived. The
hand was unmistakable.

"Fordham College, June 15, 1847

My dearest Bride,
How can you ever forgive me my transgressions? I
am sorely ill and deprived as I am of all power of
thought or action, I know only that I have no doubt
offended you to your core. How can you ever forgive me?
But forgive me you must.

You have been the truest friend that ever a man
could want for and I have loved you for all eternity. As
you are aware, I was demented over the loss of our dear
Sissy and almost neglected my love for you. For all those
years I held both of you in my heart and continue to
think of you when each day I take up my pen.

I must see you, my Bride. You must allow me to beg
your forgiveness and to once again place my head on
your dear breast so that I may feel your strength and
vitality. Please tell me when next we can meet.
I remain always, your beloved, Ned"

I was inclined to think that Ned had now lost all sense of propriety and sanity and considered tearing up the paper and forgetting that he and I had ever met. I could live out my life here in comfort and quietude, but somewhere in my mind, Sister Eulalia's words rang true, and I knew that I must do as Ned asked and see him again. So, I wrote to him telling him that I would be most happy to see him, inviting him to visit with me in due course.

I did not hear from him. Summer turned into autumn and autumn into winter. The flowers that had bloomed so beautifully and had provided me with a sensual symphony of pleasures had died and returned to the earth. The winds blew hard that December, and the driving snow came to blanket all the earth, it seemed, in silence. Silence.

I began to read all the books I could find about the great religious traditions of the world, learning what it was to be on one's path. I lit a candle each day and sat for a long time, just calming my mind. But I did not hear from Ned.

I gave up hope of ever seeing him again and wondered from time to time if he had succumbed to his rather nasty habit of drinking himself into a stupor and gone too far. I had no way of knowing.

Then, without warning, as he had done in the past, Ned Poe arrived on my doorstep. My (new) housekeeper, Ernestine Little, who greatly admired my independent life as a woman in Baltimore society and had told me this more than once, announced his arrival with a kind of sour expression that reminded me of eating astringent pickles.

I was anxious to see him, and when she let him into the parlour, he immediately threw himself into my arms while Mrs. Little stood under the archway with the most disapproving expression on her face. She had her arms folded across her chest and I could almost hear her "tsk, tsk" as she quietly clucked her tongue and tapped her foot. I was acutely aware of being watched.

"My dearest Bride," Ned said, his arms still clasped firmly around my neck, "how I have longed to see you."

I wondered at this admission, as he had been singularly unable, it seemed, to contact me in months.

Finally, he loosened his noose-like hold on my person, and we sat down, his hand still holding mine while I gestured to Mrs. Little to leave us alone. She closed the parlour doors with a flourish as if she needed to protect herself from our antics. I noticed that Ned's dark hair, now beginning to gray at the temples, was wild and uncombed and that his eyes were bright. As I looked even more closely, I noted that his pupils were wide.

As we talked, it became clear to me that his thinking was not quite right. Appearing to be irrationally concerned about the recent criticism of his work, he arose and began to pace around the room frantically while he talked, his hands moving about as punctuation.

"Do they not understand their own tedium? Do they not see how it is they, themselves, who are inadequate? They are all jealous, jealous I tell you!" He whirled around and, seeming to make himself dizzy, grasped for the edge of the settee.

Sitting on the settee, I calmly waited for him to finish his monologue, thinking all the while about what I might say to assuage him. Then it occurred to me that I ought not to be mollifying him at all. It was not my job. I had seen him like this before – many times, it seemed, far too many.

Ned withdrew what appeared to be a manuscript from the breast pocket of his jacket, and noticing its condition, I wondered how long it had been there. It was crushed and dirty, but in Ned's usual form – a scroll of paper, pieces fastened together end on end, in an endless, never-ending script of words, words, words. And in that moment, I knew, as much as I loved this man in an odd kind of way, that I could see his essence in my life. He was nothing but words whose power I had yet to see and doubted that I ever would.

Ned finally sat down on a chair across from me and hung his head in his hands. "Will they never see the genius, Bride? I fear I can take their slurs no longer."

I looked down at my hands, loosely clasped in my lap amid the folds of my dress and weighed my words.

"Shall you take your life, then?" I said quietly.

He looked up at me, his eyes wet with unspent tears.

"My life?"

I met his gaze evenly and said nothing for a moment. The silence hung in the air between us, a tangled jumble of unspoken thoughts and emotions.

"My life?" he said again, louder this time.

"Will you take your life?" I repeated myself, emphasizing each word in its turn. "With all this outrage and hopelessness, surely you have contemplated this course of action recently."

Ned looked at me and said nothing.

"Ned," I said, "they have criticized you before. Genius, as you put it, will always meet with suspicion and resentment. If you choose not to cope with it, then you must put a stop to it. You do not have control over your detractors, only over yourself. It seems to me that if it is your choice to see your circumstances this way, your path is clear."

"Perhaps you are right," he said quietly.

I waited for him to take in my words. I knew that he had contemplated such drastic action before, but I also knew that contemplating taking one's life was one thing, while acting upon it was quite another. I wanted him to know that it was serious business and that he needed to confront it in so many words.

Finally, he got up. "Perhaps I will not do it today, Bride. Perhaps another day. I shall think about your words, but I feel I must go now."

And so he did. I thought about this encounter for a very long time after Ned had left Baltimore, and I wondered if I would ever see him again, or even hear of his circumstances.

Then, on a bright day in July 1849, I opened the newspaper to read of a lecture tour by a certain poet and editor named Edgar A. Poe. I read the piece with great trepidation about what might be included. Then, there, buried halfway down the page, was the announcement of the engagement. Ned was to marry a certain Elmira Royster Shelton of Richmond, a widow.

A great wave of anger, such as I had never felt before, welled up inside me. All of Ned's protestations of unending love seemed to be as much a part of his imagination as the mournful characters in his stories. Had he been in my presence at that moment, I believe I could have killed him with my bare hands. Elmira Royster! This was the love of his adolescence, he had told me about when first we met in Charlottesville all those many years ago. And now he was to marry her? It was outrageous.

I threw down the offending paper and crushed it under my feet. There were no tears, only disgust. Perhaps it was now finally over.

TEN

There were six Baltimore ladies sitting around my dining room table, sipping tea from my finest china on that early autumn afternoon. I was chairing a meeting of what had now become a kind of charitable foundation for the support of the Hospice of Hildegard which had truly become a Baltimore fixture. Indeed, many of the finest ladies of the city clamoured to sit at this table and to do their good deeds in support of women less fortunate.

We had just completed the plans for the New Year's Ball in support of our move to larger quarters when Mrs. Little appeared at the door and cleared her throat.

"What is it, Mrs. Little?"

She cleared her throat again. "I must speak with you in private, Mrs. Ryan."

I excused myself from the table, leaving the conclusion of the meeting in the capable hands of my vice-chairman, the mayor's wife.

Mrs. Little backed out of the room and closed the heavy oak doors behind us. She looked about as if to ensure that no one was listening. "Mrs. Ryan, he's here again," she said, *sotto voce.*

"He? Who is he?" I no sooner had the questions formed in my head and the words out of my mouth when I knew of whom she was speaking.

"Mr. Poe?" I said, my hand finding its way involuntarily to my mouth.

"The same," she said. "I have sequestered him in the kitchen for the moment. I did not know if you would wish the ladies to see him." She hesitated a moment. "Indeed, I did not know if you would wish to see him."

I thought about this turn of events for a moment. "No," I said, trying to think. "No, I suppose not... still..." I looked at Mrs. Little, who seemed less flustered than she usually did when Ned made these unannounced appearances. "How does he seem?"

"Actually, Mrs. Ryan, if you ask me, I would say that he is the most competent I have ever seen him. He is calm and well-mannered. He even apologized before I bid him enter. And he looks impeccable – in an impoverished sort of way, if I may be so bold as to say. He asked me to give you this."

She thrust a daguerreotype of Ned's likeness into my hands. He looked more handsome than I had seen him in many years. I examined it for a moment, then thrust the small picture in its gilt frame into a drawer of the hall table. I was unsure of my feelings. I knew that I ought to have him removed from the premises forthwith and that Mrs. Little would be only too willing to assist. But something stopped me.

"Mrs. Little, please provide Mr. Poe with some lunch and make him comfortable in the breakfast room. I shall complete my meeting and see to the ladies. Please tell him that I shall see him presently."

I knew that I should have been angry at this precipitous appearance. After all, the last time I had heard of his circumstances, he was engaged to be married, and I was furious. Somehow, the months had blunted that emotion, and I was reminded of what we had meant to one another. Then the thought struck me – was he already married to Elmira? I took a deep breath and returned to the ladies, placing a smile on my face as I opened the dining-room door.

It took almost half an hour to bid them all farewell at the front door. I then took another few moments to rearrange myself in preparation for seeing this old friend of mine.

It was the 29th of September.

Ned was sitting at my usual spot at the breakfast table when I entered the room. He did, indeed, look rather well – calm and smiling – if a bit tired. He got up the moment he saw me, but instead of his usual frantic embrace, he came over and took my hand in his, then calmly raised it to his lips.

"Hello, my darling Bride. You look radiant. I am exceedingly happy to see you once again." He stood back and looked at me, still holding my hand. "You have changed little since we first kept company at the university all those years ago. Time has been very good to you, my darling."

As he followed my lead into the parlour, it was as if all occurrences of the most recent correspondence had never happened. This was not the Ned I had experienced in recent years. It was not the Edgar Poe who was angry at the critics, hysterical at the death of his wife, enraged at life and death. This was more like the young poet with ideals and imagination, haunted but not tormented by his hauntings. My resolve to berate him for his transgressions melted away like the wax of a candle illuminating a long and languorous lovers' encounter.

"What is it that brings you to Baltimore, Ned?" I sat down on the settee and smoothed the folds of my dress.

Instead of joining me as I thought that he might, Ned walked over to the fireplace and leaned his elbow there. Looking at me carefully, he said, "You."

I looked at him, not understanding his meaning.

"Bride, it is you who brings me here. In fact, I was to have proceeded directly to my wedding –"

At this pronouncement, I must have gasped, for he immediately came to my side, taking my hand tenderly in his again.

"Bride, I am not to marry – at least I am not to marry Elmira. I cannot. I love another. In truth, I have loved another since I was seventeen years old. Since first I gazed upon her face across the stacks of books. Since I first walked with her among the grass and trees of Albermarle County. Since then, she has invaded my every thought, my every action. It is because of the thought of her that I have joined the temperance society."

I was impressed. I knew that Ned, in his own reckless way, had loved me, but I had no idea that I was such a part of his every thought. Indeed, I was equally touched by the notion that thoughts of me could cure him of his tendency to drink. But, did I believe him?

We talked for a long time. It seemed that Ned's so-called engagement to Elmira had been an on-and-off kind of arrangement, although it seemed clear that this trip ought to have taken him to his own wedding. People were expecting him, or so he said. He also told me that no one, not even Maria, knew that he was in Baltimore.

"I have come to a kind of peace in my life, Bride. And I wish to spend my remaining time in your company.

This worried me. Whereas I did like the idea that Ned seemed more like the young idealist I had met so many years ago, I was uncertain how our lives might now intertwine at this late stage in our lives. However, he was reasonable and calm, and seemed to be in complete control of his life for the first time since reaching adulthood. I was smitten.

That night, after Mrs. Little had gone off to visit her sister for several days (although Ned's presence certainly had made her reconsider her prearranged plans), Ned came to me. It was as if we were young students again and were now able to fulfill the desires of our hearts and our bodies.

He was a lover like no other I had experienced. His poet's nature seemed to fill him with a kind of passion that made me feel as if I were falling deeper and deeper into a cocoon of delight and obsession.

For two days, we talked, even laughed and planned our days together. We never once left the house. The realities of our lives never entered its four walls. I had never seen him this free of his constant melancholy of simply being alive.

On the morning of October second, I awoke to find that I was alone in my bed. I shook out my hair and found a dressing gown that had been discarded at the foot of the bed. I crept down the stairs to find my love.

As I neared the kitchen, I could hear rustling and humming. Opening the door, I was completely dumbfounded by the sight that greeted my barely open eyes. There sat Ned Poe at the table, bottles and packets in front of him. His eyes were wild, and he was wearing what appeared to be my gardener's old clothes that usually hung on a hook in the porch that led from the kitchen to the back garden. They were dirty and worn, and along with the unruly hair and the brightness of his eyes, he had the appearance of a demented lunatic.

When at last I was able to make some sense of what I was seeing, I realized that Ned had taken my key and opened my herbal cupboard. For a moment, I was angry at the obvious mess he had made of my precious substances, but it quickly faded as I realized the full extent of the situation. By my reckoning, Ned had already imbibed several herbal preparations as well as what appeared to be my entire stash of laudanum. His speech was slurred, and I feared for his life.

"What are you doing?" I said, frantically trying to collect bottles and packages.

"Bridget," he said, his words slow and garbled, "I promised you I would stay with you until the day I died. That day..." He got up from his chair and grabbed onto the table for support. " ...that day has arrived."

He made his way past me and out into the hallway. Before I had a chance to decide what I ought to do, he was opening the front door. I reached him just in time to grab his hand.

"Ned, where are you going?"

He pulled his arm away from me and stumbled down the front steps. It was still very early, and none of my neighbours were about.

"I am going now, Bridget Ryan, and I thank you for what you have done for me."

He then began walking and swaying down the street. I began a pursuit, but realized that in bare feet and wearing nothing but a dressing gown, I would not be very effective. I looked to see what direction he had chosen and went back into the house to dress as quickly as I could.

When I was ready, I took the carriage out myself and began my search. I found not a trace of him.

As dusk fell that night, I visited an old friend of John's, Dr. Cochrane, whom I knew still had contacts within the local hospitals. He told me that he would make some enquiries about the possible admission of my friend to a local hospital. And then I went home.

My sleep was visited by all manner of terrifying creatures of the night – all of them parts of myself. When I arose the next morning, I felt as if my own horse and carriage had trampled me. I could hear activity downstairs, and for a moment wondered if Ned had returned. But then I realized that it was not Ned but Mrs. Little who had returned and was likely preparing my own breakfast.

I spent the entire day walking around in a kind of trance. I was unable to sit still and unable to focus. I walked for several hours through the streets, half expecting to see Ned at any time, but fearing what I might find. I did not, however, wish to be gone from the house for too long in case Dr. Cochrane had been able to find out anything.

Unable to do more than move the food around on my plate that evening at dinner, I sat wretchedly drinking my coffee when Mrs. Little appeared to announce the arrival of a Dr. Cochrane. I arose quickly to greet him in the parlour.

"Mrs. Ryan," he said, extending his hand, "I have word of your friend the poet."

We sat, and he told me what he knew.

Evidently, Ned had been found outside a seedy tavern, Gunner's Hall, in Lombard Street, apparently drunk and delirious. A Dr. Snodgrass had taken him to Washington College Hospital, where he now resided in a room in one of the hospital's towers devoted to caring for drunkards.

"He is in the care of a young Dr. John Moran," Dr. Cochrane said. "He is in good hands, but according to the report I have gleaned, I am sorry to tell you that your friend is not expected to recover."

It was no worse than I had expected. I alone knew that it was not drink that had put Ned in such a stupor. The only thing that surprised me was that he had not yet succumbed to the combination of poisons that now circulated through his body. Given Ned's health history, I, too, expected he would not recover.

"Do you think that Dr. Moran would allow me to visit with my old friend?" I said.

"I shall make the necessary arrangements myself, Mrs. Ryan. It is the least I can do for an old friend's widow."

And so the next morning, the fourth of October, I made my way to Washington College Hospital, high on a hill, to find out the condition of my poet.

Dr. John Moran had been expecting me. He was young, under thirty years or so, I reckoned, and very business-like. Dr. Moran's assessment of Ned indicated that he did not believe Ned to have been drinking at all. Indeed, Dr. Moran seemed to think that Ned was suffering from some kind of brain congestion and might well have been beaten up into the bargain. There was bruising around the head.

"He comes in and out of consciousness," he said in answer to my question about Ned's current condition. "He has even refused the brandy I offered him to help stimulate him in some way. I must tell you that I believe his condition to be terminal, Mrs. Ryan."

"May I be permitted to see him?"

Dr. Moran hesitated. Finally, he decided that I could do no harm and that it might do his patient some good to see a friend.

When I entered the room where Ned lay, I was only a little surprised at his condition. He was drenched in perspiration and was as pale as Virginia had ever been on her worst days. He was clearly unconscious at that moment. We were never able to speak again.

I lingered for a quarter of an hour, gazing at his countenance, remembering better times when our lives lay full ahead of us. Finally, I kissed his damp forehead and left him, closing the door gently behind me. I took my leave of the hospital, knowing that I should never see my friend alive again. On my way out, I asked Dr. Moran to send word to me if his condition changed.

On Sunday morning, October 7, 1849, as the church bells rang out across Baltimore, a young boy arrived at my door bearing a note from Dr. Moran. Edgar Poe was dead.

I sat with the note in my lap for some time, then I tore it up and scattered the remnants on the hearth. I went upstairs to my room and retrieved the raven's feather from where I had hidden it these long years. As I turned it over and over in my hand, I attempted in vain to divine the source of Ned's anguish. Finally, once I had committed it to memory, I wrapped it in several layers of a linen handkerchief and placed it on my bedside table next to Ned's picture, which I had put there before going to the hospital to see him.

On Monday afternoon, with little fanfare, Ned was buried in the small Presbyterian cemetery on Fayette Street. I counted only eight other mourners.

Then I went back to my home to contemplate my past and present, but most importantly, my future.

* * *

In the middle of a sticky thunderstorm on the 15th of July, 1850, Catherine Ryan made her boisterous entrance into the world, and I was struck with wonder at finally meeting the love of my life. I finally knew why I was here. I made the years count.

On May 10, 1872, Catherine Ryan graduated from the medical college of the New York Infirmary for Women and Children. It was, without a doubt, the proudest moment of my long life. She had been able to accomplish what had been denied her mother.

On October 7, 1880, I took my old trunk, the gift from Mr. Bowness so many years ago, down from the attic. I meticulously cleaned it and placed a number of objects inside. In the deepest reaches of the trunk, I placed the linen-wrapped package, then covered it with three layers of lace. When the objects were neatly placed, I took up my pen and wrote a note, placing it carefully inside my journal. This was the final item I placed in the trunk before locking it and placing the key with my will, which had been amended with a codicil regarding its beneficiary. One last time, I ran my fingers over my initials engraved on the brass plate and wondered how long it would be before it was once again opened. I placed the trunk at the foot of my bed.

I knew that I had completed my life's work, and took action to meet my God.

ELEVEN

I awoke stiff and freezing. The open window that had seemed so magical the night before now enabled an icy wind to blow across my face as I lay across my desk. I shivered and shook my head, trying desperately to remember why I was here and not in my bed. I looked at the clock on the wall to find that it was nine-fifteen, and suddenly it occurred to me that the year ought to be 1849. But it wasn't.

I had Bridget's diary clasped tightly in my hand, and I realized that I had read until close to six a.m. before falling into a troubled stupor. And I didn't seem to have a hangover, which was rather surprising, given the copious amount of liquor that I believed I had drunk the night before. Then, when I attempted to get up off my chair, I realized the reason for my lack of a headache – I was still drunk.

The glass in front of me wasn't even empty, but the rum bottle beside it was. I made it to be only about three hours since my last drink.

I wobbled toward the window, and with as much effort as I could exert in my inebriated condition, I managed to slam it shut. It was an old window and usually stuck. I shivered and wrapped my arms around myself while I looked for a blanket of some kind.

I had a kind of tattered sheepskin rug thrown on the floor and thought that this would do quite well. I sat down on the floor beside Bridget's trunk and wrapped myself in the rug. I had gotten no further than uncovering her diary, a scent bottle and the haunting daguerreotype of Edgar Poe the night before and now had so many questions spinning about in my brain. What else was in that trunk?

I picked up the picture again and was even more riveted by it than I had been last night. What a bizarre story! Is fact more unbelievable than fiction? Could he really be my...what? Great-great-great-grandfather? Was that enough 'greats'? My muddled brain couldn't take in that possibility yet.

I picked up the scent bottle, turning it over in my hand. I unscrewed the cap and opened it once again, this time being a bit more cautious as I sniffed gingerly. Could it be old jasmine scented weakly with hemlock? Surely not. I replaced the cap.

Then, uncovering several more objects at the bottom of the trunk, my hand touched the cover of a book. I picked it up and turned it over in my hands. It was unmistakable: a first edition of Edgar Allan Poe's poetry. The title was "Tamerlane and Other Poems" by "a Bostonian." The date on it was 1827. My stomach did a wrenching turn, and I had to put the book down as if it had had this physical effect on me. How much must it be worth?

When I picked it up again, the letter fell out of it – the letter from "Ned" to Bridget when he had sent her this book – in his own hand. Then I remembered something.

Under the book lay a layer of yellowed, stiff lace. Then, beneath all of this was the linen handkerchief with the initial "R" embroidered in the corner. Carefully unfolding the pieces of linen, I uncovered what it protected. For there, amid the folds of fabric, was a black feather. The Raven. I began to shake uncontrollably.

This was all beginning to be a bit too much for me when I heard a banging on my front door and a familiar voice shouting.

"Sean? Sean, are you there?"

I heard the door open and then footsteps coming toward the den.

"What the...? Sean, are you all right?"

It was Alyssa, my young neighbour from next door – the high school student who had a major crush on me and whom I lusted after in the months since she had presented herself at my front door. I had only restrained myself from having my way with this luscious piece of jail bait based on the knowledge that she saw me as her ticket out of the bay, and into what she presumed to be the glamorous world of the university professors – and writers. I had stupidly told her that I was really a writer and would be giving up teaching as soon as I sold my first novel. For some reason, the sight of her conjured up in my mind a picture of Virginia Clemm and Edgar Poe. I shuddered at my own folly.

I looked at her now, standing in the doorway wearing her signature cable-knit sweater purchased from LL Bean on her one trip outside of Canada to Maine and a prized possession. Suddenly, it occurred to me that I must look very peculiar to her at this moment. Then, instinctively, I shoved the book and other objects back into the trunk and slammed it shut, then attempted to get up.

"Sean, what's the matter with you?"

I wasn't sure if she was worried about my appearance or angry at me.

"Alyssa," I finally managed. "How are you?"

"I'm great, but I can see that you've been better. What are you doing?"

I grabbed onto the arm of the nearest chair and tried to pull myself into a standing position.

"You look like hell," she said when finally I was eyeball to eyeball with her.

"Yeah, I'm sure I do," I said, running my fingers through my unruly black curls. I was in desperate need of a haircut. I had even noticed Dr. Tomlinson, the head of my department, giving me what I thought to be the evil eye last night at the party. I surprised myself for having remembered even that little detail of the faculty party.

"I kind of fell asleep over some work last night."

313

Alyssa looked at me, then over to the empty bottle on the desk, and back to me. "Sure. What kind of work were you doing?" She sounded surprisingly unconvinced.

"Oh, some research for my writing." My eyes fluttered briefly over the trunk, which I suddenly felt a deep need to protect. It seemed somehow private, as if for my eyes only. But, I thought suddenly, if I am Edgar Poe's only descendant, can I keep this to myself?

"Well," said Alyssa, breaking into my thoughts, "you don't seem to be in any condition to go to Peggy's Cove with me today." She peered at me closely. "You don't remember, do you? We were supposed to go hiking," she said, clearly snorting at my obvious incapacity, "and then to lunch at the Sou'wester. You'd probably fall off a rock and drown." She sighed.

"Sorry," I said weakly, not knowing how to placate her.

"It's okay. We can do it another time. I'd better get home – unless you need my help." She looked around.

"No. But thanks," I said. "You go ahead. I'll just take a shower.

She turned toward the door, then turned back to me. "Oh, I almost forgot. Mom told me to tell you that there's an old man looking for you."

"An old man? What kind of an old man?"

She shrugged. "I don't know. Anyway, he said he'd be back this weekend. Mom told him you'd probably be going to the States for Christmas. I don't know if he's coming or not."

I wasn't sure what to make of this news. An old man looking for me? Well, I had other things to think about, not the least of which was thinking up an excuse to placate my mother about my sudden decision not to go home for Christmas, especially since I'd been there this fall for the funeral. Anyway, I had too much to think about, and I needed to do it alone.

I spent the next few days walking around in a kind of trance – it was what I imagined suspended animation might be like. I was awake and doing things, but both time and space seemed almost non-existent.

In fact, I thought a lot about time during the days that followed my first encounter with Bridget's trunk. I kept going back into my mind to the night when her story came alive for me, and how it almost seemed as if I had been able to watch it. A long-time "Star Trek" fan, I laughed at myself as I truly considered the existence of a space-time continuum. And what about all that nonsense about parallel timelines I had read about? Maybe they weren't so far-fetched after all.

But the other image that played itself out in the background of everything I thought about was the image of me as the descendant – perhaps the only descendant – of Edgar Allan Poe. Could it be true? The facts were all there, laid out for me in startling detail by my ancestor. I even wrote out my family tree going backwards from myself...

Sean O'Hara... me...

Son of Catherine O'Hara... Mother was born a Donohue in 1927...

She was the daughter of Cecelia Donohue. Grandmamma Cecelia was born a Flynn in...1900.

Grandmama Cecelia had a brother at one time, as Mother told it. His name was Liam, but he died in the 1940s.

Then the line goes fuzzy. Who was Grandmamma Cecelia's mother? And when was she born?

I sat down at my computer and opened a new document. I began typing out all that I could remember. I thought if I looked at it carefully, I might see something and remember. Then I remembered Pete.

Pete was Dr. Peter MacDonald, one of my few new friends at the university. Our friendship was based on our mutual terror of being "found out" as we liked to say over a beer or two... or more at the pub in the student union building. Both first-year professors, we liked to remember our student days and blend into the background on Irish pub night. We had yet to be spotted by any of our students – at least that's what we thought.

Pete was a new faculty member in the history department, but genealogy was his personal passion. Maybe a genealogist could point me in the right direction to uncover the missing link in my apparent line of ancestry.

I managed to track him down just as he was packing up to trek home to some small town in rural Ontario for Christmas with his own extended family.

"What's up, Sean? If I had known you hadn't left yet, I would have given you a call for a last drink before the holidays."

I told him – carefully – that I was tracing my family tree and was looking for guidance about where to find the family name of a great-grandmother who probably lived in the Baltimore area at the turn of the century. As I had expected, or rather feared, he asked me what had brought on this sudden interest in my roots.

"Oh, nothing specific," I said, trying to evade the issue. I was very glad we were on the telephone, so he couldn't see me squirm. "I've been reading some things about the history of the eastern seaboard, and it occurred to me that I didn't really know much about my own ancestors who lived there during that time." It wasn't really a lie.

"You're not still doing research on Poe, are you? Didn't you already decide you'd spent – no, I believe 'wasted' was your exact word – enough time on a...what was it you called him?"

I sighed at remembering my drunken tirade about my doctoral work.

"Oh, yes," he said, "I remember. You called him a demented genius who squandered his life on hallucinatory substances. So, what's the deal, Dr. Sean?"

I knew that I couldn't tell Pete the real reason for my sudden interest in history, so I agreed with him that I was continuing my search for information about Poe. It wasn't really a lie.

316

Finally, he let slip the name of a woman at the University of Maryland who did that kind of work and who knew research assistants who might be persuaded to do the footwork for me. I wished him a happy holiday and made another phone call. There was no answer.

So I stewed for another twenty-four hours and tried her again. I hoped that she hadn't left for her own holiday break yet.

The second call brought more success. In fact, although she herself wasn't there, her research assistant was. I thought, how sad – probably a poor, underpaid, overworked grad student who can't even get away for a decent holiday. But she was bright and cheery, and when she heard I was calling from Canada, she was positively enthralled. I was almost as delighted as she seemed to be when she agreed to do the search herself – if I promised to let her stay with me sometime when she came to Canada for a visit. Since I knew that the likelihood of that happening was not great, I readily agreed,

Two days later, she called. She had most of the information, but had run into a bit of a stumbling block as she called it.

She had found Grandmama Cecelia's birth records from the baptismal registration in 1900 in a church in Baltimore. Her mother was listed as "Lydia Flynn, nee Casey." I completely ignored the information she provided about the fathers, since I remembered that Grandmama's will specifically said the trunk was to be given to the first surviving male offspring. Clearly, the men were unimportant.

Lydia's birth had also been recorded in baptismal records. She was born in 1877 in Baltimore and was buried there in 1935. It seems that they had all lived in the same house for all those generations, a fact that I already knew. Thus, it was easy to find that her mother was a "Dr. Catherine Ryan" and her father a "Dr. Ian Casey."

She had also found Dr. Catherine's birth registration from 1850, but it didn't appear she had been baptized, and this was where the young research assistant had become confused.

"There was no mention of her father at all," she said. "But it did list her mother as 'Bridget.' Isn't that peculiar? I mean, wouldn't you give a last name on the record? Didn't you have to? Especially back then?"

I didn't care, but I suspected I knew the answer anyway, and I had the information I was looking for. Catherine Ryan was my great-great-grandmother. And she was Edgar Allan Poe's daughter.

I could barely get the words out of my mouth to thank her and tell her that she could send me a bill for her services.

I sat down and wept.

TWELVE

The old man finally found me. It was Christmas Eve, and I was sitting alone in my living room, gazing out over the bay, my books and papers on the coffee table in front of me. The fire crackled, or to be more accurate, hissed since I was trying to burn damp wood. There was no snow yet. The knock was strong and determined.

I took a sip from the lukewarm coffee that sat on the table and got up from the sofa. When I opened the door, I was face-to-face with a tall, elderly man dressed completely in black. His grey hair curled over his collar and around his pointed face. He was holding a satchel.

"O'Hara?" he said in greeting.

"Yes, I'm Sean O'Hara. I understand you've been looking for me."

"Been in town for a week now, waiting for you to be home." He peered into my face as if trying to memorize its features.

"How can I help you?" I said, inexplicably hesitant to invite this unusual man inside immediately. I noted the silver-tipped walking cane he held in his left hand and hoped he did not intend to use it as a weapon. Such a silly notion, I thought.

"You're Cecelia's grandson?"

I nodded.

"I have something I need to talk to you about before I die."

Die? Was he planning to die? Here? Now? I fervently hoped not. How would I explain a dead old guy whose name I didn't even know? But he knew my late grandmother, so I ought to let him in, I thought. So I did.

He seemed to fill the small house with his height and something else about him. There was a kind of regal bearing about his size, but it was more about his carriage. He looked around and gestured toward a chair.

"Mind if I sit down? I'm eighty, you know, and not as robust as I used to be."

"Please," I said, moving some papers out of his way. "Please sit down. Sorry, I don't appear to be hospitable. It's just that you've taken me a bit by surprise. I don't get many visitors out here." I too sat down. "So, you knew my grandmother?"

He looked around as if taking in every detail of my surroundings. "Yes, Cecelia and I were friends for some fifty years."

It was then that I realized that I had, indeed, seen this man before. How could I have forgotten? He had been the tall gentleman with the bowed head at the back of the church during Grandmama's funeral. When the service was over, I had looked back to see if I might have a word later with one of her few remaining friends, but he had disappeared.

"You," I said, "you were there. At the funeral."

"Yes, I was. I am sorry I failed to remain to meet you, but I was too overcome with grief." His eyes misted over even now at the memory. "Forgive me. My name is Aaron Goldberg. I'm from Baltimore."

Then he told me his entire story. He and Grandmama Cecelia had known each other since their early twenties. They were in love and had planned to marry, but because Aaron was Jewish, her father wouldn't allow it, instead finding her a nice, Catholic man – evidently, whom she did not love. They kept in touch for years, but clandestinely.

When Grandmama was forty-three years old, her brother Liam, three years her junior, whose existence I barely knew about, had died. In fact, according to Aaron, it was a commonly held belief among Baltimore society that he had killed himself, although the family would never admit to it. My grandmother had been close to her brother and had been devastated, finding little solace in the arms of her husband, something of a drunk. I seemed to have quite a family legacy. At that point in Aaron's story, I wasn't

320

at all certain I wanted to hear any more. I offered him a beer – it only seemed fitting – but he declined. Instead, he opened his satchel and pulled out a bottle of Martel cognac. Even better, I thought as I went to the kitchen to find brandy glasses.

We both took a drink before he continued. Several years after Liam's death, specifically on New Year's Day in 1949, my grandfather died. I'd heard that he had some kind of liver problem, and I was now convinced that he must have suffered from cirrhosis. Aaron nodded in agreement at this pronouncement.

"It was a blessing for Cecelia, though," he said. "She was like a new woman."

"Did you and she pick up where you had left off all those years before?" I asked, drawn now into another foray into history. I was wondering why, if my grandmother had had such a close friend for so many years, I had never met him. Or even heard anything about him.

"Not quite." Aaron cleared his throat and refilled his now-empty glass. As I watched him swirl the amber liquid around in the glass before taking a sip, I remembered that Grandmama Cecelia had served cognac whenever she wanted to celebrate anything.

"My wife, you see."

And suddenly I did see. He was held by his own obligations.

"But I am ashamed to say that I did not always keep sacred the vows of my wedding."

I nodded in understanding and felt no need to press him for details. I could see how painful this was for him. I was anxious, however, to find out how he came to be here in my living room on St. Margaret's Bay in Canada on this Christmas Eve.

"Liam had been dead several years, and when her husband died, Cecelia came to me with a request. She warned me that it would be a strange one, and she was right. Indeed, I thought that she had taken leave of her senses that night. I remember it clearly. I can't remember what I ate for breakfast yesterday, but I remember that day in 1949. Oi! Imagine! That's what happens with age, you know. It was January 18th."

I was impatient for him to continue. Finally, he did.

Grandmama had asked him to humour her and to do her a favour. She wanted him to take three roses and the remainder of the bottle of cognac that they were sharing on that cold January evening, and go in the early hours of the following morning to the southeast corner of the cemetery at the corner of Fayette and Green streets. He was to place the roses and the cognac on the grave of her great-grandfather, whose birthday was January 19.

"She told me that her grandmother Catherine's will had specified that in the year that marked the 100th anniversary of his death, her male offspring were to begin this ritual, keeping their identities a closely guarded secret. Of course, at the time, I did not know the name I would find on the grave marker."

I drained my glass and could feel the hair on the back of my neck starting to creep up.

"You know who I'm talking about, don't you?"

Grandmama Cecelia had asked him to visit me after she died.

"I am here to pass the baton as it were." And he actually handed me the walking stick. "In three and a half weeks, on the morning of January 19, I shall be in the darkness with the Poe museum curator, awaiting the annual arrival of the mysterious stranger. No one will molest or disturb you in any way." He looked at the half-full bottle of cognac. "Take that. Oh, and the three roses you'll need. One is for Virginia, one is for Maria and of course, one is for Edgar."

"None for Bridget?" I said, my head swimming.

He shrugged. "She never said one for herself."

He drained his glass and disappeared from my life.

EPILOGUE

I'm sitting in my hotel room overlooking Baltimore's inner harbour. It's snowing again. I have my laptop open, and I'm scanning the local newspaper headlines online. I find the one I'm looking for.

"Mysterious stranger makes his usual visit to Poe's gravesite."

So, I made the headlines again. Beside my computer on the desk proudly lies a copy of my new book – it's about Bridget Ryan, but of course it's fiction. No one knows I'm her great-great-great-grandson, and no one ever will. I've kept the family secret all these years and plan to continue the tradition to my grave.

I finally became a Canadian citizen last year. My son, the patriot of the true north strong and free, thought it was about time. After all, Dad, he had said to me, you've been living here and working the system since you fled a war you didn't like. I could hardly argue with him there. My adopted country had been good to me. Anyway, he had continued, you have no ties to America.

My son, Edward O'Hara, but we call him Ned. He turned twenty-one yesterday. He's working out now in the hotel gym on the eighteenth floor, but he'll be back soon, and we'll go down for breakfast. Then I'll explain to him where I had to go at 4:30 yesterday morning. Research, I had said.

But he'll keep the family secret, too. I know this. Because he's Edgar Allan Poe's great-great-great-great-grandson, and soon it will be his turn.

ACKNOWLEDGEMENT OF SOURCES

Although a novel is, by nature and design, fictitious, it still requires research to get the details right. This is a novel, and all the characters are creations of my imagination, except for Poe and members of his family, whose characteristics and personalities can only be recreated from often differing fragments of history and musings that have gone on for well over 100 years. In the end, however, this is my Edgar Poe, a fictitious recreation of what might have been.

The locations where Poe lived and worked are as accurate as research would allow, while Bridget's homes, places of business, acquaintances and relatives are completely fictitious. Indeed, any resemblance that Bridget might have to any person who really lived in history is purely coincidental.

There are many versions of Edgar Poe's life and little agreement about many details, especially about his addictions and untimely death. Indeed, there is no information at all about what he was even doing in Baltimore from September 29, 1849, until he was found in the street on October 3, several days before his death.

I take full responsibility for any quibbles that any readers might have with the "facts" as presented. Indeed, this is a work of fiction, and all "facts" must be taken as literary devices only and not commentaries on actual events.

Of all the materials I consulted through the course of writing this book, the following materials were most helpful to me in understanding the life and times of Edgar Allan Poe:

- Kenneth Silverman's 1991 biography of Poe: "Edgar A. Poe: Mournful and Never-ending Remembrance," is well researched and eminently readable.
- Marc McCutcheon's 1993 reference book: *Everyday Life in the 1800's.*
- Dr. Robert Patterson's 1992 article in the *Canadian Medical Association Journal*: "Once Upon a Midnight Dreary: The Life and Addictions of Edgar Allan Poe." This article, in fact, was my inspiration for filling the gap and answering the question of how Poe *might* have died.
- The 1818 publication *American Ladies Preceptor: A Compilation of Observations, Essays and Political Efforts to Direct the Female Mind in a Course of Pleasing and Instructive Reading*, published in Baltimore,
- The website of the Edgar Allan Poe Society of Baltimore
- Cornell University's *Making of America* website

...and, of course, Poe's own words. *PJP*

ABOUT THE AUTHOR

PATRICIA J. PARSONS started her writing career as a freelance health and medical writer. Her almost three-decade academic career began accidentally when she stumbled into teaching writing and corporate communication strategy to undergrads, eventually establishing herself as an expert in communication ethics and strategy. Two of the textbooks she wrote during her academic career are still used today.

She is also the author of half a dozen nonfiction trade books. More recently, she defected to writing women's fiction, humour and the occasional mystery or thriller. Her novel, *We Came From Away*, was short-listed for the 2025 Stephen Leacock Medal for Literary Humour.

After spending most of her career in Halifax, Nova Scotia, she now lives in Toronto, where she writes and travels to exotic places so her characters can do the same.

OTHER BOOKS BY PATRICIA J. PARSONS

www.ingramcontent.com/pod-product-compliance
Lightning Source LLC
Chambersburg PA
CBHW030642260626
47157CB00007B/2447